3

Praise for the novels of Heather Graham

"An incredible storyteller."
—*Los Angeles Daily News*

"Graham wields a deftly sexy and convincing pen."
—*Publishers Weekly*

"A fast-paced and suspenseful read
that will give readers chills while keeping them
guessing until the end."
—*RT Book Reviews* on *Ghost Moon*

"If you like mixing a bit of the creepy
with a dash of sinister and spine-chilling reading with
your romance, be sure to read Heather Graham's
latest...Graham does a great job of blending
just a bit of paranormal with real, human evil."
—*Miami Herald* on *Unhallowed Ground*

"Eerie and atmospheric, this is not late-night reading
for the squeamish or sensitive."
—*RT Book Reviews* on *Unhallowed Ground*

"The paranormal elements are integral to the
unrelentingly suspenseful plot, the characters are
likable, the romance convincing, and, in the wake of
Hurricane Katrina, Graham's atmospheric depiction of
a lost city is especially poignant."
—*Booklist* on *Ghost Walk*

"Graham's rich, balanced thriller sizzles with
equal parts suspense, romance and the paranormal—
all of it nail-biting."
—*Publishers Weekly* on *The Vision*

"Heather Graham will keep you in suspense
until the very end."
—*Literary Times*

"Mystery, sex, paranormal events.
What's not to love?"
—*Kirkus* on *The Death Dealer*

Also by HEATHER GRAHAM

HEART OF EVIL
PHANTOM EVIL
NIGHT OF THE VAMPIRES
THE KEEPERS
GHOST MOON
GHOST NIGHT
GHOST SHADOW
THE KILLING EDGE
NIGHT OF THE WOLVES
HOME IN TIME FOR CHRISTMAS
UNHALLOWED GROUND
DUST TO DUST
NIGHTWALKER
DEADLY GIFT
DEADLY HARVEST
DEADLY NIGHT
THE DEATH DEALER
THE LAST NOEL
THE SÉANCE

BLOOD RED
THE DEAD ROOM
KISS OF DARKNESS
THE VISION
THE ISLAND
GHOST WALK
KILLING KELLY
THE PRESENCE
DEAD ON THE DANCE FLOOR
PICTURE ME DEAD
HAUNTED
HURRICANE BAY
A SEASON OF MIRACLES
NIGHT OF THE BLACKBIRD
NEVER SLEEP WITH STRANGERS
EYES OF FIRE
SLOW BURN
NIGHT HEAT

* * * * *

Look for the next Krewe of Hunters novel
The Evil Inside
by Heather Graham

HEATHER GRAHAM

SACRED EVIL

MIRA®

ISBN-13: 978-1-61129-780-5

SACRED EVIL

Copyright © 2011 by Slush Pile Productions, LLC

Printed in U.S.A.

For NYC—an amazing place,
and for a few of the people who have also
made it more amazing by being there.

For Aaron Priest, and all those at the agency:
Lucy Childs, Lisa Vance, Nicole James,
Arleen Priest, and John Richmond.

And, of course, for my MIRA Books editors
in the Big Apple: Adam Wilson, Leslie Wainger,
Margaret Marbury, and Krista Stroever, who
went above and beyond and walked the streets
of the old Five Points region with me. Thank You!

Yes, ready for my cemetery tour now…!

Prologue

Someone was following her.

Stalking her.

She'd heard the footsteps. Among the deserted streets and the canyons of tall buildings; the sound seemed to echo from everywhere.

The night was extremely dark, and, Ginger Rockford thought, *you would have believed that the streets* were *lit by centuries-old gas lamps, as they'd supposedly been during the filming that day.*

A hot afternoon had turned into a chilly, misty night, and a fog was rolling in from the river.

The area seemed ridiculously quiet—except for that sound she heard now and then, a *click-click,* like a footfall, and then a shuffling noise, as if her stalker dragged a foot.

Great. Chased through the streets by a gimp.

It was New York City, for God's sake. Millions lived on this tiny island.

So where the hell were they all now?

Ginger turned around to look back in the direction from which she had come. She could still see the row of trailers on Whitehall Street; she had just left one.

Sammy Vintner, fat-old-ex-cop studio guard, was still on duty, but she saw that he was on the phone.

He was the only living soul she saw.

There were markers where the tape had been that had held the crowd back during the day, separating the filmmakers from the plebs hoping to catch a glimpse of megastar Bobby Walden.

She cursed Bobby Walden. While she'd waited, believing that he was really going to call her, Bobby had surely been picked up by a big black limousine.

Bobby was a *somebody*. She was a *nobody*.

But at least Bobby had spoken to her. The female lead, Sherry Blanco, had almost knocked her over, and she hadn't even apologized. Well, maybe Sherry would learn. Ginger had done a lot of studying up on actors and their careers. She estimated that Sherry Blanco had about three years left—she was nearly thirty-five, and it was starting to show. Sherry was pretty, but she couldn't really act. Nor had she been known for any kindness to the young hopefuls with whom she had worked. Ginger hoped with her whole heart that she might be a rising star when Sherry was a burned-out has-been.

At least Angus Avery, the up-and-coming director, had noticed her. Okay, so his words weren't every girl's dream. "Perfect! I mean, damn, do you look the role of the immigrant prostitute, her dreams already vanquished!" That was how she had gotten to be the one on Bobby's arm, and how she had managed to flirt with him.

And then he had said that they needed to hook up, and taken her phone number.

So she had sat in the trailer well past time to leave; Missy Everett and Jane Deaver—who had played the other two young prostitutes in the scene—had begged her to leave with them. Their day of extra-stardom was over. They should celebrate, and wonder if they'd wind up on the cutting-room floor.

She, like a fool, had refused to leave; she'd been waiting for Bobby. And she should have left. The set was a construction site. The ugly old building that had been there had been razed to the foundations and a few structural walls. There were rumors about the site; bad things had happened there. She didn't really know what—she wasn't into history. Maybe it had been an old burial ground. But it had been perfect for the set designers when they had installed their prefabricated backdrops and facades, and it had been right next to Blair House, a truly creepy old place. She hadn't been spooked during the day. The day had been chaotic with actors and crew, one shot being set up while another was being shot, sometimes over and over again if Avery didn't like the lighting or the camera angle.

How had she managed to be the very last one on set? Oh, yes, waiting and praying that Bobby would really call her.

Sammy had emerged from his guard post. "Hey!" she called back, hoping that he would pay attention, see her and wait for her to come running back. She'd even take a ride with disgusting fat Sammy at this point.

He wasn't looking her direction. He was going off duty, heading away from her. She should have accepted a ride from him when he'd offered, but she'd been convinced she'd find a taxi right away.

Who the hell knew that the area dried up like a prune once it got late at night?

The guard disappeared behind one of the trailers; he'd been anxious for her to go, of course, once she'd refused to ride with him. She'd been the last one near the trailers, the only one left who had been working on the on-location day-plus shoot for *O'Leary's,* a tale about crime and prostitution in the eighteen hundreds in New York City. One of the pubs in the area had had the right interior, and the buildings—except for the gap where the old Darby Building had so recently stood—were perfect. The gutted area and the work tents set up on the old site were shielded by a blue screen for the moviemaking; New York was not a city to make do without the income a permit for such work would secure for the city. Nor, with the preservationist-supporting liberals to be found in the area, could a recently discovered historic site be disturbed.

Even so, the area around the demolished building was surrounded by cheap wire fencing that any school-boy could scale, and closed by a gate with a two-bit combination lock. It looked like a war zone in a third world country.

She was beyond it, though, and she hurried; the gaping hole in the landscape seemed alive, mocking her for her fear of darkness and shadows.

Now she cursed Bobby Walden. Megastar—jerk!

So, maybe, she had been too easy, too wide-eyed and too hopeful. But he'd really been into her during the shoot; he'd whispered such cool stuff to her between takes that day. She was ready; she knew how to get her name in the paper, and how to move ahead. In film, in the real world, perception was everything. She wasn't a fool; she didn't expect a happy-ever-after with Bobby Walden. Just a date—or a night in his hotel room, a place she could pretend to slip out of while being sure that she was spotted by the media. That was all she needed. Her picture on Page Six, maybe. People would start talking about her, and it would make it worthwhile that she'd slept with the pimple-faced assistant at the casting agency to get the job as an extra—a down-and-out historical hooker—for the movie. And, she should still be glad, because she'd wound up with *a few lines,* enough to quality for her SAG card.

B movie. That was okay. Many a star had gotten his or her start as an extra-suddenly-given-lines. It took something like being singled out by Bobby Walden to get noticed.

"Hey! Hey, Sammy!" she called, walking back toward the site and Sammy. But Sammy didn't appear from behind the trailer that was just about two blocks away now. He had to have heard her, but even if she ran, she'd never catch him. "Sammy! You fat ass!" she muttered.

Sammy was gone. Probably down in the useless-to-her Whitehall subway station already.

She thought she saw a man; a different man standing by the trailers. He must have been an actor; he seemed to be wearing a stovepipe hat and a long black all-encompassing coat. Whoever it was would be in big trouble with the costume department.

The moon shifted; there was no man standing there. She was making herself bizarrely nervous; it was simply because she'd never imagined that anywhere in New York could become so devoid of people.

She turned and retraced her steps. If she reached Broadway and started running…

She was almost at the corner when she heard the noise again. *Click-click-drag.*

Was it coming from behind her? Or before her?

She turned the corner and screamed; there was a man standing there. He looked dazed. He was in dirty jeans, a dirtier denim jacket. He hadn't shaved in days, and his hair was tangled and greasy.

"Hey, lady, you got a dollar? Just a dollar—or some change? Anything—a quarter?" He took a step toward her with his hand outstretched, and she suddenly knew the direction from which the *click-click-drag* had come. She could smell him; he was absolutely repulsive.

"No!" she cried. "Get away!"

"Lady, I'm just a vet—"

"You're just an alcoholic or a junkie—and you're disgusting! Take a bath!" she said. She didn't even want to touch him to shove him in the chest, but she did so. She was desperate to get past him.

He fell against the wall of the building she was passing. She didn't look to see what type of office it was; she hurried on for a block, turned around. The ratty old homeless man was gone.

She leaned against a railing where she had stopped, panting, to stare back hard. She wanted to make sure that he was gone—really gone. She needed to get a hold of her fear. As soon as she got a little bit farther up Broadway, she'd start to see people. Ha! Stalked by a derelict who would fall down in a breeze. Well, the louse-ridden bastard was gone now. She kept looking down the street, making sure.

It was amazing; she could hear the traffic on West Street, albeit in the distance. Battery City was no more than a few blocks away. Wall Street was mobbed with cutthroat brokers during the day, and tourists thronged Trinity and St. Paul's. But now the streets were dead, as dead as those rotting in the old graves and tombs of the city's churches.

Yes, the derelict was gone, too.

She turned to hurry on up Broadway.

She hadn't heard a thing; she hadn't suspected anyone might be in front of her—she had been looking behind, back to the dark abyss of the site.

Her turn brought her directly into *his* arms. Before she could open her mouth, his hand clamped over it, and he twisted her viciously around until she was flat against his body.

She tried to scream, but the sound was muffled by the gloved hand. She strained to see, to kick to fight...

She barely even felt the knife across her throat; the blade was that sharp and the slice he made was swift and hard and sure. She was aware that, as the blood began to flow, he dragged her. She saw the lights of the street.

Seeming as pale as old gas lamps.

As she died, the world growing dark and cold, she was dimly aware once again that it was all a matter of perception. Blood was rushing from her throat, and she was dying. She was even aware of the irony—that she might become really famous at last.

Somewhere, not far, car horns blared, neon illuminated the city and millions of souls worked, played and slept.

But to Virginia Rockford, the world beyond was no longer of any consequence.

Her last vision was that of a shadow-man.

A man in a long black cape wearing a stovepipe hat. A shadow-man, coming at her again with the long wicked blade of his knife...

But she felt no more. Death became a gentle blessing.

1

One great thing about New York City—tourists.

And residents who behaved like tourists, every time he came to the scene of a murder.

Jude Crosby flashed his badge to the officers on duty and ducked beneath the yellow crime scene tape that was stretched across lower Broadway.

The murder site had acquired more onlookers than a movie premiere. Traffic downtown had grown to a snarl that was just about impassable even with the extra traffic cops manning the detour, and the sound of cursing drivers threatened to drown out the sound of their horns.

Fortunately, it was only just dawn; most finance workers weren't even on their way in yet.

He made his way to the circle of men around the body. He was glad to see that the medical examiner who had been on call was Wally Fullbright, a man in his late fifties with ruffled white hair and big-rimmed glasses; he looked like an aged Beaker, from the Muppets. He was, in Jude's mind, the finest in his profession. Yet, he never considered his own expertise as the zenith of knowledge, and was known to probe to the depths of any anatomical mystery.

"Crosby!" Fullbright said, acknowledging Jude without looking up. He knew he had a distinctive height, and in his off-hours he practiced at the ring. Pounding away at punching bags helped him release the tension that often bubbled up after dealing with some of the more bizarre crimes that plagued the city.

Even then, he had to make his way through more men; officers had formed a curtain of bodies, hiding the corpse from the view of the crowd that looked on.

He quickly saw why.

"Lord," he said quietly, hunkering down across the body from Fullbright.

He'd seen a lot as a homicide detective in New York City. Dead drunks, prostitutes, drug addicts, mob hits and victims of domestic abuse. He'd seen the derelicts who had died in Dumpsters, in alleys, atop mountains of trash and he'd seen the floaters who had popped up in the East River and the Hudson.

He'd never seen anything like this.

"Do we know who she is?" he asked.

"Sir!" one of the uniformed men—Smith, according to his badge—said. "She had her ID on her, in her bag. Found next to the body. Her name is Virginia Rockford, twenty-six years old. We believe that she was an actress working on location last night, but that fact still has to be verified. We formed ranks around her as fast as we could when we reached the scene. We called it in to Major Crimes because of…because of the way you see the body."

"You found her like this?" Jude asked.

The officer blushed and shook his head. "There were people coming around, staring. I threw the coat over her."

"And I carefully threw it off, again, in favor of the screen of blue," Fullbright said.

Jude nodded. He understood. The black trench coat now at the victim's side had apparently belonged to Officer Smith.

He doubted Officer Smith would ever wear the coat again.

Smith shouldn't have changed the crime scene in any way, but, under the circumstances, Jude knew why he had felt compelled to do so—even if the officer had known better.

He looked at Fullbright. "Tell me, please, that she wasn't—gutted—alive?"

Fullbright shook his head, indicating the thick pool of blood at the victim's throat, and the way it had poured down the front of her dress. "It's my belief that she was seized, her mouth muffled, though God knows who might have heard her scream down here at night, and that her throat was slit ear to ear immediately. I think, and it's my theory, but, logical, if you will forgive me, that she was nabbed on the corner, and quickly dragged into the street as she died. There are two slashes, but I believe the first would have caused her to bleed out. The mutilation of the body occurred after death."

"I've seen some bad ones in my day, but this seems exceptionally sick, don't you think, Detective Crosby?" one of the other uniformed men asked.

"They come in very, very, very sick sometimes," Jude said quietly.

He looked at the victim again, feeling his own stomach curdling. There was bruising on her face, which might have come from a blow, or from the force the killer used to hold her while slashing her throat. Her legs were bent at the knees slightly, and falling outward in a sexually implicit line. Her stomach appeared to have been sliced deeply several times, but there was now such a mass of congealed blood and ragged flesh, there was little he could tell about any precise injury that had been done to her.

"How long has she been here?" he asked Fullbright.

"I'm estimating time of death to be around eleven," the medical examiner told him. "Give or take an hour."

Smith offered, "I was on duty down here, Detective Crosby. I had just come on duty. I came running when I heard a woman screaming." He pulled out a pad and read from his notes, nodding toward a woman who was on the sidewalk, surrounded by officers. "She's Miss Dorothy Hannigan, and she runs the bakery on the corner. She came walking from the subway exit—" he pointed down the street "—and started screaming when she saw the body. I called in dispatch for help and they called you." He swallowed hard. "It was barely light… I thought she was a mannequin, a movie prop, at first."

Jude Crosby studied the body a moment longer; he wasn't sure it was necessary. The details seemed to be etched into his mind.

He was sure that Fullbright was right—she had been nabbed while walking on the sidewalk, and dragged out to the road to die. He wondered how long, even with the light traffic at night, it had taken the bakery worker to discover the body. Time of death wasn't exact, and a number of cars had to have driven by at sometime.

He started to rise.

"The Ripper," Fullbright said.

"Pardon?" Jude looked over at the man he sincerely respected.

Fullbright looked at him and spoke dryly. "Jack the Ripper. London murderer of the late eighteen hundreds. Come on, Jude, you were sent to study criminal history and crime-fighting methods across the pond. The Ripper. Jack the Ripper. His first victim—well, the first victim agreed upon by most criminal experts and Ripperologists—was Polly Nichols. Found on August 31, 1888. She was found...just as we've found this girl."

Officer Smith made a sound at the back of his throat. "That was well over a hundred years ago, Doctor. I doubt the same man could have killed this girl. And, hell, that was London, not New York."

"One theory regarding the cessation of the murders after the Mary Kelly grand finale was that the bastard came to the United States," Fullbright said, looking at Jude.

Jude asked Fullbright, "You think we might have a whacked-out murderer who is also a Ripperologist—one dedicated to the point of re-creating the crimes himself?"

"I hope not," Fullbright said. "They just got worse," he added softly. "The murders just became more and more vicious. Until Mary Kelly, and then..."

And then...

Of course, no one knew what would happen next. Jude was far from a Ripperologist, but he'd attended a lecture at a British forum on "Historical Crimes, Modern-day Solutions: Crimes That Would Have Been Solved in the Twenty-first Century." He knew that theories abounded. One was indeed the idea that the Ripper had come to the United States. But, of course, wherever he had gone—to America, Africa, South America—or hell itself—that had been over a hundred years ago. And Jude didn't believe that he was a Freddy Krueger-type monster who had returned to roam the streets.

And still, he felt a deep unease sweeping over him. Last week, they'd found the remains of a girl in the Hudson; she was still a Jane Doe, but her throat had been slashed. A pleasure boater had reported the remains; police divers had brought her in. Two weeks before, there had been a victim who had died en route to the hospital without ever being able to speak or point a finger even vaguely in the direction of her attacker; she'd been cut—slashed and stabbed.

But not like this.

Not like this poor girl.

Probably a once pretty girl, who had been alive just last night. Filled with hopes and dreams. She might have been nice; she might have been a scrapper, one of the thousands of hopefuls who came to the big city each year to strike it rich in the Big Apple. The open chart of her life was closed, and it didn't matter if she'd helped old ladies cross the street or snubbed the geeks who had stared at her when she had walked by, oblivious. No one deserved this kind of end.

He noted the position of her body, and that she had certainly been positioned and displayed; he was sure the killer had worn gloves, and been careful *not* to let his victim catch any skin cells in her fingernails. Still, there was always hope.

Jude stood up and started going through the initial motions. He ordered that his victim's hands be bagged in hopes she'd gotten her nails into the bastard that had killed her somehow or somewhere, but he knew he didn't even have to say the words. Fullbright was on the case.

Photographs were taken of the body. He watched that procedure, making certain that the techs took every angle he might need.

He spoke to the uniformed officers on the street. Buildings were to be canvassed in hopes that someone had been somewhere doing something. The crime scene unit was called in to search the area for any possible minuscule clues.

Fullbright stood, giving additional orders to the officers and his assistant. He looked at Jude while the gurney and body bag were brought over, everyone there moving quickly and efficiently.

"You're working alone on this?" Fullbright asked him.

"I don't have a new partner yet. I haven't had anyone assigned to me since…since Monty took a bullet," Jude told him.

"How's he doing?"

"He's having another surgery on Friday. They're hoping he'll walk again," Jude said.

He tried to keep his voice even, and free from the

resentment he couldn't help but feel. Niles Monty had been doing the right thing—he had been the perfect officer, trying to talk down the drugged-out vet who had just shot and killed his wife. His partner had been doing all the right things, and the soldier, in tears, was ready to hand his weapon over to Monty. Instead, a frightened vigilante neighbor who'd snuck up the fire escape had taken a shot and missed; the frightened vet had fired at Monty, before turning the gun on himself.

Jude had been waiting quietly next to Monty who had been doing a damn good job talking the man down. He felt the bullet whistle by, but too late to stop the lethal action that had all taken place in less than ten seconds. He'd managed to stanch the flow of blood emitting from his partner while praying for the medics to hurry.

The vigilante was walking the streets, his case having been dismissed, portraying himself to the press as a hero. How he was managing that, since his actions had caused the crippling of a veteran cop with twenty years' experience and a slew of medals, Jude didn't know.

God, he hated the press.

And the press was going to have a field day with this.

He looked through the crowd of television vans and camera crews setting up near the scene. He noticed Melissa Banks, who tended to be a responsible newspaper journalist in a world where sensationalism had become everything.

He strode straight for her. "Ms. Banks," he said, acknowledging her. "We have found the body of a woman on Broadway, and look, I suppose that's evident, but it's all I can give you at the moment. Headquarters will make a statement later. Pending notification of next of kin, I can't release her name."

"They're saying that her throat was slashed and that she was—ripped to shreds. Do we have our own Jack the Ripper in the city now, Detective Crosby? A Jack the Slasher, as it were?" Melissa asked him. He winced. His killer had a name now.

"We don't know if this was an isolated incident or not, Ms. Banks. As soon as we have information, we will certainly bring it to you in the best interest of the public. Now, if you'll excuse me…?"

The officers who had been first on the scene had done their best to keep the details hidden, but it was New York. People had seen. They'd seen beyond the crime scene tape and the wall of bodies, and they had seen the amount of blood around the victim. People were going to talk; speculation would run high, and if his killer was a sensationalist trying to prove a point, he would be savoring the attention he was getting this very minute. He would be somewhere, watching, and gloating over his victory.

"Should women in this vicinity be worried to walk about at night?" Melissa Banks asked him.

He stared at her; she tended to be an intelligent woman. "Women should always be careful walking about at night. However, since the financial district is relatively quiet at night, yes, I would definitely take extra care."

One of the other reporters had heard his words and

moved in. "Did you just say that it's not safe to walk the streets at night?"

Jude stepped toward her. "What I just said was that any single woman should take care at any time—anywhere. Sadly, there is evil in this world, and there are those who will hurt others. I'm suggesting women not be alone late at night on quiet streets. Period. I'm also suggesting that journalists be responsible and not create panic where panic will avail no one. I'm promoting common sense, and if you'll really excuse me now, I have work to do."

Jude walked back to the body, and looked at the corner. He paused, and motioned to a crime scene tech, who hurried over. "Blood, I'm pretty sure," Jude told him, and the fellow nodded gravely and went to work. On the sidewalk, he found more drops of blood, and motioned as well.

A photographer followed the techs, taking pictures as they took samples of the substances on the ground.

He was certain that Fullbright had been right; his victim had been walking uptown, as if she was trying to find a busier spot on Broadway, perhaps to hail a cab. The assailant had waited for her on the corner behind the building. Jude didn't like his audience, though the uniforms were doing the best they could to control the scene. He was still downtown on a busy Monday morning, and blocking off an entire street in the vicinity of the stock market, city hall, Trinity, St. Paul's and the Woolworth Building was not easy. Still, he called one of the young officers over, took a position behind the first building and had the officer walk toward him.

He couldn't be seen until the last minute. When he

stepped out, it was easy to accost the man, spin him around and ascertain that a strong man could have certainly caught a woman so; he would have had to have dragged her as she bled, and thus the trail to the street.

Why leave her in the street?

So she would be found, and found as she was.

He scanned the crowd, wondering if any of the men hovering about in their business suits, construction vests, chef's outfits, messenger tees or other attire might be a killer. He wouldn't be bloody anymore; he'd be fitting in with the crowd.

Jude walked down the sidewalk to where the bakery manager still stood, trembling with two officers. She was shaking badly.

Dorothy Hannigan was a woman with a thin face and thinner body; she obviously did not indulge frequently in her bakery's items. She looked at him with wide brown eyes and an expression that still denoted the horror of her discovery.

"Ms. Hannigan, I'm Detective Jude Crosby. I know you've already given the officers your statement, so I really just want to thank you for so quickly summoning help, and for all that you've done to assist us in the investigation." She hadn't really done anything—she'd screamed instinctively. But he had discovered that the right tone of questioning always produced more than dismissal or rudeness.

She nodded, seeming to get a bit of a grip. "Shall we have some coffee?" he asked her.

She looked nervously at the corner bakery. "I open. I gave the keys to one of the boys…but I guess no one is really going to be hungry around here for a while."

He smiled. "They'll be hungry," he said. *Don't kid yourself,* he thought. *People will be converging to talk. When the crime scene tape is gone, they'll be fighting each other to get in the street and photograph the position where the body lay.*

"But come in...the police will clear this with your boss." He nodded to Smith, who hurried on in ahead of him. He ushered Dorothy Hannigan to a booth at the rear of the bakery. Apparently, the boy she had given the keys to had gotten things going; customers were already in the shop, but other than Dorothy Hannigan's white face, little gave away the fact that Jude was anything other than an ordinary customer. His suit was a good one, not that a homicide detective in New York made the big bucks, but he had a great apartment in Hell's Kitchen, thanks to his father's savvy with real estate, and it seemed, lately, that he lived to work. That meant decent suits—and suits that blended in well with the business attire in the moneyed district where he worked.

"So, Dorothy, please, tell me exactly how you came upon the body this morning," he said quietly. He lifted a hand so that she would wait. Officer Smith had apparently seen to it that the owner, now in, was aware that his manager was helping the police; a waiter brought them two cups of coffee and quickly disappeared. She shook her head. "I saw...the body. It was barely light, you know. And there was no traffic—no, wait, there was one car, but it was in the other lane, and it just drove on by. You can only go the one way, you know."

He nodded, taking a sip of his coffee.

She shivered suddenly. "I come off that subway

every morning. I'm the only person who gets off half the time. That could have been me."

He set a hand on hers. "She was killed late last night, Miss Hannigan. I don't think this killer was looking to stalk victims in the morning—someone would have come. You saw how quickly the streets got busy."

She swallowed audibly.

"Is there someone you can ride in with for the next week or so?" he asked her.

She stared at him. "You're going to catch this freak in a week or so?" she asked. "Half the cases go unsolved, from what I've heard."

"That's a gross exaggeration, really. Half the murder cases we go out on are—well, sadly—domestic. And they're solved," he said.

"But—how? There are twenty million people on the island of Manhattan on a workday—that's the statistic I've heard."

"Give or take a million," he agreed. "Please, that's why I'm asking you—describe exactly what you saw."

"I was walking down the street. I saw the car go by—oh, yes, of course. I saw the body in the middle of the street because of the headlights. The car just kept going. I was afraid it might have been an old derelict, passed out in the street. I have a little laser light I carry, and a whistle—I'm not stupid, you know—and so I shone the light and hurried out, hoping that nothing was coming barreling up Broadway. And then I saw her—and then I started screaming."

"Did you see anyone else—anyone at all? A bum, a shadow…anyone?" he asked.

She shook her head. Then she sat straighter. "Wait—there's old Captain Tyler."

"Old Captain Tyler?"

She nodded. "A sad case. Everyone keeps urging him to go to a shelter, but he shows up back on the streets, begging. I mean, of course, God help us, we get a lot of homeless guys down here. But Captain Tyler is kind of sweet. He's an older fellow, Vietnam vet."

"Did you see him this morning?" Jude asked.

"I might have."

"You might have?"

"There was a pile of rags and a sleeping bag at the entrance to the subway. I remember thinking that it *might* have been poor old Captain Tyler. But I didn't disturb the pile."

He nodded. "But nothing else? No one watching you?"

She shook her head. "No, not that I noticed." She fell silent again. "I'm going to get killed on my way in to work one of these days despite my whistle, aren't I?"

"Come in with coworkers, Ms. Hannigan, if there's any way. I'll talk to your boss. It's prudent to be extremely careful until we know what we're up against," he said. "I've got to get my men looking for Captain Tyler. Can you give me a description?"

Tyler, according to Ms. Hannigan, was tall and thin, wore a shabby army-surplus jacket and dirty denim jeans, and had long white hair and a scraggly white-and-gray beard.

"He told me once he suffered from shell shock," Dorothy Hannigan told him. "Sad, huh? Can't hold a job, and his benefits don't really keep a roof over his head." She gasped. "He couldn't have done this, could he have?"

"If you see him, call me. I don't think, however, that shell shock, even after years, would suddenly turn a man into a vicious murderer. But when we find him, we'll find out what we can. We have some truly wonderful psychiatrists with the department. They'll be able to deal with him," Jude assured her. As he spoke, his phone rang.

It was Norton, from headquarters.

"Assistant chief wants to see you, pronto," Norton told him.

"I'm at the scene," Jude told him.

"I know. I told him that you'd been dispatched by orders of the lieutenant. But he says that you've had time to do what you can do there, and that he wants to see you about a task force."

"No other murders today, huh?" Jude asked dryly.

"Not like this. Film is already rolling. The news is shooting through all five boroughs, the country and the world like the spew from a geyser. *Jack's back.* That's what they're saying. Anyway, he wants you in here, now."

The twenty-first-century media was amazing, Jude thought. He barely knew anything about the crime, but rumor was running rampant, and he understood that One Police Plaza wanted this solved as quickly as humanly possible.

Two other murder investigations were open on his slate; this seemed to be the one that mattered. Naturally. The other two had also been stabbed, but one had died on the way to the hospital and one had been dragged out of the river. This had been public and sensationalist. The victim was a spectacle on Broadway. They were both his cases because he worked specifically for the chief of police; he and Monty had been "detective specialists" for years, which meant they could cover all of New York City as needed.

He wished that they hadn't been his cases; he'd gotten nowhere with them. The other two women had died quietly, apparently without friends to miss them. They hadn't been discovered in such a bold and gruesome state, with all the world watching.

Except that he wondered if the deputy chief was thinking along the same lines that were now plaguing him. He wasn't a Ripperologist, as Fullbright considered himself, but he did know about the case a fair amount since he'd spent the month of August in Britain last year for an experimental exchange police procedural program. The program had included a study of the Ripper files, with one of Britain's top historians discussing police work now and then. Jude had looked at the archives available. Five victims were accepted as the Ripper's, but the London case files had started with the deaths of two women who had been killed before what was now deemed by experts to be Ripper murders.

They had the girl from the river, and the girl who had survived her attack long enough to make it to the hospital. Neither had carried ID; neither had been reported missing. All efforts to identify the two had been to no avail. Both had come from New York or to New York…and met sad ends.

And now…

Virginia Rockford.

"I'm still at the scene, working it," Jude said.

"Crime scene folks are there. And they're good at what they do. That's what the assistant chief said. Get in here."

Jude clicked his phone closed. Great. He'd find himself besieged by the reporters stationed at "the shack" on the second floor of headquarters before he could reach the deputy chief's office.

He wished he hadn't been called. He wished any other cop in the city had come on for this case.

But they hadn't; he had been on duty, and he had been specifically ordered down here.

He thanked Dorothy Hannigan and left her his card, and started out, wishing that he could look for Captain Tyler himself. But he told Smith to get more men on finding the homeless man; and he gave the officer the task of connecting with the producer for the movie being shot down the street and getting him a list of anyone involved in the production. He wanted the beat cops to keep a presence on the street and their eyes open.

There had probably been a number of young women involved in the shoot the day before; the cops could start with them. He stressed the importance of their notes, and Smith looked at him, hesitant. "Crosby, you know I'm a beat cop, right? Not the boss down here."

"Smith, I think you'll be fine," he said.

He headed down Broadway. It was far easier to walk around Lower Manhattan right now than to get his car.

He managed to reach the deputy chief's office without being waylaid. The offices were huge, and he was just lucky that the elevator he was in didn't stop on the second floor where he might have been detained by an avid reporter.

He stood in front of the desk, but Nathaniel Green, "D-Chiefy," as the men called him affectionately behind his back, wasn't a browbeater. He wasn't a political appointee, either. He'd earned his place, moving up the ranks.

Green indicated the chair in front of his desk and Jude sat.

"Are you taking me off this new case?" Jude asked him.

Green smiled grimly. "Sorry, no. But I'm giving you a team, a task force. Who do you want?"

Jude was quiet for a minute. He wanted to work with Monty, his partner of the last five years. But Monty was still in the hospital, and the last thing he needed, still clinging to life and praying to walk again, was a sensationalist murder case on his mind.

"Ellis Sayer and his group."

"You've got them. You have priority access to whoever you want in the Technical Assistance Response Unit. And I'm bringing in the feds."

"The feds? As far as I know, the killer didn't kidnap the women and cross state lines." Jude was truly puzzled; he wanted to believe that when it was important, law enforcement agencies did know how to cooperate. But they could also be possessive and territorial. The NYPD usually wanted to solve their own cases. They didn't mind help from other agencies, but they wanted control.

Green grimaced dryly. "You just said women. I believe we're thinking along the same lines."

"That we have a killer trying to emulate one from the late 1880s? That's a stretch."

"We have a killer who left a woman slashed to shreds on Broadway. The other women in those two earlier cases—both seemed to have come from nowhere. They were murdered, and they're still trying to hold on down at the morgue to see if the bodies will be claimed." He hesitated. "Look, Jude, this is my call. The second that body was found, the media went crazy, and, before the public puts the puzzle pieces together, I want to be on it—a step ahead. Think about the way our Jane Does were ripped up."

"*Obviously,* sir, since I arrived at the scene of last night's crime, I've given it some thought. But I've also been trying to give the first two victims my full attention. No one seems to miss them—as you said. They appear to be lost creatures. Maybe prostitutes," Jude said. "And maybe the three murders are all connected—at this point, we just don't know. If you say we should bring in the feds, fine. I'm not sure I see where federal jurisdiction is warranted yet."

"What we're bringing in is a special federal unit. We're not handing over jurisdiction. They'll work with you—you work with them," Green said.

"Sure. Though again, I'm still not seeing a federal connection. And we have FBI offices in the city. Why is a *special* unit coming in?"

Green looked at him with a certain degree of exasperation. "Jude, this is coming straight from the top brass. The mayor's office. We can't have tourists terrified of coming to New York City. We've done a good job in the past few years. Giuliani cleaned up a lot of the theater district and visitors can actually catch cabs that take them where they want to go. We don't need a return to the seventies—or back to the days of Five Points, when a walk near where our own building stands meant tripping over the bodies of the starved, diseased—or murdered. We have to work hard and fast. The media is already having a field day with this one. If a special unit can help, I'm all for it."

Jude winced inwardly. Special unit? He wasn't sure what that meant. But it was fine. He was pretty damn sure that they weren't going to find anything to point them straight to the killer. New York City cops were good; they had learned to deal with just about every-thing the world could throw them. But they were also faced with a population that was staggering. Finding leads was going to be like looking for the proverbial needle in a haystack.

"Well, hell, yes, I'm glad for anything that can help," Jude said.

"You want not just this murder solved, but the other two as well. I know you, Crosby. You've been beating the pavement and harassing Tech Support every day for help on the two victims you pulled in the last couple of weeks."

"We don't know that these killings are connected in any way."

"Stabbings with sharp knives or utensils, same place on the bodies, each attack growing more violent…"

Jude looked down, not wanting Green to see that

he was irritated about being called off the street at the prime moment to make discoveries.

"We do have good cops. Our forensics people are cops, too, Jude. They won't let you down. You know you aren't going to find clues on the street…you know this is a serious situation being created by an extremely organized killer. This is going to take time, manpower and all the behavioral profiling help we can get."

"I can be a team player, and you know it."

"That's why you're in charge, Jude. Have you seen the news already?" Green asked.

"Oh, yeah." He looked at Green across the desk. "Yes, the media is giving the bastard just what he wants. Notoriety."

"That's true. Now, as to the team… This unit was established by a man we worked with down here years ago. Adam Harrison. Similar crimes. Attacks on historical properties, and a perp who was in love with Edgar Allan Poe and started killing people like the victims in Poe stories. Anyway, it's a different thing to go after a man like this, and the head of this team is an agent who worked the behavioral sciences aspect of crimes for years. One of the team is already in transit—the others will be here tomorrow. I'm setting them up with an apartment in Blair House. You'll actually meet…" He paused for a minute, looking at a memo on his desk. "You'll meet Miss Whitney Tremont at Blair House at two, get her settled in and then head for the autopsy."

"I'm taking her to autopsy?"

"Yes."

"I thought Blair House was closed for renovations."

Green nodded. "It is—the preservationists won't let

the place be torn down, and it's not due for construction crews to begin work for another few weeks. I want the team in the area. I'll set up a meeting for you tomorrow with the team and the team head, Special Agent Jackson Crow."

Jude stood. It was decided, and he knew it. So much for his social life. Wait—he didn't really have a social life. Since he and Jill had parted last spring, he'd enjoyed three one-night stands and a two-week dating whirl. Actually, he'd had three one-night stands—enjoyed two.

"All right. I want Hannah Mills in Tech."

"She's yours."

Jude nodded again. "And I have priority at autopsy—now, and if this does go further?"

"I just called Fullbright. He'll be your man, and he will be ready to meet with you at three this afternoon—the autopsy is already scheduled."

Jude nodded again. "I'm going back to the scene until then. I'll meet your Miss Tremont at two, and we'll be at autopsy together at three. And don't give me that resigned look. I'll call Ellis and get his team moving, too."

"You're the best I've got, Jude. And I'm giving you priority all the way," Green told him.

Jude wasn't sure he was the best that the deputy chief had. Hell, he'd just watched his partner get shot in a situation that should have never ended as it had.

But this was what he did; he'd known all his life that, like his father and grandfather—and great-grandfather before that—he'd wanted to be a cop. He'd been lucky; he'd gone to college and gotten degrees in criminology and psychology, something his father and grandfather hadn't been able to acquire. But they'd both been good cops. The kind who put the bad guys away.

This was one bad guy they were going after and they all knew it.

"I'll do my absolute best, sir," Jude said.

"I know you will."

He had been dismissed. He headed straight to Tech Support, where he discovered that Green had put through a call to Hannah Mills. Hannah was excited; she'd never actually spoken directly to Green before.

She was a whiz with computers, and if a piece of information was available anywhere, Hannah could find it. At one time in history, she would have been called a spinster. She was a slender woman with bottle-thick wire glasses, brown hair worn in a bun each day and a mind that could work as quickly as a computer.

"I'm making printouts for you, they'll be popping out as we speak," she told Jude.

"She was with the movie crew?" Jude asked.

"She was portraying prostitute Mary Green. She was an extra, I believe, but she had a fair amount of screen time. Maybe even a line or two. Anyway, I have a list for you. The producer, the director, the name of the off-duty officer patrolling…a liaison with the movie and television unit. I think it's all here. And when you want more, you call me, day or night!" She stood up in her little cubicle and planted a kiss on his cheek. "Thank you, Jude! Thank you for asking for me."

"Thank *you* for being a good tech. I do have something for you. I want you to find out all you can about a Captain Tyler, a Vietnam vet."

"Oh, that Tyler. I thought you meant one of the thousand others on the island of Manhattan."

"Very funny. This one would have been in and out of local veterans' hospitals."

"On it," she assured him.

"And one more—I want everything you can find about a government group put together by a man named Adam Harrison. Team head is Jackson Crow."

"The name is familiar. I'll get right on it."

Jude returned to lower Broadway, opting to walk back to the scene. On a television screen, through an appliance-shop window, he could see that Deputy Chief Green himself was speaking to the media. He urged citizens to calm down and be vigilant.

He put a in call to Ellis and let him know that he and his group were to join Jude and the feds. Before he had reached the scene of the crime again, he had everyone in motion; they would start with initial interviews of everyone on the movie set. He looked at the list Hannah had given him; he could get one of the feds to make sure that this list and the list that Smith was able to garner matched. Like it or not, he was working with the feds. Might as well make use of them.

With careful steps, he walked from the set to where the body had been found, reimagining the victim's probable search for a cab, and how the killer had come upon her. All the while he searched for Captain Tyler as well. But though he made new acquaintances with several of the homeless people on the streets, he didn't find Tyler.

He felt a growing sense of anger.

Someone out there was either amusing himself at

the expense of the police, or sincerely thought himself the reincarnation of a legendary killer.

The victim probably hadn't had time to scream. New York had been teeming with life just blocks away—the population was huge.

Just as it had been in the crowded tenements of Whitechapel and the East End of London.

The killer had probably surprised her; choked her to unconsciousness before slitting her throat.

His phone rang. It was Hannah.

"What's up? What have you got?"

"Info, but not on the victim—on your *team*," Hannah told him.

There was a strange excitement in her voice.

"They're a special team, all right. They've barely been around a year, but they've already solved a number of really bizarre cases. Jude—they're a paranormal team. They don't just investigate, they appear to talk to ghosts. They're highly respected for what they've done, but they're also a bit on the outside, even of the FBI itself. Only the head guy, that Jackson Crow, has been a special agent for a long time. But he's supposed to be one of the best behavioral guys out there. They sound good, really good. But weird, too. You must have heard something about this group. They solved a creepy murder in New Orleans that had to do with all kinds of political corruption."

"I might have heard something," he said. He winced. Leave it him to wind up with the "special" team. Which reminded him...

"Thanks, Hannah. I have to meet one of the agents now, and it's good to be forewarned."

He hung up. On to meet his spiritualist or medium or whatever. He'd been told he had to work with the team; he would. He'd be polite. He'd spend the days and nights reminding himself that all help was needed at the moment.

The days and nights ahead suddenly seemed extremely long.

Be polite. Collect the "special" agent. And then on to autopsy.

2

Blair House.

It stood behind a wall and next to an area where a massive construction project seemed to be under way—except that the construction crews didn't appear to be out. The house was barely a block away from Wall Street, and another block from Broadway, within easy distance of St. Paul's, Trinity and the World Trade Center site.

Blair House itself was as out of sync with the current pulse of the city as the churches with their early American graveyards.

As far as the financial concerns of humanity went, it only made sense to tear down the old to make way for the new.

But, Whitney Tremont had been glad to hear, Blair House was not going to be torn down. It was slated for a great deal of renovation; federal money was coming in to tend to a federal project—it was said that among the many places George Washington slept, Blair House was one of his favorites.

A low brick wall obscured much of the facade, while

wrought-iron detail, tangled with ivy, rose from the wall. She could see the house from the sidewalk only because the driver who had picked her up from the airport had provided her with keys, and she had opened the gate while awaiting her NYPD liaison, Detective Jude Crosby.

The brick path to the house was overgrown, as was the house's yard area. To the left, there was a charming pagoda overrun with ivy and flowering plants and to the right, a fountain that no longer trickled water was in a similar state.

The house itself was Greek Revival—several steps led up to a porch with fine Ionic columns. The front door was double-wide with etched-glass porticoes.

The off-white paint was peeling. The columns obviously needed help as well.

"It's not as bad as it looks."

She turned, startled. She had been giving the house so much attention that she hadn't noticed the tall man who had walked up to her on the sidewalk.

He was actually hard not to notice; he was a good six foot three and built like a linebacker.

"I wasn't thinking that it was bad," she told him. "I was just thinking that it's beautiful, and I'm glad they're not tearing it down." She offered him a hand. "Special Agent Whitney Tremont, Detective Crosby. Thank you for being here."

He shrugged his broad shoulders. "Sure. The situation is bad. Whatever it takes. Need a hand with your bag?"

She shook her head. "I'm fine. We can just head on in."

He hadn't exactly been warm and cuddly, but he wasn't being rude, and he seemed to be sincere. Other agencies sometimes resented FBI involvement in a case—they weren't always fond of the fact that someone over them had invited the feds in.

She'd never exactly intended to work for the federal government, but she didn't mind. As long as they were left to work alone, it just didn't matter. And since the head of their unit, Jackson Crow, had established himself as an agent with an exemplary record before he'd been given his current team, she was more than willing to accept the occasional snickers that came their way. Jackson could stare down any man and silence him within a matter of seconds.

"I believe they had a cleaning crew come in already—a good thing, since I don't imagine that you and your team would want a lot of people around." Jude Crosby told her. "Also, if I know my superiors, they had staples brought in, so you should have essentials."

"Thanks."

He studied her for a minute; his face gave nothing away. "Well, I guess we should get you settled." He actually grinned. "You know it's a haunted house, right?"

"What self-respecting house this old isn't haunted?" she asked.

He was still sizing her up, of course, given the team's reputation. She smiled, not saying anything. They were all welcome to wonder. Detective Crosby would meet Jackson Crow soon enough. Jackson had a tenet he lived by, and the team followed its simple sentiment— use logic, and then feelings.

"The rest of your team isn't arriving until tomorrow?" he asked her.

"That's right."

"So you're staying here alone tonight?"

"Yes, and I'll be fine. Let me take a quick look
around, drop my bag and we can go to the autopsy."

He pointed to the area next door. "That's where they
were filming the movie and that's where the victim
came from when she was leaving. I'm surprised that
they sent you in alone."

"You shouldn't be. I went through a lot of sessions
at the shooting range. I passed," Whitney told him.

"Can you shoot a ghost?" he asked. The question
seemed pleasant enough, but she realized she was being
mocked. She wondered if he was more concerned that
she was a ghost-hunting special agent, or that she was
a small woman.

"I'm quite competent, thank you," she assured him.

"All right, your call… Just remember, please, it's an
NYC case with NYC police heading the investigation.
I'm impressed that a unit was asked in immediately.
Somebody thinks that your ghost hunting—that your
team—is top-notch. Thing is, there's nothing really
around you at night, unless you want to count the dead
in Trinity's and St. Paul's graveyards. Last night, that
crew working this area so late was unusual. But that's
film for you."

He didn't wait for her reply; he started up the walk.

Whitney stepped into the main hallway, which was
long and extremely broad. A slim curving staircase
against the western wall led to the floor above, and she
could see down the hallway to the door that opened to

the back. She wanted to stop, to try to sense the place, but she didn't; not with Jude Crosby watching.

"They say the foundations of this old place date back to the last decades of the eighteenth century. There were lots of fires back then, though, and not a lot of control. I think the current structure is from 1810. I have to say, I'm glad they're preserving it, too. Wonder what it was like back in the day. I mean, New York moves like a bullet. I love the city."

"It's a great city," Whitney murmured.

Whitney noted that the hallway had probably been the grand meeting room of the house; parties had probably been held right there with indentured servants or slaves walking the room at times with silver trays. A grand piano sat against the wall at the rear; she wondered just how old it might be.

But she'd have to explore later.

Whatever happened with the New York City police, she wanted to make sure that she was there from the get-go, and that her prep work had been done. They were there to assist the police, not to take over an investigation, no matter how much pull they might have with different power structures. She'd spent the trip reading email on the current murder—preliminary notes only—and, since the cry was out that the murder seemed to be mimicking that of a long-ago Ripper victim, she had spent most of the time during her flight on her iPad, downloading the best books she could find on the elusive killer from the past.

"I've only been in this house a few times," Jude told her. "When I was a kid on school tours, before it was closed down for renovations. I'm going to suggest you snag the first room up the stairs on your left. The last owners—who gave it to the government about twenty years ago—had a nice bathroom installed up there."

"Thanks," she told him.

"Go on, take a peek. I'll carry your bag on up, and then I'll get you down to the morgue."

"Thanks," she told him again.

He was an imposing presence. His features were as rugged as his muscled form—handsome, masculine, strong, with the right amount of rough around the edges.

Not a good thought, she told herself. She had to be blunt and strong herself; in fact, she was going to have to make sure that she remained smoothly professional in every way. They needed his respect. In her case, at five-three, she was fighting physical odds right from the start.

"I can really carry my own bag—"

"Simple courtesy, Agent Tremont. We're not without it," he said.

The bedroom was nice. She glanced in the doorway as Jude Crosby set her travel bag on the footrest at the end of the bed. She took a minute to dig into her overnight bag for her better camera to be added to the shoulder bag.

"You're a photographer?"

"Film is the best record of what we see, isn't it?" she asked.

The room smelled sweetly and lightly of lavender cleaning solution. It was a beautiful room, and she was convinced that it did have a feel for the past, just as venerated old churches and other historic buildings often seemed to have.

Would it be more than just the sacred feel of history? she wondered.

"Great," she said. "Let's go."

Jude arched a brow. "That's it? You don't want to look around longer? Settle in?"

"Nope." She was grateful that she'd been able to come so quickly; they'd received the call almost immediately after they saw on the news that a gruesome murder had taken place in New York. While Jackson had calmly spoken about travel arrangements and equipment, explaining the circumstances in which they'd be working, she'd been online and discovered that if she left within the next ten minutes, she could be on a plane to LaGuardia that was scheduled for departure at ten, and would have her on the ground in New York by one. She'd jumped at the chance, although not without a few minutes of stern warnings from her associates. They mostly consisted of: *Be careful. We'll be right behind you. You know not to take chances. Remember that we work best when we can earn the cooperation of the local police.*

"Okay," Jude said. "You need anything else?"

She tapped her shoulder bag, a big soft leather sling she hadn't released since she'd gone through the security lines at the airport.

"I'm good. I have everything I need for the moment."

He gave her a crooked smile. "You travel light for a woman."

She felt her own smile tighten just a bit. Was he mocking her? She was fairly small and slim, she knew.

Her appearance and gender often worked in her favor. She wasn't threatening in size and, sometimes, that was good.

Get along with the locals, she reminded herself.

"Don't think of me as a woman, Detective. Think of me as an agent," she said. "And I won't think of you as a boy or a man—I'll think of you as a top-notch NYPD detective."

He laughed. Apparently, he did have a sense of humor. And he could laugh at himself.

As they left Blair House, Whitney found herself pausing to look at the large construction site next door.

"I'm assuming whatever was there wasn't protected by any historical society," she said.

"No, there had been an ugly building there from the 1920s, or something like that," Jude said. "Before that, it had been some kind of society building—not like high society. I mean…I don't know. Some people claimed that it was a spiritualist house, or a place for Satanists, or something like that. Odd, though. Construction there has had to halt several times. A few workers were injured. I think one was killed. And then, of course, last night happened. The film company had acquired permits to use the area. They bought mega-insurance for the shoot, but I don't think it helps, because the murder was off-site."

"And the woman who was murdered had been working there," Whitney said.

"Yep, playing a gaslight prostitute, I believe. Honestly, it's really no wonder that folks are crying 'Jack's back.' Poor girl. There's been some insinuation in early news reports that our victim didn't always get along with the other actresses. But maybe that's not a fair assessment—we haven't even really begun the investigation. From what I've learned, the old Jack the Ripper found victims who were used up, missing teeth, old and ugly, but I guess none of his victims had a reputation for not being nice. Now, that's an interesting question. Does being *nice* or *not nice* have much to do with being a victim?"

Whitney glanced at him. He was thoughtful, really thoughtful. She decided that he might have made a decent behaviorial scientist himself.

"That *is* an interesting question," Whitney said, still looking at the cheap mesh fencing and the occasional ugly green plastic sheets that surrounded the construction site. It appeared that the majority of the old structure had been demolished; there were planks over what looked like foundations that were still in the process of being dug out and cleared. There were also piles of new timber lying about—remnants, she presumed—of the sets that had been hastily constructed for the on-location shooting that had been done the day before.

She thought the site was empty and then she realized that there was a gate around the other side, and by the gate there was a small section with a tented roof. Sitting beneath it, watching the entrance and reading a magazine, was a guard.

"One guard watching the area," Whitney murmured.

Jude pointed to a row of trailers on the other side of the street. "Yesterday, throughout the day, there was tons of security. That's the tail end of the movie crew. There was no shooting today, and the producer announced, after the report of Miss Rockford's murder, that they were done with the location." He glanced her way. "I spent most of the day down here off and on, trying to get a real feel for what was going on, and what the situation was last night."

"What is your feeling about it now?"

He glanced her way and actually smiled. "I have a feeling—ye olde cop gut feeling—that it does have something to do with the movie and the movie crew."

Whitney mulled over his words as he drove her down to the morgue. She listened to the constant honking that was as natural as conversation in this city. She watched the rush of pedestrians along the busy streets. People flocking through the intersections, the occasional dog walker pausing along the sidewalk with a Baggie.

She'd been a film student herself in the city, and she knew the area. But now, she felt as if she was seeing it all through different eyes. She thought about the age and the history of the city; the city buildings forming a concrete tomb over the iniquity and depredation of what had been the Five Points region. Wall Street— once where the old wall built to protect the tip of the island had been. Few places rivaled New York City as a place where the sheer velocity of life trampled the pivotal spaces of history.

It all seemed new to her now: the slash of Broadway, the one-way streets, the parks, the people, the old and the new.

Well, her eyes *were* different now; she was different. And all because, once upon a time, she had determined to hold her own ground.

Life was different.

As was death.

As they headed for the morgue, Jude tried to forget the woman at his side.

Whitney Tremont. Special agent. Very special agent.

But, she did know how to be quiet. She was distracting, but that wasn't her fault. His. He set his mind back to the situation, and tried not to think that she was definitely an interesting and arresting individual.

Captain Tyler. Now, there was a dash of cold water. He wanted to find him—and he would. Rush hour— that time when citizens took their lives in their hands just to step into the subway—would most probably bring Captain Tyler back to his home haunts; the subway station where those who knew him would be kind enough to drop spare change or a dollar his way. The autopsy would be finished by that point.

He had spoken with many people who talked about how strange downtown could be at night. By day, the world itself hummed because of all the activity that occurred at the New York Stock Exchange. By night, restaurants closed. The gates to the churches were locked. Office workers were gone, and the major hotels were by Battery Park and the South Street Seaport. Nearby Tribeca and Soho entertained nightlife and housed hundreds of thousands of people. But here, at this end with the financial district and the government buildings, the night brought on a haunting quiet, as if the little area needed time to recoup from the madness of the light.

His only hope was in finding Captain Tyler, he thought. Or someone else who was like a ghost, left to eke out an existence from those who passed hurriedly by day, and forget them once darkness fell.

Jude parked his car, still lost in the case as he did so, and hoping against hope that it might be one that was solved quickly. Though he had his task force questioning the hundreds of people who had been involved in the film shoot, and he knew that they'd be eliminating those with airtight alibis, they'd also be making lists of those he needed to interview himself, or who needed to be investigated further. He almost forgot Whitney Tremont; in fact, he might have if she didn't give off a soft, underlying perfume, and if he didn't just feel the warmth of the body beside his own.

She was out of the car door, though, before he could walk around to open it for her. She was pure motion and energy.

"Keep your thoughts going and don't worry about me, Detective," she said. "I'm right behind you."

He grinned. So she was.

Jude Crosby was known at the morgue; he had no difficulty navigating the structure of the building, Whitney Tremont following closely behind him.

"OCME," or the Office of the Chief Medical Examiner, was housed on First Avenue. New York City held many firsts in the investigation of death; the Office of the Medical Examiner was established in 1918, the first of its kind in the country. OCME established the first toxicology laboratory and the first serology laboratory as well, at Bellevue Hospital, rather than the six-story headquarters where the executive offices, mortuary, autopsy, X-ray, photography and many labs were housed now.

Attending a victim's autopsy was always paramount to him; no matter how great a medical examiner might be at a report, there was always something to be gained by attending. Many medical examiners did consider the autopsy to be the victim's last chance to speak, and Jude believed them. You never knew just what a victim might "say."

He knew that time had made him jaded; he'd seen the dead so often. He noticed the odor of decaying flesh, and the stronger odors of the chemicals that were used to mask the smell. He noticed them, but he barely thought about them. He thought of the place as sterile. He wondered if his religious teachings as a child kicked in when he saw the dead; *the spirit didn't reside in the flesh. The dead were far from feeling pain. They had gone to a better place.*

He wasn't sure if he completely believed that. He did believe that they suffered no more in the fragile shell of the flesh.

There was a saying on the wall outside the autopsy room, there for all to see, a Latin motto: Let conversation cease, let laughter flee. This is the place where death delights in helping the living.

He hoped that Virginia Rockford could help point them toward her killer.

There were eight steel tables in the room, and three of them had occupants. Thousands passed through the doors of the morgue yearly, but not all were murder victims. Suicides came here, along with those who died in accidents, and those who died while in apparent good health. There were those who had died "by violence," and those who had died unattended. There were many reasons to come to the morgue. It was a big city; people died in strange ways.

Two assistants were working with Fullbright when they suited up to join the procedure. The body had been stripped and cleaned by the assistants, and somehow, that made the injuries done to Ginger Rockford all the more macabre. He could clearly see the gashes in her throat, and the hideous slashes that had been made in the lower abdomen.

He was aware of everyone around him, and especially, Whitney.

Whitney worked with her camera; he wanted to stop her. He had to remind himself that she was an agent, and not a gawker. Whatever photos and digital film she took would be for the purposes of the investigation.

Clothed in scrubs, Whitney might have blended in with the workforce, except that he could see that she was also wearing a pair of neat little fashionable heels that weren't usually worn by techs in the morgue. When he had introduced her to Fullbright, she'd stood a slight distance back as well, as if trying to make herself unobtrusive.

When he looked at her, curious as to whether or not she could really watch the autopsy and learn from it, he discovered that he was almost transfixed by her eyes. They were nearly gold. The color had to be hazel, but the green and brown blended so remarkably that the color was almost like the sun. And her skin was the most amazing shade of golden copper he could imagine. It seemed as if every race into which humanity had divided had recombined in her, and that mixture was arresting; she was a beautiful young woman, but much more as well. She stood still, and yet seemed to be brimming with energy. Character, curiosity, passion and a certain appearance of honor seemed to be imprinted in the very structure of her face.

And she was young; too young to be jaded. He had the feeling she still believed in "Truth, Justice, and the American Way."

"Jude, look well," Fullbright said, and he clenched hard on his jaw, returning his full attention to the sad matter at hand. "The two great lacerations to the throat severed both the major blood vessels in the throat—just as in the case of Polly Nichols, the woman most detectives—past and present—believed to have been the Ripper's first victim. And if you'll note the mutilations on the abdomen, you see how jagged this first cut is, and you'll see how violent and savage the rest are. Jude, these are nearly the exact wounds as perpetrated by a killer over a hundred years ago."

He stared at the woman, holding back a groan. He didn't discount the idea that they might be looking at a mimic who had an agenda that would send the city into a real panic, attempting to re-create the slayings of a long-gone killer.

But he didn't discount the idea yet that they were looking at an isolated incident, and that Virginia Rockford had managed to really anger someone intent on killing her specifically. And solely.

Whitney spoke up. "I spent the hours on the plane here reading up on the crimes, since the press seems to believe there's a copycat out there." She walked to the side table where she had left her shoulder bag and dug in it briefly to produce a piece of paper with a picture on it. "Polly Nichols—a morgue photo. Care to compare the medical examiner's report with our corpse?"

Jude looked from her unique eyes to the photo, and despite his determination to keep an entirely open mind, he had to give the comparison credence.

The Ripper's victim had been older; life had not been kind. The image was not that of a pretty young woman.

Whatever else Virginia Rockford might have been, she hadn't been old. She had been attractive; killed when it seemed that the world was waiting for her.

But, despite the difference in the living appearances and situations of the women, the wounds on the bodies were the same.

Exactly the same.

The autopsy had just begun. He thought they had already learned what they needed to know.

3

She was losing credibility, Whitney thought, and doing so by proving a point.

But learning how to work with Jude Crosby wasn't going to be easy.

He was a hard-boiled cop. And the perfect vision of one. So tall, so leanly, ruggedly muscled. He had dark hair, with no signs of gray yet, neatly clipped. She estimated that he was in his mid-thirties; a man with gray eyes that had seen too much; he was weary, and yet he still seemed to have the look of a man who wanted to change the world.

Whitney thought that he must have grown up reading every old detective novel that had ever been printed. He didn't have to speak a word; she could tell by his body language that he wasn't happy about her being on the case.

Maybe she shouldn't have been so pleased that she'd been the first of her team to arrive on-site, or that she should be the one to dive headfirst into the macabre killing. Perhaps it would have been better if they would have started out with Jude Crosby meeting one of the

guys; Jackson Crow, Jake Mallory or Will Chan might
have made a better impression. She doubted that Jude
Crosby had ever worked with a female partner. He kept
looking at her as if she were a little mosquito that had
gotten in his way. She wasn't out to prove anything;
she and the others were a team, and each member was
always glad to make use of his or her gender, color or
any perceived edge when it meant getting done what
needed to get done.

"Let's move through this autopsy before leaping to
any conclusions, shall we?" Jude Crosby suggested.
His voice was even; his tone was cool.

Doesn't play well with others! she thought.

Too bad. Fullbright seemed fine; he accepted her
simply as an FBI agent, and he was interested in the
photo of Jack the Ripper's first canonical victim. Fullbright was intrigued by the puzzle before him, and
it seemed evident that he was an armchair detective
himself, fascinated by the mystery of old. The medical examiner was convinced that the killer had, at the
least, studied the modus operandi of the mysterious
nineteenth-century killer.

*Crosby wasn't happy. Maybe he was always that
way. Maybe he felt that the federal government was
encroaching upon his right as state law enforcement.*

Well, that was all right. They had worked with cops
who were grateful to have them around—and cops who
didn't want them at all. They were learning as they
went, and so far, their odd mix of a team had done very
well.

She could step back.

"Definitely," she replied, and did step back, clearly defining her role as observer.

Whitney had seen many horrible things, but nothing like what had been done to the young woman on the gurney. She didn't want to blink or blanch as the doctor reported his findings in a dispassionate voice; she couldn't appear too weak to stomach it. The only thing she could do was force herself to take a huge mental step back as well. In truth, that wasn't so hard. It couldn't be *real* flesh on the table; that was too terrible to accept.

But she had known what the findings would be. Not exact, perhaps. But close. There were two grievously deep slashes across the throat, cutting the windpipe and vital veins and arteries; the woman had nearly been decapitated. There was bruising on the throat. There was a ragged gash right beneath the ribs, and followed down on the right-hand side of the body to the pelvis, displaying the kidneys. There were two cuts to the genitals, deep, and violent.

It was all so frighteningly exact.

Down to the wounds, the direction of the wounds, everything.

She felt Jude Crosby's eyes on her, over the body of the dead woman, and she met his gaze. *Steady, but not challenging,* she warned herself. They'd been asked in, through Adam Harrison's nudging, but it was still best to keep things as copacetic as possible.

"Doc, you scraped beneath her nails?"

"Of course—but we're not going to get anything. She didn't have a chance to fight him. She doesn't have a single defensive wound on her."

"Fibers? Threads? Hairs?"

"She went fast—the lab has her clothing."

Jude nodded. "All right. We'll leave you to close her up. Call me if anything—"

"Yes, of course, Jude. If anything, whatsoever. I'm not expecting anything on the toxicology reports, but, I promise, I'll let you know immediately." He hesitated, looking at Jude. "I still have your Jane Does in here," he said. "Are we getting anywhere with them?"

"We've sent out the picture of the girl who died on the way to the hospital—we've sent it everywhere in hell, and nothing," Jude said. "The second girl...the one from the water. Well, you saw her face. Not even a mother's love could help her recognize that child. I just asked my lieutenant yesterday about getting a graphic artist over. I'm not great on computers, but I know that a good graphic artist can do an amazing job with a likeness."

"Well, I'll get with you as soon as I have...anything," Wally Fullbright assured him grimly. "Miss Tremont—a pleasure, even if we're meeting under sad circumstances."

"You, too, Dr. Fullbright," Whitney said. "Thank you. Except...would it be possible for me to see the two girls who died last week?"

She thought that Jake would step in and proprietarily inform her that they had nothing to do with this case, and that he had it covered.

Fullbright did look to Jake.

Jake nodded.

"My assistant will escort you," Fullbright said.

"Thank you," she told him.

They followed a fellow in scrubs out and down the hall. In another room, there were rows and rows of steel drawers. Apparently, despite the number of deaths that came through the morgue, the murders of the two unknown girls were remembered. The assistant knew right where he was going. He glanced at Jake apologetically. "We're calling them Jane Doe wet and Jane Doe dry. The more recent body was pulled from the river," he explained to Whitney, something she already knew. Jackson Crow was thorough when he briefed his team.

He pulled out the drawer and pulled back the shroud-like sheet covering the corpse.

Whitney locked her jaw.

The flesh on the girl's face had met with the elements and any number of hungry river carnivores. The skull peeked through in many places. The skin that remained was a mottled gray-blue color, where it wasn't pulpy-red.

She glanced at Jake. "I'd like to take some photos. One of my teammates is a true whiz on a computer. He can work any graphics program invented, and I think he can get us a likeness of this girl's face by tonight. He's flying in tomorrow, but if he can get something right away, you can have the image by morning."

He was still wearing a mask over his mouth; maybe that made his eyes seem all the more intense.

He nodded.

She looked at the M.E.'s assistant. "I need a tape measure or a ruler," she told him.

"We have excellent photos at the station," Crosby told her.

"I can email these straight from my phone," she told him.

He obliged her with a nod, and she drew out her little high-megapixel phone/camera, and began shooting from every conceivable angle. Both men waited for her, and she worked quickly. On the one hand, she felt as if, in this steel and sterile environment, nothing was real. On the other hand, the girl in the drawer was far too real. Eventually, the police would find out who she was, because although Whitney hadn't known Jude long at all, she was certain that he would never give up. She had to keep snapping pictures; the police could find out *who* she was. Her work was to find out who had done this to her and why.

And hopefully before more died.

When Whitney was done, she nodded grimly. The assistant gently covered the dead girl's face again, and closed the drawer while Whitney prayed that she had a signal, so she could email the photos to Jake Mallory efficiently—and quickly.

Jude thanked the attendant and started walking on. Still hitting the send key, Whitney followed in his wake.

All the drawers were numbered. That seemed incredibly sad to Whitney. They were people in the drawers, not numbers.

In contrast, the second victim looked serene, as if she were sleeping. She might have been, if it weren't for the deep gashes on her body, visible when the sheet was pulled back.

"We've had her picture out everywhere," Jude said quietly. "And no one has claimed her body yet. She'll stay here a few more days, and then they'll house her in the morgue in the basement—and then she'll go to a potter's grave at City Cemetery," he told her.

Whitney took just one picture. The assistant covered the body and shut the drawer.

As it closed, Whitney felt as if she was surrounded by steel, the scent of formaldehyde and other chemicals, and realized just how cold she was.

"Well, I have a witness to find, Miss Tremont," Jude told her.

"Of course. I'm here to follow in your footsteps," she said.

He paused. She knew he really just wanted to tell her to go away. He didn't. He shrugged. She'd been assigned to him; he'd been told to accept the team's help. "All right, fine."

He turned and walked quickly. She hurried to keep up with him. He was tall. She was—not.

Outside, horns were blaring, pedestrians moved about the street and it seemed that everything in the world was small and slow next to the size and speed of the city. Jude Crosby, however, knew his city well. He maneuvered the sidewalk in a long stride; he'd parked his car on the street. That in itself was quite a feat—she was a good driver, but she'd never figure out how he parked his car in the tiny space where it was wedged. He started to walk around to the driver's side, but then remembered her. He turned and opened the passenger-side door.

She slid in quickly. She had the feeling that if she didn't move fast enough, she was going to be left behind.

"Who are we looking for?" she asked him.

"Captain Tyler," he said briefly.

"A cop—a sea captain?"

"Old veteran. Vietnam," he said. "He wanders that area at night. The woman who found the body thought that he was sleeping nearby when she came out of the subway. He might have seen something."

"Have you spoken with the last people to see Virginia Rockford yet?" Whitney asked.

"We'll be going through the cast and crew from the movie next, and those who were working at the on-site location," he said. He glanced at her. "Obviously, a sensationalist murder like this, I'm not the only cop on the case."

"But the two earlier victims—you were assigned to them?"

"My partner and I were assigned as the lead detectives on both cases. We've had a decent record, even when we've come up against unknowns. How anyone can live in this day and age and not be missed by *someone,* I don't know."

"Well, they must be missed by people who can't imagine they'd be in New York," Whitney said.

He stared straight ahead; she didn't blame him. In school, she hadn't kept a car in the city. She wondered if she'd actually be capable of driving when everyone seemed to think that they belonged in every lane, when the streets stopped up and people were everywhere.

"I suppose someone, somewhere, misses them. But you'd be amazed by the amount of people who really don't seem to belong anywhere," he said.

"I understand your partner is in the hospital," Whitney said softly, realizing she was probably treading on dangerous ground.

"He was shot. Mainly because people who don't know what they're doing need to stay out of police business."

"But he's going to make it," Whitney said.

He gazed at her then. His eyes could be as cold as jagged gray ice. "Yeah, he's going to live. Whether he'll ever walk again or not, I don't know."

"Medicine has come far. I'm sure he has the best doctors in the world."

He didn't reply. They drove in silence, except when he cursed beneath his breath at the other drivers on the road.

He glanced over at her as they moved south. "Have you been to New York before?" he asked, as if remembering that he had another person in his car.

"Film school," she said.

That drew a frown. "You are here now, with me, but you went to *film school?*"

"Yes."

"But now you're an agent."

"Yes."

"Don't you usually work with film, then? Surveillance systems, that kind of work?"

"Sometimes. In many ways, I still work with film. We're a specialized unit, working with bizarre situations. But you know that. You've had someone look up information about the team."

He ignored that. "This is homicide. And, sadly, homicide is horrible, but not—ghostly."

"And you don't think it was a bizarre homicide?"

She had him there, and he knew it. He didn't reply. She knew he wasn't happy that his partner was in the hospital, and he was working with a girl who looked as if she might have only just gotten her degree—in film. He wasn't pleased.

Crosby seemed to have a talent for parking in New York City—of course, he drove an unmarked car and didn't have to worry much about parking tickets. Still, he seemed to be able to find the only street parking on Broadway, and they were quickly walking down the major street, weaving their way through the mass of humanity.

Crime tape was gone; a woman had been murdered, and speculation was on everyone's lips—but Broadway could only be stopped so long.

Jude knew where he was going; they walked to the subway.

His pace decelerated as they reached the entrance. "Captain Tyler!" he said politely.

Whitney looked around Jude's imposing form and saw that there was a man sitting by the entrance. He was wearing a worn peacoat, denim jeans and a cap. He had nice gray eyes—that appeared as if they had known much better days.

"Yes?" the man said. He heaved a sigh and stood up. It seemed that he did so because he had been addressed by name, and standing was the proper thing to do. "Do I know you?" he asked Jude. "Can I help you in some way?"

"Sir, you can help me, yes. I'd like very much to bother you for some of your time. I'm a detective with the police, and—"

"The murder," Captain Tyler said. He nodded. It appeared that his thinking was clear; he didn't seem to have been drinking, nor did he have bloodshot or dilated eyes that would indicate he was taking drugs.

"Yes," Jude said.

"I saw her," Captain Tyler said, staring at Jude, then noting Whitney and looking at her, his smile becoming a gentle one. "Ma'am," he said, touching his cap. "Yes, I saw the young woman last night. She was not very nice."

Whitney frowned; she desperately didn't want this man to be the murderer. She didn't know him, of course. He smelled like the street, but that didn't matter. But there was something about his gray eyes and grizzled face that seemed to speak of dignity beyond misfortune.

"Captain Tyler? You're certain you saw the woman who was killed?" Jude asked.

"Oh, yes, her picture has been all over the news." Captain Tyler smiled, seeing Jude Crosby's frown. "Pete's Appliances, up on Reade Street. He keeps the news on all the time in his shop-front window," Tyler explained. "They've been blasting that girl's face over the airwaves all day."

"Can you tell us, please, about when you saw her last night?" Jude asked.

Captain Tyler nodded gravely. "She was walking up Broadway. I asked her for change, or for a dollar. She was rude. I think she said that I was an old junkie. I have never sold drugs. I took some drugs. I was in the jungle. It was the only way to stay in the jungle." He shook his head. "They say she was ripped up bad.

I've seen men living and breathing and running into battle, and then their young bodies literally blown to bits, their limbs here and there. But they are saying that the girl was gutted... She wasn't nice, but I hope she went quickly."

"Captain Tyler, would you come with me to the station?" Jude asked him. "I'd like to get your statement down on paper."

"Statement?" Captain Tyler said, confused.

"Yes, everything you have to say can help us," Jude told him.

Whitney looked at Jude, frowning. He couldn't believe that this dignified old man, down and out as he was, had hurt anyone.

"But—"

He glared at her fiercely. So much for cooperation; this was *his* case.

Captain Tyler nodded, looking at Whitney with a smile. "Free hot coffee, even if it's bad," he said.

"I'll get you *good* coffee," she promised him. "And, are you hungry?"

Captain Tyler was hungry. Jude seemed impatient, but when she started into the nearest coffee shop, he muttered and eased past her, buying Captain Tyler a large coffee and an Italian sub, and paying for it himself.

At the station, Jude moved through the offices, pausing only briefly to rattle off a few names in introductions she couldn't possibly remember. He directed her to one door while he directed Captain Tyler in through another door. She found herself in a small room behind one-way glass. She saw Jude sit Tyler down, and he asked the man his first name. It was Michael. As Jude politely laid out the lunch and waited for Michael Tyler to eat, an older man joined her in the room, offering his hand. "I'm Deputy Chief Green. I know that they call me D-Chiefy behind my back, and I answer quickly to Green," he told her, his tone pleasant and easy as he studied her. "And you're the first of the feds?" he asked.

She smiled, offered her hand in return and told him, "Yes, I'm the first of the feds. I'm Whitney Tremont."

"Well, glad to have you. I spoke briefly to Agent Crow. He said not to be fooled by your size, that you're as strong as a diamond. Is that true?"

She arched a brow. "Well, I'm not sure about that. I'm fascinated enough by what I do to walk boldly into the fray."

He nodded with a small smile. "Jude met you at Blair House?"

"Indeed."

"You and your team will be all right there?"

"It's beautiful. We're grateful for the lodging," she said.

"Well, we're glad to have any and all help on this one. We have to nip this thing right in the bud," he said, turning to watch through the glass. She thought that he might be one man who had been raised to the right position; he had an easy manner about him, but he watched the proceedings with sharp eyes, and she didn't think that he missed much. He'd done an assessment of her, she was sure, and he'd probably come to his own conclusions, with or without comment from Jackson Crow. But then Jackson and Angela Hawkins did have an edge over the rest of the team. Jackson had been an agent for years before becoming head of their team; Angela had been a cop in Virginia. She, on the other hand, had been sought out because she'd refused to doctor film that she'd taken of an actual ghost—because it hadn't been doctored to begin with! And Adam Harrison, who had put them all together, had been fascinated with her abilities with film and video, and her background, perhaps. However, after they had proved themselves with the Holloway case, they'd all received training, and she was confident in the training she'd received.

However, a man like Jude Crosby would consider her too inexperienced and too young and maybe even, eventually, too emotional; maybe she was, in a way. A way that she hoped stood her well. Emotions came along with instinct and intuition, and she and the team relied heavily on intuition. When she watched Captain Tyler, she was still somehow convinced of his innocence. The man's hands shook, perhaps due to Parkinson's or something, but she was certain that he wasn't on drugs. She wasn't sure what she expected; she had never conducted an in-office police interview. The only interviews like this that she'd ever seen had been on television. But Jude was never rude to the man. There were none of the softly spoken questions followed by yelled accusations or hands beating on the table that she had seen on television shows. He just asked Captain Michael Tyler to remember everything about the night and his meeting with Virginia Rockford.

He grew very serious, though, leaning forward as he asked, "Captain Tyler, after Miss Rockford passed by you, what did you do? What did you see? She must have been murdered right after she passed you. If you saw or heard anything else, we need to know."

Whitney was surprised when Tyler paused like a man who did have something to contribute. He shivered—or trembled—and then shook his head.

"I'm not always…right. You know, I mean…in the head. I hear explosions when they're not happening. I see…I see enemy faces in a crowd. I'm not always—right."

"That's okay. I understand. But anything you saw or heard or thought that you saw or heard will help me. Anything."

"A man," Captain Tyler said.

"What did this man look like? Did you see him with Miss Rockford?" Jude asked.

Tyler shook his head and closed his eyes. He seemed to be in pain. "I'm not sure he was real. He seemed tall in the night, but it might have been his hat. He wore a tall hat. And—and a cloak. And he was carrying something. A bag. Like…"

"Like a backpack?" Jude pressed.

"No. Like an old doctor's bag," Tyler said.

Jude sat back a moment, and then asked, "Did you see the man with Ginger Rockford?"

Tyler said, "No. I saw him under the street lamp. I saw him from a distance—he was down Broadway when the young woman was telling me I was a junkie. I've never been a junkie. I didn't see his face, but I did see that he looked strange—as if he didn't belong there. As if he had…stepped out of the mist from some other time." He winced again, and gripped his trembling hands together. "I told you—I go to the hospital now and then, but...when I'm on the street, I see things."

Jude nodded. "Thank you. Captain Tyler, can you still write?"

"Yes."

Jude passed him a legal pad. "Please, write down everything that you thought you saw. We deeply appreciate your help."

Tyler looked at the pad and held the pencil awkwardly for a moment, and then started writing. Jude waited patiently with him, and then excused himself while Tyler set about finishing his task.

Jude entered the small chamber where Whitney stood with Green.

"He's not our killer," Jude said.

"No," Green agreed. "From my experience, this man wouldn't be capable."

"You've introduced yourselves, I presume?" Jude asked. "Deputy Chief Nathaniel Green, Whitney Tremont."

"We've met, thank you," the deputy chief said. "What do you think about the man he saw? Sounds like the image of the Ripper. Do you think that the media is going to cause everyone out there to start seeing men in stovepipe hats and cloaks, carrying medical bags, around the city?"

"Probably," Jude said wearily. "But I still wanted to talk to Captain Tyler myself. We believed that he was in the area, and so it was important to know what he had to say. He's not the killer. From what he's said, it's looking more possible that we do have a psycho out there who wants to be the new Jack the Ripper."

"Ellis Sayer called in right before I joined Miss Tremont. He's talked to Angus Avery, the director on the film Miss Rockford was working on at the site. He's arranged to meet you at the old diner up in Soho... He should be here in the next half hour."

The deputy chief nodded. "Sayer also told me that you've set up a meeting with the task force in the morning—let's hope it's a quiet night."

"Let's hope. We have anything from Forensics?"

"We will soon."

Jude started out of the room, and then paused. "Sir, do you think we could get someone to—"

"I'll get an officer to see if we can get Captain Tyler into a shelter for the night. He may refuse our help, but I'll offer what we can," Green said.

Jude nodded. He sighed, as if he'd forgotten to pick up a brick he had to carry around his neck.

"Agent Tremont?"

"Sir," Whitney said to Green. *It was nice to meet you* or *it was a pleasure* just seemed wrong under the circumstances.

"Good to have you here, Agent Tremont," Green told her, and she thanked him.

Once again, she had to hurry to catch up with Jude. He was already moving through the building.

She realized quickly that he didn't intend to ditch her—brick around his neck or no, he'd been given his orders regarding her federal involvement along with the rest of the team, and as long as she didn't get in his way, she'd be fine. He simply assumed that she'd follow at his speed.

And so she kept up. She was at the passenger's side of his car again before he could open the driver's side.

She buckled in silently. As they pulled out into traffic again, she realized that he glanced at her.

"You heard him, of course."

"Captain Tyler?"

"Yes."

"Of course. I hear very well, Detective. Young ears, you know."

She thought that he almost grinned. "I'm not sure exactly what insights the specialty of your team might provide, but I don't believe that the ghost of Jack the Ripper has come to murder people in New York City."

"I don't believe that, either," she assured him.

"But you do believe in ghosts," he said. Lord! She'd heard that tone often enough.

"I believe that, frequently, by looking at the past, we can understand what's happening in the present," she said evenly.

He made some kind of snorting sound that was *almost* beneath his breath.

Whitney held her silence.

"Ghosts," he muttered after a minute.

She turned to stare at him. "Do you have any religious beliefs, Detective? Are you an atheist?"

She thought his jaw hardened, but it was difficult to tell with him. He hid his emotion well—unless he meant for it to show.

"Do I believe in God? Yes, I suppose I believe in a higher power."

"Hmm." She allowed herself a small sniff.

"And what does that mean?"

"Crosby—Irish. I'll bet you grew up Catholic," she said.

"Tremont—French? Hmm. New Orleans. Catholic—Baptist, voodooist, vampire Buddhist...Wiccan?"

She shook her head, offering him a smile with just a slight edge. He wasn't happy that he was saddled with a small woman. She was also a woman of mixed heritage who came from a city known for its alternative beliefs—voodoo, mumbo jumbo, as some thought. "Obviously, my background is mixed," she told him. "But, you see, my point here is that anyone who grew up Catholic, or in many of the Christian religions, already acknowledges a 'holy' ghost in the Nicene Creed. Most of us worship a higher, unseen power. Most people worldwide have some kind of faith in an afterlife, and if we can believe this without seeing what lies beyond, why does it seem so ridiculous that the energy that was life can stay behind?"

His eyes were on the road ahead of him. She saw the muscles in his face twitch. He didn't believe that energy stayed behind.

"Hell," he said, glancing her way, "if you can solve this case with ghosts, just go right on and be my guest."

Whitney smiled, not responding. There was something she liked about him, despite his curt manner with her. He had a good strong jawline and steady eyes. She thought he probably hit a gym now and then and she wondered if he spent time with a punching bag—he had callused knuckles.

"Angus Avery...I know the name. He's not as big as a Spielberg, but he's not an unknown," Whitney said.

"That's right—your expertise is film."

"Yeah, I'm good with it—you wait and see," she told him. "I worked with some excellent people—filmmakers from several of the major educational channels. I'd intended to make documentaries. Eventually, I would have found my own projects."

"But you woke up one morning and decided you wanted to be an FBI agent?" he asked.

She looked over at him. He glanced her way, but his attention was for driving.

"I like where my life has gone," she said. "And even you will like Jackson Crow and some of the others."

He laughed. "Even me?"

"You're not pleased to have me hanging around."

To her surprise, he was quiet for a minute. "Sorry. It's just that Monty—my partner—was like another half of me. We had a situation under control, and some idiot vigilante walked in and one man wound up dead and my partner may never walk again. You're fine. In fact," he said, and he grinned broadly, glancing her way again, "I think I'm happier to have you than whoever they might have assigned me. You're a guest of the city police. You won't be trying to second-guess me."

"I may be."

"Still, you'll have to bow to my decisions—I'm lead."

"I'm sure the task force will all bow to you," Whitney said.

He swerved slightly, avoiding a taxi that didn't seem to realize that there were lanes on Broadway. A few minutes later, in Soho, he pulled into a spot that had looked too small for the car.

"Diner is up there, on the corner," he said. He took

her elbow, directing her toward the end of the street. Keeping up with him meant long strides, and she took them.

They entered the touristy diner, which was decorated in red plastic and chrome with old movie posters on the walls. Looking around, Jude pointed down a row of glitter-red plastic booths.

"Is that him?" he asked Whitney.

She looked. A lone man was sitting in one of the middle booths. He was on his phone, and he'd doodled all over the napkin at his place setting. He had dark hair that was swept over his forehead in a strange way—*hair transplant, gotta keep young,* Whitney thought—and gold-rimmed glasses and he seemed to be thirty-five or so.

"I think so," she said. "Directors don't have their pictures out there all that often, and I don't think he's been nominated for an Academy Award yet."

Jude edged her ahead of him and she walked toward the booth. "Mr. Avery?" she asked.

He looked up and waved a finger at her, pointing at his phone. She held still politely.

Jude did not.

He flipped out his badge, and reached for Angus Avery's phone, snapping it shut and returning it.

"Sorry, Mr. Avery. I know that time is money in your line of work, but time could mean someone's life in mine. I'm Detective Crosby, and this is Agent Tremont."

Avery took the closure of his phone with little more than a frown, but he seemed perplexed by Whitney's appearance. "Agent?"

"Agent Tremont is with a special unit of the FBI, Mr. Angus," Jude explained, urging Whitney into the booth and taking the seat beside her. "Thank you for agreeing to meet with me," he said.

Angus Avery nodded, and then shook his head sadly. "Hey. This is horrible. But, I have to tell you, I think it's almost my fault."

"You killed Miss Rockford?" Jude asked.

"No! No, of course not!" Avery protested. "No, no—I should have stayed away from that location. I should have shot anywhere else in Manhattan—or Brooklyn, the Bronx, New Jersey or Hollywood, for that matter. It's that damn location. It's haunted—and it's cursed. And God knows—the creature haunting the place might just be Jack the Ripper—the real Jack the Ripper!"

He leaned forward. "Don't you understand? Jack the Ripper left London and came to the United States. And when he did, that's where he lived!"

4

Film people.

Great. He couldn't help it, he glanced at Whitney.

She smiled. "Surely, Mr. Angus, you don't believe that Jack the Ripper has lived all these years and that he's just starting out to murder women again? At age one hundred plus."

"I knew all about the history of the location. I just doubted all that mumbo-jumbo ghost stuff, just the way you do."

"I heard something about the location this morning, but I don't really know much about it," Whitney said. She smiled at him. "I went to the film school at NYU, Mr. Angus. I loved living and working up here, but somehow, I never learned about the location you were using for the film shoot yesterday."

"Well, let me tell you about it," Avery said, leaning toward Whitney.

Maybe the young woman would turn out to be an odd asset, Jude decided. Angus Avery seemed to like her. She was encouraging him to talk. He did believe—gut feeling—that the movie had something to do with it all. Maybe her background was going to be a good thing.

"The building they just tore down had no history. The Darby Building. It was an ugly old thing—built in the 1920s. No character, no class whatsoever. It should have been torn down. But what was on the site before— that's where all the trouble comes from."

"And what was there before?" Whitney asked. "A friend of mine told me that it had been some kind of spiritualist church."

"An offshoot group of some whacked-out folks— now, I suppose it would be some kind of nondenomi- national thing—started out building a church. Plain church. Simple pews, no statues, no stained-glass win- dows. They began in the 1840s, but it was too close to St. Paul's and Trinity to make the powers that be happy. Anyway, it became a 'home.' But it was a home for believers. I think it spent about twenty years becom- ing an old-fashioned halfway house for the homeless, immigrants, addicts, you name it. But by the end of the last decades of the nineteenth century, spiritual- ism was coming heavily to the fore, and along with spiritualism, you had devil worshippers, pagan cults and all that rot. So, imagine, you've got the House of Spiritualism here, and the Five Points area just blocks away. Slums and a cesspool. So. They start to clean up the Five Points area, and where do you think the real crackpots are going to come? Why, right over to the House of Spiritualism."

Angus Avery sat back, looking pleased with himself, as if he'd solved everything.

"And the so-called American victim of Jack the

Ripper was killed in the Bowery, and again, we're talking about a matter of blocks," Whitney said.

Jude spoke up. "Carrie Brown was killed in an old hotel."

They both looked at him, as if surprised that he was in on their conversation.

"Yes, she was killed in a hotel room. But Jack the Ripper killed Mary Kelly in her apartment. He was better—in his own mind, I'm sure—at his task of 'ripping' when he had time and privacy on his side. Well, here's the thing—and, Detective Crosby, I believe you'll find this in old police records or in memoirs of the officers of the time—they believed that the Jack the Ripper mimic or *Jack the Ripper* himself found lodging at the House of Spiritualism."

"So you believe that by renting the location for your film shoot you awakened the ghost of Jack the Ripper—or Jack the Ripper himself," Jude said, trying very hard to keep his tone low and even.

Angus Avery shook his head unhappily. "We were finished with the site after that day's shoot—we'd broken down. We were already planning on moving. But I called off *all* shooting for today—everywhere in the city. Can you even begin to imagine what that will do to my budget?"

"What made you choose the location?" Jude asked.

"Ah, well, the real shots we could get. And the fact that the financial district is actually shaped more like the Five Points that once was than the area that was Five Points! The movie takes place in the late eighteen hundreds. Shooting there, we could use the streets with some editing and CGI. And I had a great, almost barren landscape for the set designers to create facades. You'd be surprised at what you have when you black out modern additions to downtown."

"There's a giant pit at the location—dangerous," Jude said.

Avery waved a hand in the air. "We had it barricaded during the filming, and all kinds of people keeping watch. Production assistants and city engineers. We had a permit that included working a large section of Broadway," Avery said. "I knew about the location, but, as I said, I thought it was all a bunch of hogwash."

"And right next door, you had Blair House. It's pristine—you could have done some great shooting there," Whitney said. "I—"

Jude squeezed her hand beneath the table; he didn't want her announcing that the team was staying at Blair House. Especially since the team wasn't all here yet. As the day went by, he found himself more concerned that they had Whitney Tremont housed at Blair House—alone—for tonight.

"Blair House is under federal jurisdiction at the moment. I don't know exactly which historical association is in charge, but it's on the national list of historic places. I don't believe that a permit would have been given out for the use of it right now, no matter what was promised to the city," he said.

"Precisely," Avery said with a sigh. He brightened. "But, we did get some great footage of the facade. In fact, the Blair House facade—cleaned up, CGI—will be the house of ill repute where our movie prostitutes were settled."

"Just what was the movie you were making?" Jude asked.

"*Am* making. *O'Leary's*. I'm afraid the loss of an extra doesn't stop the giant wheels of a movie turning forever. And don't think badly of me, please. Movies have been completed when the featured stars have died. Everyone can't take the hit. Lord knows, in this country, we have to keep people employed and the money moving these days."

"You're a humanitarian," Jude said.

Whitney kicked his ankle.

"And the movie is?" Jude asked.

"A love story," Avery said. "A love story set amidst the squalor of the final days of the Five Points region of New York City. I mean, seriously, it's hard to imagine what it was like. Tenements were so crowded that the living often walked over the dead. Gangs were kings... politics were crooked. Sewage was a real killer—disease ran rampant. My movie, *O'Leary's,* is about two young people who rise above the horror and corruption to make it to the top."

"Ah. They moved to Gramercy Park!" Jude said.

Finally, he'd managed something that the filmmaker could seize upon. "Precisely!" Avery said with pleasure.

"Mr. Avery, what time did you leave the set yesterday?" Jude asked him.

Avery was thoughtful. Many people immediately shrank suspiciously from the question, aware that it was not harmless. But the man seemed to be remembering his day. "I left by five. One of my assistant directors worked on a few last shots with the prostitutes.

I headed to midtown. I gave a speech to a class from the fashion institute at their dinner at six."

Jude didn't ask Avery if there were witnesses; he'd check on it himself.

"Mr. Avery, we have a witness who saw a man in costume on the street—a nineteenth-century cloak and tall hat, like a stovepipe hat," Jude said.

"Was your witness a wino living on the streets? Or was your witness the killer?" Avery asked.

"You have nineteenth-century costuming on your cast, Mr. Avery," Whitney said. "Perhaps the killer is stealing from your wardrobe department?"

Avery shook his head. "You may speak to my costume designer and the wardrobe mistress. I insist on all costumes being returned at the end of the day. If a costume wasn't returned, I'd have known it. I might be making a movie, but any half-baked costume shop in town might have a cloak and a stovepipe hat! Look, please, check my alibi—and check my work record. It couldn't have been me, and I guarantee you, my wardrobe mistress would have been fired if there had been anything missing."

Avery's alibi didn't actually clear him. He might have given a speech—and returned, Jude thought. New York traffic—always a major "if" factor in the city. And, still, by the time Virginia Rockford had been killed, there had been very little traffic downtown. Avery could have well done everything exactly as he had said—and still arrived back on Broadway in time to commit murder.

"How well did you know Miss Rockford?" Jude asked.

"Know her? I didn't know her at all," Avery said.

"But she was working on your film," Jude said.

"Directors seldom hire the extras," Whitney said quietly.

"Oh, right, well, of course not," Jude said.

"Her death, however, devastates me," Avery said.

A waitress stopped by their table; Jude ordered coffee and Whitney did the same. Avery already had a cup before him.

When she was gone, Avery became businesslike. "I've asked my office to make sure that your fellow officer—Detective Sayer—has a list of everyone associated with the film, and what their position is. Except for poor Miss Rockford, of course."

"Of course," Whitney murmured.

"Do you have an idea of anyone else who might have stayed behind last night?"

"We have a guard who stays on until the last actor, costumer, production assistant—*even caterer*—has left the set for the day. Last night that would have been a fellow named Samuel Vintner. My offices have given Detective Sayer everything he could possibly need—phone numbers, addresses, even social security numbers. We desperately want to see this murder solved."

"Thank you for your help," Jude told him.

Angus Avery wagged a finger in the air again, directed at them both. "You mark my words. It's evil land. I think that they were burying people in the walls and foundations. I think that you'll find that Jack the Ripper—the real Ripper—is buried somewhere on that location. You have to find the corpse and burn it and say lots of prayers. Maybe that will stop this."

"We're hoping to catch a flesh-and-blood killer before anyone else dies," Jude said.

"Mr. Avery, there might have been someone—someone working on your movie—who had a grudge against Virginia Rockford," Jude said.

"There might have been. I told you, I didn't know the girl," Avery said, sounding impatient at last. "You have the names and office address of the casting directors. Madison and May Casting—they're actually on Madison. They can tell you all about the extras." He stood. "If there's nothing else, I have a date with a bottle of blended scotch whiskey and a friend. This is becoming a nightmare, what with my actors in a stew and the press all over everything in the world…forgive me. Order dinner on my tab, if you like. I need to go now."

"You noticed nothing unusual on the set at all?" Whitney asked.

"I told you—the location is cursed. We had a fellow die of a heart attack when he was moving set pieces. That was unusual. Natural causes, though, that's what they said. And we had a few injuries, too. It's the location. Go dig up the Ripper, burn his bones and the world will be back to normal. Down to a few domestic, drug and gang murders a week!" Avery had grown really impatient. "I'm easy to find, Detective Crosby. But, please, I'm a busy man. Call me only if you believe I can really help you."

"Sir, police business does take precedence. Rest assured, I don't like to waste my time. But if I feel that I need you, I will find you, no problem. Wherever you are," Jude assured him.

Avery's lips tightened as he rose and walked out, a clipboard in his hands. Jude watched as he headed out to the street—and a waiting stretch limo.

"Are we having dinner on him?" Whitney asked him.

"Nope, and I'm not seeing his movie, either," Jude said, rising. He looked at the three cups of coffee and laid a bill on the table, and then lifted a hand, hailing their waitress. When she arrived at the table, he said, "Miss, I need that cup, please."

"What?"

"I'm a police officer. If you need to get the manager, do so. That cup is evidence in a case I'm working."

"You need a Baggie?" she asked. "The cup is all yours!"

"Thanks. I carry my own," he told her.

In a few minutes, he'd secured the cup that Avery had been drinking from. "Let's go." He flipped his phone out and put through a call. "Ellis? Hey, yes, I've met with Angus Avery. I want the limos that worked that film site yesterday impounded. You'll need warrants, but you won't have a problem getting them now. I want Forensics going through them."

He listened for a minute. "I know everyone is working around the clock. Get the limos in anyway. They'll get to them." He listened again. "Yep, thanks, Ellis." He hung up and looked at Whitney.

"Where to now?" she asked.

Jude hesitated, and then offered her a twisted grin. "I'm going to drop off the cup at the lab, and then I'm bringing you home to meet Dad, Whitney. Seems like the thing to do after this conversation."

* * *

Andrew Crosby lived in Hell's Kitchen, also known as Clinton, which, for some reason, had become a more politically correct term for the area. His home was in a building that appeared to have been built in the late eighteen hundreds. Flowers grew in little patches of earth that might be called a yard, and when they entered the hallway and climbed the stairs to the two second-floor apartments, one of the doors was open.

Jude actually lived in the same building; his was the apartment next door. Years ago, when the place had gone co-op, his father had purchased the apartments. His dad's foresight was something for which he was eternally grateful. Living in New York was expensive.

At first, too, after his mother's death, he'd been glad that he was so close. And now, with the life he led, it was still good to be next door. Andrew had never been the type to intrude; he was there when needed.

"Jude, been expecting you all day!" his father said in a booming voice, greeting them at the entry.

"Whitney, meet my dad, Andrew Crosby. Dad, this is Whitney Tremont. She's with the feds who have been sent down on this case."

"A fed! Nice," Andrew said, greeting Whitney warmly. Naturally, Whitney still seemed lost, since he had told his dad that she was there, but hadn't told her anything about his father other than that he was good at puzzles, knew the city like the back of his hand and would be expecting him. "I have pasta ready for the pot, and I've been brewing up a sauce all day. It's meat sauce. I'm sorry, I wasn't expecting you, Agent Tremont. I hope you're not a vegetarian."

"I'm not, but I do have a team member who is, if you ever need to host us all for some reason," Whitney told him. She was smiling. Well, his father was likable.

As they chatted, Jude saw that Whitney learned that Andrew Crosby had worked his way up the ranks without benefit of higher education, and he had reached the rank of lieutenant. He'd worked the worst streets, the most unusual crimes and, been commended for bravery several times. He'd retired just a decade ago, when Jude's mother had first been diagnosed with cancer. He'd spent every day at her side until she had slipped away.

"Since you're having me to dinner, I hope I'm able to return the favor," Whitney told him.

"Well, I must say, seems that I'd like that, if the rest of your team members are anything like you. But, of course, we've got a situation going," Andrew said. "You two haven't been watching television, I take it?"

"What now?"

"Here, I'll show you," Andrew said.

He led them past the entrance. The apartment was just as it had been a decade ago. Jude had finally convinced his dad—when his mom had been gone two years—that she would have been angry with him if he hadn't given her clothing and shoes to Goodwill. But the throw she had knitted remained on the couch; her doilies still covered the occasional tables. The only concession his father had made to modern living was the entertainment center; he had a good flat-screen television, a sound stereo system and even Rock Band and a Wii Playstation.

As they followed him into the living room, Andrew

picked up the remote control and hit a play button on the television.

Jude frowned, not certain what he was watching at first. Then he realized that the two beautiful young people on the screen were giving a press conference.

"Bobby Walden and Sherry Blanco," Whitney said.

"Yep," Andrew said.

"The leads in Angus Avery's movie?" Jude murmured.

"I knew her only briefly, only in passing," Bobby said. "But Ginger Rockford was a beautiful person, and we're all horrified at her death."

"This movie is dedicated to her memory!" Sherry Blanco put in, dabbing at a tear.

"But aren't you afraid? Aren't you afraid to continue filming?" one of the reporters asked. Jude squinted. It appeared as if they'd done the press conference in front of the Plaza. They were standing on red-carpeted steps, and the press was kept at a distance by velvet ropes. It was almost like a premiere night.

"We can't be afraid," Bobby said. "We owe it to Ginger to finish the film."

"And, of course—" a man in a suit—one of their agents?—stepped in front of the microphone "—*of course,* we're increasing security on the set. We're cutting all night hours and doubling up on our security personnel. And we've negotiated new locations for the rest of the shoot, though! Rest assured. We will remain in this great city!"

Those words were greeted by a roar of applause.

"There's a murderer on the streets—a heinous killer—and what really matters is that America's sweethearts are going to finish a movie," Jude said thoughtfully.

"Nothing you can do about pop culture, son. I just thought you should see this," Andrew told him.

"She didn't do it," Whitney said.

"Too small. I don't think she could have managed the kind of strength needed," Andrew agreed.

Jude looked at the two of them. They had taken up positions on the sofa, watching as Andrew ran the recorded version of the press conference.

"That's great. You two have eliminated a suspect. Now we just have to eliminate about another eight million people or so," Jude said.

"You'll get it narrowed down," Andrew said with confidence.

Jude lowered his head, hiding a smile. His father always had confidence. He'd never given up on one of his own cases, though it was true that far too many went unsolved, despite the best work of dedicated people and excellent forensics labs.

The press conference ended with a public service announcement: Sherry Blanco begged the women of New York City to be careful, and to be safe. When two anchors came back on, talking about the celebrity of those involved, Andrew shut the television off.

"Dad, I need anything you have on the construction site down by Blair House. The director—Angus Avery—just told us that it had been a kind of church for devil worshippers at some time before the recently razed structure was there," Jude said.

"Ah," Andrew said thoughtfully. "Well, then. Come into my den," he said.

His father loved history; always had. In fact, sometimes, when he'd been a child, his father's love of history had driven both him and his mother mad. They'd had to tent one time with the rebels at Monmouth, canoe down rough water in the wake of Teddy Roosevelt and follow the path of George Washington. Most of the time, however, his father's love of adventure had been wonderful.

And it could prove very helpful now.

The apartment was designed in an ell, and they followed Andrew through the kitchen and dining room to the room that had once been the extra, or guest, bedroom and was now his father's library.

He noted that his dad didn't show Whitney his old room, now kind of a back parlor and not much different than it had been. Apparently, Andrew had silently decided that whatever Jude wanted to tell Whitney about his father's place and his own was Jude's call.

There was a large accountant's desk in the center of the room, a number of overstuffed chairs and the walls were lined floor to ceiling with books. One wall contained fiction, his father's favorites, from Poe and H. G. Wells down to more contemporary authors like Robert McCammon and F. Paul Wilson. He had a fine collection of works by Dickens, Defoe and others as well; this wall also contained his fictionalized history.

The back wall was totally dedicated to fiction and nonfiction on the city and state of New York, while the last wall offered books on American and world history.

"Wow," Whitney murmured.

"Books—my weakness," Andrew told her, looking through his titles. "Here! *The House of Spiritualism.*

It's a first edition, written by a fellow named Magnor Honeywell in 1910. He was on the police force in Lower Manhattan from 1880 to 1905. He had firsthand experience of everything going on in the city, and he was there during the final days of the Five Points dismantling. This book can at least give you an insight into what was going on back then."

"This is fabulous!" Whitney said. "It's a first edition, though—"

"And it's nothing, if it can help," Andrew assured her. "Besides, I'll bet you take care of your books."

Whitney immediately started thumbing through it and let out a pleased cry, scanning information here and there. "It's the best description I've seen on Carrie Brown," she said. She looked at Jude. "She was—"

"I know who she was," Jude said. "She was a prostitute found dead in room 31 of the East River Hotel, mutilated—in the manner that Jack the Ripper's victims had been mutilated. Since she was found on April 24, 1891, it was easy for the reporters camped out on Mulberry Street to determine that the Ripper had left London after his horrendous mutilation of Mary Kelly at the end of 1888, and come to America. Oh, by the way, check my exact figures on this, but I believe she was something like the forty-fifth person to die violently that year—even with the Five Points region having been cleaned up. A man named Ameer Ben Ali—aka Frenchy—was arrested and convicted of the murder, and later exonerated. Chief Inspector Thomas Byrnes made an ass of himself, since he'd claimed that if the Ripper ever came to America, he'd catch him in twenty-four hours. Byrnes practiced a form of psychological torture on criminals that really created the term *the third degree*. He was supposedly larger than life, but totally corrupt, amassing a fortune of over a quarter-million dollars when he was only making a salary of about two thousand. He was forced to resign in 1895 when a new president of the New York City Police Commission came in—Theodore Roosevelt. Whether Carrie Brown's murder was or wasn't the work of *the* Jack the Ripper, he was never caught."

Whitney stared at him, smiling slowly.

"Don't be too impressed. He went to a police symposium in Britain, kind of like a look at how to improve things for detectives on both sides of the briny," Andrew said, but Jude saw that his father was grinning. He smiled in return. His father was a good man; at seventy, he was spry and dignified, almost as tall as Jude and straight as an arrow. "Keep flipping those pages, and you'll find info on the House of Spiritualism itself," he told Whitney. "I'm going to set out dinner."

"I can help," Whitney said.

"I'm sure you can. It's just pasta. You read," Andrew told her. He left them both, heading to the kitchen.

"He's an impressive man," Whitney told Jude.

"Thanks."

She started reading, sinking into one of the chairs. Jude excused himself, walked back out to the living room and pulled out his phone to put through another call to Ellis Sayer.

"Anything?" he asked.

"Do you know how many people were on that set during the day?" Sayer asked him over the wires.

Jude liked Ellis Sayer. He was the most thorough man Jude had ever met; he was glad to have him on the task force because he was so anal that he checked out every little tiny detail—and that sometimes mattered.

"Yeah. A ton. I've got the lists."

"Hundreds. We've sifted through the caterers, and eliminated them from being on set past six o'clock. Most of the actors were gone by seven, the designers, camera crew, lighting…they were all out by eight-thirty. Here's the thing, of course—they could have come back. You met with the director—Angus Avery?"

"Yeah. The ghost of the Ripper killed her, according to him. He's convinced that evil lurks on that construction site—Jack the Ripper did come to America, and was buried there, and has now been dug up with the demolition of the building. And the ghost is pissed."

"Yep, that's what he told me, too. But I knew you'd want to speak with him yourself. I've spoken with the principal actors, and limos picked them both up early. But I'm sure you want to speak with them, too. They'll be at the station tomorrow."

Jude rubbed his forehead. "Yes, that's going to be important," he said.

Sayer was silent for a minute. "Jude, we're not going to get this guy tonight, that's for sure. I'm not going to call Fullbright again…he'll never answer my calls again if I do. All he'll tell me is that she *was* butchered like a Ripper victim. I think Fullbright is actually excited about the possibility. Scary. But I guess he spends his days with bodies. That's what's so scary to me—people are *excited* by this murder. You'd think the movies would be enough for them," Ellis added with disgust.

"Do you know, by the way, if Captain Tyler went to a shelter?" Jude asked.

"The old vet who saw a man in a dark cloak and stovepipe hat, carrying a medical bag?" Sayer asked dryly.

"Hey, it's the only description we've gotten of anyone in the vicinity," Jude said.

"Except for Captain Tyler himself, who admits to being there," Sayer reminded him. "But, yes, the old guy is fine. He agreed that he might need a breathing treatment, so he's at a place that's kind of a halfway house for vets—it offers some medical assistance, and rooms with more of a homelike atmosphere. Hannah did some research on the place, and she seemed to like it best. She said he could be happy there—not living in the midst of the urine and antiseptic smell of a shelter."

"Glad to hear it," Jude said.

"He's really our only suspect."

"No. If you didn't see him, you didn't see how his hands trembled. No way he could have held a knife and carried out the murder," Jude told him.

"I haven't seen him. The deputy chief filled me in on him. So, he's not a viable suspect. Okay, so I'm looking for Jack the Ripper?" Sayer asked.

"More or less. Keep your men questioning cast and crew," Jude told him.

"That'll be a full-time job for the team."

"We've got patrol cars doubled up down there, right?" Jude asked.

"Please! Come on, you asked for me because I'm good," Sayer told him.

"Thanks, Ellis. Keep me posted."

"Will do."

When Jude hung up, he heard his father call, "Chow's on. And, hey, you want to be good at your jobs—you got to fuel the human engine."

Whitney joined him from the library as he headed for the dining room. Andrew had set out the pasta and a salad and bottles of red wine and soda. "Didn't know if you wanted to indulge in a glass of wine this evening," he said gruffly.

"I'd indulge in a lot more," Jude said, but he reached over to pour them each a glass of cabernet. "Thanks, Dad. This is a nice break. We do have to eat."

"Mangia, mangia!" Andrew said. "I had an Italian grandmother," he told Whitney.

Whitney thanked him for the meal, but couldn't hold back her excitement over her reading. "Did you know, when the city started the demolition of the tenements in the Five Points region, a lot of plain old thugs became interested in the House of Spiritualism? The movement—or modern spiritualism—began to rise in 1848 with the Fox sisters claiming to communicate with the dead, and from then on, it grew. There were all kinds of charlatan mediums taking people for large sums, and that's what went on mostly at the House of Spiritualism at first. But then it took a twist. By the later 1880s and into the 1890s, those who were less than scrupulous were joined by those who had downright *devilish* desires. It was still a time when orphaned and immigrant children were barely valued. Only occasionally did the papers mention that a child had disappeared, or a young woman. While the police suspected that a number of murderers and sadists were taking refuge at the society, they couldn't prove anything. A raid in 1890 produced nothing at all. *But,* there was a rumor that Carrie Brown's killer was a member of the so-called church, a mysterious newcomer who had arrived from Britain. It's suspected that he died there, but everything about the man was rumor. There were no records of his arrival or even his existence, but the police heard that he was so sadistic that he scared the people there, and that they killed and buried him secretly somewhere on the property. They *found* Carrie Brown, but there were still nearby alleys and overcrowded tenements, and it's believed he killed more victims, but in the overcrowding, constant crime and corruption of the time, they were probably immigrants and their bodies were decayed when discovered, and treated like refuse. Oh, you will like this. He went by the name of Jack. Jonathan Black."

"Sad, very sad," Andrew said.

"Right. Thank God corruption no longer exists," Jude said.

"Hey!" Andrew protested. "We've come a long way."

"Yes, we have. But, then again, as human beings, it seems that we haven't come so far." He hesitated. "Look at the victim we found today," he said quietly. "And I don't believe that we've unearthed the body or soul of Jonathan Black and that he's terrorizing Lower Manhattan. There's someone out there, a psychotic but organized killer, with an agenda."

"Agreed—but what if he is someone who knows all

the history of the area?" Whitney asked. "Someone who is working to re-create the crimes."

"Angus Avery seems to know all about it," Jude said.

"And this will give his movie more publicity than money could ever buy," Andrew noted.

Don't argue with the man! Whitney warned herself.

Jude wanted to bring her back to Blair House after dinner; she didn't have to stay up with him. He was just going to make the proper calls to assure himself that Angus Avery had indeed spoken at a dinner that took place in Midtown, and talk with the driver who had been assigned to get him around the city. He was going to have records pulled on the major players in the movie, and also get an interview with the ex-cop who had last been on duty at the site.

"I don't do shift work—I'm here to work the case," Whitney told him.

"I know. I'll pick you up at seven-thirty for the task force meeting," he assured her. "I'm on to paperwork and phone work, mundane telephone stuff. There's no reason for you not to settle in and get some sleep."

When they arrived at Blair House, though, he hesitated in the car.

They'd passed several patrol cars—the police were making their presence known in the area.

But Blair House was dark, except for the slender porch light, and the street lamps illuminating the construction site were sadly lacking in strength.

"Hey, I'm not afraid of the dark," she told him.

"Maybe you should be."

Whitney grinned. "You don't believe in ghosts, and they're not going to bother me. And if there's a real human threat, remember, I have a gun, and I know how to use it."

"No one is ever invulnerable," he said.

"I'm all right, really," she assured him.

As she was about to get out of the car, she felt her phone buzz. She paused to see the message she was receiving.

Whitney sucked in her breath.

"What?" Jude asked her.

She passed him the phone. There was a likeness on the screen. "I know you have police artists, and that they've surely worked with what you have. But Jake Mallory is really a technical wizard. He's worked every angle of the pictures I've sent him, and this is the likeness he has created from 'Jane Doe wet' that I sent him today."

Jude stared at the image. "You've got a computer in the house?"

"Of course. And I have a mobile broadband card, so we can connect anywhere you like."

He seemed to be appraising her with new eyes; she had proven that the team might just be of use.

"Let's go."

She still had all the keys for the team on the band that the driver had given her, and it took her a minute to open the gate and then the front door to the house. Once inside, she told him that it would take her a minute to set up her computer, but he assured her that it was no problem. She moved quickly, racing upstairs to the room she had chosen, hurrying back down and finding that she could easily set up in the broad hallway at an old desk situated below the stairs. In another minute, she had the image on the large screen, and it was so good that it looked like a photograph. Jake had sent her a note next to the image: *Naturally, don't know about eye color, but from what you sent, computer said her hair was brown. Hope this helps; see you tomorrow.*

Jude leaned over her shoulder, staring at the image on the screen. The woman pictured appeared to be in her mid-thirties. She looked a little the worse for wear, as if she had spent long years abusing alcohol or drugs.

"Just about thirty-five," Jude said as if reading her thoughts. "That's the age Fullbright estimated as well." He looked at her. His face was close; the lamplight gave his skin a bronze cast. She felt a little tremor shoot through her. She liked his face. She wished that she didn't.

"Our next step," he told her, "was going to be to remove the head, dissolve the flesh—Fullbright likes maggots, actually—and then send the skull to a woman down at the Smithsonian. But…may I?"

"Of course."

She stood, letting him take the chair at the desk. She watched as he emailed the likeness to someone, typing, "I know it's late. Use any newspaper contact. I need this out there—neighborhood websites, flyers, too. Copy should just read, 'Do you know this woman?'"

A second later, he got his reply. "On it, Jude. Not too late. I can get it in for tomorrow morning."

"I'm sorry to bother you now."

"Hey, I was up. I've kind of got a guy, Jude. We have coffee. We chat. Who knows… I was on the phone with him when you emailed."

"Good for you, girl."

"But don't worry—I'm always your girl first, Jude."

Jude replied, "You're a good egg, Hannah."

"I'm the best."

He eased back in the chair, and then sat forward again, emailing the likeness to himself. Then he rose, looking at her strangely. "Thanks. Yes, we've had some sketches done. But...this is—detailed. It's as if she could walk off the page. I don't know if we can find out who she was, and if we do, if that can help us catch her killer, but...hey. Everyone deserves a burial, and no one deserves to die like that."

Whitney nodded. "Sure. I agree."

She felt as if they shared a bizarrely awkward moment. He had discovered that he didn't dislike her and she just might be useful.

She had just discovered that she liked way too much about him.

"Listen, I have a two-bedroom place in Hell's Kitchen and you're more than welcome to come back with me. I'd appreciate it, actually. I don't like thinking about you down here by yourself."

"You live in Hell's Kitchen, too?" she asked him.

He laughed. "The apartment next to my father. He was bright enough to buy when things went co-op a couple of decades ago, and I just pay him a minimum rent—his pleasure money, as he calls it. I think he charges me because he knew I wouldn't accept the place if I didn't pay him something. And, hey, I'm sure he'd be happy to have you for the night, too."

She was tempted. Really tempted. She wasn't afraid of Blair House, or of being alone. She was afraid that the more she was with him, the more she liked him, and the more she was close to him, the more she realized that he was really an attractive man—and she was attracted to him. Not a good thing on the first day of a new investigation.

Whitney certainly had no desire to appear to be afraid just to be with him—or anyone.

And he probably didn't understand that she *needed* to be in the house by herself for the night.

"I'm all right, honestly. Like I told you earlier, I'm not the fearful type. And I have some work to do tonight. I have to decide where I think we'll need our camera equipment, and just what we may want to film or record on tape…"

He stared at her blankly.

"We always keep track of what happens around us," she said. "And, of course, we'll want to watch the property next door."

He still stared at her.

"Oh. For shadows and ghosts and things?" he asked. His tone was polite.

"For anything that's going on," she said. "Trust me—it's good."

"I believe you."

"Good. And I'm okay, really. I'm not a fool."

He smiled, and it was a real smile.

"Maybe not staying here would make you the intelligent type," he told her.

She grinned at that. "Thank you. Sincerely, thank you. But I have a phone. There are cruisers in the street tonight. I'm not going back out, and I'll sleep with my gun under my pillow."

He nodded; her words were rational.

"All right, then. I'll be here at seven-thirty, sharp. You need a wake-up call or anything?"

She laughed at that. "No, but thanks again. I have an alarm on my phone. I'll be fine. Honestly."

She walked him to the door. "Good night, and..."

"And?"

He hesitated just a minute, gray eyes guarded. "I look forward to meeting the rest of your team.

"Thank you," she said.

Again, the moment felt slightly awkward; almost as if they'd been on a strange date all day.

She made sure he heard her sliding the bolts on the front door as he left, and she watched through one of the etched-glass windows in the door as he walked back out to his car.

When he was gone, Whitney walked through the house, leaving the large hallway light on as she wandered the downstairs. She could well imagine that it would be a fine tourist attraction when the renovations were done.

She didn't have any of the equipment; that would arrive with the others. But it would be good to have a sense of where she wanted cameras and recording devices.

Upstairs, Whitney took stock of the bedrooms. There were six of them, and everything in the house seemed to be proportionate. Three on one side, three on the other.

She paused at a window that overlooked the construction site next door. The book she read that day had shown pictures of the structure that had been there when it had been the House of Spiritualism; then, a two-story building with a circular porch had stood. The steeple was still standing toward what had been the rear of the structure. People had entered from the same sidewalk that led to the path to Blair House.

Whitney stood in the darkness, watching the site. Patrol cars rounded the corner regularly, and she was pretty sure that when Jude Crosby left her, he had called in to make sure that the cars would watch Blair House throughout the night.

When the equipment arrived, she knew that they would want to keep a good eye on the site.

Pulling her phone from her pocket, she saw that it was nearly midnight. The time had gone so quickly that day. She told herself that she had to be tired; she had not known this morning that she'd be spending the night in New York City. But she wasn't tired; she was wound up.

In the kitchen, she brewed herself hot tea and made mental notes about where she wanted cameras set up. She wanted a couple of cameras looking down Broadway at all times, but, of course, they couldn't cover every possible nook and cranny and shadow. Yet the cameras would catch movement of anyone who did come onto the street.

Finally, she went back into the hallway. She stood very still, waiting. Nothing happened. No shadows moved. The old house didn't even creak.

"What? Did everyone *die* in this house in a state of absolute bliss?" she said aloud.

Nothing. Just the darkness.

Of course, it wasn't Blair House where the supposed evil had taken place; it had been next door, at the House of Spiritualism. But she wasn't an idiot, and she wasn't going to go out to explore the area until the rest of the team had arrived.

At last she convinced herself that it was time to get some sleep. She put her service revolver on the little table next to the bed, changed into pajamas and curled up to sleep.

She couldn't sleep, and so she rose, and in the quiet of the night, headed for the stairs.

Downstairs, she looked at the pictures she had taken at autopsy. They were a good record, and she would show them to the others, but at the moment, they weren't giving her any information that would help in finding a suspect.

She found the book that Andrew Crosby had loaned her. It was fascinating reading, all about the demise of the Five Points area, the House of Spiritualism and the founding of the NYPD. And the murder of Carrie Brown.

The author had been convinced that there had been other victims.

She tried to imagine the squalor of the Five Points area, so near to this one. What had happened to the sea of humanity that had lived in those tenements when they had been brought down? The area had been so similar to Whitechapel in London; filled with immigrants eking out an existence. Filled with crime—and police who increased their incomes by taking bribe money from all the establishments in the area. Money paid so that the police force would protect shop owners from thugs and criminals; money paid so that the police would overlook code infractions and other illegal activities.

She smiled; impressed and thinking about Jude Crosby. The man was truly intelligent and well read. He wasn't unlike most of humanity; he believed in what he saw, in flesh and blood. In bad people who did bad things.

"Well, yes—there is a truly evil person, flesh and blood out there," she said softly. "But, if someone *is* in this house, I'd love to speak with you!" she added.

Nothing.

Hoping she could sleep at last, she closed the book, headed back upstairs and willed herself to try to sleep. Finally she dozed, and then she slept deeply.

She didn't dream. No images flashed through her mind in the night, at least none that she could hold and retain.

When she woke up, sun was filtering through the chintz drapes.

She yawned and stretched, and looked toward the foot of the bed.

And froze.

A woman stood there, her image hazy and then solid. She appeared to be in late Victorian dress; her clothing was poor, simple cotton. A crocheted mantle sat over her shoulders. Her hair was queued, and yet tendrils were escaping. She looked to be about thirty, but her appearance was worn and tired...

Like that of the image of Jane Doe wet Jake had created from her death photos.

But she wasn't Jane Doe wet. She had lived long before Jane Doe wet.

Whitney thought that she heard something, like a whimpering. She realized that the woman wasn't alone. At her side was a large hound, a mix between a shepherd and a wolfhound, perhaps, but a large shaggy creature that stood valiantly at her side.

The woman began fading away again.

"Please, please, stay!" Whitney begged.

The dog lingered just a moment longer.

But the woman disappeared, and then, more slowly, the dog. Whitney was left to wonder if the images had really been there, of if she had imagined both the woman and canine in the desperate hope that she could learn something from the beyond.

5

It was barely the crack of dawn when Jude pulled the last of his information sheets from the printer in his home office and arranged his discourse for the task force meeting the next morning. He had pictures and every note taken on the Jane Does, and he had every note they'd thus far acquired regarding Virginia Rockford as well. And, he had drawn up a time line of Jack the Ripper in London, the murder of Carrie Brown and everything he could find on the House of Spiritualism as well. There was nothing to be found on the mysterious Jonathan Black other than what had been written by his contemporaries. Hannah was searching records, but she had found nothing that registered he'd been in the country, or in the city of New York.

It was possible, of course, that the murders were not related in any way, and that the murder of Virginia Rockford was unrelated to any past or present Ripper. But Deputy Chief Green had been disturbed enough by the similarities to call in a special unit, and there was no reason not to entertain anything that might help in the investigation.

He dreaded the thought that another victim would tell them whether or not they were moving in the right direction.

Allison, his blue-eyed mixed-breed cat, meowed, cleaning her paws as she sat at the edge of his desk.

"Too damn bad they hadn't invented credit cards back then," he told the cat.

He was startled by a knock at the side door to his office.

When his dad had bought the apartments, they'd discovered that the place had once been owned by a notorious madam, Madam Shelley, who had been a voyeur. What had appeared to be wall actually hid a door, and that door led to the apartment next door. When he'd had to fix the wall because of water damage from a leaking pipe on the floor above, they'd found out that there had been an entrance and exit between the two apartments—and a way for the madam to spy on her clients.

They'd kept the exit/entrance something of a secret door. Jude's father had never interfered with his life, and it was nice that he was close. He could feed Allison when Jude wound up working crazy hours on a case.

He stood to unlock the door, letting his dad in.

Andrew remained on his side of the doorway, hands behind his back, waiting for an invitation in. Jude smiled, looking into his dad's back parlor. A lot of the things crammed in here had been his own—a huge desk and computer and game player, for example; the shelves were crowded with books, and more. Animal skulls, comics, Star Trek and Star Wars toys and all kinds of collectibles.

"Sorry, I know it's early but I heard you rattling around in here," Andrew said. He grinned and drew his hands from behind his back, producing a large paper coffee cup. "Didn't know if you'd bothered to brew yourself any."

Jude took the cup, stepping back. "Thanks. Good and strong?" he asked.

"You bet, killer strong, just the way you like it."

"Come on in. You know I always appreciate your advice."

"The media just keeps going crazy. Slow day for catastrophes yesterday," Andrew said with a shrug. "No storms or oil spills or other such activity. The major cable stations have all hopped on the bandwagon. Everyone across the globe has to be getting information regarding Virginia Rockford. I can't help but wonder if she's happy in heaven. She found her fifteen minutes of fame—a lot more than fifteen minutes. There are even some takes from that movie on the internet—don't know how people got them. Well, barriers can only keep onlookers so far—it's gone viral. That movie is going to make a fortune!"

"Yes, I guess it is," Jude said.

"And don't hesitate, son, if you want any help on anything, let me know. There's got to be something else useful in my book collection. if you want any research done and your folks are bogged down—though I guess you have half the department on it—let me know, okay. Even if it's just coffee."

"Thanks, I'll take you up on that. And, hey, I'm going to leave my side of the door unlocked. Will you check in on Allison this evening, give her an ear rub and make sure she has water and food?" Jude asked.

Andrew laughed. "I'll even clean the litter box! I can see you gotta get out of here. Talk to you later." He turned to close the door.

"Hey, wait," Jude said.

His dad paused, brows arching with anticipation.

"Yeah, we've got lots of people, but you are a reader and you have one of the best book collections I've ever seen. Keep reading. See what you can find on the House of Spiritualism, Jonathan Black—and Blair House."

"Of course," Andrew said.

He left, closing the door between the two apartments. Jude headed out. As he did so, he picked up the morning paper at his door, flipping it over:

Have You Seen This Woman?

He was pleased to see that Hannah had gotten Jake Mallory's computer rendition of his victim on the lower-right side of the first page of the paper. Since he'd spent the night preparing for the meeting and grimly realizing how little they had to go on, it was a pleasant perk to see that the likeness was in the paper, and just as he had wanted it placed.

The paper was on the front passenger's seat of the car when he picked up Whitney; she was in front of the house, waiting for him at precisely 7:30 a.m. He couldn't help think again that everything about her was gleaming, from the pert curls in her hair to the tone of her skin and on to her eyes. She was entirely unique— and absolutely mesmerizing. She would surely draw attention no matter where she went. He did wonder if that would prove to be an asset or a distraction.

He admitted grudgingly to himself that she had probably drawn more from Angus Avery than he would have managed.

"Nice," she said, accepting the newspaper and seeing where the picture had been displayed.

"How was your night?" he asked.

"Quiet," she assured him.

"You slept well?"

"Like a baby."

"Well, I won't have to be worried tonight. You won't be alone. The rest of your team gets in today."

"I wasn't worried last night," she assured him. "But I like my team. I'll be glad when they're here. And, I think you'll like them, too."

"I'll like anyone who can move this investigation in a forward direction. The news has picked up on the unknown victims we discovered. It's a media frenzy."

"Strange," Whitney murmured. "Or maybe not so strange."

"What's that?"

"Think about the late eighteen hundreds in London. There were murders that occurred constantly, especially in the East End. But the Ripper murders were the first to really gain attention. They were so ghastly that people were forced to notice people and the horrendous conditions under which they were living."

"That's not a comparison. They don't need to notice this area. Five Points is really long gone."

"Yes, but Five Points wasn't cleaned up until the 1880s, 1890s. The Bowery was filled with seedy bars and hotels—it wasn't a nice area! And what happened to Carrie Brown turned into a huge case as well, with the media heavily involved. Some people believe that Jack the Ripper was out to draw attention to the absolute misery of life."

"Personally," Jude told her, "I don't think that Jack the Ripper was hoping to clean up the Whitechapel area of London. I think he was a psychopath with a bitter hatred of women, and there was nothing about him that should have been romanticized. I don't believe he was in the royal family, and I don't believe any of the half-cocked theories that have come out about him in books in the last few years. Possibly, he was a butcher—the degree of his anatomical skills has been argued throughout the years—who suffered from a sexually transmitted disease. And it's likely that he got that disease from a prostitute. Or maybe his mother had been a prostitute, and he'd spent his formative years watching her ply her trade. Today, he wouldn't have gotten away with his crimes—we rely so heavily on forensics now. Back then, there were slaughterhouses in the area and a lot of the population walked around bloodstained—people walking around bloodstained are noticed these days, even in New York City. The populace might be busy and impatient, but they're not blind or ignorant."

"Ah, careful! The head of the New York police force at the time made a big mistake mocking the English police over the Ripper—and then he couldn't catch the man who killed Carrie Brown, and possibly others," Whitney warned. "They were desperate—and a man innocent of the crime went to prison for years because they were grasping at straws."

"I don't knock the London police, they worked with what they had. Thing is, since I do know a lot of our less-than-prime neighborhoods well, I can imagine what it was like for them. They were amidst an absolute stream of humanity, and knifings and bar fights were the norm. Prostitution has always been a dangerous profession, and clever killers—and even not-so-clever killers—have eluded law enforcement in every age. And the New York police force was first created by the city in 1844 and reorganized a year later—and modeled after the Metropolitan force in London. It was the first police department in the United States." He glanced at her apologetically. "Can't be my father's son for nothing, you know."

"Let's pray that we get this guy," Whitney said.

The task force was set to meet in one of the spacious conference rooms. There was a large rolling poster board that Jude could use for his presentation and organization, and he began tacking up pictures, lists, maps and assignments. Hannah walked in while he was working and Whitney was reading the book his father had loaned her, having understood he really didn't want her help setting up. He liked that about her; she didn't insist.

He introduced the two women, and Hannah spoke with enthusiasm. "I can't wait to meet the rest of your team. I'm sure I will, unless we get him right away, which, of course, is impossible...sorry. Jude is a great detective, it's just that—"

"Hannah, it's all right," Jude said.

"Anyway," Hannah said, "I know just about every program out there, but I've seldom seen anyone find a computer program that could work so well with *morgue* photos. She's so real—it looks like the picture was just shot!"

"And you got it right into the paper at the last minute," Whitney told her.

Patrolman Smith arrived looking a little awed to be there, and the seven detectives working with him and Ellis Sayer filed in one by one soon after Ellis arrived, before it became 8:00 a.m. exactly.

Deputy Chief Green came into the room at eight.

"I'm only at this meeting as an observer, everyone. And to let you know that I have ultimate faith in your talents as investigators. This is our highest-priority case in the city right now, and you have access to any form of backup at any time—beat patrols, patrol cars— the mounted unit if you need it. Now, we all know that the media seized on the information regarding the victim almost before we were in on it ourselves—not much you can do to stop people from talking. I and our public information officer have given them what we can, though we will try to keep further information to a minimum to weed out the nuts. Agent Whitney Tremont is the first of the assisting FBI unit to arrive." He paused to indicate her; Jude saw a few lips tighten, but mostly the others noted her with grim nods.

Jude didn't really believe in rivalries between federal and local jurisdiction—whatever it took to get it done was important—but there had been times when local investigations and federal interests had clashed, and that did create problems.

"The team is here because they specialize in unusual circumstances and they have an excellent track record. I know you're all aware that we have two Jane Does who were murdered, and because of those two women and the especially heinous nature of Virginia Rockford's death, we're entertaining the possibility that someone is trying to re-create deaths from Victorian London. I don't believe that any journalists yet realize that we do have victims with injuries similar to those of the victims of Jack the Ripper. I realize that this killer has us by the balls, but he must be caught. Jude, I'll turn it over to you."

Jude stood before his board, pointing out the two women who were not believed to have been Ripper victims, but who coincided with their Jane Does. He reminded the team that they weren't to draw assumptions, but that they needed to be wary. He went on to describe the five victims of the Ripper—per "experts"—and then the New York victim of the 1890s, and pointed out the fact that the filming that had taken place on the day that Virginia Rockford had been killed was where the Ripper was rumored to have lived, if he had come to New York.

"All right, our one eyewitness—albeit a burned-out Viet vet—saw a man on the streets who resembled the gaslight-movie version of Jack the Ripper. Cloak, stovepipe hat, medical bag. So we do believe it's going to be important to understand the past regarding the murders in London and the murder of Carrie Brown in New York City. But we're not discounting the idea that the Jane Does and the murder of Virginia Rockford are unrelated. As yet, the medical examiner has only been able to tell us that our victim was ripped up exactly the same way as Jack the Ripper's first victim—sadly, he has not reported DNA discovered on the body or clothing, or any scrap of forensic evidence that could help us. We now have a reasonable likeness of Jane Doe wet in the paper, so we're hopeful that we'll hear from someone who knew her, or knew her identity. Our real-life suspects could be just about anyone in the state of New York. Obviously, we're going to start by focusing on the movie cast and crew. Sayer?"

"We're on it, Jude. It's just a hell of a lot of people," Sayer told him.

"We spent yesterday interviewing hundreds of people," one of his men added quietly.

"Find the costume designer and everyone in costumes. If Tyler saw a man in a stovepipe hat and cloak, I believe he exists. He's burned out—not blind," Jude said. He looked at Whitney. "Agent Tremont?"

She might have been surprised that he was asking for her input at this point of the investigation, but she didn't show it. She stood and walked forward. "If our killer is playing out a reenactment of the nineteenth-century Ripper murders, he's doing it in his own way, since he killed an attractive young woman and didn't target an older prostitute with missing teeth, as did the Ripper. I believe this discrepancy might indicate the killer is a narcissist—whatever route he takes can be twisted into anything that he wants, because he is all important. Therefore, he's doubly difficult to catch. Although it appears he is trying to recreate a time of terror, he will also consider expediency in everything that he does. He's organized, despite the savagery of the crime. I think it's going to be important that we study the past, because he likely knows all the stories regarding New York and London in the late eighteen hundreds. He may not believe that the voice of Jack the Ripper is in his head...he may just be using the crimes of the past because of their shocking brutality. This killer is going to prove to be the average or even handsome next-door neighbor. If you knew him, you'd probably want to talk about the crimes with him— you'd never suspect him of being a functioning psychopath. Also," Whitney said, and paused, glancing over at Jude, "I don't believe that this man is acting alone. Although I don't particularly subscribe to any of the conspiracy theories, it is possible that the real Ripper worked with a partner. In with the royal conspiracy theory is the concept that a carriage came and took the Ripper away from the crime scenes, and thus he wasn't seen walking around Whitechapel covered in blood. Obviously, then, the carriage driver was in on the killings. Others claim that there were so many butchers and slaughterhouse workers at the time that people were accustomed to others walking around covered in blood."

"True. The East End of London was crawling with butchers and slaughterhouses," Jude said.

"But, the truth doesn't matter as much as what the killer *perceives* to have been the truth, so, please, it's important that we all review everything that went on back then."

Sayer shook his head, looking at Jude. "Does everybody really believe this? That a modern-day

Ripper has come to New York? Or, should I be working off the newspaper accounts—and assume that the Ripper did come here in the eighteen hundreds, and that his ghost has risen to attack the women of our city?"

"Sayer, no one in this room believes that a ghost killed Virginia Rockford, I assure you. But," Jude said, once again pausing to look at Whitney, "one of the most logical theories we have at the moment is that someone either wants to emulate the Ripper, or perhaps believes that the voice of the Ripper's ghost speaks to him and tells him what to do."

Hannah groaned softly and started when they all looked at her. She grimaced. "Sorry. I just think of all the defense strategies criminals have— The violence on TV made me do it. The abuse I suffered from my alcoholic mother made me do it. The dog spoke to me in Satan's voice. And now, Jack the Ripper made me do it!"

Every detective in the room seemed to nod, but only Jude spoke. "We all know the system is imperfect, Hannah, but we have to catch the guy, and leave it to our prosecutors to get him locked away forever. Him—or them. But, in most cases, and I believe we'll discover this to be true here, if there is an accomplice, one of the killers is still driving the action and the killing."

"I have booklets for everyone," Hannah said. "History of the Ripper in London, the murder of Carrie Brown, info on the House of Spiritualism and, everything we have—basically the autopsy results—on our

Jane Does." She glanced at Jude, too. He nodded to her and she handed out the booklets. Sayer looked at Jude. "You want us to read all day, or keep up with the interviews."

"Hey. You all passed the exam to get where you are," Jude said evenly. "And you know street work, and how to go with gut-level thinking to solve this. I have complete faith in you. And Jackson Crow, who will be at our next meeting, has a reputation as one of the finest minds in criminal behavior."

"You say solve *this,* Detective Crosby," one of Sayer's men, Alex Lacey, said. It always seemed to Jude that his surname was misapplied since he was a brick wall of a man. "What if we are putting puzzle pieces together that don't really connect?"

"You mean the murders of the Jane Does and Miss Rockford?" Jude asked. "We could be wrong on that. We're talking theory here now, too. But, we all know that as soon as the body of Virginia Rockford was discovered, the cry of *Ripper* went up in the street. And I know I've hit a dead end with every possible lead on the Jane Does. Maybe we *are* looking for several killers."

"And maybe there won't be any more murders," Sayer said.

Jude later thought that Ellis Sayer couldn't have spoken on cue more completely if they had scripted the meeting. As he was still speaking, there was a tap on the door. Lieutenant Nelson, Deputy Chief Green's assistant, beckoned him gravely to the door.

Green listened to her, and then turned back to the

group. "I'm afraid, Sayer, that the question of more victims has just been answered. Melody Tatum, a local escort, has just been discovered in an alley in the Bowery."

The NYPD was given a bad rap sometimes—all cops were given a bad rap sometimes, just for being cops—but he was proud when he reached the scene to see the first officers on-site had quickly taken control of the crime scene, and there wasn't just tape protecting the area—a narrow alley in back of a number of buildings—there were barricades. There was again a human wall of officers as well, protecting the mutilated body of Melody Tatum from the curious stares of onlookers—and the press.

"Crosby!"

"Hey, Crosby!"

"Detective!"

He heard the shouts of the press as he arrived and ducked beneath the tape and made his way through the officers, nodding a grim appreciation to several of the men as he did so. For the moment, he ignored the press. Whitney and Sayer followed closely in his wake while other members of his task force interviewed the first officers at the site and began to work a door-to-door canvass in the area. They were once again in a section of the city where the dark alleys could be quiet, while just blocks away, nightlife teemed. But they were in the midst of some residential buildings, and the police would knock on every door.

He hunkered down by the body, hands gloved.

Melody Tatum had been in her mid to late thirties;

she might have been "plastically" attractive. Her face was bruised and swelling, but he could see scars in the puffed skin that indicated she'd already had cosmetic surgery.

Her eyes were open. Blue eyes that seemed horrified, and still surprised.

She hadn't been missing teeth, nor had she been old or ugly, like the Ripper's usual used-up ha'penny whores in London. And yet there was something similar about her, he thought. Illusion was gone from those dead eyes. Once upon a time, she'd had dreams. Life had taught her that not everyone made the big time. In her case, the word *escort* had certainly been a euphemism. There was a look about her of someone who had gotten hard around the edges. She'd learned the truth about the fairy tale, and she'd dealt with it, but not without losing a little piece of her soul.

There was no mistaking the fact that the woman was dead. Her insides had been removed and arranged around the body. The garish fur of her coat rose against her throat. Jude inspected the coat, and saw where the fur had hardened at the throat. Using his pen, he gingerly flattened the fur, and when he did so, he saw the slash that had nearly severed the head from the body.

He stepped back, allowing the police photographer to do his work. In the background, never getting in the way, Whitney took her own photos as well. He felt cold himself. He was accustomed to crime, brutal crime. But the disembowelment of this woman was something that could twist the most cast-iron stomach. He looked at Whitney; he could see in her face that the crime appalled her, but he could see the same thing in the grim expressions of everyone around him. He heard one old seasoned cop yelling at another not to disturb the crime scene, and to move on quickly. The retching sounds made by the younger officer proved that he was moving away as quickly as he could.

Whitney was obviously affected, but she quietly did whatever she felt she must, always a step behind so as not to disturb the work of the local police. She was professional; he wasn't sure if she was taking still shots or videos, but she intended to chronicle the crime scene. She seemed so small there; fragile and delicate, and he was surprised by the desire to drag her away from a scene so horrible. Perhaps he would have felt that way about any young woman. He steeled himself; she was an agent. And, at that moment, if the agents could prove a ghost was guilty and stop the horror, he'd be happy to see it happen.

Fullbright came through and hunkered down opposite him. "My, my. Our Ripper is a busy boy," he said.

Jude frowned at him, but Fullbright didn't notice. He was shaking his head. "Have the photographers finished?" he asked Jude. "Has she been touched or moved in any way?"

"No. Officers Lewis and Jentz found the body at eight forty-five; her purse, with her identification, credit and business cards, was found about twenty feet away. If anyone else came across her, they didn't report the discovery. Jentz said they saw the heap from the sidewalk when they were heading to the café down the street to start their shift with some espresso. When they started toward her, they thought that she'd passed out, or been mugged or injured. Lewis went to feel for a pulse, saw the organs displayed around her and then called it immediately and set up the barricades. We're in an alley. We can keep this site closed up all day and into the night," Jude said. "And thank God," he added gruffly, "they stopped the media and the internet and Facebook crowd from snapping any photos."

Fullbright acknowledged his satisfaction with an inclination of his head. He eased the coat she had been wearing from her lower body.

Jude steeled himself; he almost had to turn away.

Whitney went a pale shade of gray and another officer turned away, making the same horrible retching noises as the previous young officer.

"Get it out of here!" Fullbright warned with a growl.

"Can you give me a time of death?" Jude asked.

Fullbright waved away a swarm of flies that were now buzzing around the victim.

"Give me a chance, Detective. Give me a chance."

Jude stood unmoving. He felt the air and it felt chill, but not cold. In fact, it was warm. Thankfully, there had been no rain the night before.

"I'm going to estimate 4:00 a.m., or between 3:00 and 5:00 a.m.," Fullbright said, taking the body's temperature and moving an arm to find the state of rigor. He looked around. "I believe that at that time of night, he would have been all alone in the alley, but I don't think the young woman ever had a chance to scream. It's hard to see, I realize, with the face in the shape that it is, but you'll note that beyond the bruised lips and the blood—there, her tongue is protruding. I need to get her to the morgue, but I believe that she was strangled. She blacked out before he killed her...she might have gone without so much as a whimper." He cleared his throat. "From a cursory examination, I can tell you that the intestines are on the shoulder. I believe that several of her organs are—gone."

"Gone?"

"Yes, but, of course, I won't know more until the autopsy."

"Which will be soon?"

"I'll have her ready at the morgue in three hours, Jude," Fullbright assured him.

Jude felt Whitney looking at him.

And he knew what she was thinking.

Annie Chapman, the second of the Ripper's canonical victims. She was found in just such a display, her tongue protruding, her body disemboweled—several organs missing entirely.

The weight of the world—or at least the entire steel empire and granite of Manhattan—seemed to be weighing down on him. He'd thought they could concentrate on the area where the construction site had been utilized by the movie crew. He'd thought they would find the killer in the midst of the filmmakers. But now, they were in the Bowery. Melody Tatum had been an escort, not an actress.

The killer's sphere was widening.

Yes, he'd suspected himself, as an itching, back-burner thought, from the moment he had come to the site of Virginia Rockford's murder, that the slashing deaths of his Jane Does were associated with the murder of Virginia Rockford. He just hadn't wanted to believe that a modern-day Ripper could be at work in his streets.

Sayer called out to him. "Forensics is asking if they can move in. They've been working the perimeter. Are they good?"

Jude looked down at Fullbright. "Five minutes. I want the hands bagged. I want her body-bagged just as she is—we've a better chance of preserving evidence on the clothing and all if we get her down to the morgue."

Jude walked over to Judith Garner, a woman he considered to be one of the city's best forensic detectives. She was like an iron horse; wild red Irish hair turning gray, eyes silver, face gaunt—mind like a computer.

"Garner, anything and everything from the perimeter here. With any luck, the alley hasn't been disturbed."

"Cigarette butts, gum wrappers, dog hairs, coffee cups and the entire contents of the Dumpster—I got it, Jude. Hairs, fibers, footprints, but now we'll have to take those of half the police force. I will be thorough…you know that," she promised him. "We've got the purse, too. Doesn't look as if the killer ever opened it, but this guy is wearing gloves. Oh, by the way, her business cards identify her as 'a premium date for the businessman on the move.' She might have been a high-class hooker, but it seems that her employment is on the books. She's with Harold Patterson's Elite Companions."

He nodded. "Thanks," he told her. She studied him, shaking her head. He knew, of course, that most of the force was feeling very sorry for him. This killer wasn't leaving behind any evidence; he was apparently aware that any trace could help the police discover his identity. This was the kind of case where the suspects might be limitless, and if the killer wasn't apprehended, he might as well leave the state and hide behind a gigantic tiki beverage on a distant island, under an assumed name.

He saw that Whitney was still back by the body. He could see her golden eyes and the empathy within them. She hunkered down by Fullbright as he bagged the hands. Fullbright nodded at something that she said.

Jude felt his muscles constrict.

Ripperologists.

He knew that they were making comparisons.

But this wasn't the East End of London.

No, it was the East End of New York.

How in the hell did he get every woman in Lower Manhattan to stay off the streets at night? And how would Manhattan itself survive, if the killing continued and the panic increased?

His phone buzzed and he answered it.

"Crosby."

"It's Green. When you can, head in to the station."

Jude was puzzled. "Sir, I'm on-site with the victim. When I leave here, I'm heading off to the victim's place of employment—Harold Patterson's Elite Companions."

"We have a woman here named Daisy Harding who knew your Jane Doe wet. She recognized her from the paper. The young woman's name was Sarah Larson. She wanted to be a Broadway dancer. She started turning tricks when that didn't pan out. The girl was an orphan from Kansas City, Kansas. No family and only a few friends. Get on down here as soon as you can,

Jude. The murder you're covering is on all the news stations already."

"They can't have gotten that much information. The two officers who discovered the body did everything right—they barricaded the entire alley immediately."

"Yeah, and I know they tried to shield the body as best as possible, but this is New York, Jude, you know that. That alley has windows and the neighbors have camera phones."

"I can imagine exactly what the reporters are using as a headline," Jude said wearily, aware that his search revolved around a nutcase who thought he was the mysterious and infamous Victorian killer.

"Jack's back," he said.

And, in a way, the killer was proving that it was true.

Life was all about perception.

6

Daisy Harding was a slender young woman with large brown eyes and short-cropped brown hair. She moved with tremendous grace, and Whitney wasn't surprised to learn that she was a dancer. She had just gotten into the chorus of an off-Broadway play called *The Girl Next Door,* and she was quick to tell them that she'd been about to head back to her native Arkansas, since she'd been barely surviving.

She was distressed but articulate as she spoke to them, telling them how she had met the victim, Jane Doe wet, now identified as Sarah Larson, when they had both auditioned for a show the year before. Sarah had been a dancer, a good one, but the city was filled with hopefuls from all over the country who were auditioning for Broadway shows.

"I know that she did some extras work, and she got a job at a coffee shop," Daisy said. "And then the coffee shop started cutting down on employees and hours, and everyone else was doing the same. She took a job at a place called Not Your Mama's, and she *thought* she was going to be a dancer, but it turned out that it was a strip club. She actually started making some money, but she was miserable. And then…" Daisy paused, shaking her head. "Then she started taking drugs and drinking to cope. And then I think her drug habit got expensive, so she started working on the side." Again, Daisy hesitated, wincing. "Hooking. The last time I saw her was about a month ago. She knew that I was upset for her, and she told me not to worry. She was going to get it together. She was going to go out and get more movie and television work as an extra, and she'd finally get out of what she was doing." A large tear rolled down her cheek. Jude pushed a tissue box closer to her.

So she, too, had been involved in the film world, Jude thought.

"You were trying very hard to be a good friend, Miss Harding. I'm sure that you did everything that you could," Jude told her.

"No, no, I didn't. If I had, she'd be alive," Daisy said.

Jude looked down for a minute. "That was a computer image we had in the paper, Miss Harding. But, now that you've given us a name, we can verify that she is your friend. She must have someone somewhere."

"No," Daisy Harding said. "She told me that she'd been in a home with dozens of kids, all of them just waiting to be eighteen and get out. She'd spent a couple of years working different places to get to New York. And…she had the kind of friends you look at when you're at an audition and hope they break an ankle so that you get the job. It's competitive out there. I don't mean that we—as a whole—are hateful or would really hurt anyone. It's just there are so many people trying to get work."

"Of course," Whitney said softly.

"Miss Harding," Jude promised, "we'll find out what happened to your friend. I promise, I won't stop until we do."

Daisy started to cry again softly. Whitney left her chair and walked around to the young woman. "You're doing everything you can for her now, Daisy," she said. "You're helping us find out about her, and that will help us find out about her killer."

"Please, yes, oh, please, at the least, get some kind of justice for her! I had a home and a family, and now, I've been lucky here. We weren't rich, but my parents would send me money when I couldn't get a show, or when I couldn't get any kind of job at all. Sarah...she had no one. No help. It's not...it's not fair."

Whitney saw Jude's mouth tighten grimly; she could almost read his mind. *No, life wasn't fair. But what had happened to Sarah Larson went far beyond that sentiment, and he didn't mean to let her die without catching her killer and bringing him to justice.*

"You think..." Daisy began, her voice hoarse, "you think that the same man killed that actress in the street, and that he...he's killed this new woman, too?"

"We don't know, Miss Harding. We're investigating every angle," Jude said.

Tears still bright in her eyes, Daisy finished telling them everything she could about Sarah Larson. When she left the station at last, Ellis Sayer threw some sheets on the table in the conference room where they'd been speaking with Miss Harding. "Limo drivers of interest, six of them," Sayer said. "I sent Alex Lacey and two other men to go through the company. The time cards, mechanics and bosses match on most points, but these guys were the last on the job, if you want to speak with them."

Jude nodded. "They're here?" he asked.

"Am I your second in command for nothing?" Ellis asked him dryly. Whitney liked Ellis Sayer; he always looked a bit down, sad and weary, but he seemed steady. So far, he'd followed through like a bulldog on the tasks he was given.

"Get Lacey in here with me," Jude said. "That way he'll catch any contradictions."

He looked at Whitney. "I'd like to stay for this," she said.

When Ellis walked out, she noted that Jude seemed anxious. "You want to get to the strip club, right?"

"Yes," he said, rubbing his temples. "But Sayer has the drivers here. I know Lacey does a thorough job of questioning, but...we'll keep the pressure on. There's a lot I want to get to during the day. Melody Tatum's *boss, pimp* or *whatever*. The strip club—it's going to be damn hard to stay hot on a single trail when victims are popping up all over. But one thing I've learned is that people *don't* like coming in. They feel that if we're questioning them, we think they're guilty, not just looking for information. The drivers are here...we'll speak with them now."

Jude spoke to the drivers one by one, asking them first, in a friendly fashion, if they minded being recorded. Baskin, Lumis and Finn had been told to take whoever Angus Avery told them to take anywhere Avery said they were to go. Baskin had wound up running errands for Avery himself—buying tobacco, a special mineral water and picking up his glasses, which he had left in his apartment. Lumis had run with the costume designer to a fabric shop, picked up special makeup for Sherry Blanco at a Fifth Avenue shop. Finn had spent most of the day sitting in his car; at four he had made a run, collecting costumed extras from a theatrical agency. All three had returned their cars and clocked out by six. A man named Joe Hutchins had been assigned to Sherry Blanco; he returned her to her maisonette on Park Avenue at four-thirty, and returned his car. Sam Eagan had driven Bobby Walden; Walden had left the set at seven, and the car had been turned in right after. Eric Len had driven Angus Avery, and he verified that he had taken the director to speak at the dinner, and then brought him home and returned his car. Nothing that any man said contradicted what any other said. All cars had been returned before nine-thirty the night of Virginia Rockford's murder.

When the interviews were over, Whitney asked Jude, "We're heading to Not Your Mama's?"

"Yes."

"Before following up on Melody Tatum?"

He nodded. "I'm trying to ascertain if we are seeing a pattern," he told her. He shook his head. "Ellis Sayer will make sure that no one leaves the city—and that Harold Patterson is available when I'm ready to drop in on him," he added dryly. He actually offered her a grim and weary smile. "Let's go."

It seemed that today was going to go just a little bit differently; Jude actually waited for her to grab her shoulder bag before heading out with his long strides.

As they walked down to the car, he was on the phone

with Hannah, having her draw up the address of the establishment. It was in the Bowery, on the edge of the old Five Points area. It wasn't just a strip club; it was one of the seediest joints Jude had ever seen. The interior was dark and filled with curved back booths covered in some kind of black velvet that reeked, most probably there since the early seventies. When he and Whitney entered, blinking to adjust their eyes to the darkness, it looked as if rats scurried away. Giant rats; the clientele who had been in the club who, in all likelihood, had pockets full of drugs. There was one woman dancing; she had the look of someone very young—and far too slim to be an exotic dancer.

Cocaine. Cocaine took that kind of toll on the body, he thought.

A woman walked forward; either a waitress or a manager. She was the opposite of the woman dancing—tall and buxom, over forty and if he had to pick a single word to describe her, he would probably think, *blowsy.*

She seemed to have radar for cops and was well on the way to absolute belligerence as she approached them.

"You've just ruined our business for the day," the woman complained. "Our permits are in order. What do you want?" She looked from Jude to Whitney as she spoke, and she was obviously sizing Whitney up as a new morsel to put on the menu.

"I wish I could ruin your business for eternity," Jude said, keeping his tone even. "Are you the owner? Owner or manager, I'm thinking, because it doesn't look as if you're on the drugs you get your girls taking—free, at first, I imagine. Then you get them hooked and they're yours until they're all used up."

She was angry, of course.

"I am the owner, Myra Holiday. What is it that you want—Officer?"

"Detective, Ms. Holiday. Detective Crosby. And this is Agent Tremont, FBI. Congratulations. You're a suspect in a murder investigation."

That at last brought a real reaction from her. "Murder? No way in hell could we be associated with a murder investigation."

Whitney arched a brow and lifted the newspaper with the picture of Sarah Larson.

"Sarah quit. She had some big-time offer, and she was quitting. She told me that she'd gotten a real chance. You're in the wrong place—you ask the other girls—she left here about two weeks ago, full of herself. She said that she couldn't tell us what was going on, but that we'd be seeing her soon enough, and that we'd all be pea green with envy."

Whitney was angry, he saw, looking at the woman with fury and loathing. "You saw the paper—you saw the paper and you knew exactly who the woman in the picture was—but you had no intention of helping the police!" she said indignantly.

"Hey, I don't want any trouble. And you say she's dead? Well, she was always after something, always after somebody with money. And she was willing to go anywhere with anyone. She was gone from here, I swear it! You can ask any of the girls. They'll tell you that what I'm saying is true."

"She was willing to go after anyone with money

after you turned her into a junkie," Jude said, his voice soft.

"I didn't kill anybody!" the woman protested.

"Actually, I'm pretty sure you've managed to kill a lot of women throughout the years, Ms. Holiday," Jude said. "I'll need a list of your regulars."

The woman started to laugh. "My regulars? I don't have a list of any regulars. What, do you think customers sign in or something? I don't have any lists. And I didn't call the police because Sarah Larson was just trouble. A little bitch. I haven't seen her—I'm telling you that she was out of here weeks ago, and no one has heard from her since."

"I'm going to suggest, Ms. Holiday, that you get something together for me, because we are in the middle of a major murder investigation—and I'm going to have a team out here to rip the place up looking for evidence. Some of them are really good friends with some of the vice and fraud guys, and…"

His voice trailed; the woman was suddenly white, and not because he had threatened her with a vice squad. She was horrified.

"You—you think that Sarah's murder had something to do with…the women who were butchered. You think that she was a victim of the *Ripper?*"

Jude shook his head with disgust. "She was murdered and dumped in the river, Ms. Holiday, and you couldn't even bother to identify her for the police. We don't know if her murder was associated with the other murder. We do know that she's dead, throat slashed, and that you're going to cooperate in any way humanly possible. I have a team coming in to speak with your girls, and to go over this place with a fine-tooth comb, and if you make me have to waste the time to get a warrant, I'll make sure that I take so much of your time, you'll be ready for retirement when I'm done."

"Whatever you want, whatever you want," Myra told him.

Whitney brushed by her and headed for the skinny woman dancing on the stage.

"Hey!" Whitney called. The skinny woman didn't notice her at first. She was just swinging around the pole, eyes lackadaisical, moving only vaguely to the music.

"Hey!" Whitney called again.

The girl blinked, noticing her. She smiled curiously. "Hey, sugar. You don't look like the kind of woman who likes women, but, hey, you are a pretty thing and I promise I can make you real happy."

"I need to speak with you," Whitney told her, flashing her badge.

The woman froze, and looked backstage as if she wanted to run. Whitney quickly hopped on stage and showed her the picture of Sarah Larson. "Was she your friend?" Whitney asked.

Again, the girl looked longingly backstage, dying to flee.

"Look at me—talk to me," Whitney said firmly.

The young woman's shoulders slumped. "That's Sarah," she said softly. "She was my friend. She's dead, isn't she?"

"I need to know who she was seeing," Whitney told her.

The skimpily clad girl winced, shaking her head.

"She wasn't seeing anyone. She said if you closed your eyes and dreamed, it didn't matter that they were smelly creeps. She wouldn't have seen anyone here, I mean, not beyond work. She told us all that we had to be strong and keep dreaming, even when…she was going to be a star. She was a real dancer."

"And she left here, to go somewhere else?" Whitney asked.

The girl nodded, slowly at first, then strenuously. "She said she was going to go off and be a star."

"Where? With and for whom?" Whitney persisted.

"She wouldn't tell us. She said that she'd been promised a role."

"As a dancer?"

The girl nodded, looking past her at Myra.

"Think, please, it's very important," Whitney persisted gently.

"I swear, that's all that she would say," the skinny woman said.

"What's your name?" Whitney asked.

"Candy."

"What's your real name?" Jude said, coming forward.

"Debbie. Debbie Mortensen," the girl said.

Whitney started to hand her a card; she realized that the girl had nowhere to put it, except in the string of the ridiculous studded thong she was wearing. Jude drew out his own card and joined it to Whitney's, then stuck both cards in the band of the thong. "The police need your help. Anything you can think of might be important. Other officers will be around questioning everyone here—talk to them, or call us."

He turned and strode out. Whitney followed him. He dialed Sayer and told him to get officers down to the place to question everyone involved. He called Hannah and told her to get on the business records.

"You don't believe Myra or Debbie?" Whitney asked.

He sighed. "No, I do believe them. And one of those girls will notice if someone was in here who was a bit above the usual clientele."

As they stood there, Debbie Mortensen, now wrapped in a red, faux-silk housecoat, came rushing out into the street.

"I thought of something!" she told them. In the garish light of day, her age was visible. Debbie Mortensen wasn't a girl. She had to be at least thirty-five. And, like Myra, she was scared. Her face was white and pinched.

"Thank you," Whitney said gravely.

"Talk, please," Jude told her.

"There was a guy that she was into, not long before she left," Debbie said. "He—he was weird. He looked like he came off a movie set. I mean, he was wearing some kind of weird hat and a cloak. Like...like..."

"Jack the Ripper?" Whitney offered.

Debbie's eyes widened and she nodded. "I never really saw his face because he kept the hat low and he sat in one of the back booths all the time. Sarah was kind of amused by him. She gave him a—a lap dance. Then it seemed that they were talking. I noticed her close to him in the back booth. In fact, when he left, she did a leap off the pole and went running after him. I remember, because when she came back in, I teased her about it. She said that he'd disappeared—it was like he went out to the street and vanished into thin air. But she wasn't worried—she was going to see him again."

"Did she say that he was going to make her rich and famous?" Jude asked.

Debbie shook her head. "But it wasn't long after that Sarah left, and when she left, she did say that we'd all see her soon—we'd see her rich and famous. She disappeared. She disappeared, just like he did, I guess." Debbie hugged her arms around her chest and started to shiver. "I mean, for real, just the way that he did. I'd forgotten to give her back a necklace. I rushed into the street, and she was gone. Just as if she'd vanished into thin air." She backed away from them suddenly, her mouth gaping. "He *was* Jack the Ripper!" she said, hysteria rising in her voice. "Oh, my God, we're all in danger here. I don't know what to do. I have to pay rent…I have to eat."

You have a cocaine habit, Jude thought. *Yes, that has to be fed.*

"There are shelters," he told her. "If you come to the station, we can help you get your feet back on the ground. There are programs to help women in your situation. You can clean up."

Debbie Mortensen stared at him as if he was crazy.

She shook her head. "That's what I know!" she said, and she turned and raced back into the club.

On the sidewalk, Whitney looked at Jude. "It seems that the victims are all practicing prostitution in one way or another," she said.

He looked at her and sighed. "She was going to make them all pea green with envy," he said.

Whitney nodded. "The movies," she said quietly. "We're back to the movie that was being made downtown—gaslight era. The site where the House of Spiritualism once stood."

He couldn't help but smile at her. "We're back to the movies, Agent Tremont. Someone involved with that movie is totally insane, or..."

"Or?"

"Has a very strange way of trying to make sure it has promotion," Jude told her. "Come on," he said, taking her arm. He realized that it was too easy to touch her. And that it wasn't bothering him to have her with him. She was bright. She listened, and she stepped in just when it seemed that she should.

He liked her.

And he was fascinated by her. He was certain he'd never met anyone quite like her. Anyone who looked like her, with such a unique and compelling *golden* beauty.

He gave himself a mental shake. He was a cop, she was an agent. And women were dying.

"Where are we going now?" she asked.

"Coffee and lunch—with the lists of those involved in the movie. Coffee because I need it. Lunch because I have an autopsy coming up, and I'm not sure I'll want it after."

"Where are we going?"

"Somewhere I know we won't be disturbed."

Twenty minutes later, they sat across from one another at the dining room in his apartment. Coffee was brewed, and sandwiches and chips lay on a plate between them.

Whitney liked his apartment; it was neat, comfortable and eclectic. Like his father, Jude Crosby had books—his were everywhere. He seemed fond of old leather and hard wood, organization and comfort.

She looked at his books. Many were obviously works he had acquired because of his obsession: histories of law enforcement, a book on truly comprehending the Constitution, forensics books and more.

He was a mystery fan, too, so it seemed; shelves were filled with books by Childs, Ellroy, Connelly and several more contemporary authors. Again, like his father, he seemed to be a fan of the classics, and he had beautifully bound collections of Shakespeare, Dickens and more. His shelves were strewn about the apartment; even the dining room had a bookshelf.

Jude had apologized to her, leaving her to make the sandwiches while he collected information on the movie crew and cast with the notes Sayer and his group had entered into a file that he could reach on his computer. He checked his watch, aware that the hour for the autopsy was approaching. She didn't think he was late to any event often.

Whitney, reading over the list in front of her, frowned, looking at Jude, who sat across from her at his handsome mahogany dining table. He had loosened his collar and it was obvious he had been running his fingers through his hair. She looked back to the list she'd been reading quickly; the case was riddled with urgency, and she had found herself thinking that he was a remarkably attractive man, somehow rugged and macho, and still courteous and aware of those around him. It was a strange mix and in it all, he came off, she realized, as ridiculously sexually appealing. She blinked, trying to refocus. She'd been busy in the last months, learning a new life. Training had been rugged for a film major, and she'd given it all her effort. She hadn't stopped living; she and the team had become close, almost like a well-oiled machine that could think as one. They'd learned to work, and still smile and even laugh sometimes as they did. But she hadn't really thought about *sex,* much less a particular man, in forever, so it seemed.

And, no matter what the sizzle he seemed to create in her bloodstream, she was working. And it was doubtful that he was really thinking of her at all—except as the agent with whom he was forced to work.

"The newest victim, Melody Tatum," she said. "We don't know that she was associated with the film in any way, Jude."

"Sayer has team members at her escort service. When the autopsy is over, I'm heading there to speak with the owner-slash-manager of the business." She saw him check his phone, reading his text messages. "Nothing much is ever what you expect. The strip club is owned by a woman—we met that charming opportunist already—and the owner-manager of the escort service is Harold Patterson. I knew that of course, but, I guess I'd still have thought it was going to be a woman. Someone who'd done the *escorting* herself before reaching a point where she could live off the backs of others."

"Hey, you wouldn't want the world to discriminate, would you?" Whitney asked him. "Maybe Harold Patterson did a little escorting himself. Don't be biased now."

He grinned, an actual, easy grin. "Nope. It's just interesting, that's all," he said. "I wouldn't ever want the world to discriminate in any way, shape or form. But what I want isn't going to change expectations. I look forward to meeting one of the others of the profession."

Whitney smiled, lowering her eyes and looking back at her notes. She was beginning to *really* like Jude Crosby. She'd been lucky in her life to hit very little prejudice herself, but she was a mixture of races, and she wasn't a fool—there were people out there who still couldn't really deal with the idea of an equal world. Jude Crosby wasn't just paying lip service. She felt that he'd seen an awful lot in his years working the streets, and that his mind was set. He didn't judge a person by gender or color and probably not by sexual orientation, political or religious affiliation, or any particular choice in life that didn't cause injury to others.

Not good, she warned herself. *There was no way out of the fact that he drew sexual attraction by his very existence.*

It hadn't been good that he was such a strong individual. Liking him so much was a whole different story.

People had died, she reminded herself.

"Samuel Vintner. The guard was apparently the last one on the set. He is an ex-cop. Two other girls had tried to hang around—they'd wanted Virginia Rockford to leave with them. Missy Everett and Jane Deaver. They left together, and were lucky enough to find a cab. There was still one down that far on Broadway, and they grabbed it together, afraid that another wouldn't come. They said that Samuel Vintner and Virginia Rockford were the last people on the set."

"Yeah, and, sadly, having been a cop, or even being a cop, doesn't mean that someone is legitimate. But it's not the cop," he said.

"Oh? And why not?"

Jude hesitated. He grimaced. "Gut feeling," he told her. "And—I just don't see an old used-up cop on duty as the last guard at a movie site as having any kind of stake in anything that's going on."

"He would know how to avoid detection," Whitney pointed out.

Jude looked at her. "Anyone can get online, and everyone watches television. Most people are aware that sometimes perpetrators can be arrested because of DNA, trace evidence, skin cells...assuming, of course, that we have some kind of comparison to make. And you do have just cause for search warrants, DNA and so on. You know that. The thing is—this guy will make a mistake, whether he's insane or a person with an agenda."

Whitney was silent.

"What?" he asked her.

"Jack the Ripper got away."

"Jack the Ripper might not have gotten away. Anything we know about the killer is really a theory, and nothing more. Supposition. And Jack the Ripper was busy in London in the 1880s. We've come a long way."

Whitney jumped, suddenly hearing a rapping sound that seemed to come from the walls. It was followed by a "Hey!"

She was instantly ready and alert, but didn't draw her weapon; the "hey" didn't sound threatening.

"Dad," Jude explained. "Hey," he called back. "In here."

"Do you want company?

"Dad, come on in. We're thinking aloud with each other. Another mind won't be a bad thing at all," Jude said.

Andrew was still a little hesitant when he came in the room.

"I never mean to interrupt," he said.

"You're not interrupting at all," Whitney replied, grinning.

"Dad, sit, do you want a sandwich?"

"I—I heard voices. I was just checking to make sure that it was you," Andrew said. He shrugged to Whitney. "That's the best you can do when you live next door to your son. Stay away when you should, check up on his interests when you should."

"And you do a great job of it," Jude assured him.

Whitney thought that his affection for his father was real and admirable. They did treat one another as equals, even though the parent-child connection existed as well. Their bond was tight, and she was only sorry that it made her like Jude Crosby even more. He was really far too easy to like.

Jude set down the papers he'd been looking at and shook his head. "But, if you heard voices in here you didn't think were mine or a friend's, you needed to stay on your own side and dial 911."

"Son, I was patrolling the streets when you were still in diapers, remember?"

"So, okay, Dad. Do you have anything for me?"

"Yep, yep, I do," Andrew said.

"And that would be…?" Jude asked.

"Blair House!" Andrew announced with pleasure. "I have a book that lists as its sources a number of books at the NYU library. In the history section there's a copy of a ledger that's at the Pierpont Library. The family who owned Blair House from the 1860s to the 1890s was in financial trouble by the end of the century. They kept the place as a boarding house. And guess who stayed there?"

"Jonathan Black?" Whitney asked.

Andrew stared at her again. He nodded, mesmerized anew. "How did you know?"

"Lucky guess."

"There's a signature—Jonathan Black—of a man who signed in as a guest in March 1891. One month before the murder of Carrie Brown. So, before he wound up at the House of Spiritualism, Jonathan Black checked into Blair House. That had to be one really bad, creepy dude. I wonder if he watched the people over at the House of Spiritualism, and then moved in on them!"

As they listened to Jude's father's announcement, Whitney's phone began to buzz. She quickly looked down at the text that had come to her. It was from Jackson Crow. As usual, he was brief. "Have arrived. Settling into Blair House."

"What is it?" Jude asked her.

"My team has arrived," she said. She thought that something passed through Jude Crosby's eyes. Was it regret? Something just a little bit sorrowful? She felt something of a strange regret herself.

She'd liked working with him. They'd begun to... bond, after a fashion.

And now...

"Well, Jackson is just the man who can really add experience to the investigation," she said briskly.

"We need to finish up here then. I have my own agenda," Jude said. "There are five from the film I want to interview personally—the two stars, Blanco and Walden, Samuel Vintner and the girls who saw Virginia Rockford last, Missy Everett and Jane Deaver." Jude paused, looking at Whitney. "I don't give a damn where the Ripper might have wound up. I'm certain Jonathan Black, Jack the Ripper or whoever the fellow might have been did not arise from the grave to start murdering people!"

"But," Whitney said, "Jude, we do need to know who researched Jonathan Black and the murders that happened in that age. It is obvious now that someone is repeating them. Checking the library records at NYU and Pierpont might help us find out who."

Jude took a deep breath, staring at her.

"Yes," he said. "It does seem apparent now." Disgusted, he shook his head, and leaned toward her, his tone like solid steel as he said, "One thing, however, is true. Jack is *not* back. There is a killer out there, and I swear, this time, he's *not* going to become a mystery for the ages. I'm going to find the bastard."

7

"Come on, clue me in on everything," Angela said, and walked down the hallway and through the door to the kitchen. There was a little table in the breakfast-nook area. She poured herself a cup of coffee and headed toward it. "I want more of a feel for what's going on."

Ellis had made the trip to the airport to collect the rest of the team—and all their equipment. But he left them to settle in with Jude after they stopped by the station to introduce the team around. Whitney wasn't sure about her own feelings toward Ellis. He always appeared weary and tired. But Jude seemed to believe in him. And if Jude believed in him, he had to be one of the good ones. He was different, though. He didn't seem to have much of an open mind regarding anything that wasn't hard evidence. He was a cop who worked by the book. He would be methodical and thorough, she thought.

"Tragic, scary events," Whitney assured her, but she poured herself a cup of coffee and walked over to join Angela at the table.

"Well, I know that. But, you believe that whatever's going on calls for our skills set? I was surprised that Jude whisked Jenna away with him to the autopsy, but she might bring out the answers about that death," Angela said.

As Whitney had suspected, Jude and Jackson had hit it off immediately. They were both no-nonsense and determined, low-key and yet as steadfast and persistent as a pair of bulldozers. When Jude left with the two agents, Jake Mallory paired off with Will Chan to set up the equipment as she had determined it should be.

"The cops seem to be treading water—all we have to go on is the similarity to the Ripper and a possible link to that movie," Whitney told her.

Angela nodded. "Whatever the reason, I'm glad to be here. The house is quite beautiful, and it's amazing that it has remained as untouched and pristine as it has all these years, what with the continual progress and rebuilding in a city the size of New York," she said.

Whitney was glad to see Angela, as she had been glad to see the rest of the team. They had come to a point where they worked wonderfully together; they knew one another, and they were actually something of a family. And, of course, if they were a family of any kind, Angela was the matriarch even if she was in her early thirties. But she'd come from law enforcement, and despite her lovely and fragile blond appearance, she was tough as nails, and wasn't afraid of her talents dealing with the past—including the dead.

"If I'm reading and understanding all the information correctly, it's the property next door that is so notorious. And still, Blair House has been here forever. It must have some salacious history somewhere in there!"

"It might all be connected, you know. Jude's dad was a cop, and he's an amazing researcher. He has a library you wouldn't believe. Anyway, he found a copy of a ledger kept at the Pierpont Library—the family took in boarders...among them, Jonathan Black."

"Interesting," Angela said. "We'll need to get to the library and see what we can find out. But Blair House itself doesn't have a history of terrible violence or the like."

Whitney shook her head. "Not that I've discovered yet."

"Have you come across the unusual?" Angela asked Whitney.

"Not what we would consider unusual," Whitney told her. "But..." She thought Angela Hawkins the most intuitive in their group. If there were spirits—or energy—left behind, Angela was the one who could usually sense them first and open her mind to the pain and loss of the past, drawing them out.

They'd all learned quickly to respect one another's talents. Jackson was still the one to insist they find the flesh-and-blood truth in any situation, and he tended to be quiet when it came to his belief in his own *intuition,* but he respected the opinions, feelings and intuitions of his group.

"Ah! You *do* know. You just doubt yourself," Angela told her. She shivered. "Though, it's really strange down here—with that...abyss next door. I can only imagine the night, the darkness, the loneliness... I might imagine a thing or two myself. What did you see?"

Whitney laughed ruefully. "I tried all night, speaking aloud to any ghosts that might be around, and they totally ignored me. But when I woke in the morning, there was a woman looking at me. She never seemed solid—when I blinked, she was gone. She was in late-Victorian attire, and if I had to guess, I'd say she'd been around in the 1890s. So, I might have wanted to see someone so badly that I imagined her, or she was someone who does haunt this house." She hesitated a minute. "And, I saw a dog—her dog, I imagine."

"A dog?" Angela sounded curious. "How interesting!"

"We've seen animals before," Whitney reminded her. "Civil War soldiers on horses."

"I'm not doubting you at all," Angela assured her. "It's possible your vision might have died by violence, and that the dog might have died first, trying to protect her."

"Well, they both disappeared quickly," Whitney told her.

"Hmm." Angela ran her fingers through her mane of blond hair thoughtfully. "Sometimes, as we know, ghosts are shy, terrified of the living, or they don't know how to communicate, even when you're open to them. When we can get closer and closer to the reason they've remained, we can coax them out… I'm going to spend the early part of the afternoon just getting to know the house. Later, maybe before sunset, we should explore the property next to us—en masse, of course."

"Have *you* felt anything about the house?" Whitney asked her.

"I'm not sure yet, either," Angela told her. "Places this old always seem to speak to something inside us—give us an inner awe—whether they're inhabited by spirits that can't move on or not. They're filled with history and time. But I can't say that the local ghosts ran out to meet me," she said, smiling. "Patience is needed. And, as we've all learned, we don't know why certain people…communicate with other people. Dead or alive," she added. "Where do you feel we're going to be as a team? I liked Crosby—very much. And he seemed perfectly willing to have the team on his task force."

Whitney shrugged. "Relatively accepted, no one smirked at me too visibly at the task force meeting. And you saw how intrigued they all were to meet you at the station house. They've had to have seen the press about us being ghost hunters, but our solve rate always has a perfectly rational explanation. Jude wouldn't believe in a ghost if the entire population of Trinity Cemetery crawled out of their graves to say boo. But he's a decent guy."

"Are you still convinced that it all has to do with Jack the Ripper and someone obsessed with him?" Angela asked.

"Angela," Whitney said, "yes, I'm convinced. There were two pre-Ripper murders—Polly Nichols and Annie Chapman—and those coincide with the Jane Does. And now, Virginia Rockford and Melody Tatum. I was there when the medical examiner gave his preliminary on Melody. I don't think there's a doubt that this killer intends to carry out the same streak of murders as Jack the Ripper."

"Then Jude's father's library might help us."

Angela laughed suddenly. "I just realized—you met the detective's father. Have you two set a date yet?" she teased. "He's impressive. His size alone must intimidate the criminals in his world from the onset of any investigation. Quick work."

"No, no," Whitney protested. She hoped she wasn't blushing. If she was, she hoped that her biracial coloring was hiding the fact. "Like I said, Jude's father is a retired cop. I think Jude often speaks with him about his cases. Anyway, I'm still reading the book, but it was written by a retired cop who was in New York when Carrie Brown, the so-called American victim of Jack the Ripper, was murdered. What's difficult is that there are no records on the man, Jonathan Black, who this author suspected of the crimes—and of being the Ripper. The only real mention of him seems to be in that ledger. I haven't had a chance to verify that no other records exist on such a person coming into the country, or living at Blair House, or at the House of Spiritualism. But one theory is that he became so debauched and terrifying that he scared the devil worshippers he lived with, and that they killed and interred him somewhere at the site."

Angela was thoughtful. "If there's more information regarding either of the properties to be found on the computer, Jake Mallory can find it," she said. "And we can get a list at the library—they take names before allowing people to handle rare books."

"Oh, there's a tech at the police station Detective

Crosby seems to believe in implicitly. Her name is Hannah Mills, and I get the feeling that if he asked for her to be on the task force, she had to be good."

"I'll have Jake get down to speak with her. If they combine their efforts, I'm sure we'll be better off," Angela said. She glanced out the window at the construction site.

"Jude's father is pretty good, too, so it seems," Whitney said.

"The more I think about it…he's a civilian now… we'll keep track of his findings, but we can't really bring him on this," Angela said.

"Andrew's not afraid of much," Whitney said.

"We always take any help—we just need to keep civilians safe, you know?"

"Of course."

"And I'm sure that Jude is grateful, and that he's also careful to see that what information he receives from his father is kept under his hat," Angela said.

"Do you know what Jackson is thinking about the situation?" Whitney asked Angela. She hoped that her team leader would agree with the psychological assessment she had made of the killer at the task force meeting earlier. Jackson had worked with behavioral science units for years, had a firm understanding of psychology—and was extremely familiar with that of killers.

This case had become personal somehow. Maybe because she empathized too much with the victims. Maybe because she had been the first to arrive in New York; Jackson had figured that she knew Lower Manhattan well since she'd gone to NYU, and that she'd make an excellent team representative while the rest of them gathered information and equipment.

She'd never walked the streets as a hooker, she thought dryly, but she had seen a lot of pain and desperation in the streets of her native New Orleans, and she had seen how easy it could be for people to become desperate for the simplest necessities of life.

"The killer is so controlled," she murmured, shivering suddenly. "Angela, the two Jane Does were killed like Emma Smith and Martha Tabrum—murders that are accepted not as Ripper killings but as precursors to the events, precursors that wound up in the police files of the time. Down to the one being attacked, and dying en route to the hospital—the other was pulled from the river. Assuming that we have someone trying to reenact what happened in Victorian London, he is still willing to take major chances, because the one girl was left alive, though so near death that she couldn't really help the police. That takes nerve—I mean, killing someone that way was such an incredible risk! I'm worried this killer could go on and on, because there are other victims in the original investigations and old files as well. Today, the cops and experts who study the files seem to agree on the five nineteenth-century victims—but that's not the point. There were so many other victims who were being investigated at the time. Then, of course, there's the belief that he came to the States and killed Carrie Brown here. Police records say that Carrie Brown was the only woman butchered like a true Ripper victim, but that didn't mean that there weren't other murders—or that the Ripper did die in New York if indeed he came here."

"That's a lot of killing for someone to reenact," Angela said.

Whitney nodded, frowning. "There were 'accidents' at the site, too, when they were setting up to film the movie. Angus Avery, the director, believes beyond a doubt that there's something evil about the site. There's something going on, but, of course, I don't know what. I do think that once we've had a chance to explore the construction area, we'll...well, we'll be on to something."

Angela rose to put her coffee cup in the sink. "No one goes there alone, Whitney."

Whitney laughed. "Trust me! I have no wish to wander around there alone. Ugh! But I do think that we need to get some cameras going in that area."

"I agree. Tell Will, and the two of you decide just what equipment you're going to need and we'll all be your grunts this evening," Angela said.

"There is something very different in the contemporary murders," Whitney said, looking at Angela.

"Yes, this is far more than a century later," Angela said.

Whitney shook her head gravely. "The Ripper's second victim was found more than a week after the first. But this man has killed two nights in a row. He's accelerating."

"I think we should get to the library," Angela said.

"Let's do it," Whitney agreed.

"Our poor girl was already suffering from cirrhosis of the liver, but she hadn't been drinking the night she was killed. Stomach contents were well-digested, suggesting that it had been some time since she'd eaten. I don't believe that the murderer had to have had a medical degree, but he definitely had some knowledge of anatomy—the uterus and its appendages have been removed. The incisions have no hesitation, and are clean. There is no injury to the *cervix uteri*. The rectum has been avoided, while the upper portions of the vagina and two-thirds of the bladder have been taken from the body. They were not discovered on or anywhere near Melody Tatum." He paused, looking at Jude. "To my knowledge, they have yet to be discovered anywhere."

Jude shook his head. Dr. Fullbright had been meticulous. Officers had canvassed the entire area. The forensics team had been over the entire alley. Dumpsters had been pulled apart; not an inch had been overlooked.

He heard Fullbright's voice drone on; it didn't matter what he was saying. The woman on the autopsy table had been brutally butchered—that much was apparent to the most untrained eye. And Jude knew as well that everything that Fullbright found was going to be consistent with the findings on the body of the Ripper's second victim, Annie Chapman.

The city was filled with possible suspects.

He had to narrow it down.

No matter what, it seemed to come back to the movie. He didn't know about Melody Tatum yet, but he was sure that he would discover that she'd been promised a role in it—or that she...

Had she slept with someone involved? Plied her trade upon the actor who had an agenda?

Time! They needed more time; even with the task

force relentlessly questioning people for hours, there just wasn't enough time.

Fullbright finished the official autopsy after removing sections of tissue and drawing fluids for analysis. He stepped away from the table, stripping off his gloves and lifting his mask. He spoke to Jude, Jackson and Jenna.

"You know, Jude," he said, "that I'm one of those armchair detectives, always trying to study the newest on the Ripper case. I swear, it was almost as if the killer had an old autopsy diagram of Annie Chapman on him when he killed and mutilated this woman."

Jude nodded. "I want the details kept confidential; I talked to Sayer just now, and he and his people have wasted hours listening to the confessions of petty criminals and plain old nutjobs, all just trying to get their names in the paper. And it's even harder to deal with the true mental patients who begin to think that they're evil. Sayer had one call from a prisoner who said that his astral self committed the murders, and another who told him that Jack the Ripper had scooped him up in a spaceship and then sent him down with instructions on what to do."

Dr. Fullbright nodded sympathetically. "My office will refer to the police spokesperson on any matter, Jude. But, I'm afraid that the public will grow into a frenzy anyway. They'll think what they want."

"True enough, but let's not give them any validation," Jude said. He looked over at Jackson Crow. The man was his own height, with straight ink-black hair that gave credence to a Native American background. He had been quiet and grave during the autopsy, respecting Jude's position as the lead detective. Jenna Duffy, soft-spoken, her words musical with the hint of an old-world lilt, had been equally respectful, but her green eyes had been ever watchful as the autopsy had taken place.

Now Jude wanted an opinion; he knew all about Jackson Crow. Hannah had filled him in during a quick phone conversation just outside before he'd joined the others in the autopsy room. Crow had an interesting background with the feds, having saved two team members who should have died with the others. He'd been on leave after that, and then given the position to head the special team. He'd had years of experience at Quantico before his current position, and was reputed to have a bull's-eye ability when it came to pegging the traits and psychology of a killer.

Jackson said, "Whoever you're dealing with is organized and intelligent. You certainly wouldn't see him on the streets dripping the blood of his victims. He has a plan, and he's carrying it out. This isn't Victorian London, and he knows it. Whether he believes that Jack the Ripper came to the United States or not, he is working on that theory as he carries out his crimes, which makes him very dangerous. He's going to go for the next accepted step in the career of the past killer. Next up, you can expect a double event. One woman will be found quickly with her throat slashed. Then he'll find another, and he'll make sure that he has the time to carry out the mutilations."

"How much time does he need?" Jude asked, looking from Fullbright to Jenna Duffy.

The two looked at each other. "Fifteen to thirty minutes?" Jenna asked Fullbright.

"Give or take, depending on his skill," Fullbright said.

"What kind of weapon is he using?" Jude asked.

"That's hard to say—the blade is at least six inches," Fullbright told him. "But there are so many knives available today...might be a military weapon, or it might be a chef's knife. Six inches at least, and very sharp."

"Thanks," Jude said. "Keep me posted, if anything," he told Fullbright.

"Of course," Fullbright said.

As they left the building, Jude's phone rang. It was the deputy chief, suggesting another meeting for the next morning with the task force, and a briefing with the precinct beat, with a thorough briefing to be recorded for every law enforcement officer in New York City. Jude agreed, and told Jackson Crow the plan.

"In the morning, fine. Then I'll have you drop us back off at Blair House so that Whitney can walk us through the murder of the starlet, and we'll start exploring the area where the filming took place."

Jude agreed.

When he dropped the agents off, he was surprised that he wanted to go in, or ask that Whitney come out, just so that he could say hello, or make sure that she was...

Safe. She was an agent. She had sworn to lay down her life, just as he had.

He'd liked her as a partner; he wasn't sure when he had realized that. He wasn't easy. It had taken him a long time to get used to Monty, and when they had bonded, they had bonded. In a day, it had become easy to have Whitney at his side. As he drove away from Blair House, he made a call and made sure that his next interview subject—the jerk who owned the escort agency—would be waiting for him.

"Oh, it was so exciting!" Janice Hodge said. They stood in her office at the library. She was the librarian and historian charged with the care of archival documents. "I can't help it—I do tend to be starstruck, though, you just wouldn't believe it, we get so many celebrities here! But, then, of course, look at the payback some wonderful actors give the city. Think of what De Niro did with the film festival. And you can just honestly be walking down the street, and there's Nathan Lane in front of you!"

She was an attractive young woman in a jacket, pencil skirt and stilettos—not the old image of a librarian by any means.

But Whitney gently led her back to the subject at hand. "What we need is to find out about research done on Jonathan Black. There's supposedly a ledger here—probably in one of the rare-book rooms—with information regarding the old House of Spiritualism, and Jonathan Black."

"Yes! Well, of course, that's what I'm trying to say. We had—supervised, of course—a number of the people from that shoot in here. The director and the two leads in the movie. Oh, and a prop man, and a set designer, and—"

"Sherry Blanco, Bobby Walden and Angus Avery?" Whitney asked.

"Perhaps you could give us a list," Angela suggested.

"Yes, of course, but I can't tell you exactly what they read. We supervise the rooms, naturally, and many books are kept under lock and key beneath glass, but when people are studying the history of the city in a certain room, we're not always sure which books they were looking at."

"We'd be really grateful for your most recent list," Whitney said.

"Yes, of course. Oh, that murder was horrible," Janice Hodge said, shaking her beautiful, long brown hair. "And so sad. Can you imagine how wonderful it was, though, before the dreadful business began?" She sighed and then smiled. "Mr. Avery even suggested that I should be in the movie!" she said.

"And you didn't take him up on it?" Whitney asked her.

She shook her head. "I was actually at a library conference the last few days—in Houston. But...I'm a single mom of three. I can't afford to leave the day job. I can't even take a chance on losing the day job, no matter how starstruck I might be. If you'll hold on just a minute, I'll copy off the list for you."

When she returned, Whitney thanked her and she and Angela left.

"I'm amazed you didn't study it right away," Angela said.

"If we'd had a reaction, I'd just as soon it not be seen," Whitney said.

"But let's look at it now!"

Out on the street, Whitney studied the piece of paper. "Amazing, really," she murmured.

"What's that?" Angela asked.

"The number of people who seem to care about history," Whitney said.

"Well, the number of people in the city is amazing," Angela reminded her.

"Of course," Whitney said. She kept reading. "So we know about the principals in the movie, and it's not a surprise, and they can certainly explain being there."

"You think? Actors would be in on the research?" Angela asked.

"Not usually, but Angus Avery probably dragged them in—made it like a promotional thing. He doesn't seem to miss a beat. So, we have the three of them... and there's a whole group here associated with the movie."

"And who else?" Angela demanded.

Whitney looked at her and shrugged, still feeling a bit of unease. "Andrew, Jude's dad, was in here about—" she studied the dates on the sheet "—three weeks ago. And here's another name I know." She broke off and dialed her cell phone. Jude answered, and she told him where she and Angela had been.

"Anything unusual in there?" he asked her.

"The movie people paid a visit," she said.

"And I'm not surprised."

"And your father—a few weeks ago."

He laughed. "That's not a surprise, either. Dad is always at the library."

"And Dr. Fullbright."

"Hmm," Jude said. And that was all.

* * *

"According to Detective Magnor Honeywell," Whitney told the others, "the House of Spiritualism began benignly enough—the spiritualism rage was still going on, and all kinds of tarot readers and mediums took up residence here. It was an abandoned church, more or less put out of business because of St. Paul's and Trinity. Whatever the Constitution might say about freedom of religion, the people still weren't tremendously accepting of anything beyond their own Protestant beliefs. The foundations became a basement, and at first, because it was rather dark and eerie, most of the séances and readings were done in rooms in the basement. The police did raid the place, but when they arrived, there was nothing to be found, other than tarot cards, books and a lot of tea—I believe a number of the spiritualists read tea leaves as well. But, according to rumor, when the mysterious Jonathan Black moved in, the devil worshipping began, with markings on the floor, black masses, worship of relics—having belonged to an infamous historical personage—and all that kind of thing. The black masses also took place in the basement. Magnor Honeywell writes a truly gut-wrenching portrait of the era and the final demise of the Five Points sector. In the tenements themselves—without benefit of anything that might be construed as devil-worshipping evil—they were constantly finding the bodies of children dead of disease or starvation. There were hundreds—perhaps thousands—of immigrants pouring into the country on a daily basis, and therefore, record keeping was poor, and there can be little documentation of the fact that many people ever lived much less died."

"So, on to the basement," Jackson said. "Everyone is armed...and hard hats and lights? It *is* a construction zone, and the mayor is apparently terrified that one of us is going to kill him or herself. The only reason we can legally go in unescorted by a contractor is that the mayor is so desperate to find the killer, and I think he believes he's grasping at straws himself to think that we might find anything in the rubble that can help us now."

"Okay, so let's head on over," Jake said, grinning sheepishly. "These may be feather-light cameras and recorders, but they're damn heavy."

"Ah, quit whining," Will said. "You've seen the heavy stuff."

"Yeah, I have," Jake said lightly. "And I think I'm going to need a masseuse on the expense account."

"Sadly, you won't get one," Angela teased. "You're going to have to hope that your beloved Ashley is able to make a trip up here, if this goes on too long."

Jake was engaged now, but he and his fiancée both knew that his work and his dedication to the team would frequently make for separations. He'd found the perfect woman: Ashley Donegal understood his situation completely. But then Ashley had been involved personally in one of their investigations, and if she were to join them at any point, she'd be an asset.

Jenna murmured, "We need to do this. Jackson is right, the next time the killer strikes, it's going to be a double event."

"Onward to the House of Spiritualism," Jackson said.

He led the way; the last out of Blair House, Whitney made sure that she locked the door as they departed, and she locked the gate as well. She wasn't sure if locking the gate—or even the doors—could protect them if someone was determined to break in, but she had no intention of making it easy for anyone. She looked back at Blair House as she followed the others.

That afternoon, they'd finished positioning their powerful magnifying cameras toward the property next door, but even so, Whitney knew, the darkness and shadows would stop them from discovering what she was expecting to find in the basement area of the House of Spiritualism. She and Will had discussed their options, and they had ten of what Jake described as the "feather lights" to be set up in the foundations along with an equal number of recorders; until they explored the site, they wouldn't know if they'd figured accurately.

The gate at the construction site meant little. It was a bad lock, and the fencing around the site was chain link. Around the block on the other side, they saw that a single night watchman was on duty at his canvas-covered tent. She was sure that he made certain no pedestrians or cars entered through the main gate, yet she was equally sure that he remained at his post through the night, and didn't wander into the vast expanse of the property.

Jackson waved his light toward the guard to let him know that it was the team entering the property. Then he set his powerful beam on the ground that lay before them, and started toward the abyss of the foundations.

"What the hell is that?" Jenna demanded suddenly,

pointing her own beam toward what appeared to be a lump to their right, near the deconstruction of some scaffolding. Jackson quickly turned her way, approaching the site. A tarp lay over what might have been a body.

Jackson drew the tarp aside.

For a moment, Whitney's stomach twisted. There appeared to be a female in late-nineteenth-century dress, white button-up blouse and navy skirt, face-down in the dirt. But Jackson quickly hunkered down, touched the form and let out an audible sigh of relief. "Mannequin," he said. "She must be left over from some kind of shoot."

They moved on. A treacherous flight of steps led downward into the gaping hole of the foundations. Plywood covered some areas over the foundation support walls, and in other areas, they could look up to the night sky. They moved on down, Jake and Will warning one another to be careful with the equipment.

The original structure must have been very large, perhaps a good ten thousand feet just on the ground floor. While their lights displayed the usual—hard earth for the floor, with remnants here and there of brick and wood, along with brick support walls—they also created shadows and proved the fact that the foundation itself had been broken up in many areas.

"I think this is the largest section, right here, at the base of the stairs," Whitney said. "And if Magnor Honeywell was right in his assumption of where black masses might have been carried out, I believe it would have been right here."

"Let's set up two of the cameras," Will told her.

"Thank God!" Jake said, setting down his burden.

"All right. We'll do this in threes," Jackson said. "Jake—"

"Yes, of course, hang with Will and Whitney and help unpack," Jake said.

Jackson grinned. "Angela, Jenna and I will venture around the walls," he said.

For once in her life, Whitney wished she could be the one exploring rather than working on the technical side. But she set to work with Will, unpacking their cameras and recorders.

"Will these broadcast on the screens back in the hallway at Blair House?" Jake asked.

"Yes, each camera has to be set, but each camera has a dedicated screen," Whitney assured him.

"One at each end?" Will asked.

Whitney nodded, and then realized that he might not see her; his flashlight was angled on the boxes.

"Yes. Jake, grab the tripod there for me, please?" she asked, heading toward the far wall with one of the cameras. "These batteries are supposed to last twenty-four hours, so we'll have to change them again tomorrow evening, starting out a little earlier."

Jake came with the tripod and she set up the camera. She hit a switch, turning it on. She heard a little whir; she'd poised the camera angle on the stairway, but the little whir assured her that the motion detector was working. The lens would follow them while they were in the foundations. It would later direct itself toward anything that moved.

They did get a lot of shots of rats that way, but

they'd also managed to capture unusual phenomena in the past.

A green light came on, assuring her that the remote was feeding into the screens back in the main hallway of Blair House.

Jake walked over to where Will was setting up, straightening out the legs of the tripod being positioned on the opposite side of the room.

Whitney started to follow him, when she froze, aware of a sound behind her. She turned quickly.

At first, she saw nothing.

Then she heard the sound again. It was a soft whining.

The camera clicked and whirred, turning itself.

There, against the shadows of the far rear wall was a dog.

No. *The* dog. Huge, furry and beautiful. It was the mixed-shepherd hound she had seen when she had awakened this morning.

The phantom dog that had guarded the phantom woman.

He trotted up to Whitney; she hunched down and stroked his massive head, and it seemed to be real. She watched and *felt* it as he licked her fingers.

And faded into the night.

8

Harold Patterson wasn't much of a surprise.

He was tall, slim and fit, with a head of rich dark hair that was as sleek as his designer suit. His office was posh, on the twentieth floor of a renovated building in Tribeca. Before entering the man's office, Jude read the notes that Sayer had texted to him. *Fellow is slimy as a rat but has a law degree; he can carry off prostitution as legally as the Catholic Church hires nuns. Melody Tatum was not scheduled to escort anyone anywhere last night; she'd asked him to leave her off the bookings, but I'm obtaining a warrant anyway to check out his client list, and what bookings were made for last night.*

Now Jude looked at the man himself, sitting across the elegant, polished cherry-wood desk that was the centerpiece of an office designed to make a wealthy client feel that he or she was among equals, and as such, safe.

"This is truly horrible, which I told your comrade Detective Sayer. Melody was a beautiful woman, and she had such a touch of class about her. And you realize, of course, that congressmen, businessmen, *busy* men come to this city and they're expected to make appearances at cocktail parties, dinners and all manner of social occasions. Not to mention the fact that a man with numbers spinning in his head might just need a night out at a theater or a concert, and desire a companion with whom to discuss the event. Melody was an amazingly kind and sympathetic woman—she wasn't just beautiful," Patterson said.

Jude leaned forward, not about to be intimidated by his surroundings, and certainly not about to believe the spiel about his escorts being nothing other than educated sounding boards or eye candy.

"I'm not concerned with anything that has to do with your real business practices, Mr. Patterson. You're a pimp in a suit, and your girls are better-dressed hookers."

Patterson's face mottled and he looked as if he was going to explode with a denial, but Jude rose to his full height and stared down at the man. "I don't give a damn about that at the moment. If I did, it wouldn't matter. But you can spout your legal rights and the Constitution at me for hours. The city is in crisis, and we can acquire all the warrants we need. There is just cause. I'm concerned with the death of Melody Tatum, and the fact that a modern-day madman is at work in the streets of New York trying to prove that he's Jack the Ripper reincarnated. I want to know who Melody was seeing the night she was killed. Unless, of course, she happened to be with you."

Patterson, clearly tongue-tied, opened his desk drawer and produced a ledger. "My God! I've never

even hit a woman! I didn't kill her—I was with Holly
Blum, another of my employees, all night. She'll tes-
tify to that, swear on a dozen bibles! I don't know who
Melody was with! Honestly. And I've handed over the
list of clients who come through here. Honestly. And
they can take my computer—you can bring in all your
techs." He hesitated. "Only thing is…."

"The only thing is?" Jude demanded.

"Nothing, really," Patterson mumbled quickly.

Jude leaned on his desk, and brought his face down
close to Patterson's. "Only thing is *what?*"

Patterson winced. "I, uh, I'm not always sure they
give their real identities."

Jude eased back. Patterson hadn't killed anyone; gut
instinct.

"Congressmen, yeah, accountants, sports stars—
movie people?" he asked.

"Probably," he muttered. "Guys with money who
want a girl who doesn't look like a two-bit floozy come
here. It's not like they hand me their personal credit
cards," he said. He looked up at Jude. "You said I was
a pimp and my girls were hookers. Well, a john is a
john as well, whether he's a horny teen looking for a
quick hookup, or a guy in a designer suit who wants the
illusion that he's with a do-over 'Pretty Woman.' Producers, directors, presidents—they all have the same
basic biology."

Jude drew the man's ledger over to him, flipping
through the pages, looking at the names, running his
finger down the pages.

His finger stopped. He looked over at Patterson.

"Who is this?" he asked hoarsely.

Frowning, Patterson looked at the entry.

Jonathan Black.

"Um…" Patterson said.

"Who the hell is it?" Jude demanded.

"I don't know."

"What the hell do you mean, you don't know?"

"He was just a phone call…and you can see by the date—he was scheduled to go out with Melody more than a week ago," Patterson said.

"Just a phone call? You don't demand payment in advance?" Jude asked.

"Cash," Patterson said.

"You just send a woman out on the streets with a man who promises to pay cash?" Jude said incredulously.

Patterson seemed to be shrinking in his chair. "Many men don't want their identities known."

"Did he come in with the cash?" Jude demanded.

Patterson winced again. "It was in an envelope under the door."

"God help me, by any wild chance, do you have the envelope?" Jude asked.

Patterson, as he had expected, shook his head. "I tossed it," he said apologetically.

"And the cash is in the bank, right?" Jude asked.

Patterson brightened. "Oh, no!" Again, he practically bit his own tongue shutting up. He couldn't have been much of an attorney, Jude decided.

"Right. It wouldn't be in the bank. It would be under-the-table income," Jude said. He leaned toward the man again. "I need it."

Patterson looked a little ill again.

"Well?"

"You're kind of looking at it," Patterson said. "I—uh—I went out and splurged on this suit."

"The whole thing? Patterson, damn it, do you have anything left?"

"Maybe...maybe." He stood and reached into his pocket and drew out a slim leather wallet. He dug in it and leafed through his bills, producing one. "This... well, I've mixed up money, but I wasn't carrying any other hundreds...this is the last, I think!"

Jude reached for a tissue, took the bill from him and wrapped it. He doubted they could really gain anything from it; a killer organized and meticulous enough to have gone this far had probably worn gloves when he'd handled the money. They were likely to get dozens of prints, and possibly, none of them the killer's.

But he was grasping at straws. And he'd found one.

"Whitney?" She stood and turned around.

Jake, tall, handsome and lanky, was staring at her with concern.

She winced. "Did you see it?" she asked.

"See what?"

"The dog?" Whitney let out a breath. "You didn't see it," she said.

Jake walked over to her and set his hands on her shoulders. "Whitney, because I didn't see it doesn't mean that it wasn't there. You mean a ghost dog, right?"

She nodded. "I guess seeing a ghost dog isn't all that helpful, is it?"

Jake affectionately touched her cheek. "We don't

know yet, do we? You may have a key to many pieces of information through that dog," he assured her.

Whitney heard a shuffling sound from the stairway. Startled, she and Jake spun around.

Jude Crosby was coming down the stone steps that remained on the ground that led into the foundations.

"Hey!" he called.

Whitney was surprised to see him there. She was equally surprised that they hadn't heard him coming; they had to be more vigilant.

"Is anything new?" Whitney asked, breaking away from Jake and walking toward him. "You met with the guy who runs the escort agency—Patterson?"

Jude nodded. "I'm on my way to another meeting with the director, Angus Avery, and a few members of his cast and crew."

"You found something that points to the film crew?" Jake asked. Will walked curiously toward them.

"Maybe." He paused a minute. "I found the name *Jonathan Black* written in Harold Patterson's ledger. Naturally, whoever he is, Patterson never saw him. He dealt with him over the phone, but he had an appointment with Melody Tatum a week before the murder. Jonathan Black can't be that unusual a name, but under the circumstances..."

"Under the circumstances," Whitney said evenly, "I'd say that our killer definitely believes that Jonathan Black was Jack the Ripper, and that he's taking on his persona."

"It's a sound theory," Jude agreed. "I'd hoped that knowing who had been in to study the rare books would be more helpful. I'm not surprised that either my father's name or Fullbright's name were on the list. Fullbright is an armchair detective, fascinated by the Ripper and the past—and the possibility that he came to the States. And my father is such a history buff. And I'm not surprised about the film crew. Angus Avery claimed to be working on accuracy. He's an excellent excuse for having looked into the past."

"Along with his key actors," Whitney added.

"Accuracy again, I guess," Jude said. "The list is important."

"Yes."

"But," Jude told her, "I'm sorry to say that we still don't have a real shred of forensic evidence against anyone—though I'm now trying for a print on a hundred-dollar bill. The only witness we had to the night that Virginia Rockford was killed is Captain Tyler, and I doubt he'd do well on the stand, even if he had actually seen anyone he could identify—other than a cloaked figure that looked like Jack the Ripper. But, yeah, I think someone who has something to do with that film is involved—gut feeling, if you will. We'll go over what we've discovered, the autopsy reports and discuss the psychology of the killer further at the meeting in the morning." He paused, looking at Whitney. "I knew you were here, so I thought I'd stop by and see if there was anything you needed—or anything you'd discovered."

"So far, we're just on setup," Whitney told him.

He nodded, but she was pretty sure he was thinking that it hadn't taken a special team to arrive at the Ripper theory. He was skeptical that cameras in the foundation of an old building—even a building where terrible things had once been done—could really make a difference.

Yet, he had been told to work with their unit of the FBI; he would do so.

"Jude, if we can discover more about the person this killer is trying to emulate, it will tell us more about him, and hopefully, help you trip him up," Whitney said.

"Of course," Jude said politely. "Profiling a killer can be extremely helpful."

It's not exactly profiling when you get the information from a ghost, Whitney thought. But she kept silent.

Jackson appeared with Jenna and Angela and greeted Jude with, "Anything?"

Jude briefed Jackson and the others on his meeting. "I'm praying we don't get another victim tonight," Jude said. "I've got patrol cars doubled up all over Lower Manhattan—the Bowery isn't that far from the south end of Broadway, and I have a feeling the killer is going to stick to the area. It's a gamble, but if this killer is working on the identity of Jonathan Black as the Ripper, then he will keep his murder spree down in this area." He shrugged. "I see that you're busy, and I know that Whitney's expertise is film, but that's why I really came by—Angus Avery seemed to have some kind of rapport with you, Whitney. I thought it might work well if you accompanied me to talk to him."

She was surprised; she tried not to show it. "I can finish up here with Jake's help," Will said. "And I'm sure the police consider the interview far more important than our work down here with cameras—always a long shot," he said evenly.

"Whitney, yes, go on with Detective Crosby," Jackson said. "We'll finish here."

She nodded, and was surprised at how glad she was to leave the foundation of the old building, and the miasma that seemed to loom there.

Or maybe she was just glad to join Jude again.

It didn't matter; Jackson had assigned her to go.

Tonight, Angus Avery was simply annoyed. His two young stars, Bobby Walden and Sherry Blanco, were nervous, anxious—and bored. Missy Everett and Jane Deaver, the girls who had been prostitute extras and had last been with Virginia Rockford, were scared, huddled together on a couch. They seemed so nervous, in fact, that they didn't even seem excited to be in the company of greatness—Angus Avery, the director, and Walden and Blanco, the two stars of the movie *O'Leary's*. Which was good; they were unaware that the two spoiled celebrities seemed to think nothing of them at all. The security guard, Samuel Vintner, sat by himself, rolling his hat and looking awkward in the plush lounge of the five-star hotel that housed Avery.

He was sure that all of them would have bolted when he was on his way over if it weren't for the two members of Sayer's team who had escorted them to the lounge and held sentinel at the door until Jude had arrived with Whitney.

"Detective, I'm happy to help with this investigation, but I'm a busy man. I'm the director, you know. The producers are under the gun to come in under budget. I'm naturally horrified that young women are being murdered, but you're a cop and I'm a filmmaker.

I need to be making my film. We're already going to go over by several days and several million dollars," Avery complained. He looked toward the two men at the door and added in an aggravated tone, "My costume department has been ravaged, our wardrobe mistress is in tears daily and I met with you immediately to tell you what I could."

"I just want to get a real picture of what went on that day," Jude said. He smiled pleasantly. "You're quite something, Mr. Avery. Impressive, the way you look into realism."

Avery frowned. "Thank you."

"Not only did you look up information at the library—studying rare ledgers—but you brought along your lead players."

Sherry gasped. "How did you know that?"

They hadn't actually known just which document the trio had studied, but now they did.

"You signed in, right?" Jude asked.

"Of course," Avery said, waving a hand in the air. "It's important that we give the film the edge of realism. And I'm a tough taskmaster as a director. It's not *who* you are all the time, it's also what you want in a situation. And if you understand your situation, you can be passionate about it. The film is about a time in history. I wanted Bobby and Sherry to understand history."

"It was—great," Sherry said.

"Ditto. I enjoyed the library," Bobby said.

"The fact that we went to the library makes us suspects?" Avery inquired, frowning. "If an interest in special documents makes us suspect, then you're going to have a lot of suspects."

"True," Jude said easily. He changed his line of questioning. "Agent Tremont has worked in film. She'll understand anything you have to say when I may not."

"Yes, and frankly we're intrigued by the set, and the information you gave us previously, Mr. Avery," Whitney said. She offered him an easy smile. He seemed somewhat mollified.

"I don't know what else I can tell you. The movie is a major production, you know. And we were filming that day, before breaking down to set up at the next location. I should have never chosen that location, never! It might have been the so-called Darby Building that was recently brought down, but it was once the House of Spiritualism, and I don't like to be a superstitious man, but I honestly feel that there is something simply evil there."

"I didn't feel a thing," Bobby muttered. "Sorry, Mr. Avery, I just didn't."

"I didn't like it. I wouldn't have been hanging around that place once it got late!" Sherry Blanco protested.

"It was creepy," Jane Deaver said. "I hated being there. And we tried to get Ginger to leave with us. We tried!" Huge tears formed in her eyes.

"Did you see anyone lurking around the set? Did you feel as if you were being watched? Was anything out of the ordinary?" Jude asked.

Missy said, "No."

"Yes. No. I mean, it was just creepy!" Jane said. "When night came, the lighting was so low and there were shadows everywhere, and the shadows seemed to move."

"Shadows move when the object casting them moves," Bobby Walden said quietly. "There were people all around—until late." He looked at Whitney. "You know, the wardrobe folks, the crew. Breakdown calls for a lot of workers, and the camera crews were wrapping up. Production assistants were wrapping up...and then it's the end of the day. People get the hell out of there."

"Who was left at the end?" Jude asked.

"Sammy was still there," Missy said, pointing at the retired cop. "Sammy was with us on the sidewalk, just outside the chain-link fence, until the cab came."

Samuel Vintner, ex-cop, going to ruin, with gin blossoms on his cheekbones and a paunch, grew red and shook his grizzled head. "I'd have been there for Virginia Rockford, too, but she—sorry, don't mean to speak ill of the dead—but she just bitched at me. I even offered her a ride home. She didn't want me around her, so I went to make sure that the crew was out and that the gates were all locked again."

"With the cheap padlocks," Whitney murmured.

"Hey—that's the city, not us!" Sammy protested. He looked at Jude. "I swear, yeah, I may have been one of the last people to see her alive, but I tried my best to make sure she was safe, and when she was on location, she was safe. I offered her a ride. She told me no, she wouldn't drive with me if I were the last creep on earth. She was in a huff, angry about something. She left, headed straight to walk north on Broadway and when she was locked out, and I went to the guard on the other side of the block—the city fellow—and told him I was leaving. The place was empty. I'd seen to that!"

"Where did you go from the site, Mr. Vintner?" Jude asked.

"Home, where my wife warmed up my dinner. My sister-in-law—who hates me, by the way—was there. They'll both tell you that I was home thirty minutes after the set closed for the day. Miss Rockford was angry—and, sorry, it's true, she wasn't the nicest person in the world—and she left in kind of a huff, treating me like I was a gnat in her way."

"I didn't even speak with Ms. Rockford!" Sherry Blanco said. She was an attractive woman, extremely pretty, blue-eyed and blonde and slim as a reed. Her words betrayed little empathy, despite the public service announcement she had done.

"Not once? Not once during the shoot?" Jude asked.

"No. I wasn't in the scene she was in. I was on set that day, but I left by three-thirty. Look, I'm sorry, truly sorry for this woman. But bad things happen in this city every day, and I can't let them all tear me apart. I left the set early. Detective, you can't possibly suspect *me!*" she said.

He smiled, not agreeing that it would be impossible. "Ms. Blanco, we were hoping that you might have met Miss Rockford, and perhaps exchanged a few words with her. Or that you might have seen someone perhaps watching her on the set?"

"Well, I didn't speak with her." She waved a hand in the air. "Detective," she said, fluttering her lashes at him, "I'm afraid that you just don't understand a movie set, and the logistics that go with it all. There might have been another major player in the movie that I didn't meet. It depends on your call times and scenes, and who is in the scenes. You just don't understand."

"But I do," Whitney said sweetly.

Sherry Blanco stared at Whitney, irritated. "Look! I didn't speak with her! I didn't see anyone hanging around her. Bobby talked to her, though. She and Bobby were in a steamy scene together, one of the last filmed that day."

"I was nice to her," Bobby said, startled, and edging away from his costar. "We were working together. Of course I talked to her!"

"She was waiting for you!" Missy Everett said, suddenly bolting to her feet as if she'd erupted from the couch. "You had to know it—I knew it!"

"What?" Bobby gasped.

"She was waiting for you! She thought that you were going to call her to hang out with you for a while when the filming was done," Missy said.

"That's right," Jane Deaver agreed. "When we tried to get her to leave, she said that she was going to hang out with you."

Bobby reddened to the shade of a tomato. "I—I talked to her. I didn't make a date with her or anything."

"Well, she sure thought that you did," Jane said, staring at him accusingly.

Jane caught her friend by the shoulders and drew her back to the sofa, whispering something.

Bobby suddenly seemed distraught. "Look, I'm sorry if she believed that. And, I hate to say it, but if she planned on spending time with me, it's not because she was bowled over by me—she probably thought it might get her attention from the right people."

"Jane, you know that's true!" Missy said softly.

Jude was pretty sure it was a warning that if she wanted to work again, she needed to calm down about Bobby Walden.

Missy said, "Look, we *liked* Ginger, and we weren't happy about leaving her, but she insisted. We didn't see anyone—Sammy walked us to the street and we got into a cab together. I didn't see anyone watching Ginger in any weird way during the day, except, of course, the actors, who were supposed to be sizing up the available prostitutes. And they all turned it on and off. Detective, you know that we really have spoken with other cops—they were all over us and everyone else who had been at the site, down to the limo drivers."

Jude smiled. "That's their job, you know," he told her. "They check and verify everything. They even know that a cabdriver named Abdel Mohammed picked you two up and dropped you at the B-Way Café up in Midtown."

Missy and Jane looked at each other with wide eyes. "I didn't know his name, did you?" Missy asked Jane.

"Well, when there are two of us, I don't usually go getting chummy with the cabdriver!" Jane said.

"Excuse me!" Angus Avery said. He tapped his watch. "Time. Time is money. Directors who come in way above budget don't get hired again."

"Mr. Avery!" Whitney said, her eyes golden and luminescent. "I don't think that you have to worry. We'll be sure that the media know just how helpful you've been. That's going to be tremendously important when your work is judged. You can be the man who helped the women of New York City."

"The whores of New York City," Sherry Blanco muttered.

They all turned to look at her. "I do read the papers, you know!"

"Yeah, she reads *People* and *US Weekly*," Bobby muttered.

"Bobby, you're just being cruel. And I'm not being stupid or mean, just truthful. This has been all over the news. They identified the girl from the river—in fact, I heard that one of the educational channels is going to do a sob-story thing on her called *The Girl from the River!* What was her name? Sarah whatever. She couldn't get real work, so she started stripping. I saw Virginia Rockford on that set, and she may not have hung up a shingle, but she was for sale. And now that poor woman this morning…Melody Tatum. High-priced escort! Well, in truth, they were all whores. That's who the Ripper went after, right?" She looked at Jude hopefully.

Jude felt tension searing him like a blade; Whitney set a hand on his arm and squeezed lightly.

"Ms. Blanco," Jude said, "no one really knows for certain who the killer will target next, and it doesn't matter if anyone knows those who were killed, or is like those who were killed. With this killer, he seems to be moved by his *perception* of the victim, and God alone knows how he might perceive anyone out there. Especially a high-profile actress."

Whitney jabbed him in the elbow as Sherry Blanco's face whitened. No, he didn't want her to walk the streets shaking; he did want her to give a damn that women were dead.

"The point is," he continued, "they were brutally murdered. And we need any piece of information, no matter how trivial, that anyone can offer to help us catch him."

Sherry leaned forward then, pale, and looking somewhat contrite. "Honest to God, Detective, I just never spoke with Virginia Rockford during the day. But that site was creepy."

"Really creepy when it turned dark," Missy said. "The lights aren't all that great down there, you know. I mean, the real lights, the streetlights, not the set lights. If anyone moved on the street, it cast giant shadows over the stage flats that were up. We had all kinds of facades going during the day, but they were mostly just painted wood, put up and pulled down for the shots."

"We will be using the exterior of Blair House for a number of green-screen shots we took that day," Angus explained slowly to Jude, his tone indicating that since Jude wasn't in the film business, he was most probably dense. "That means that we'll edit the image of Blair House into the action shots."

"I think I got it," Jude said. "We had an eyewitness down in the area when Virginia Rockford was filmed. The eyewitness saw a man in a cloak, or a coat with caped shoulders, on the street." Inwardly he winced. "He was carrying a medical bag—and wearing a stovepipe hat, or something similar. Was there an extra on the set in that attire that day?" he asked.

They all looked at each other. "Everyone's in period costume. The movie is called *O'Leary's* and it is about the destitution and dire situations in Lower Manhattan and how it was cleaned up at the end of the nineteenth century," Bobby said. "But no one had any kind of medical bag, I don't think," he said, looking at Angus Avery.

Avery sighed. "Detective, I just don't think you understand the scope of what went on that day. Sets went up, and sets came down—that meant hundreds of crew members. We had gangs fighting in the streets. That meant more than a hundred extras. You must know all this—the police have lists of every single person hired that day."

"And a number of the extras would have worn that kind of cloak and hat," Jude said.

"But I don't remember that the costumer gave anyone a medical bag—or that anyone in Wardrobe handed any of the extras any kind of medical bag," Bobby said.

"I've told you, though, that I wished I'd never chosen that location," Angus said, shaking his head.

"Why *did* you choose the location, Mr. Avery?" Whitney asked. "Feeling the way you do about it—I mean, you were the one to tell us about the structure that had been there *before* the recently demolished building."

Avery lifted both his hands and rubbed his fingers together toward the ceiling. "Money! Everything in film is money. We could set up easily, and break down easily, and the city was willing to rent it for a song. If I could only go back…"

"But the woman found this morning wasn't on the set and wasn't in the movie," Sherry said. "So, Angus, for you to be upset with yourself over the location isn't at all necessary. You're not to blame. The killer was out there." She walked over to the director, and gave him a consoling hug.

Jude knew that he wasn't getting anywhere that evening. He stood and told them gravely, "Thank you all for meeting here and speaking with us. The station number and my cell is on my card. Please, if you think of anything that can help us, call. Day or night."

"Of course!" Avery said, standing. It almost seemed as if he was shaking Sherry Blanco off as he did so.

Avery looked around the room. "We're done here," he said, wanting the extras, his two stars and Sammy Vintner out—leaving him alone.

There was an awkward pause as everyone stared at Jude in silence. He nodded, looked at Whitney and turned to head out of the room and to the elevators.

"Avery wants them all out," Whitney said.

"Yes, I got that feeling," Jude told her.

"But it seems they all want to talk to one another."

"So, we'll wait and watch them," Jude said.

"Where will that get us?"

"I'm not sure, but let's see who leaves first."

Downstairs, they went to Jude's car parked on the street. He slid into the driver's seat and she walked around to the passenger's side.

They had barely closed the doors when Samuel Vintner came out and strode in the direction of the subway.

Not sixty seconds later, Missy and Jane came out together.

Next, Bobby Walden. Jude picked up his cell phone and pressed a single digit. "Sayer, you're near the hotel?"

"Yes, in back of you about a block," Sayer told him.

"Bobby Walden is out."

"All right. I'm tailing him."

Whitney sat quietly at his side. "Bobby Walden?"

He looked over at her. "His alibi had him home alone. He said his driver picked him up and brought him home, and when the task force queried the car company, the driver verified that he'd brought him straight home. That doesn't mean that he didn't go back out. He's a principal in the film, and the girls said that Virginia Rockford thought she had a hot date with him. I'd just like to make sure that he does go home and stays home tonight."

She was quiet. They were both hoping that the killer didn't strike again that night.

They waited.

"So, Sherry Blanco is sleeping with the director, and not her costar," Jude commented.

Whitney laughed softly. "And see, you didn't even have to major in film to figure that one out, Detective!"

"But he didn't seem to want her clinging to him," Jude commented.

"Maybe she got him to change his mind," Whitney said lightly.

"Well, I do imagine she could be persuasive," he said.

"Oh?" Whitney queried, a teasing note in her voice.

He turned and looked at her, and smiled suddenly. The tension of the past two days had seemed monumen-

tal. Though his job meant much more than just something to do for a living, sometimes he had to remember
that he was still kicking and breathing himself.

"Not my type at all," he assured her. "That girl has
a streak of ambition sharper than a blade and she's...
I don't know. I imagine her walking around her own
house in little heels that click on the floor with some
kind of a froufrou yappy dog in her arms, making sure
at all times that everyone around her knows that she's
a movie star. I don't think that she's stupid—she just
doesn't care about the rest of the world."

"Interesting! And harsh," Whitney said.

"And how would you describe Miss Blanco?" he
asked.

"She might keep a cat instead of a froufrou dog,"
Whitney said. "A Persian, perhaps. Or a designer cat."

"Designer cats exist?" he asked.

"I'm sure."

He leaned back, still smiling.

"I do believe that Sherry Blanco was having a thing
with the director, but I'm willing to bet that the 'thing'
is no more," Whitney said. "She is scared, and I think
she's trying to be honest. And it's better that she's
honest than act as if she's lost her best friend."

"She's still too ambitious for me." He laughed.
"What do I know? I have some friends who have
worked Broadway, and they're all really nice. Sherry
Blanco doesn't seem to be nice."

"Some actors and actresses are nicer than others.
And some cops are nicer than others," Whitney pointed
out.

"Touché!"

Whitney turned to him. "What difference does it make if Sherry Blanco was sleeping with Angus Avery? The fact that he can act like a lecher wouldn't make him a murderer."

Jude said quietly, "No."

"Then?"

"It might show where alliances lie. She was ready to throw Bobby Walden to the wolves tonight. We were supposed to believe that he had planned to meet Virginia Rockford."

"You've spoken about an accomplice," Whitney said. "Do you believe that Sherry Blanco could be that person?"

"No. But I believe that if Angus Avery needed an alibi, Sherry Blanco would lie through her teeth for him, smiling and fawning all the while," Jude said.

"Ah, but when you're an actress, you need to know the directors, not so your fellow actors," Whitney said.

"Right. Directors cast movies, not actors."

A few minutes later, his cell phone rang. It was Ellis Sayer.

"A limo picked Bobby Walden up at the cross street and drove him straight to his place up by the park. I saw him get out and go into the building."

"Thanks."

"I'll have a patrol car sit on him," Sayer told him.

"Yeah, let's keep an eye on him tonight," Jude agreed.

"Done," Sayer said.

He hung up. Whitney was frowning in thought.

"What is it?" he asked her.

"Old Shakespeare," she said.

"What?"

She looked at him. "Carrie Brown, the American victim who was killed in like manner to the Ripper victims… What I was thinking was that they called her Old Shakespeare because she was always quoting Shakespeare, and she either performed in the theater at some time, or, at the very least, had experience with plays in one way or another. She seemed to have been well educated, even if she had become an alcoholic and a prostitute before she died. Maybe the killer isn't targeting *prostitutes,* but actresses—or would-be actresses!"

9

Whitney debated mentioning the fact that they hadn't eaten; it was late.

She was tired and hungry, and she was curious about anything that the team might have found in the foundations of the House of Spiritualism, but she also felt as if she had been saturated with the sadness and horror of the murders. Bobby Walden had been taken home that night; Angus Avery had spoken at a dinner. That didn't mean that one of them hadn't driven back downtown. She needed a break to clear her head and step back, and wonder just what it might all have to do with the past.

What they had to do was pray that they could find a piece of evidence that truly pointed them in the direction of the killer—before he struck again.

She wasn't known for being shy, and yet, she felt somewhat awkward around Jude. Her first impression of him had been that he was just a hard, cold, macho cop, and that she had to stoically and quietly hold her ground. But the more she was with him, the more she *liked* him, and the more she accepted that fact, the more she accepted that she was physically attracted to him. She also had to accept that he was extremely attractive in all the right ways; many women probably felt the same—simple biology, he was rock solid, tall and strong, the kind of man whose survival instincts would have made him most appealing once upon a time—and that he appeared totally indifferent to his effect on those around him. He was confident, but not cocky, and could be aggressive, but also careful in his treatment of people, as in the case of Captain Tyler. If he had something to go on, she was certain he could be harsh but fair in an interrogation room as well.

"Food," she said.

"Pardon?" he asked. Apparently, he'd been deep in thought.

He looked at her and she smiled. "Don't you feel the need to stop—refuel?"

"Oh, yeah, food," he said. He smiled in return, and shook his head. "You know, it's true, the first forty-eight hours in any case usually points to whether or not you will solve a crime, but even then, and in the midst of some pretty bad cases in New York, I usually have a sense of self-preservation. You can't turn off the *thinking* about a case, but you still remember to live and breathe. With this—" He broke off, shaking his head. "We have dozens of capable men and women out there working around the clock in one way or another, but I still feel as if it's all on me. Food, yes. Food would be good. There's an all-night diner on Avenue A that's pretty decent. Are you good with your team?"

"They can reach me anytime they want," Whitney said. "And if they haven't gotten hold of me yet, they're doing fine without me."

He nodded, looking toward the road again, and he was back in thought. But when they reached the restaurant, and they'd chosen a booth and ordered food, he looked at her with a polite grin. "Miss Whitney Tremont, FBI agent with a special investigative unit. Tell me more about yourself."

"Ah! An interrogation," she said, nodding gravely.

"No bright lights, no fists thumping on the table, no mirrored room," Jude said. "Just the facts, missy, just the facts."

"Hmm. Well, I did major in film at NYU, but I'm from New Orleans, born at Tulane Medical Center." Her smile deepened. "And my great-grandmother is one of the most respected voodoo priestesses in New Orleans—she doesn't raise the dead or sell love potions or stick pins in dolls or anything like that—the dolls are for tourists to buy. She is a brilliant and fascinating woman. My mother was a teacher, my father was a philosophy professor, and his background was French. I was raised attending Mass at the cathedral in Jackson Square every Sunday morning, but I also really respect my great-grandmother's beliefs. Her life is all about balance, and she has tremendous faith. She's a wonderful woman—you would really like her. It's pretty obvious that I come from a complete ethnic olio, and I believe my mom's father was a Cherokee, though Dad's folks arrived off a boat from Marseilles. Voodoo has a lot in common with Catholicism, and the two worked well enough together in my family."

"I don't have a problem with any faith—Christian-

ity, Judaism, Islam, Buddhism, you name it," Jude said.
"Not when it's a faith that brings people through life
respecting life and his fellow humans, believe me. All
New Yorkers don't think that a voodoo priestess has
to be a quack." He grinned. "I watch the Discovery
Channel!"

Whitney laughed. "Maybe I do get defensive sometimes. Far too often, people do mock each other's beliefs."

"Face it—wars are fought over minor differences in
belief," he said. He drummed his fingers on the table.
"Film to the FBI. And you're not in the audiovisual
department. How did the career segue come about?"
he asked her.

She hesitated again, and then shrugged. He knew
they set up cameras everywhere; he knew they looked
into the past. He'd surely read up on Adam Harrison, and knew that many people considered them to
be quacks. He'd known from the beginning about the
cameras—he'd already asked her if she filmed ghosts.

"I was working on a project for one of the educational channels, but, of course, they, like everyone—so
it seems these days—have to bring in the advertising
dollars, and so you have to have shows that lure in an
audience. *You* may not want to believe this, but while
we're often looked on as *imaginative* or quacks, the
majority of American people do believe that the paranormal exists in one form or another, so ghost shows
are immensely popular. Anyway, I filmed some truly
strange phenomena, and the producers were convinced
that I'd rigged the film, and I hadn't done so. I refused
to unrig what wasn't rigged. They'd been planning on

doing more of a storyboard, with ghosts appearing and disappearing, and they were dismayed that what I caught was *something,* but not a woman in white fluttering across the screen. I was young—"

"Was?" he asked her with a teasing note in his voice.

She laughed, giving him the point. "I'm not *just* out of high school," she told him. "I'm short and look younger than I am. I'm twenty-eight."

"A vast age," he said gravely.

"Age is irrelevant—it depends on where you've been and what you've done in your time on earth, my friend," she told him.

"Then I think I'm feeling about a hundred and eight right now," Jude said.

Whitney grinned. "Well, you're well preserved."

Their food arrived; they'd both opted for omelets, which seemed a fitting meal since it had gotten so late that dinner and breakfast might be combined.

"Anyway," she told him, "I resigned from the project. I was lucky, because I had a book on the market about the philosophy of world religions, and although it was never on any bestseller lists, it has steady sales, and those sales saved me from poverty while I mulled over my next move. I'd pretty much decided to go into filming my own documentaries when I was called by Adam Harrison and asked to join the team. Jake Mallory had been an agent for almost fifteen years, but the rest of us were drawn from other walks of life. I think our first case was an experiment on Adam's part, but the six of us worked well together. They sent us through training and we all became agents officially."

She grimaced. "I admit, I've never worked with any other agents, and even in the bureau, we are unusual."

"Ghost busters?" Jude asked.

She couldn't really read the tone of his voice. "We have an amazing success rate on the cases with which we've been involved. Ordinarily, it's not just profiling a killer or his victims, but a situation. That's often done by discovering what went on in the past."

That brought Jude back around to the case. "All right, then, let's take our situation. A tough one. You may be right, that *actresses,* not prostitutes, are being singled out. Which brings us back to the film. Except, of course, we could all still be wrong on this—Jane Doe dry might have died because she was randomly attacked, and Sarah Larson might have met with your usual run-of-the-mill heinous killer. We had nothing to go on, nothing at all. The thing is, when we discovered Virginia Rockford's body, she was so mutilated, and she had been left so blatantly in the open, that it does seem like the killer is demanding attention—*Ripper*-style attention."

"Ripper-style—but if there is one killer and the victims were all his, he's really starting to escalate on the rate of the murders," Whitney said to him.

He nodded thoughtfully. "Very scary thought. To be honest, I wasn't convinced that the women were all killed by the same man until it began to appear that there was a pattern between the victims—they were all women who *wanted* something. They wanted the dream. They wound up doing what they needed to do, in their own minds, at least, to get by. But they wanted to be entertainers—*stars.* Each of those women might have been easily seduced by someone who was prom-ising them a role in a movie. What someone could do that better than the director?"

"The producer," Whitney told him dryly. "In this case, as in many, there are half a dozen producers, but not one of the real money people is in New York, from what I've read about the shoot. So, yes, the director. And, as far as extras go, they're often brought in by a casting agency. But…"

"But Angus Avery would certainly have the power," Jude said.

"Yes. But, remember, you pointed out that we don't really have to work with facts—perception would work just as well. Anyone involved with the shoot could probably convince a woman who was dying to break into films that he had the power to get them a small role."

"True," Jude agreed.

They'd finished their omelets; the check came. Whitney reached for her wallet. "Hey, please, it's my pleasure to take you to dinner," he told her politely. "Contrary to popular belief, NYPD cops are paid enough to eat," he said lightly.

She laughed. "Agents, too. But I doubt either of us is going to get rich in this."

"Probably not," he agreed.

She didn't fight for the check. She thanked him, and they walked back out to his car. The night was clear and beautiful.

And quiet.

She felt his hand at the small of her back. "I should get you back to Blair House." The sound of his voice was husky. The touch of his hand seemed to send electrical currents along her spine.

"Yes," she said simply.

Jude walked Whitney into the house.

Will Chan was seated in front of the bank of computer screens they'd set up in the broad hallway of Blair House. He rose, smiled and stretched when they came in.

"Thank God!" he said. "I need a breather."

"Will, I'm sorry. How long have you been sitting there?" Whitney asked.

"About fifteen minutes," Jenna announced, coming into the hallway from the kitchen. "Don't let him give you a hard time… We've all taken turns at the computers since we've been back at the house."

"Fascinating," Jude said, walking to the bank of screens. "What's causing the shadows?" he asked.

Whitney came to stand by him.

The feed from the two cameras set in the main sector of the foundation next door seemed to show some kind of motion. Dark shadows appeared close to the ground, almost as if a dusty fog had settled close to the floor, fog that undulated and breathed.

Jude looked at Whitney. "What is going on over there?"

"We'll know in a minute," Will said. He pointed at the screens. "There they are now—Jackson and Jake."

Whitney saw that her teammates had returned to the foundation; the motion-sensing cameras had turned toward them when they entered. Will spoke into the remote microphone. "Well? Anything?" he asked.

Jackson and Jake were wearing clip-on receivers

and transmitters. "Nothing," Jackson said. "There's nothing here at all."

"Do you see anything that would explain the darkness we notice moving around on the screens?" Whitney called to them.

Jude's gaze was set on the screens. His features betrayed no emotion other than curiosity. Whitney had to wonder if he was skeptical, thinking that they were setting up some kind of a show.

"Nothing. We're going to walk around here for a minute, going from section to section. Let us know what you're seeing—that darkness persists, right?" Jake asked.

"It's that area, that area right there, in the main section of the flooring."

To Whitney's surprise, Jude walked to the screen. "Look," he said, touching it. "There are the boundaries of that darkened area. Look at the floor. It's got strange discoloration," he said.

"That's not surprising," Will said, sitting down and watching the screen. "There was a structure there that was demolished, and then another that was demolished as well. You can see the structural walls, but there might have been nonstructural walls that were broken through over time. Both buildings might have had different layouts."

"No, but look," Jude said, his finger moving in a pattern over the screen. "Something was drawn on the floor with some kind of paint or dye at some time."

"He's right," Whitney said.

"What is it, do you think?" Will asked.

Whitney narrowed her eyes, watching Jude's finger move.

"A pentagram," she said. "A downward-pointing pentagram."

Jude straightened. "I'm taking a walk over there," he told her.

Whitney wanted to go with him, but she thought that she shouldn't. Whatever he did or didn't experience, she thought it would be best if he did so on his own, or with Jackson and Jake being the only members of their team present.

He left them; Whitney joined Will in one of the rolling chairs in front of the bank of screens. She spoke with Jackson as Jude walked from Blair House to the property next door. "Jackson, Jude just pointed it out. The discoloration on the floor isn't random aging. An upside-down pentagram was drawn in there."

"That's not much of a shock," Jackson called back to her. "Not if the so-called House of Spiritualism began as a haven for Satanists."

"I suppose not." She hesitated, but Jude couldn't have gotten in there yet. "Jackson, that black miasma seems to emanate from it."

Jake was standing not far from Jackson, still, and listening. "There's someone out on the street," he told Jackson.

"It's Jude—he's on his way over," Whitney informed them.

A minute later, she saw Jude coming down the steps. He had made quick time, but she had learned that his strides were long and that he walked fast.

"It is a pentagram," Jude said, looking at Jackson

and Jake before beginning to follow the broken markings on the floor. "It looks like it was drawn with some kind of chalky brick substance or dye. There might have been some kind of flooring placed over it at one time."

"The people here when it was called the House of Spiritualism might have kept a false floor over it, something that they could easily roll out if the police came—not that having it would have been illegal. Freedom of religion applies to Satanists as well," Jake said.

"But I doubt they wanted it known that they were welcoming Satanists," Jude said. "Or that, perhaps, the 'spiritualism' in the name was their own euphemism for Satanism. To the best of my knowledge, it can often mean many different beliefs and practices, but in Lower Manhattan at the end of the eighteen hundreds, *most* of the population was Christian, and worshipping Satan would have meant, to them, sinful orgies, all manner of debauchery—and blood sacrifices. Many killers throughout the years, such as Gilles de Rais, as far back as the fourteen hundreds, committed hundreds of brutal murders with some excuse that a demon or the devil had demanded the blood sacrifice. And, of course, as the years pass, new groups make idols of such men as Gilles de Rais, Jack the Ripper and other killers."

Will looked at Whitney, startled by Jude's speech. Whitney shrugged. "His father has a huge crime library," she told Will.

"Hey, it's good to understand history, as we all know," he said.

"So they had a pentagram on the floor. They seemed to worship evil. I wonder what else was down here, and if someone today knew exactly what was here, and what was going on. Do you see any signs that anyone has been…down there lately?" Whitney asked.

All three faces stared at the camera, as if they could see her and didn't understand such an obvious question.

"I mean…does it look as if someone has been down there practicing any kind of Satanic rituals? Is there any sign of blood?" she asked.

"Not visibly or obviously," Jackson said.

"We can get a forensics team down here," Jude said. "Check it out."

The forensics team isn't going to tell us why it seems that there's a black fog that lies low to the ground on film, Whitney thought.

But she wondered if bad things had gone on down there—recently—as well as in the past, and she knew that they were all wondering if Sarah, *Jane Doe wet,* had been killed in the night in the darkness of the abyss before her body had wound up in the river.

"Well, we're coming up," Jackson said. "It's late. We'll look at everything with rested minds in the morning."

Jude returned with Jackson and Jake to Blair House, then bid them good-night, reminding them to lock themselves in and be wary.

Jackson didn't reply that he was an armed federal agent, to Whitney's surprise. As such, he knew that it was never amiss to remember to be careful.

Whitney wanted to walk to the door to tell him

good-night; she didn't allow herself to do so. Actually, she didn't want him to leave.

Or, if he was leaving again, she wanted to go with him.

But that was ridiculous, of course. They had barely met; they were both part of a task force. They hadn't met at a social function, or a bar—or even dating online.

Even so, she felt that she knew him. If she didn't know him, she knew him well enough to know that she wanted to know him better. The sexual attraction she was feeling was almost overwhelming, and since that was the case, it was a good thing that she didn't walk to the door.

"We'll all hope it's a quiet night," Jackson said, bidding Jude good-night. When the door was locked, Jake looked at Whitney, giving her an odd smile.

"Go ahead, kid, and get some rest. I'll watch the screens tonight."

"I should do some of the staring at the screens," she said. "Film is my forte. I really should—"

"Get some rest," Jake finished for her. "You've been on this a day longer than the rest of us, and these are long days."

She smiled back at him. She loved Jake—he was like a brother. But she looked at Jackson, ever their quietly strong leader, who was watching her.

Jackson just nodded gravely. "Get some rest. You've been on all this too intently for way too many hours. We've got this covered."

Jude felt odd as he left Blair House—almost as if he'd left something behind.

It wasn't a something.

It was a *someone*. Whitney.

It was amazing to think how quickly things could change; he had thought of her as *young,* and he had thought of her as *annoying* at first. Not only had they saddled him with a federal team, but they'd given him one comprised of inexperienced children.

Now…

Now, she had somehow become an important part of the investigation. Now, he wished that he'd met her anywhere except on the job, and that he knew how to take a break and let the rest of the task force run while they went out for a drink. He wondered if he needed to stop working with her, if the light scent of her perfume hadn't somehow permeated his senses and therefore his mind, so that now he was thinking about her when he wasn't even with her, longing to stroke the exotic golden-amber color of her skin, test the softness of her lips…

Killer. Serial killer on the loose, he forced himself to remember.

And he could demand that his mind return to the case, because they were following only leads and people so far, and they had nothing tangible, nothing on which they could begin to pin a case.

The movie, it all came back to the movie. Or maybe it didn't, but it did seem a viable direction.

They could all still be way off base. Not on the fact that someone had studied the case of Jack the Ripper and took it to heart. New York was a massive city. Lots of people knew all about the filming, and some of them presumably knew about Blair House, or the House of Spiritualism.

He called his father, because he knew that Andrew wouldn't call him, assuming that he was busy, but that he'd naturally want to be kept up on the case.

"How's Whitney doing with that book?" Andrew asked him. "Weird, I know, but I think that the site itself may have something to do with the case."

"The *site* made me do it," Jude said, his tone weary. He'd heard every excuse known to man in court, and it wouldn't surprise him if someone opted to use the ghosts of the past as a defense.

"Here's the thing, son, and you know it—a sick mind can grasp on to a lot, and even when someone knows right from wrong, they can certainly use some kind of knowledge as a spur to commit crimes. Take the religions of the world—the *good* ones," he said. "People can twist and turn tenets of peace into terrible mandates that somehow miss the entire message of love and goodness to one's fellow human being. So, take someone into the occult—which can just be a love of the earth, the use of herbs and so on—who is fascinated by death, cruelty and the dark side of human nature. They could twist their beliefs into some kind of house of worship for sure. We venerate the saints—they venerate blood and brutality."

He hesitated, and then told his father, "We found an outline of an old pentagram in the floor—forensics will go in tomorrow and take a look around."

"Why? Isn't the pentagram over a century old?"

"It makes me wonder what else might be there. Or, if someone is using it again. I can't help but wonder if one of the early victims might have been attacked there. I want to know if there's any blood that can be detected."

"I'll see what else I can find in my collection about old New York. Who knows, I may find something," his father told him.

"And you can always head back over to the NYU library, or connect with your friends at the Pierpont," Jude said.

He didn't realize until that moment that he was going to question his own father.

He was relieved by the answer.

"Actually, you're right. Maybe I should. But there's still so many books that I have here…I don't think I'm going to find a book anywhere that says 'read me for the answers'! It's going to be a hunt. But I'm on it!"

"Thanks, Dad."

When he hung up, though it was late, he called Hannah. Her workday was a typical nine-to-five, but she stayed up late at night, watching television—and now, of course, flirting with the new fellow in her life.

Hannah loved television and loved to compare her work and what she learned from the detectives with what was shown on the screen. One day, she told him, she was going to be a consultant on a crime show.

"Hey, Jude! How's it going—the lists are endless…"

"It's going, Hannah. I'm going to have a crime scene team out at the old construction site tomorrow. I was thinking you should be with them," he said.

"Sure!" she said excitedly. "Except…I am a computer tech, you know."

"Yeah, I know, but you've been compiling lists, checking facts…you might be helpful on site."

"Oh, yeah, thanks!" she said. Then she added, "Jude, I've found out a lot of stuff about Harrison's team."

"And you haven't called me?"

"Well, I did tell you what I knew when they were first called in—it's all just speculative media reporting really. But Adam Harrison got into finding people to help with special investigations years ago."

Whitney had told him that Adam Harrison had approached her after she had left her job. She'd been going to do her own documentaries. She hadn't lied to him about anything.

But it seemed the whole world saw the group as ghost busters.

"His son was supposed to have been some kind of psychic, and he became fascinated with the occult. You know, kind of like the magician Harry Houdini. When his mother died, he was determined to speak to her through the 'veil,' or whatever. Well, here's the thing—in all the instances his teams worked on, the case was solved and the stranger occurrences proven."

"The ghosts did it?" Jude demanded skeptically.

"No, no…but to have been asked onto that team, well, each member had to have some kind of psychic ability, and it looks like it's real. I mean, neither any of the people he worked with previously or the members of this team have gone on record that there are ghosts involved—in fact, the leader, Jackson Crow, has always been one of those people out to find the real cause, but…"

Great. He really was working with ghost busters.
That should help him keep his distance.

But it wouldn't. He felt something like a body burn when Whitney was near. Natural, he tried to tell himself. She was young, she was beautiful, she was as sensual as…spun gold. He was human.

"Guess what they're called—off the books?" Hannah asked him.

"What?"

"Krewe of Hunters. K-R-E-W-E," Hannah spelled out. "Their first case together was in the French Quarter, in New Orleans, and I guess that's what they wound up calling themselves."

Krewe of Hunters, of course, mysterious old New Orleans. Filled with ghosts of the past, aboveground cemeteries…cities of the dead. Where else would ghost busters want to get started? he asked himself, his mental tone a mocking one.

"Jude, you there?" Hannah asked.

"Yeah, yeah, Hannah. Sorry. Meeting at 8:00 a.m., remember, every day until we catch the bastard or the task force is disbanded. I'll see you then." He hesitated, trying to remember that they all had lives, too. "How's it going with your fellow, Hannah?"

"He's not exactly my fellow, Jude. But, it's nice. He calls every once in a while, and sometimes I find him waiting for me at the coffee shop."

"Sounds like a budding relationship to me!"

"Maybe. But work comes first."

At his apartment, he threw off his jacket and sat in front of his own computer.

There was a tap at the connecting door.

"Come in, Dad," he said.

Andrew entered, bearing a glass."Thought you could use this."

"Oh?"

"Bourbon and soda," Andrew said.

Jude laughed. "Bring it on in."

"You sound worn out. You okay?" Andrew asked him sympathetically.

"Yep. We'll catch him," Jude said grimly. They had to catch him.

"They never caught the real Ripper—and they never caught the fellow who really murdered Carrie Brown."

"They didn't have the investigation capabilities we have now," Jude said. "And they didn't have ghost busters."

"What are you talking about?" his father asked.

Jude stared at his dad, smiled slowly and shook his head. "I'm willing to bet you've known all along that everyone on the special team must have psychic ability."

Andrew shrugged. "Well? Surely you knew that."

"I knew that they investigated using local stories and history. I knew that they looked into people who thought that ghosts existed, or that ghosts told them to murder people or... I didn't really accept the fact they all believed completely in spirits themselves!"

"Son, you need to get off your high horse," Andrew told him. "There's a lot to the world we don't know, and a lot we'll never know. So, you think you're all procedure and facts, just the facts and nothing more. But I've heard you say a dozen times that you have a gut feeling about something. It's all the same. Don't throw away all the good you may get because you're so convinced you're right that there's nothing in the world that isn't totally solid."

He was startled; his father seemed almost angry.

"Dad—they're ghost busters."

"Good for them. And if ghosts can solve this horrible case, let them!"

Jude stared at him silently.

Andrew went on. "I've been reading up today. Stuff I guess you know, but still good to think about. Most serial killers today come from working-class backgrounds and kill because it gives them a sense of power. But, historically, many people who had power and wealth killed because they considered themselves above mortal men. They killed because in their minds they had a right to kill. I guess that's part of the psychopathic personality, and still, obviously sick, these people can be organized and good-looking and brilliant—as in the case of Ted Bundy."

"Thanks, Dad," Jude said.

"Of course, you're the one with the degree in criminology," his father said with a smile. "Well, I'm going to go back over to my side."

Jude lifted his glass. "Thanks for the drink."

"You bet. Good night."

His father went through the door and closed it. His

cat leaped up onto his lap and purred. For the moment, he wished he was the damn cat.

That night, they studied the video that had been taken at the site next door.

There were definitely shadows to be seen; strange shadows, the kinds without the light sources to have been created on a natural level.

Whitney touched the screen. When she did so, she felt a strange surge of electricity sweep through her.

She had seen the dog there.

She was certain that the dog had protected the woman. She kept staring at the screen, and she saw something behind the dog.

"Could this be the shape of a woman?" she asked softly.

"Yes, of course it could be," Angela told her.

Will pointed out, "It's definitely something. And none of us was there to cast that shadow...we're on the right track."

They could see the shadows, but they really had no answers at the moment. They all needed sleep.

Whitney was wound tightly when she first tried to lie down and sleep. But as she lay staring at the ceiling, she heard a tap at the door. Angela walked in, bearing a teacup.

"Herbal tea? Or a bit of caffeine so I can better lie awake?" Whitney asked with a laugh.

"Decaf with a shot of whiskey," Angela told her, handing her the mug and curling up at the foot of the bed. "I thought I'd help you get to a REM sleep where maybe your subconscious will let you sort out some of the things running around in your mind."

"Or open it up to voices from the past?" Whitney asked her.

Angela nodded.

"But you're our great communicator," Whitney told her. "And, of course, Jenna is wonderful."

"Ah, but I think that you're the one these ghosts may talk to," Angela told her. "I ran through the footage from the site next door. There was a shadow when you bent down. You saw the dog again, didn't you?"

Whitney nodded.

"Dogs are our greatest companions, you know. Take Greyfriars Bobby, the little terrier who sat on his master's grave daily until he himself died. Anyway, I'm going to bed, too, so scream like a banshee if you need any of us or even if you're frightened…it's just us, and not one of us will think a thing of it if you see a ghost."

Angela stood and left her and Whitney started to sip the tea.

She picked up the book that Andrew Crosby had loaned her, the Honeywell book about the House of Spiritualism. She found herself looking in the index for the word *dog,* but didn't find it. But she found several pages listed under the name Annie Doherty. Curious, she began flipping through the pages. Annie Doherty had come from a stable home in Westchester, New York; her father had been a preacher. But Annie had fallen in love with a seafarer. She had run away from her father's strict dominance to follow her lover, a man named Leland Robinson, and come to the tip of Manhattan, where he had promised her he would be staying, near the docks. By the time she reached Manhattan, Leland Robinson had left on a ship. With the few funds she had, Annie found lodging at Blair House. While most of the theaters had moved north up Broadway, a small playhouse, the Travertine, had still been open just north of Wall Street, and Annie had tried to make a living selling oranges in front of the building. She had longed to become an actress and would sing in the streets as well for whatever pennies those coming and going from the theater would throw. She lived there almost a month before she disappeared, leaving behind her large shepherd-mix dog. The then owner had been furious since he'd been left a sizable bill, and he'd reported her for skipping out. But Annie hadn't gone home, and she hadn't taken her meager belongings. Nor had she taken her dog, a pet she had seemed to love deeply. The police assumed she fell into mishap, but nothing was ever discovered on the whereabouts of the young woman.

Whitney set the book down. She knew that many murder victims, caught up in the overcrowded tenements, had disappeared or died—their decomposed bodies eventually found—with little or nothing done for them. Police reports had sometimes been written up, but more often their sad lives had simply been forgotten. In the cases where the bodies had been discovered, they had usually wound up in paupers' graves.

Whitney marveled that so little had been done to find the mysteriously vanished young woman. Honeywell, the cop, seemed disgusted by the situation as well. But he did excuse the department at the time, writing,

"Immigration was massive; half the immigrants were in the country illegally. Handling one of the about-to-be-demolished tenements was like going to war each day."

But Annie Doherty hadn't disappeared from a tenement; she had been living at Blair House. She'd left her clothing and her beloved pet behind.

She set the book down. "Annie?" she said softly. The owners of Blair House had supposedly been decent people, running a very decent boardinghouse. Could Annie have died here?

The dog she was seeing had to be Annie's, which would mean that the woman who appeared with the dog had to be Annie.

She picked the book back up and rifled through the pages again.

Annie Doherty had disappeared in April 1891, the same month in which Carrie Brown had been murdered.

She took a long swallow of her tea, the questions in her mind driving her crazy. Why would these alleged Jack the Ripper victims simply disappear, or be discovered as refuse, decomposed corpses, which the police would not recognize as victims, when he left his London victims so blatantly exposed? Had there been a copycat killer, not getting it quite right, at the House of Spiritualism at the time, and had that person been Jonathan Black?

Could such a man possibly have been organized and intelligent enough to switch his modus operandi, and dabble in Satanism, or pretend, at least, to be a great leader in the psychic realm to gain power at the House of Spiritualism?

And, if so, she asked herself wearily, did the past actually have anything to do with the current killer's blood spree?

Yes, quite possibly. If it had been some kind of sacred venue for Satanists, with symbols...maybe more, icons there that had been worshipped. Yes, someone knowing all that history could well warp it into a new murder spree.

At last, despite the frenzy in her mind, the tea and simple exhaustion began to weigh on her and she began to doze.

That's when she felt the wet nose on her fingers and heard the dog's soft whine.

"Hello," she said quietly, and sat up. His head rested easily on the bed. He looked at her with huge, mournful brown eyes.

She stroked his head, and his fur felt soft and real. "What is it, boy? What are you trying to tell me?"

She looked beyond the dog. Her bedside light was still on, but the corners of the room were in shadow. She searched to see if the woman—Annie Doherty?—had appeared with the dog. But she didn't see anyone, and she forced herself not to be afraid of the fact that a real dog seemed to be imploring her for help.

"What is it? Help me—I want to help you," she told him.

He ran toward the door, barked softly and wagged his tail.

"Okay, you want to go out?" Whitney asked.

The dog ran back to her, and then back to the door again.

"Okay."

She got out of bed, grabbed her terry housecoat and slid her feet into her slippers, and walked to the door. The dog pawed it, continuing to wag his tail.

Whitney opened the door, and the dog ran out into the hallway, and then down the stairs.

Jake was seated in front of the computer screens; he started when she ran down the stairs. "What?" he demanded, blinking, jumping up.

"It's the dog," she said.

"Where? Where's the dog?"

"There!"

She pointed to the door. The dog had now raced to the front door, where he looked back at Whitney and wagged his tail. Then he pawed the door.

She saw Jake's frown. He might not see the animal, but he'd heard the sound of the door moving slightly in its frame.

"He wants to go out. Jake, he's leading me somewhere."

Whitney started to rush for the door. Jake grabbed her arm. "Wait!" he told her.

He had his cell out and he dialed a number. She could hear Jackson's sleepy voice come through the phone. "Whitney wants to follow a ghost dog."

Jake listened and snapped the phone closed. "He's coming."

Jackson, with Angela behind him, came hurrying down the stairs. Jackson had thrown on jeans and a shirt, and he wore his agency-issued Glock in a shoulder holster. He carried a wide-beam flashlight. Angela had merely thrown on her robe.

Jackson told them curtly, "Angela will lock behind us. Jake, you and I will go with Whitney. And the—dog," he said, pausing to frown. Jackson clearly didn't see the dog. "Angela, keep watch on the screens and warn us if anything shows up."

Angela stared at Whitney, nodding.

"Do you see it?" Whitney asked her.

"I see…something," Angela said.

"He's there. I swear it!" Whitney told them.

"Go, go on!" Angela said.

Whitney was glad that Jake had stopped her; she wasn't going to take the time to dress or arm herself, but she'd be safe with Jackson and Jake.

She unlocked the bolts on the front door. The dog raced out. Whitney followed him; the others followed her.

The dog took them where she knew it would—the construction site.

The ghostly animal that had felt so real slipped through chain-link fence as if he were mist.

Jackson opened the padlock and they went in.

The dog raced to the old foundations, and disappeared down the stairs.

Whitney ran after him, mindful of the rubble-strewn ground, and came to the great gaping chasm and the stairs that led down to it.

Jackson arrived with his wide-beam flashlight, and Whitney started down the steps. She came to the central room, where, despite her training, she felt chills snake along her spine and a sense of fear tremble in her limbs.

Instinct! she thought.

The dog stood in the middle of the pentagram, looking at her expectantly. He turned and raced around the supporting wall, and disappeared into the dark.

Whitney ran after him, and, with each step, she felt a greater sense of choking fear. She knew. She knew that beneath the ground and remnants of flooring, they would find the body of Annie Doherty.

10

Jude woke as suddenly as if had he been slapped in the face.

He reached for the Smith & Wesson that he kept on his bedside table at night and jerked to a sitting position, trying to ascertain what had awoken him. There was nothing in his room; there was nothing at all that hinted of an intruder or any kind of danger. He silently walked through his apartment, barefoot and in boxers, but there was nothing amiss.

He returned to his room and quickly stumbled into his jeans and a pair of loafers, shirt, holster and jacket. Still, there was nothing, no unusual sounds in his apartment, or coming from the streets. It was a quiet time in Hell's Kitchen, but New York never really slept.

Dressed, his gun in hand, he walked through the living room, looked in his computer room and carefully and silently opened the door to his dad's apartment. Andrew was in his room, snoring softly. Nothing seemed to be amiss.

But Jude was so disturbed that he knew he wasn't

going back to sleep, and despite himself, one word, a name, kept ripping through his mind.

Whitney.

Not even sure what he was doing, he headed for the street. A cab had just stopped at the avenue; it would take time to get his car out, so he started to run to the intersection, whistling loudly and waving his hand. The cab waited.

When he was seated in it, he wondered if he wasn't a fool, or if the workload was really playing with his mind. He was heading to Blair House and the construction site in the wee hours of the morning because something in his sleeping mind had made him think that Whitney might be in danger. What the hell. He'd heard of stranger things. He could have called one of the team; should have called one of the team.

But he was already in the cab. He'd just head down and see what he could see. And if there was nothing—which was likely—he could still talk to Jackson. If they were ghost busters, as the rumor mill seemed inclined to call them, they wouldn't think that he was that crazy. Or maybe they would. What the hell, he was started on the way now, might as well see it through.

He realized that the feeling she was in trouble, in danger, was persisting in his mind. Despite getting in a cab in the middle of the night, he was still afraid that he wouldn't be there in time. He had the cab stop in front of Blair House; the hall lights were on.

They were always on; someone was always watching the screens.

As he leaned forward to pay the driver and ask him to hold on, he noted that there seemed to be a spot of brightness that rose above the meager illumination of the streetlights in the area. "Move down the block, please," he said.

Yes.

There was someone in the foundations of the House of Spiritualism.

"Here—let me off here."

The padlock wasn't unlocked, which should have been reassuring. If Whitney had come here in the middle of the night, as insane as that might be, she would have been with someone else; they had a right to be there, and they would have unlocked the padlock.

They were trained, he reminded himself.

Of course the padlock was locked. They wouldn't have left an easy entry for an intruder.

If it was indeed the Krewe of Hunters who had come here.

Jude crawled over the fence, cursing as he did so. The chain link was poor, and the tips were bare. He tried his best to protect his body parts, hoping his insanity wasn't going to lead to partial dismemberment. He leaped to the ground and hurried across the stretch of rubble to the stairs.

The light was emanating from below. Drawing his gun, he started quietly down the stairs.

He gritted his teeth and gave himself a mental shake.

He was afraid for Whitney.

There was something wrong with this place; he wasn't prone to unease, nor was he superstitious, or afraid of the dark.

But there was something like a miasma here, some-

*thing that felt heavy in the air, something that seemed
to hint of death and decay and even...*
   Evil?

The dog walked to the rear of the room. He sat—
almost leaned—against the far wall and began to
whine.

"I hear it," Jake said softly.

"He's there," Whitney said, pointing toward the wall.
"There's something there he wants us to see, or find.
Jake, I was reading Andrew Crosby's book. A young
woman named Annie lived in Blair House at the time
of the Carrie Brown murder. I don't know why, exactly,
but I think the dog has something to do with her...and
he wants us to find something."

"You mean, you want to dig up the ground," Jackson
said.

"Uh—yeah, I'm sorry, I do. Can we?" Whitney
asked.

Jackson frowned, drawing a finger to his lips. He
and Jake drew their weapons and eased against the
wall.

They heard Will's voice come to them softly over
through their radio setup. "You've got company—"

And then they heard, "It's the police!" The deep,
rich voice boomed then echoed in the cavernous space
of the foundations.

"It's Jude," Whitney said, though she was sure that
Jackson and Jake realized who had come upon them
as well.

"FBI!" Jackson called back. "Jude, it's us."

As Jude came around the structural wall, everyone sheathed their guns.

He appeared in the glow of Jackson's light, hair tousled, looking tired and confused.

"What are you doing down here?" he asked them.

"It's what we do—investigate," Jackson said.

"In the middle of the night? In a dark hole in the ground?" Jude asked. "Don't you have cameras going?"

"We do," Whitney said, looking at him with her huge golden eyes luminous. "What are you doing here, though? Is there something new, a lead?"

"No," Jude replied with the single word. Something passed through his eyes, but so quickly she might have imagined it. And yet, for that moment, she almost felt as if he had reached out and touched her, and the hot arrows that flew through her bloodstream were shocking, alarming—and seductive. But he had already turned to Jackson. "A hunch. Or less. I couldn't sleep. I just decided to slip down to the area myself, and when I saw an extra glow of light from this place…I came on down. But what did bring you here?"

Jackson said, "A hunch."

Jake stepped in to clarify. "Whitney has been reading that book your dad loaned her. She found a reference to Blair House, and a young woman named Annie who disappeared at the same time as the Carrie Brown murder."

"The author believed that she disappeared here because, of course, he hated everything going on at the House of Spiritualism," Whitney said, staring straight at Jude.

He nodded, frowning. "I have a forensics team coming out in the morning—a crime scene unit."

Jackson cleared his throat. "No new victims tonight, correct?"

"Not yet," Jude said. He wasn't distracted. He kept staring at Whitney.

"Just what do you want to dig and what do you plan to dig with?" he asked her. He groaned softly before she could answer. "Construction site, and though the work is on hold, I figure under the tarp in that back section we'll find some pickaxes and shovels."

She smiled. "Just this area, right here."

"A hunch?" Jude asked her.

She nodded.

She thought that he groaned softly again, but she couldn't be sure. "Well, let's see what's here, shall we? I can call in backup, you know. Even at this hour. For once, I can have what I want without question."

"Let's work this alone, and see what we get," Jackson said.

"Because, if it's nothing," Whitney added, "then…"

"We'll just do it," Jude said.

He headed farther back into the foundations, where plywood made something of a roof over the gaping pit, and waterproof canvas tarps had been molded over equipment. Jackson arrived with his wide-beam powerful flashlight, and they ripped away one of the tarps. They'd found of cache of tools, including spades, picks, shovels and saws that had all been stowed.

"I'm surprised the construction workers left these," Jake said. "They usually value their personal tools."

"City of New York," Jude told him. "Look at the

handles—these are city property. That means be careful. They're probably old and overused."

Whitney watched as the three men chose picks; they found a small spade for her. "Be careful of our little site as well," she said.

She caught Jude's hand as Jackson and Jake headed toward the section of floor where the dog had led her. "I know why you didn't call for backup or help just now," she said quietly.

"Oh?"

"If I'm wrong, you don't want to appear to have been part of a ghost-hunting expedition," she said, wishing an edge of bitterness hadn't risen in her throat.

He looked at her for what seemed like an eternity. Then he offered her a wry smile. "Well, there is that."

"And?"

He shrugged. "Maybe some things should just be kept tight. I know about your team, and I myself have nothing but suspicion and theory."

She looked at him and nodded gravely. "Jude, we have more than that. There was and is a Jonathan Black. I don't know if the historical one was the real Ripper or not, but he was a murderer who used the House of Spiritualism for his own ends. He might have killed women—Annie Doherty at least—with the excuse of it being a Satanic sacrifice. I think he killed them in the area of the pentagram, and buried them in the floor in the next room. I don't know where that will lead, or if it can really help us, but finding the truth can't hurt us."

He nodded. She was surprised and he offered her a

small, grim smile and lifted a hand to move a strand of stray hair from her forehead.

"Let's dig, shall we?" he said.

"Thanks."

The dog had disappeared; maybe Jude's arrival had been just too much for him.

For a few moments, the only sounds down in the foundations were grunts and the sound of the pick hitting hard earth.

Then, Whitney cried, "Stop!"

They all stopped and stared at her. "You didn't hear it—there was something different, something hollow sounding—right where Jude is!"

He hesitated. He tentatively struck the earth. The sound was different.

Whitney rushed forward with her spade and began digging more gently at the earth. In a moment, she had her hands in the dirt, dusting away. In areas, brick remained. In other areas, there was just dirt and earth.

She revealed brick; a pasty-colored, poorly laid area of brick. Jackson grabbed the flashlight from where he had set it on the floor. "Different flooring," he said.

Jude fell to his knees and carefully began to lightly chisel with the tip of his pick at the mortar between the homemade bricks. One began to loosen, and Whitney fell to her knees across from him, gingerly prying it away as Jude released it at last. He was able to grab a second brick before it fell, and she reached past him for another.

"Lord!" Jude stared at Whitney across the hole they had created.

"What? Did you find Annie's bones?"

Jude looked over at Jackson. "Yeah, maybe," he said. "Maybe?"

"There must be at least a dozen skeletons in this hole!"

Despite the very early hour at which they had found the skeletons, the sun was up by the time the right people had arrived to start working the site. Because the poor souls in the hole had long been buried, they were down to skeletal remains and bits of clothing. Forensic anthropologists and archaeologists joined the crime scene unit arriving on the scene.

Jude worked with the techs in the area of the pentagram, where, he believed, if a modern-day Jack the Ripper had twisted history, he might have brought his earlier victims as he felt his way into the murders.

Sean Meyer, head of the unit, tried to ascertain just what Jude was trying to find; Jude pointed out what he assumed were the lines of the pentagram in the ground, and explained that he believed, due to the killer's determination to emulate Jack the Ripper, that he had certainly looked into the history of the House of Spiritualism, and though police had never proven foul play had taken place at the time, the killer believed that it had. He might have practiced the art of murder at the site.

Meyer's people went over the floor for trace evidence, which might mean nothing; construction crews had been at the site, movie people had been at the site, members of the New York Film Commission had been at the site and safety officers had been there as well, since a movie crew was setting up at a dangerous location. Those working on set construction had been given strict boundaries, but the city was in the midst of budget cuts, which meant that protecting the integrity of the rules might have been nearly impossible. Not to mention that the one guard might not have seen teenagers who scaled the poor chain-link fencing—which did have signs in many areas warning of injury and death, to keep the curious out—or idiots who thought of themselves as a cult and also read the history regarding the place.

"Meyer, I understand all that," Jude told him quietly. "What I want to find out is if we have any evidence of recent violence having taken place here—murder. If it happened, I believe it happened on the pentagram."

Meyer nodded. "I'll let my people work on trace first, and then we'll bring in the Luminol and the cameras. You know, I'm sure, that Luminol can destroy other evidence, so we'll go there last. And you know, too, that it will also pick up feces, animal blood...and if someone has bleached out the place, that will give us problems as well. What we pick up is the iron in blood, so there aren't any real guarantees, and, as I was saying, we may pick up other sources of iron."

"Humor me," Jude told him.

"Of course," Meyer agreed.

Police photographers now waited for the go-ahead with their long-exposure camera equipment to capture the blue chemiluminescent appearance of any blood spray near the pentragram.

Hannah arrived at the scene, assuring him that Deputy Chief Green had seen to it that the time for their task force meeting had been changed, and the time was now TBA. She bore the gift of a cardboard tray with cups of coffee. Jude accepted his gratefully, and walked around the supporting wall to observe the forensic anthropologists at work. He mused wryly that where they had taken pickaxes to the ground with a vengeance, the work was now being done with tiny picks and very small, soft-haired brooms. Angela had joined her team; he assumed Will and Jenna were watching the proceedings on the screens back at Blair House, since he had asked that their cameras and recorders not be disturbed.

Hannah hovered near him, but, eventually, she struck up a quiet conversation with Jake, growing more animated as she talked to him. Eventually, she walked over to Jude and said, "I'd like to go over with Jake to Blair House and see his trail of investigation."

Jude nodded. "Sure. Two heads are better than one, so they say." He glanced at Jake with a shrug. "Especially two brilliant heads."

As they left, Jude heard Hannah say to Jake with awe, "Your fiancée owns a plantation? A *real* plantation?"

They left; the digging went on.

He noted that Angela and Whitney hovered together, speaking softly now and then. Jackson, arms folded over his chest, watched the proceedings.

Eventually, the crime scene unit finished all the initial photography and trace, and sheeting was rigged over the pentagram to create darkness.

Jude walked over to the section, taking a position where Meyer said he could observe and be out of the way. The photographers were ready; the Luminol had been prepared. Jude knew it was important that it be sprayed expertly and evenly.

And it was. And in the thirty seconds that followed, he saw the floor light up.

The cameras caught the glow and the patterns.

The room lit up like blue lightning.

The rigging was moved.

Meyer looked at him grimly.

"You were right. There was a bloodbath down here."

There were three members in the team who had come to remove the bones, one with the New York Police Department, and two from the museum. A no-nonsense woman named Dr. Mary Drew was calling the shots; Whitney quickly learned that she was one of the most admired experts in her field. She supervised the removal of the bones. Years had gone by in which they'd lain undisturbed, but the conditions had been right for some preservation, she informed them. Simple biology, soft tissue decayed, and the decay created the browning they saw on the remnants of fabric that really didn't seem to go to any of the skeletons. It had also seeped into the earth, so they'd be taking dirt samples along with the bricks that had housed the skeletons in the hole within the hole.

While Dr. Drew was talking to them, Dr. Wally Fullbright arrived at the scene. He quickly assured them that they would have all the facilities they needed at the morgue to work with the bones. Mary Drew frowned, certain that her facilities at the museum were better when they were working with remains that were certainly well over a hundred years old. They bickered politely, but Fullbright held the trump card; the deputy chief of police wanted the remains studied at the New York City Morgue because they might be part of a current investigation.

Fullbright didn't interrupt the proceedings; he didn't even put on gloves, but he hunkered down by the bones that had already been painstakingly removed and looked at Dr. Drew. "They were beheaded?" he asked.

"Hard to say until we've had a chance to study them," she said. "By now, the disarticulation is almost complete."

"All women?" Fullbright asked.

"So it appears, so far."

"How many?"

"We've discovered thirteen skulls, so I'm going to assume that thirteen were buried here," Dr. Drew told him.

"Fullbright, did you read anything that would indicate what happened here?" Jude asked.

"What?" Fullbright asked, frowning.

Jude smiled. "You spend a lot of time studying old documents at the Pierpont Library. Did you glean anything that might help here?"

"You checked up on *me?*" Fullbright asked him, clearly puzzled.

"Your name was on a list," Jude explained.

Fullbright chuckled. "You know that I'm fascinated by all this. No, actually, I didn't find anything more than we already know. Most of the references are vague—the outside world speculated, but they didn't really know what was going on here. All I can say is that someone was heavily into the concept that human sacrifice was necessary."

"Yes, so I'd say," Jude agreed.

He walked over to Whitney, and nodded. He was excited to think that she knew about the history of the Ripper in America, and he seemed thrilled to find that the House of Spiritualism had hosted incredible horrors.

"But there was nothing that ever suggested Jack the Ripper was a Satanist," she reminded him.

"No, of course not, he was just a butcher, and the police were so inept back then. In London, the Metropolitan police were pitted against the City of London police, and the investigation was hampered entirely by politics—I mean, who erases evidence because it might cause someone to be offended?"

"'The Juwes are not the men to be blamed for nothing,'" Whitney quoted. In London, they had discovered the words written over a doorway after the night of the "double event" when two victims had been killed.

The words may or may not have been written; they were never even photographed. They had been ordered removed; the words, it was feared, would cause racial rioting among those of different beliefs crowded into the East End at the time.

"Personally," Jude said, joining them, "I'm afraid that our killer will reenact the double event—the Mary Kelly killing and then the Carrie Brown murder. They happened the same night those words were written. And no matter how ridiculous the theories out there may be, he'll kill as many people as armchair detectives and historians have credited to the original man."

* * *

By late afternoon, both teams were wrapping up. Jude realized that his back hurt, his muscles hurt, and that he was exhausted.

Ellis Sayer and a number of his team arrived. Ellis eyed him for a few minutes and then said, "You look like hell, Jude. You've got to have some faith in me and the others—get some rest. We're a task force, remember? I'll alert you to anything I learn."

Jude nodded. "Thankfully, so far, we don't have another victim."

"Not yet," Ellis said. He still had a dejected-basset-hound look to him. He reached into his jacket pocket and produced a notepad. "We've interviewed everyone on the set by now, and we've made it through the security company and the limo drivers as well. I have the names of the six limousine drivers who were assigned to the director and the stars. They've all been interviewed and, according to the drivers, they picked up and dropped off the major film entities just as we were told. But you may find something I haven't. One drove Sherry Blanco, one drove Bobby Walden, one was assigned to Angus Avery and three were on call to drive anyone back and forth as requested."

"Thanks," Jude told him. Whitney was walking over to him. She greeted Ellis courteously, looking at him as if waiting for something new. Ellis recognized the look and quickly informed her, "No, sorry. I haven't anything else. Well, other than the fact that they should make a giant hotel out of this place—people seem to love ghoulish crap. They'll pay the big bucks for such a haunted property. I imagine the movie will really make a fortune—the publicity it's getting is going to make it spiral right off the charts."

"True," Whitney agreed. She looked at Jude. "We have food next door."

Ellis sniffed. "He hasn't noticed that he hasn't eaten."

"I'll come over, thanks," he said.

He started to walk with Whitney, leaving Ellis in charge, but then he hesitated. "Ellis, can you get a rush put on the forensics on the limos that carried people from that set? We had them taken in, but I haven't heard anything back from the team that was inspecting them."

"They've been on the crime scene evidence. I'll push it on the limos," Ellis told him wearily. "It's damn hard when everything is a rush. They're calling out the troops, and bitching about overtime all the same." He shook his head and walked away, ever the good cop.

"Simple, quick—and we can feed tons of people, if need be," Jenna Duffy said, tucking a stray strand of light auburn hair behind her ears. She flashed Jude a smile. "Shepherd's pie, a rather good early dinner, if I do say so myself. Will is our expert sushi chef, but it's hard to feed the masses that way. Help yourself, please. Beer and soda are over there…"

Whitney slid up behind Jude, taking a paper plate from the pile on the kitchen counter and handing him one. She was surprised that she'd gotten him to leave the site and come over; she felt that there was nothing more either of them could do there at the moment.

"Hey, eat up. You have a large machine there to keep going," she told him.

"Large machine, eh?" he replied. "Are you suggesting I need to diet?"

"Not at all, you seem to be doing well with the machine. I'm suggesting you dig in, and make way for those behind you!"

He grinned, offering her his place. The others, except for Jenna, had already filled their plates. Walking into the hallway, he saw that Angela and Jackson had their plates at the bank of screens, and were watching the continuing action at the site next door. Hannah was with Jake in the den, enjoying his computer and programs, and Will Chan was waiting politely with Jenna so that she would prepare a plate of food for herself. Jude tried to wait politely as well, but Jenna and Will shooed him and Whitney out of the kitchen. "TV is on in the front parlor, you might want to take a look at the news programs," Will told them.

"We hooked up the cable while you were at the site today," Jenna explained. "You can get over eight hundred channels from I don't know how many companies."

"Wonderful—I guess," Whitney said. She dared to catch Jude's arm and steer him in the right direction.

The front parlor was filled with period furniture—except for the television and new cable system. They settled on the sofa in time to catch the weather, but then local news came back on. A pretty anchorwoman announced, "More shocking news today from downtown. Experts are now excavating the construction site off Broadway in the lower East End because skeletal remains have been found on the site. The Darby Building was slated for demolition last month and imploded, but the foundations had been deemed sound. However, before the Darby Building, a reputed destination for the city's Satanists known as the House of Spiritualism occupied the land before the turn of the twentieth century. Speculation is running high. Murder victim Virginia Rockford, working on a movie at the site, was found killed Ripper style just days ago. A little over a mile away in the Bowery, the body of Melody Tatum was also discovered. Police spokespersons have little to offer the public at the moment. We'll bring you Deputy Chief Green, taped this afternoon, right after our commercial break—*and* an exclusive interview with the beautiful actress Sherry Blanco regarding the upcoming epic *O'Leary's,* with a clip from the movie."

Jude let out a groan and winced.

"The movie just became an epic," Whitney said.

"And who would cash in on that?" Jude asked rhetorically. "Angus Avery, Bobby Walden and the ever-caring Ms. Sherry Blanco. Women are dead, bones have been dug up—and the public is still going to want to see Sherry Blanco," Jude said.

Whitney nudged his arm. "Eat."

"Before I lose my appetite," Jude agreed.

His gaze didn't leave the television screen, but, mechanically, he took a bite of the shepherd's pie. It was good—Whitney already knew, having had Jenna's shepherd's pie before. The aroma had been enough to make her realize she was starving.

Jude's second bite was far more energetic, and while they went through commercials that sold floor cleaners, cars and a product to extend a man's penis, he wolfed down the food on the plate.

The anchorwoman came back on; Deputy Chief Green announced that every policeman in the five boroughs was on high alert, that a task force was working all hours and that the FBI had a special unit on the case as well. The chief ended the interview by accepting a question about the House of Spiritualism, and saying that the police were exploring all possible angles. He tried to leave the podium, but one reporter demanded to know if the deputy chief believed that Carrie Brown had been a victim of the Ripper, and he paused, obviously irritated. "I have no personal beliefs on the matter. I'm concerned with what's happening on our streets right now."

"Is he targeting prostitutes?" another reporter called out.

"All women should take great care with any new acquaintance. It's a time for extreme vigilance."

"But," cried the same reporter, "it does seem true, doesn't it? This killer isn't after affluent women or mothers of kindergarten children!"

"We still can't say who the killer will target. Excuse me, that is all I have right now!"

Deputy Chief Green managed to escape. The anchorwoman came back with a perfectly coiffed Sherry Blanco at her side. Sherry was visibly distressed. "Poor Ginger!" she said, and tears formed in her eyes; one slid down her cheek and she dabbed at it with a tissue. "We were all so heartbroken!" She shivered. "And it could have been any of us!"

"Will the movie come out as scheduled?" the anchor-woman asked.

"We filmed today in Brooklyn, so, despite what we all have to bear, we're working hard to see that the fans and our producers are happy," Sherry assured her.

Jude made a sound.

"Hey!" Whitney protested softly. She took his for-gotten dinner plate from his hands and set it on the table. "Don't blame an entire industry. I know a lot of actresses who are really nice, and would be making real announcements, begging people to be safe."

"Luckily, it seems that everyone really kept mum at the site today," Jude said. "It's important that all the details don't get out there."

"Well, since it's in off the street and teeming with cops, the reporters couldn't get close," Whitney re-minded him.

"Yet," Jude said dolefully.

The anchorwoman directed her audience to watch the clip; it wasn't one in which Virginia Rockford was featured. Sherry Blanco, in period dress, was trying to head home from O'Leary's, the fictional pub in the Five Points district, when she was accosted by thugs. Bobby Walden appeared, dominating the screen, send-ing them off. Sherry's character looked at him with love and uncertainty in her eyes, and turned to run away while Bobby gazed after her in turn.

"Enough!" Jude rose, found the remote and changed channels until a National Geographic show on great blue whales appeared. Jude sank back down on the sofa, closing his eyes. Whitney set her own plate down, and took her seat by him again.

"You'll find the truth," she told him. Her voice was filled with certainty.

He took her hand and squeezed it. She remembered thinking that it would be nice to close her eyes as well.

The next thing she knew, she woke up.

Jude was slumped against the end of the sofa. She was slumped on top of Jude. No, she was cuddled up, curled against Jude. He felt warm and solid, vital and alive.

Someone had put a blanket over them.

He was still holding her hand, long, strong fingers threaded through her smaller, slimmer ones.

As her eyes opened, so did his.

Briefly, there was something different in the gray gaze he gave her.

Something soft, and electric, at the same time.

Desire.

She knew that it had been mirrored in her own.

And yet...

There was wariness in his eyes as well.

She looked away quickly. Well, he was a solid, white cop who was all hard evidence and facts; she was a woman of mixed heritage that included voodoo, and—oh—a ghost buster as well.

No hope, no future...she thought.

But, she realized with sadness, desire remained.

11

"Crosby! Hey!"

Startled, Jude sat up, easing Whitney with him to a sitting position just as Ellis Sayer came hurrying into the room.

"Yes, what is it, Ellis?" he asked. Whitney was trying to compose herself, smoothing down the now-wrinkled cotton blouse she wore beneath her tailored denim pantsuit.

"I think I have something. Someone. I came here first—you didn't pick up on the phone, and I figured you might be here."

Jude stood. The detective was making no sense. *"Who* do you have with you, and *what* did you find?"

Ellis's droopy hound-dog features actually shone for once.

"Come to the porch," he urged them.

Jude stepped by him. In the hallway, Angela was still standing by the door, and Jude realized that she had opened the door to Ellis, who hadn't said a word to her, but had surely seen him and Whitney on the sofa, and just marched right to them. Will was sitting at the bank of screens, looking as surprised as Angela.

Angela still even had the door open. She stared at Jude, and then followed the trio out to the porch.

Captain Tyler was standing there wearing a coat that had caped shoulders, much like the kind seen on the killer in every Jack the Ripper movie ever made.

Captain Tyler's eyes lit up as he saw Jude, and then Whitney.

"Captain Tyler," Whitney said. "You're supposed to be at a veterans' shelter."

Jude asked, "Captain Tyler, where did you get the coat?"

Tyler looked confused, not sure who to answer first. "Do you have coffee? Food?" he asked hopefully.

"Yes, of course," Whitney said, taking his arm and glancing at Jude. He knew he could be too brusque, and that she had the right touch with Captain Tyler. Whitney had incredible sympathy for the downtrodden, and it seemed that her instincts were usually on the money. He nodded; he understood her silent warning. They needed to take this slowly.

"First," Jude said huskily, "we need that coat."

"We'll find another one for you," Whitney assured him.

Tyler looked at them, and then shed the coat. Whitney quickly secured a garbage bag for the garment, hoping to preserve what evidence might be left.

When it was safely sealed, Ellis Sayer let out a sigh of relief.

"In this case," he said quietly to Jude, "I didn't want to drag him in, and we needed the damn coat, but he wouldn't give it to me. I knew he meant something to you and to the case, of course, and that's why I came straight here."

"Thanks, Ellis," Jude said.

"Of course," Ellis told him.

Jude set a hand on his shoulder.

"He's not our killer, but he may be an essential witness. And you'll notice his condition. His mind is shot and we'll have to handle him with kid gloves, so to speak."

"I figured," Ellis said.

Jackson was in the hallway when they entered the house. He glanced at Whitney, and then walked forward. "Welcome, sir," he said to Captain Tyler.

"Thank you, sir!" Captain Tyler offered a hand to Jackson. "Captain Tyler, retired, sir! And you are…?"

"Jackson Crow. Please, we'd love to have you join us for breakfast."

Breakfast? They'd slept through the night? Jude wondered.

That was bad, very bad. Except that it had been good. He could still recall his dreams. She'd been with him, and he'd been weary, but she had touched him, and in his dreams, she'd been naked, crawling over him. They'd made love passionately without a word, and he'd felt her against him, the pressure of her breasts against his arm, the softness of her body curved to his…

The last had been true.

The first…

Good God, he could only pray that he hadn't….

What the hell was he thinking? They were as far apart in thought and belief as the sun and the moon.

"Right this way, Captain Tyler, please!" Jackson said.

They seated Captain Tyler at the breakfast table in the kitchen. Coffee was placed in front of him. "I'll start the eggs," Whitney said. "Do you like cheese in them? Ham?"

"Oh, that would be delightful," he said.

Jude sat down across from the man. Ellis stood in the doorway, watching and patiently waiting. Whitney quickly went about scrambling eggs while Jackson popped bread in the toaster and Angela took a seat at the end of the table.

"Captain Tyler, this is very important. You went to a veterans' home, right?" Jude asked him. "The deputy chief told me that he'd make sure that you were helped there, and that someone would see to your records and a permanent shelter for you."

"Oh, yes, thank you. The police were wonderful," Captain Tyler said, sounding entirely lucid.

"So where did you get the coat?" Jude asked.

"In a Dumpster off Broadway," Captain Tyler said. "Of course, it's not exactly up to standards in today's style, but it's warm. It's a wonderful coat."

"Yes, it's a wonderful coat," Jude told him.

Tyler stiffened. "Sir! It was my only coat now. I gave the pea jacket to old Harry, who hangs around the new subway station."

"I'm going to make sure you have a coat, maybe

even a stylish new coat," Jude told him. "But it's very important that you tell me the exact location."

"In a Dumpster. About a block north of Trinity," Captain Tyler said.

"Thank you. Now, one more question, Captain Tyler," Jude said. "How did you wind up back by Trinity if you were at a shelter in another borough?"

Tyler's white brows arched high, and then furrowed. His hands began to shake around his coffee cup.

Jude reached out a hand and gently touched his. "Captain Tyler?"

Tyler looked up at him. "I—I don't know. I don't know. I don't remember anything. I was at the home… there were very nice people there. I had a very long shower, and it was so good. I went to sleep, in a bed, with clean sheets. I…"

"It's all right…drink your coffee, Captain." He looked down the table at Angela. "Jenna Duffy is an RN, right?"

Angela nodded, rose and went into the hallway. They could hear her calling up the stairs. "Jenna? Are you awake? Could you come down, please?"

The eggs were cooked; Jackson added toast to the plate Whitney prepared and she set it in front of Captain Tyler. "Don't be upset. Just relax."

"Yes, just relax, Captain. Your memory will be better if you don't force it."

Jenna Duffy came into the kitchen. Angela indicated Captain Tyler.

"Captain," Jude said. "This is Agent Duffy, and she's a nurse. She's going to take a look at you, if she may."

Tyler saw Jenna and his eyes lit up with appreciation. "Yes!" he said simply.

Jenna walked around the table to him. "I'm not going to hurt you, Captain Tyler. I just want to see your eyes, if I may?" She lifted his lids, studying the man's bloodshot eyes.

"Thank you," she told him.

"As you wish, young woman. Beautiful accent! Irish, of course," he said.

Jenna nodded.

"My mother, bless her soul, was an Irishwoman!" Captain Tyler said.

Jenna took his eggs away, and he stared at her like a child who had been slapped—through no provocation—by a parent. "He's been drugged," Jenna said. "I can't tell you what is in his system, but I'd get some tests done on him before allowing him to eat anything."

"What?" Captain Tyler demanded.

Jude stood. "Sir, I'm so sorry, but this is incredibly important. I have to take you to see a doctor."

"But I'm not sick! I'm hungry," the man said, indignant.

"I know, and I'll get you food just as soon as I can." Jude took Tyler's arm and started out of the kitchen and along the hallway.

"Ellis, can you drive us?" Jude said. "I'd thought we were dealing with his usual loopiness, but Jenna believes he was drugged."

"Of course. I go where you send me. Where to? Headquarters?"

"The Office of the Chief Medical Examiner," Jude said.

Captain Tyler balked. "But I'm not dead yet, young man!" he protested.

"No, sir, of course not. They have wonderful laboratories there. And it won't take long. And then we'll get you something to eat."

"All right, all right. Just so long as you know that I'm really not dead yet," Tyler said.

As they walked, Jude spoke to Ellis, telling him to get his men busy on the Dumpsters that needed to be searched.

"Jude, you know that we had Forensics all up and down the street the day that Virginia Rockford's body was discovered. I swear, there was no Dumpster left unturned that day," Ellis said.

"I know. But it needs to be done again," Jude told him.

He got to Ellis's unmarked simple black sedan and looked back. Whitney was at the door. He realized that they were both a mess; they hadn't changed since they'd made the discovery in the foundations, dug into the earth, worked all day and fallen asleep on the sofa. If he was a mess, maybe she didn't mind being a mess.

"Agent Tremont?" he said.

He saw Whitney look at Jackson; their team was tight. Jackson nodded, and Whitney hurried down the steps.

"Agent Tremont will be with us. I'm getting accustomed to working with her," Jude told Ellis.

Jude slid into the backseat with Captain Tyler while Whitney sat up front with Ellis. It didn't take them long to cover the distance to the Office of the Medical Examiner, only this time, Jude didn't head for the morgue.

Instead, he headed to the lab of Dr. Gil Sullivan, with whom he had worked many times before. Of course, he had usually brought him mysterious substances, rather than a living subject.

Jude explained how Ellis had found Captain Tyler downtown, wearing the coat, and that, as Dr. Sullivan could well imagine, they needed the coat tested as well as Captain Tyler himself. The coat he would bring to One Police Plaza, but he was pretty certain Captain Tyler needed to be tested quickly.

"Captain, how are you? I'll be kind and quick," Dr. Sullivan told him.

"Thank you."

"I'm retired navy myself, sir," Sullivan assured Captain Tyler, leading him into one of the rooms where the captain could lie down on a white-sheeted bed.

Jude, Whitney and Ellis were left in a small employee lounge. Jude dug in his pockets for change and found enough for three cups of watery coffee. Better than nothing at this point.

"I should get going," Ellis said. "I'll get with the men on the Dumpsters."

"Great, thanks, Ellis. But get some rest, too. Either that," he said ruefully, "or fall asleep on the job."

Ellis actually laughed. "Yeah, I'll get some sleep somewhere along the line. Keep me posted on anything you need."

Whitney was surprised when he smiled at her. "Agent Tremont," he acknowledged and nodded goodbye.

When Ellis had gone, Jude sat next to Whitney. He had to smile. There was a large smudge of dirt on her cheek. He reached out with his thumb, rubbing it off. She watched him with her huge golden eyes as he did so. He started to speak, and he wasn't sure what he was going to say, but it didn't matter, because his cell phone rang.

It was Ellis Sayer on the line already as he was driving.

"I've put a 'Crosby needs it now!' on the forensics for the limos," Ellis said. "I have the drivers on alert that you'll be talking to them. Right now, they're making comparisons to tissue and blood samples from our Jane Does to the blood we've managed to extract from the foundations."

"The House of Spiritualism?"

"We've got a twenty-four-hour watch on the property now. The bodies have all been…exhumed? Anyway, they're at the morgue."

"Well, then, I'll take a look while I'm here," Jude told him.

"I'm thinking that the coat probably came from the movie's costume department. We've gone through everything they had and haven't found a thing," Ellis said.

"And they didn't note that one was missing?" Jude asked.

"All of theirs are present and accounted for—unless someone in costuming is lying," Ellis told him.

"Interesting. Thanks," Jude said. He hesitated. "And no new victims yet?"

"Not that we know about."

"Thanks, Ellis." He was thoughtful a minute. "Let your men handle the Dumpsters. I need you to get to the veterans' home where Captain Tyler was taken. I need to know exactly what he ate, if he was given any drugs, if anyone came to see him and exactly who reported to work and was in the building in the last twenty-four hours."

When they hung up, he knew that Whitney had heard the majority of the conversation.

"What do you think?" he asked her.

"About?"

"The coat," Jude said. "What's the deal with costuming?"

Whitney was thoughtful a minute. "They keep close tabs on costumes, they're expensive. If one was missing and I were the wardrobe mistress...I have to admit, I'd think about lying. If a coat was missing and she hadn't reported it, she—or he—could be in trouble. Trouble as in losing a job if it came up later that a costume had just disappeared and nothing was done."

"Could someone fix documentation?" he asked.

She looked at him with a dry grin. "People can doctor just about anything."

Jude nodded thoughtfully. "This is crazy, though. I guess Ellis wasn't supposed to have found the guy on the street that quickly." He sighed. "With any luck, we can find out who drugged Tyler."

"With any luck," Whitney agreed. They both knew that the personnel at the veterans' hospital would be underpaid, understaffed and overwhelmed.

Jude hoped that maybe a security camera of some kind had actually worked. As he mulled that over, Dr. Sullivan came out to speak with them.

"You've something for me?" Jude asked.

"Oh, yes, your Captain Tyler was drugged."

"With what, how and when?" Jude asked him.

"GHB," Dr. Sullivan said, "Gamma-hydroxybutyric acid. Essentially, it's a date-rape drug."

"I know what it is," Jude said softly. "Easy to mix up a batch…you don't even have to be a chemistry major."

The doctor shrugged. "The government tries to control it, and it's on the same lists as LSD and heroin. But, as you said, anyone can mix up a batch in his or her kitchen."

"How did he ingest it?" Whitney asked.

"With a cup of coffee, probably. Or a glass of water, maybe even a glass of juice." Sullivan shook his head. "Here's the real problem with the drug, of course. It erases memory. Sometimes, in rape cases, the women remember snatches of events, or maybe something like a one-frame picture of where they were. In some cases, the victims remember nothing at all. People have died from overdoses, so we're lucky Captain Tyler is alive."

"It was planned that Captain Tyler be alive," Jude said thoughtfully. "Dr. Sullivan, would you see that he gets some lunch and some rest? And I have to make some kind of arrangements for him. I don't want Captain Tyler back on the streets, and I don't want him back at the home. I—"

"Hey, don't fret on that," Dr. Sullivan said. "I'll bring him home for the night." He grimaced. "My mother is in town. She needs someone to hover over other than me."

"That's above and beyond," Jude said. "I can find another shelter. I can even bring him in to the hospital for observation. I have a neighbor—"

"He'll be fine with me," Sullivan assured him. "Honestly. I like the old codger. Who knows, maybe Mom will like him, too. She's driving me insane, that's for sure. I'm not expecting him to have any recall, but in case he does, I'll know how to talk him through whatever memory may come back up, and I'll contact you the second that I do."

"That's great, then, thank you. I want to drop the coat off at my office, but I want to check up on the skeletal remains as well."

"Ah, yes! I heard about the find," Dr. Sullivan said. "We've got bags here."

The remains from the House of Spiritualism were in an autopsy room, lined up one after another. The remnants of clothing had been carefully bagged and tagged.

The bones looked lonely on the tables, sad and white, the empty-socket eyes seeming to stare out into space, like props at a movie set or a Halloween scare event. But they were real.

Fullbright was there when they arrived. "Wouldn't give up the supervision on this!" he assured them. "We've found plenty of nicks on the bones, and I'd bet a year's pay that they were all nearly beheaded. Jack the Ripper strangled his victims. I believe that these women were awake and aware when their throats were slit. But we've only begun the work. We'll know more when we've had more time."

Jude looked at Whitney; she appeared ashen.

"You okay?" he asked her softly.

She nodded, but something in the room was still disturbing her.

"Have you estimated the age of the bones?" Jude asked.

"Well, the clothing patterns and remnants—even stained and such by fluids—definitely appear to be late Victorian," Fullbright said. "We've estimated the age of most of the victims to be late teens to early twenties. Some have very bad teeth, which would suggest that they had been poor, immigrants perhaps. Sadly, yes! The refuse of life of that pitiable time." He shook his head. "Killing them was easy. I don't know if they were even missed with more than a passing thought. Come tomorrow, and I'll be able to give you a closer age estimate and even race, maybe nationality, of most of them. Well—" he glanced over at the forensic anthropologists, busily working "—I and my comrades of this adventure will be able to tell you much more tomorrow."

"Hey, are you really all right?" he asked Whitney as they left the building. "I can get you back to Blair House. I become obsessed, but I don't have the right to drag you along with me all day. In fact, I really don't have the right to separate you from your team at all."

"Oh, no, I'm glad to be with you, and I'm perfectly fine," she said. She looked ahead as they walked. "It was just…the skulls. The jaws on some were disarticulated from the skulls, and it looked as if they were staring at some horror."

"Yeah," he said huskily. "I can take you back to Blair House."

"No. I want to work this," she said firmly.

She was such a proud little thing, and her stature, the way she carried her body, gave her a presence that wasn't due to her size. He couldn't help feeling as they walked that he wanted to shield her from the unpleasantness at hand. He reminded himself that she was an agent.

That didn't stop them from being people. It didn't stop him from that growing feeling that they were meant to be together. So she had annoyed him at first, but that initial annoyance had turned into something else quickly. He wouldn't have been human, he'd have had to have been a eunuch, not to feel a sizzle of instant awareness when she was near. Awareness quickly became realized as basic desire, and he was a fool to keep needing her around him.

But he did. And he couldn't even say that she wasn't good with him, working the case, because she was.

And, hell, he was a cop. He had strength of purpose, damn it. He could force himself to a steel-willed control.

His dreams were his own, even his dreams of hot, carnal, naked passion. She didn't need to know that he kept imagining her naked.

Twenty minutes later, they had the coat delivered to and registered into the lab; Jude made sure it was in the hands of Judith Garner, who was still, along with her crew, wrangling the evidence gathered from both the Broadway and the Bowery sites.

Jude was fairly certain by then that he had himself—and his wandering mind—in check.

He told Whitney that he wanted to check in with Hannah, and they did so. "I don't have anything new yet," she told him. "But I started on background checks yesterday, and Jake Mallory and I divided the work—

we have hundreds of names to go through. I've got the programs situated to spit out all kinds of concurrences, similarities, mental defects, sealed juvenile records, you name it. We're working on anyone even remotely connected with the film, and with Blair House, and the House of Spiritualism."

"And," Jude reminded her, "anyone who has worked in a slaughterhouse, in an autopsy room, with medicine and anatomy in any way. And anyone who knows something about law enforcement, evidence, what we can really find and what we can't find."

"Of course!" Hannah said. She started counting off on her fingers, "The killer knows how to get around detection, the killer knows where certain body organs are, the killer apparently knows the city and the system." She sighed. "That could be a lot of New Yorkers."

"Concentrate on the limo drivers and the principals in the movie first—and look up everything you can find on Samuel Vintner, retired cop, dial-a-guard."

"I already did," Hannah said. "And you know I would have let you know immediately if I'd found anything on him. No college degree, and he passed the police academy as a C student, I guess you'd say. He was on a beat—in Brooklyn—for twenty years, and retired. He never came near the morgue, the best I can find. He never worked in a grocery store as a butcher, much less in a slaughterhouse. Detective Sayer's people interviewed his wife, and she said that he was home in time for dinner, just like he was supposed to be, and he wasn't covered in blood." Hannah paused, looking at the two of them. "You guys are a mess. You slept in those clothes, after digging all day. Ugh." She grinned suddenly. "I should have made you get up when I left last night, but you were so cute sleeping. And I'm guessing you're not getting a lot of sleep these days." She wrinkled her nose. "But, if you're representing the NYPD and the bureau, you might just want to take showers!"

"Soon, Hannah, I promise," Jude told her. "What about Angus Avery? He may be our man."

She nodded. "I did a background on him right away, Jude," she said, sounding hurt. "He went to NYU, and then to the University of Southern California. He has all kinds of writing and directing credits. As far as information I can track goes, he has never worked in the medical field, or in groceries—as a butcher, or in a slaughterhouse. He grew up in the Village, though, so, I would assume he knows Lower Manhattan well. Oh, he wrote the story—the screenplay—for *O'Leary's*. And it was considered a coup for him when he was able to hire Sherry Blanco for the leading role."

"Just Sherry? What about Bobby Walden?" Whitney asked.

"Well, they both have confidentiality clauses in their contracts," Hannah said, her eyes rolling. "I think Bobby got even more money because Sherry agreed to be in the film when she found out that Bobby was her costar. He'd been slipping, you know. That turkey called *A Slice of Christmas?* I mean, come on, a Christmas slasher film? Anyway, Bobby is still stardust, I guess. Must be all the action flicks he did.

"Sherry's a little different. She went to UCLA for one year, and then she was hired for a music-video show, and she has been working nonstop since then.

She never even had to wash a dish or bartend—her parents were putting her through. Bobby Walden was a child prodigy, and was already on the kids' channels by the time he was eighteen...tutors on set and all that stuff."

"Dig deeper," Jude said.

She might have been upset, but she was looking past him—at Whitney. He wasn't sure what kind of expression Whitney had given her, but it caused Hannah to smile.

"Your wish is my command. Go. Go get cleaned up!"

"Can't yet," Whitney told her. "We're on our way to the shelter for the veterans of foreign wars."

"Why? What happened?" Hannah asked.

"Someone drugged, kidnapped and deserted Captain Tyler," Jude explained. "And I need to get my car—can you give us a ride?"

12

Ellis Sayer had already arrived at the veterans' home and was questioning patients and workers in one of the employee lounges. As Whitney listened to Jude speak with the desk clerk, she heard the conversation recede as if she'd moved to a distant place. She felt her heart break as she looked around; no one deserved the finest the American public could give more than the men and women who served in the military. She knew that they—just as she had—signed a contract with their branch of service, one that explained that they were putting their lives on the line. Every police officer, every National Guardsman and woman, every person in law enforcement, as well as in the military, knew that they put their lives on the line.

But none did so with the expectation of facing enemy fire in the way that these soldiers had.

At first, she thought that the hallways were just busy. Then, with a chill sweeping over her, she realized that she was seeing the *dead*.

She swallowed hard, frozen at first.

It had started in the autopsy room. She had looked

at the bones on the tables, and she had imagined them rising and acquiring surreal bodies out of the air that surrounded them. She had seen the gaping mouths, opened in horrendous screams that she thought she could hear.

And now, it was worse...

They walked by her sadly; soldiers who had made it home, but not made it back to health. Men minus arms and legs, limping along on prosthetic legs, or with metal and rubber extensions where arms had once been attached to their bodies. There were those who were pale and gaunt, and had evidently died from organ damage that just couldn't be repaired, or diseases that just couldn't be cured. This was not really a hospital; it was a shelter that offered medical aid.

One man in particular stopped and stared at her. Whitney stared back, and realized that he knew that she saw him, and was surprised. She saluted him.

"Whitney?" Jude said and she started. "The night manager for C Wing is in with Ellis now."

"Of course."

She followed Jude down a long hallway. He apparently knew where he was going, because he only paused once, looking at the doors around them. He opened one and walked in.

A heavyset woman was seated at a table, wringing a handkerchief in her hands. She stopped speaking when Jude and Whitney entered, eyeing them worriedly.

"It's all right, Mrs. Dean, continue," Ellis said, looking at Jude and Whitney. He grimaced. "They're my colleagues."

"Well, all right." Mrs. Dean took a deep breath. "I saw Captain Tyler at nine o'clock—that's our basic bedtime here. But, of course, our soldiers and sailors are not forced to go to sleep then. Medications have been given out. Dinner is long over, and it's quiet time. I checked in on him because he's such a sweet man. And I think he was going to adapt okay. A doctor saw him yesterday, and he was waiting for some test results before starting on a medication regime. I gave him a mild sedative, just to sleep—an ibuprofen with an added sleep aid, doctor's orders. It wouldn't have knocked him out, and it wouldn't have done anything to his memory. And I was at the desk all night, except that if I wasn't, Mary was there." She gasped suddenly. "Except when the alarm went off in Admiral Clift's room. We both went running—he's one of the World War II vets, quite old and frail, and we both rushed in."

"What was wrong with Admiral Clift?" Jude asked.

A look of realization came over Mrs. Dean's face. "Oh, no," she said. "Nothing." She fumbled with her handkerchief. "That's when someone got to Captain Tyler!"

"Do you know why no one was notified this morning that Captain Tyler was gone?" Jude asked.

"Probably because you're not required to check out. Well, of course, we expect the courtesy of being told when our vets are leaving. We have only so many beds, and we're trying to create a place where they can find homes and receive medical help without actually living in a nursing facility. Like assisted living, with a better quality of life," she explained.

"Captain Tyler was brought in by the police. We should have been notified," Ellis Sayer said crossly.

Mrs. Dean was upset, but she was also defensive. "You'll have to speak to the day crew about the morning. I have no idea why no one was notified!"

Whitney stepped in then, smiling. "Mrs. Dean, could you show us Captain Tyler's room?"

"Of course, dear, of course."

Jude looked at Ellis, who grimaced. "Sorry," he murmured.

Whitney had longed for Angela's talent—a real ability to wait, to simply be there, sympathetically, in touch on a different plane, and allow the dead needing help or closure to see that she might see them, and come to her. Now, with the dead suddenly so apparent to her, filling the hallways, she felt a sense of overwhelming unease; she had never thought that she would see so many, so suddenly...so many...

She nearly walked into a member of the living, believing that he was one of the dead.

"Excuse me!" she told an older man. He was in uniform, and though frail, his physical health seemed to be fine. He lifted his hat to her.

"It's all right, young woman, it's all right. A lovely young woman may walk into me anytime," he said, and moved on around them. "Heading to bingo, Mrs. Dean!" he said. He paused and looked back at Whitney. "Marnie! Would you like to come to bingo with me?"

Mrs. Dean whispered, "That's Major Radison. He thinks you're his daughter, Marnie. Just tell him that you have to go to work."

"I'd love to come!" Whitney said. "I'm so sorry that I have to go to work."

"Next time, sweetheart. Plan to come on a bingo night when you can stay!" he said.

"We offer many group activities here," Mrs. Dean murmured. "Major Radison is another of our World War II veterans. His daughter, Marnie, died last year, and her family lives out in Arizona, so they're not here often. Sad, truly. For him, the Alzheimer's is a blessing. He doesn't know that she died."

She pushed open a door to a cheerful room. The bed was even made and decorated with a pretty quilt. The other furnishings offered utility with grace. There was a desk as well as a dresser, and on a counter at the back, a microwave.

"Very nice," Whitney murmured.

Jude, she noticed, had paid little heed to the room. He had gone to the window. He didn't touch it, but looked at the mechanism. "We're on the ground floor," he noted.

"Yes, we have many rooms on the ground floor," Mrs. Dean said.

"Ellis—"

"Yeah, forensics on the window," Ellis said. "I've already called—should be a team here soon. Gloves?"

He offered a pair to Jude, and Jude accepted them, and struggled briefly to get them on his long-fingered hands. He opened the window and stuck his head out.

"Footprints, too, the ground is soft, they might find something. And the parking lot is just about fifty feet away," he said. He turned. "Who is on the morning shift?" he asked Mrs. Dean.

"Gertrude, but she's gone home now," Mrs. Dean said.

Jude looked at Ellis. "We'll need—"

"I know. I'll get over to see Gertrude."

Jude appeared frustrated but resigned. "All right, Mrs. Dean, thank you for your time. No one has touched anything in this room since Captain Tyler was here?"

"The cleaning crew comes in from 7:00 a.m. through 4:00 p.m. every day," Mrs. Dean told them. "But we received Detective Sayer's call, and we were able to stop them before they came in the room."

"So, it was left like this, with the bed made?" Jude asked.

"Just as you see it," Mrs. Dean agreed.

Jude flashed Ellis a look of gratitude and Ellis Sayer nodded. "I've already been in here. There were no glasses, cups or anything else. And the crime scene unit will dust all the furniture."

"Mrs. Dean, you didn't see anyone here last night that shouldn't have been here, or anything unusual?"

"No, nothing… I didn't even think the alarm was unusual until you asked, and we knew that Captain Tyler was gone. Thank God that he's all right, but then he has been living on the streets a very long time—he does know his way around, bless him," she said.

Whitney set a hand on her shoulder. "This is a home,

not a fortress or a prison, and I can see that you try very hard to make the veterans happy."

"But I should have…I should have been aware. We take precautions with our senile guests, and certainly, with those suffering from brain damage. I should have thought about that alarm and—"

"Mrs. Dean, if you should think of anything, or hear anything, please notify me right away," Jude said, handing her a card.

"Of course," she agreed.

She turned and walked out of the room. They followed.

Major Radison hadn't gone to bingo. He was still standing in the foyer, smiling, as he looked at the pictures of the administrators. "Major Radison, bingo is about to begin," Mrs. Dean reminded him.

The elderly man looked at Whitney and smiled again. "Marnie, are you coming?"

She was about to make a polite response when she saw the first ghost who had seemed to recognize her in the hallway. He was frowning, watching her. Slowly, he pointed a finger at Major Radison.

Whitney frowned in turn, but then she wondered if the ghost was trying to help her.

"Major, before you go, did you hear or see anything unusual last night?" Whitney asked him.

"Miss," Mrs. Dean said softly, "the man suffers from Alzheimer's. I'm afraid that he can't help you."

"Shh," Jude said softly. "Whitney?"

"Major?" Whitney prompted.

"Why, come to think of it, child…" Major Radison

said thoughtfully. "Someone walked into my room with a cup and said that I needed my medicine. But then he looked at me, and said he had the wrong room, he was very sorry," the major said.

"Was he—a nurse?" Whitney asked.

"Well, a most unusual nurse, if you ask me. He was wearing some kind of ridiculous cloak—in a hospital! It's not even cold in the hospital. And he had a big hat—he looked like something out of an old-time movie! Ridiculous, absolutely ridiculous!" Major Radison said, shaking his head with confusion and disgust.

"I told you that he couldn't help you!" Mrs. Dean said.

"Major, I'm going to send a sketch artist to see you," Jude said. "Do you think he could help you draw the man you saw?"

"Why, of course!" the major told him, apparently quite happy to be of service. He turned to Mrs. Dean. "I know what I saw," he said with quiet dignity.

"Or, better yet, if you're willing, I'll send an officer to pick you up and bring you downtown. I'd like to have you look at some pictures as well, and see if you recognize anyone."

"I am willing, sir, always to serve my country!" He bowed to Whitney. "But, it must be tomorrow morning, sir! You see, now, I am on to bingo!"

"What if I sent out the artist tonight, but had you picked up to come down to the station in the morning?" Jude asked.

"I shall be happy to assist, after bingo," Major Radison said.

With a clipped bow, he left them.

"Thank you, Mrs. Dean," Jude said. Then he smiled at Whitney and opened the door for her.

Whitney turned back to see the ghost soldier who had pointed to the major when they'd been about to leave.

He saluted her gravely. She didn't give a damn what anyone thought; she saluted in return, and then stepped on out the front door, and into the gray mist of a fog-filled twilight.

Little felt as good as the hot shower Jude took when he reached his apartment at last. He scrubbed thoroughly, and the water seemed uplifting, allowing him to believe that they would sift through the haystack and find the truth. As Agent Mulder from the *X-Files* always said, *The truth was out there.* He'd been a fan of the show; seeking the truth about aliens was more entertaining than that sought in the mind of a human psychopath.

Sometimes, it did seem that the truth was hidden in a vast galaxy, but he had hope that Major Radison did have moments of pure lucidity, and that he could give them some kind of picture of the man who had come to drug and kidnap Captain Tyler.

Emerging from the shower, he longed to forget the case.

He knew that he could not. Jude had no problem believing that, whether he suffered from Alzheimer's or not, Major Radison still met the killer entering the wrong room. Somehow, he had known about Tyler, and decided that the homeless veteran would make a good scapegoat. Except that something about the situation was disturbing.

If the killer was playing Jack the Ripper, they knew damn well he wasn't done.

He felt refreshed, and yet restless.

And at odds.

He worked fine alone. When he was off, he knew how to play alone, or enjoy time with his father, friends, or even heading out for the night, when there were those times he'd meet a woman, and they'd wind up spending the night. Since his last fiasco, however, he'd determined to keep it casual, and not out of vindictiveness or bitterness. He knew cops who had good marriages. He knew more cops—especially detectives—who had broken marriages. Better to keep his distance.

He deserved a break, and he knew he had the right to take it. And that he wasn't a one-man island—the NYPD didn't work that way. But there were too many threads unraveling; he was almost certain that the blood discovered via Luminol at the site would prove that the first two women had been attacked there, at the pentagram, just as the others had been attacked before them more than a century earlier. He'd be lucky to get test results tomorrow from the crime scene unit techs working on the blood and trace at the site, and from those working on trace from the limos he'd asked to be inspected. Still, he was restless; he wanted to get into the killer's mind.

And, tonight, he didn't want to be alone. He didn't want to pull out his jazz or blues collections, and didn't want to wander the streets, or watch sports in one of his favorite bars. He didn't even want to drop in on his father—who was wonderful at helping him sort out his mind.

He wanted to return to Blair House.

And he had a very sound reason; Jackson Crow was a behavioral specialist, a profiler. And while he was forming his own suspicions, there was no one better to discuss such suspicions than the head of the crack team sent to help him.

And, of course, he'd spent the day out with Whitney, and he needed to see what headway, if any, members of the special unit had made.

As he drove, he pondered the way that Whitney had been at the veterans' home—strange. At first, it had almost seemed that her mind was wandering. Yet when they had interviewed Mrs. Dean, she had, as usual, stepped back, speaking only softly at what always became the right time.

Good cop, bad cop, he thought. *He and Monty had played that game often enough. It seemed that he and Whitney had fallen into the strategy as well. He was too curt and too quick, and she stepped in, flashing her beautiful smile with her soft green-and-gold eyes, and her words would never try to excuse his behavior, just clarify and soften.*

But her intuition in speaking with Major Radison had been uncanny.

Just as her suggestion that they dig beneath the bricks in the flooring at the House of Spiritualism. She'd found bodies; many of them.

When he parked in front of the house, he half expected to find that the team wasn't there, that they'd gone next door again, perhaps to dig in new ground. But he saw that patrol cars were sitting in front of the construction site, and that Blair House was aglow with lights.

He parked and headed up the walk. He was surprised that the door opened before he could reach it. "I was hoping you'd come," Whitney said, smiling as she greeted him. She was wearing a casual knit dress that bared the fine structure of her throat and collarbone, and the sleekly muscled perfection of her lower legs. He felt an instant heat sweep through him; it wasn't unpleasant. It was caused by seeing her there, and by the sound of her voice.

"Showered even," he said lightly.

"You look fine in the dirt of the ages, at least to me," she assured him. "Do you like sushi? Will was our cook tonight. We're having a working dinner—Jackson has a board going like the one you use at your task force meetings, and we're all discussing what we know about the case. I hope you've come with a little time?"

"I love sushi and I'm more than intrigued to see what you behavior people have to say about our killer," Jude said. Yet, at the moment, he didn't really want to see Jackson, or any of the rest of the team. He wanted to reach out and draw Whitney to him, and forget everything around them.

Dangerous, he warned himself. *Crazy.*

"Come on into the kitchen," she said.

He did so. The others greeted him as if it was perfectly natural that he had come. In fact, it seemed they'd been expecting him.

"Whitney has filled us in on the events at the veterans' home," Jackson said, shaking his hand in greeting. "Hopefully, that evidence will lead right to the killer. Take a seat, please, have something to eat, and I'll explain our board. What we've done here is connect the past with the present." Jackson pointed out the map-graph they had created.

"Yes, I think I can follow it pretty easily," Jude said. "You have Emma Smith and Martha Tabrum… the woman reported attacked by soldiers, who died the morning following the attack…and the woman whose throat was slit, whom the experts *don't* believe were Ripper victims aligned with Sarah Larson and our Jane Doe whom we still can't name. You have Virginia Rockford and Melody Tatum aligned with Polly Nichols and Annie Chapman. On the other side of the line, you have Carrie Brown—the New York victim of a like murder, and then…I'm not sure about the other names."

"These are people I've dismissed, though to some speculators they're also victims of the New York Jack the Ripper," Jackson said. "Personally, I don't believe that Carrie Brown was killed by Jack the Ripper. There were too many differences outweighing the similarities, in my mind. The Ripper's victims were manually strangled and their throats were slit. In the Carrie Brown case, she was strangled with a piece of her clothing, and her throat was not slit. The other cases are even more ridiculous. One was killed in her house in the midst of a robbery, and the mutilations didn't occur in the same manner, or at all. The Ripper never left his knife—the Carrie Brown murderer did. So, in my mind, our American 'Ripper' was not the same man.

I do believe, however, that he was the elusive Jonathan Black."

"So what the hell is our killer doing?" Jude said. "In my opinion, the Jack the Ripper of Victorian London fame was either in a mental hospital or dead after the Mary Kelly killing—if her killing wasn't just a copycat killing. Whatever it might have been, I don't see such a murderer sanely taking a break so as not to be detected. Our killer is imitating Jack the Ripper—as if he had come to America, and so, he believes the Carrie Brown killing to be attributable to the Ripper. But here's where I grow extremely wary—with the coat deliberately given to the captain, it appears that the killer is trying to set someone up to take the fall."

Jackson sat down. "I've been mulling this over all day, ever since Ellis appeared with Captain Tyler. If it didn't appear that the killer was doing his best to imitate the Ripper, I'd assume he was just trying to cast blame on someone else, in fact, to *pin* the murders on someone else. But I find it unlikely."

"Could we be looking at another person's involvement? When you consider the London murders, it's clear they grew steadily more violent," Jude pointed out. "Polly Nichols was severely slashed. By the time he got to his next victim, he hacked up her organs. He grew fonder of killing—and mutilation. I don't see such a man calmly determining that he'd better make it look as if the butler did it. So, who tried to set up Captain Tyler—and *why?*"

"Hopefully, you'll have luck in the morning when you bring Major Radison to the station and show him some mug shots, along with pictures of a few of our principal players," Jackson said.

"I'm glad you're bringing him down to the station," Will said.

"You don't think the surroundings will bother him?" Jude asked.

"No," Jenna told him. "I think he will actually feel better. Everyone will be kind to him at the station and will want his opinion."

"Yes, and I'm glad. I just wonder how much he's actually going to be able to help," Will said.

"Why?" Jude asked him.

"Whoever it was bothered to come to the hospital in a cloak, or something similar—and a hat. He might have gone all the way—with stage makeup," Will said.

"It always seems to bring us back to the movie being made—*O'Leary's*," Whitney said. "And Will is right. Anyone working around a set long enough has to learn something about makeup. So, was it really a *mistake* that the kidnapper who drugged and took Captain Tyler went to the wrong room—or did he do it on purpose? He was perpetuating the Jack the Ripper myth, even in 'stealing' and setting up Captain Tyler."

"Whitney, tomorrow you need to get to the location where *O'Leary's* is now shooting," Jackson said.

She nodded. "Of course."

"A task force meeting will take place tomorrow at 8:00 a.m.," Jude said.

"We'll be there," Jackson assured him gravely.

"How's the sushi?" Will asked.

"Pardon?" Jude asked.

"Sushi—dinner," Will said, waving his chopsticks in the air.

Jude laughed. "Sorry, it's great, and thanks."

When they finished, Will and Angela went to study the bank of screens in the hallway. Whitney urged him to come back to the den, where Jake Mallory was set up. "You know that Hannah and I are sharing our information. We've done personality studies with Jackson on some of your movie principals."

"And what are your conclusions?" Jude asked him.

"That you're looking at three possible suspects. Obviously, that's if the killer is working with someone. None of us believes that Sherry Blanco—though certainly a narcissist—has the necessary strength to pull off the murders. But it could be that she is in on what's happening, if there are two people at work, which seems possible."

Whitney looked at Jude. "You know, the royal family conspiracy theory maintained that the prince had help in the killings—his physician, Sir Richard Gull."

"Gull was the carriage driver—there to whisk the prince away," Jude said.

"So, Sherry could be the person making sure that the killer makes a clean escape," Jake told him.

"And she could just be a spoiled star," Whitney said. "And we could be barking up the wrong tree entirely."

She leaned back, stretching. A yawn escaped her. "I'm so sorry!" she said.

Jude rose. "I'll get out of here, let you have your house back and get some rest for the night."

"You should just move in here while the investigation is going on," Jake told him.

"Hey, I've got an apartment not that far," Jude said.

Move in. Nice idea. Close to Whitney. Not having to leave...

"Well, good night. I'll see you in the morning," he said.

But he didn't get out that quickly. As they started through the hallway toward the front door, they passed the bank of screens. Angela was leaning forward, pointing at something on it. "It's still there, the shadow that seems to lurk just above the ground."

Jude walked over to look. Lights set up at the empty excavation site glinted off the patrol cars now permanently parked along the chain-link fence. But despite the lights, a shadow undulated just above the surface of the ground.

"Is it the film?" Jude asked.

"No," Whitney said firmly. "It's high-speed film... captures light, shadow, movement and changes in temperature, really. Movement in the air."

"Then it's just a breeze—and the night is foggy," he said.

No one answered him.

"It's ghosts?"

"Really, there should be no activity," Angela murmured. "The bodies there were found, and they were dug out of the pit where they were buried without prayer or ceremony."

"*Those* bodies were discovered," Whitney said.

Jude groaned. "You're suggesting there are more?"

"Perhaps," she replied.

"More victims?" he demanded.

Whitney looked at him at last. "Maybe not. According to the Honeywell book your father loaned me, Jonathan Black just disappeared. The city was in an uproar; the House of Spiritualism came under so much fire that the city fathers decided that it was going to be razed, and it was. They'd lost power. According to the book, the followers had grown afraid of Jonathan Black, who, it seemed, *was* their power for some time. It is possible that they got together and basically assassinated him. And if they did so..."

"They buried him in the walls or the foundations somewhere," Jude finished for her. He stared at Whitney. "Do you know where he's buried? I mean, like you knew how to find the bodies last night?"

Whitney shook her head. "No. We don't know where his body might be, if it is there," she said. "And, of course, a new Satanist might have worshipped his body, a piece of his body...or even some kind of relic he might have used as his 'cross' for others to respect as a symbol of some kind of supernatural power."

"I can't tell you where his body might be. Not yet," Angela murmured.

Jude turned. He had to get out of Blair House. He didn't want to become known as a ghost buster, with his department snickering behind his back.

But if Whitney had been the one to ask him, he realized, *he'd have stayed through the night.*

"Good night."

In seconds, Jude was out in the street, revving his car's engine and heading home.

He hadn't even reached the house before he wanted to go back.

Tonight would bring those same dreams again.

There would be some kind of gentle breeze blowing and moonlight slipping through the windows. He would see her as she came into his arms, as they fell onto the bed together, as he felt her sleek naked flesh next to his own...

As he parked for the night, he prayed that his dad would have a bourbon waiting for him.

A big one.

And he wondered if even that would help.

The dog came to Whitney again that night. She had lain down, her mind still reeling, and closed her eyes. For once, she hadn't been thinking about the case. She was remembering that she had basically spent the night before sleeping on top of Detective Jude Crosby. His fingers, so long and strong, had held her own. She'd felt the rise and fall of his breath, and the heat and vitality of his muscles, the breadth of his chest...

The memory was interrupted by the sound of a soft whine, and then again, a damp nose against her fingers.

She opened her eyes. He was seated at the side of her bed.

"What?" she asked softly. "We found your mistress. We'll make sure that she's buried in a cemetery. I'll make sure that prayers are said. It will be all right."

She looked across her room. The bathroom light was on. In its glow, she saw the woman.

"Annie. Annie Doherty?" she said softly.

The image faded.

The ghost dog remained.

"I have to go to sleep, I really have to. You want

something else from me, but if I don't sleep, I'll never know what it is," she said softly.

The dog whined and wagged his tail.

Then she felt a sense of pressure as he jumped up onto the bed. In typical dog fashion, he circled three times and then lay down, facing her, his eyes sad.

She suddenly wondered if he had come to watch over her.

"Were you really allowed to sleep on the bed?" she asked.

The dog wagged his tail; the long furry appendage seemed to thump on the bed.

"All right, then. We're going to sleep."

To her amazement, she lay down and quickly felt dreams overtake her.

They weren't nightmares. They were sweet dreams. She was lying with Jude Crosby, and it was the most natural thing in the world. And they weren't cramped up on a couch; they were in a bed.

Her sleep deepened, and it became restful.

Until she heard her cell phone ringing in the morning, so constantly that she thought it would vibrate right off the bedside table.

She fumbled, knocked it to the floor, found it, saw that the caller was Jude and answered quickly.

"They've found trace evidence in the limo that was assigned to Angus Avery," he said. "Blood drops—the blood was Virginia Rockford's."

13

Jude sat across from Angus Avery in a situation very different from the last time they had met. There was no pleasant New York bustle going on around them now. The chairs were rigid, cold and uncomfortable, the lights harsh.

He'd been read his rights, but he still appeared to be stunned. He hadn't demanded to be left alone while he waited for his attorney to show up. Jude hoped that would take some time. It was rush hour, so it might. Angus Avery certainly had a high-powered attorney, who would get the man out on bail, unless an under-paid district attorney could convince the judge that he was a flight risk or too dangerous to be on the loose.

"This is insane!" Avery told him, shaking his head. "I'm a filmmaker, not a killer! I cooperated with your questions. You have…you have blood in a car that car-ried me to a dinner. I wasn't in that car again. This is… what do you call it? It's not proof—its circumstantial evidence, that's what it is. You have people searching my apartment now, right? You won't find anything.

And why won't you find anything? Because I didn't do it!"

Jude knew that Sayer and the deputy chief were standing behind the mirror, monitoring the proceedings. Others were surely there as well.

The limo driver, Eric Len, was cooling his heels in another interrogation room. In a few minutes, Sayer would go speak with him. They'd give him a few minutes to sweat, and then tell him that Angus Avery had implicated him. Outright lies often tripped up an accomplice.

But Jude didn't feel right. Avery was literally in tears, protesting his arrest.

"I didn't do it!" he insisted.

"How did Virginia Rockford's blood get in that limo?" Jude asked him. "Honestly, I'd like to help you out." He actually meant the words. He'd suspected that the director might be involved, but now, something about the situation seemed far too easy. "There's more, Mr. Avery, I'm afraid. There were hairs and epithelial cells that match your DNA found on the cloak that Captain Tyler was wearing when he was found after being kidnapped from a veterans' home."

"I didn't give permission for my DNA to be taken!" Avery protested. "That's my right—you didn't have just cause. You can't bring my DNA into court!"

"Mr. Avery, I took your DNA from a cup that you'd been drinking from at the diner where you met with me, and it was perfectly legal," Jude told him. "If you want to come clean with me, I can help you. We can talk with the D.A., you know that. You know that people deal all the time."

"I didn't do it! I'm being framed," he said desperately.

"It may be circumstantial evidence, but it's just about overwhelming," Jude told him. "And the city is in a panic over these murders. You're in real trouble. You need us. You need our help."

There was a tap on the door. A small, slim, middle-aged man in a crisp black Versace suit walked in. "My client has nothing else to say. We need privacy." He produced a card and handed it to Jude. "Alton Morrison III, Detective. I'll be representing Mr. Avery."

Whitney was stunned. She had expected that if the police really caught the killer he'd confess. He'd be proud of his work, though sad he hadn't accomplished the scenario it seemed he had planned. But, of course, human nature could be strange.

It was all over by the time she and Jackson arrived at the station. Eric Len had demanded an attorney immediately, but not before he had sworn that he'd returned the car to the garage just as he had said—and as records showed—and that he had gone home, alone. His wife couldn't verify that information for him because she was back in China, visiting family. But he knew nothing. *Nothing.* He had never lied.

Angus Avery was taken to be arraigned that afternoon.

His high-powered attorney couldn't get him released on bail, but he did manage to negotiate a house arrest, since the police evidence was circumstantial. He could return to his apartment with an ankle monitor. For his own safety, and the possible safety of the people of

New York, he would also be closely monitored by the police—in other words a beat cop would be assigned to watch his comings and goings.

The police were appalled; the public was divided. Naturally, there was a press conference, and Avery denied passionately that he was guilty; he was being framed, and he suspected the NYPD who were desperate to *say* that they had solved a murder—they were arresting an innocent man, just as they had arrested and *jailed* an innocent man in the 1890s for the murder of the Ripper victim Carrie Brown. In court, he swore he would prove himself innocent.

Whitney saw little of Jude that day; he was busy with the lab, with paperwork, with discussions with the prosecutors, making sure that all the evidence was in order. The team stayed at the station long enough to contribute what they could, and then returned to Blair House to discuss the arrest. Jackson didn't seem convinced that Angus Avery had committed the killings, but he didn't say that it was impossible. The police had a weak case against the limo driver at best; there was no more reason or evidence that he should have smuggled the car out of the garage after its return than anyone else. Jackson determined that they would remain in the city at least another week, helping to tie up loose ends, if need be, and also because the film they continued to see on the bank of screens from the foundation abyss at the property next door was a phenomenon they all wanted to explore. They were cleared through the bureau, the NYPD and the city.

It seemed a restless day. Whitney sat with Angela at the bank of screens that afternoon, just watching the strange shadows. But they didn't change, and they didn't do anything. She went upstairs to lie down, surprised that she was so tired when she hadn't really done anything.

In time, Angus Avery would certainly break. He would explain how he had gotten the car out of the garage, and how he had kidnapped Captain Tyler.

If he was indeed guilty.

Jude had told her briefly that the task force would remain together, gathering evidence on the chauffeur, Eric Len. So far, they really had nothing on him except that the car had been assigned to him, and he had been Avery's driver.

She felt…dissatisfied. Somehow, she had thought that they'd have a more thorough completion of the case, that they'd understand what had happened, how and why.

As she lay on her bed, she heard the dog again. She sat up. He appeared by her side again, whining softly.

"I don't even know your name!" she told him, stroking the soft ears. "Most people can't see you. Not even my friends—though Jake can hear you—but I can. I even feel how soft your fur is, even though you're a ghost dog."

The dog whined softly again. He wagged his tail.

She started, hearing a rap at her door. Angela's voice came to her quietly. "Whitney, Jude is here to see you."

The fluttering of her heart alarmed her, and she smoothed down her shirt and her hair as if to soothe it. He'd probably come about something to do with the case.

She left her room and walked calmly down the

stairs. Jude was there in the hallway, watching the screens with the others. "It has to be something in the air. Or a chemical that seeped into the floor that only shows on your high-resolution film," Jude said.

The others didn't answer him. He didn't notice. He had seen her coming down.

"Is there anything new?" she asked him. He had looked perplexed at the station, as if he, too, had found the closure of the case to be anticlimactic.

He shook his head. And then his lips curled as he gave her the grin that never failed to start that electric sensation in her veins. "I came to see if you wanted to go to dinner with me without having to discuss blood and murder—or Jack the Ripper."

Angela and Jackson looked at her and smiled like a pair of tolerant parents. Jake emitted a cough and lowered his head, grinning.

"I, uh, guess I should invite you all," Jude said.

Jake stood up, laughing openly. "Right. That's what you want. Go on, get out of here—and just give us a call if it gets too late. Shoo, children!"

She looked at Jude. He had no answer for the others; he was looking back at her with humor in his gray eyes, and more—the *whatever* that was between them that had made Jake laugh.

She met his gaze and smiled her acknowledgment. "I'll just get my purse."

She did so. Out in his car, he looked at her again. "Steak, sushi, Chinese, Japanese, Thai, Mexican…what would you like?"

"Privacy," she said.

He didn't reply. He put the car into gear and headed

straight for Hell's Kitchen. He'd barely closed the door to his apartment before she turned into his arms.

And he enveloped her in his.

His mouth was wonderful on hers, everything that she had expected and imagined. He could kiss with force and coercion, his mouth so firm but never hurtful. Just standing there, still fully clothed, she felt as if she shared a greater intimacy with a single kiss than she had known before in her life.

She felt his hands on her body, his fingers at the small buttons of her blouse. Their mouths were still locked when she touched his holstered gun and he touched hers, and they both laughed, and breathlessly removed the guns and their holsters.

They were still in the hallway, lips meeting and parting, some kisses long and deep, deliciously sloppy, hot and wet, and some brief as they parted to get a better hold on a button or a zipper. Whitney was half undressed when they heard a sound coming from the computer room.

"Oh, hell!" Jude murmured.

"Oh, hell!" Whitney agreed, trying to rearrange her blouse.

"No!" Jude protested. "The bedroom, go—I'll send my father away!"

She grabbed their guns and holsters and scurried through the apartment, listening to his voice, and hearing the sound of the door shutting between the two apartments. She hesitated in the hall, and plunged into a room. There had only been a choice of two; she'd chosen correctly.

His room was lined with books, hardwood, art deco

furnishings and a large bed that was covered with a black-and-crimson comforter. She set the holsters on the bedside table and turned, and as she did so, she found herself swept up and back in his arms, breathless, and heedless, her heart pounding and her body thrumming with expectation.

They plummeted to the bed together. Again he kissed her, trying to do away with the last of her buttons. "I've wanted this," he said hoarsely, "since I first saw you."

"And then, of course, we bonded—over the autopsy table," she said, grimacing.

"Since I first saw you," he repeated, pressing his lips to her throat.

"You're such a liar. You thought I was an annoying college kid sent to darken your day."

He paused, shrugged and grinned. "All right, well, an annoying college kid, but…" He paused, staring down into her eyes. "A golden one. I wanted to touch you. To reach out and touch you."

"You were really beautiful, too," she said softly, running her fingers softly over the hair on his forehead.

"Liar, you thought I was an annoying macho cop," he said.

"Yes," she said huskily. "But a damn good-looking one."

He laughed. His fingers entwined with hers as he leaned against her again, and their kiss then was long and passionate, filled with sweet liquid hunger. When they broke apart, they struggled with one another's clothing, as if neither could be freed from it quickly enough, as if the clothing burned, and only their naked flesh touching could ease the fire.

Not the case at all, Whitney thought, enlivened, awakened by the contact. She felt his heart, his breathing, the thrumming that seemed to pulse through his body as it did hers. He was everything she had imagined, long and hard and rock-muscled, so vibrant in his every move. *Macho man, indeed.* He seemed the leader in their urgent desire to be together, but she realized that it was only the hunger searing through him, and something of a desperate desire to please her, and make her want him as he wanted her. He need not try…

His mouth roamed her body and returned to her lips. She explored the length of his back, pressed her lips to his shoulders, delicately teased along his torso and slipped her fingers between them, cradling the rise of his erection. His body jerked and trembled, his lips found her flesh, her breasts, and he eased from her, moving down the length of her body. She trembled and undulated, and then writhed, feeling the pressure of his body on hers, and the seduction of his mouth and tongue. In seconds, a jolt ripped through her; she cried out, twisting, tugging him back into her arms, finding his mouth, and then his shoulders, feeling the jerk and ripple of his biceps and his abs, and the sheer sleek pleasure of his flesh.

In seconds they were entangled again, exploring and seeking one another's bodies, and then they rolled, and suddenly he was within her, and it was as if her mind and heart and soul stopped as one, and then began to tremble in the damp heat that arose between them, so slick and hungry and urgent. He knew how to tease and seduce, and how to give, and then give way when they reached that point where satiation was a thirst that had to be quenched. She climaxed at a point of delirium, and clung to him, feeling the volatile shudder of his body in the violence of his own, and she felt his arms around her, the coolness of the sheets and the sheen of perspiration that covered them both. And they lay entwined, he within her still, she wishing that they could remain so forever. It was long moments before he lifted her chin, met her eyes and brushed her lips with the whisper of a kiss.

"Gold," he told her. "Spun gold."

She laughed. "Sheer macho power!"

"Hey!"

"In a good way. Champagne?" she asked.

"Beer?" he countered.

"That will do, but not yet," she told him, finding his lips again and rolling onto his chest. Her turn. She kissed his chest, lowered her liquid caresses and made love to him, teasing him, telling him not to move, until he had to move, cradling her to him, rolling again and again, and making love side to side, kissing and not, moving languidly and then again with the speed of light. When they lay at last, spent again, she found herself suddenly wondering at her abandon and passion, and whispering, "Honestly, I don't do this…often."

He laughed. "Neither do I."

She grinned, and they lay there a moment. And then her grin faded. "That was so strange…"

"No, you're supposed to say something like, wow, that was great, the best I ever had," Jude told her.

She smiled, touched his cheek. "I didn't mean that.

I mean, I have wanted…well, *you,* many a time in the last few days. But this has to be the best I've ever had because it's the first time since I came to New York that I actually didn't think about the case!"

He was silent for a moment. "Beer. We do get to celebrate, I believe. Case over. Done." He stood, untangling himself regretfully from her to do so. "I actually am hungry. We can go to dinner at some point. Or call out for delivery."

"I rather like that idea," Whitney said.

Jude grinned and left the room, easy and natural in his nakedness. She watched him go, and she thought again that he was a beautiful man, and she wondered, now that she knew him, if anyone could ever be the same. She didn't want to think about that; she didn't want to think about leaving New York. She didn't want to think about not seeing Jude.

She started, feeling something leap up on the bed.

Sitting up, she stared down the length of the sheets.

There was a cat there.

She blinked. It remained.

"Are you real?" she whispered.

The cat let out a meow and padded its way toward her. She reached out. The cat came to her, happy to have its ears scratched. "You're real, right?" she asked. "I can't be the person always haunted by animal ghosts, right? I can feel you, but I can feel the dog that comes to me at Blair House, the dog that led me to the bodies."

The cat allowed herself to be stroked, and then leaped off the bed and disappeared. Jude came back a moment later, carrying a wooden tray with two beer bottles and a plate of cheese and crackers.

"Sorry, I'm afraid I don't have much. If you're hungry, maybe I should call now. There's a great Chinese place just down on the corner that delivers."

Whitney reached for one of the beers and took a long swallow. She tried to speak naturally. "Do you have a cat?"

He frowned. "Allison. Was she in here? The bedroom is supposed to be off-limits. I'm sorry—hope you're not allergic."

"I'm not. I love animals." She took another long swallow of her beer and sat up. She smiled for a moment. She wasn't sure that she'd carried through on any of her intimate dreams and fantasies regarding Jude; she had certainly never imagined how easy it would be to sit cross-legged and naked with him on his bed, drinking beer and eating cheese and crackers.

But she noted that he was distracted again, and she didn't question him.

"We're just not as celebratory as we should be," she said softly.

He looked at her, startled.

"You're right. Neither of us feels like the case is completed. What does Jackson have to say?"

"Jackson tends to be quiet and think things through," Whitney told him. "He said that he could see several scenarios. Men with wealth and power—"

"Yeah, they can feel entitled. Or maybe Avery didn't feel so entitled. Maybe his finances weren't that hot, and everything was riding on this movie. The killer was organized, so maybe Angus Avery really did plan it all out, and those girls died the way they did with him having a very special agenda."

"And here's the thing. The movie will sell like hot-cakes," Whitney said.

"It's not completed, though."

"Don't worry—the producers will bring in a director to finish the movie. No one will let go of a box-office blockbuster like this is sure to be," Whitney assured him.

Jude munched a cracker and then said thoughtfully, "Well, Angus Avery was in the city when the first two girls were killed. He did have a motive, twisted as it might be. He knew the history of the House of Spiritualism, and he certainly had the kind of movie money at his disposal to get around. Anyone out there might have studied the Ripper case, and Carrie Brown is of historical note, as well."

"You don't believe it," she said.

"It's just—it just doesn't sit right. It would have been easy enough, I think, for anyone to have slipped into the veterans' home—it's open to visitors, and it's not a prison. They're still feeling their way on how to run the place. But whoever did this seemed familiar with police procedure. I suppose that Angus Avery could have worked with any number of police consultants over the years. And he would know that he had to kill quickly—before a victim could scratch him, or get a hold of him in any way that would give us DNA. These days, I'm sure, with the number of police-procedural shows, most people are aware that DNA can be a clincher in court. He would know, too, that the law would require due process…but so would anyone. Here's what I don't get as well—he knew nothing about anatomy, as far as we can discover. Not that the Ripper murders were necessarily carried out by someone with real medical knowledge—but the killer did know *something* about anatomy."

Whitney shrugged. "Maybe he studied anatomy books?" she suggested.

"Thing is, a lot of this is harder than some people realize. You need strength to strangle someone. You really need strength to nearly sever a human head." He shook his head. "One of the limo drivers had to be involved. That, or the killer had to have an accomplice. There had to be some blood on him, and that costume would have been noticed in the subway—even in New York." He took another long swig of his beer, and moved the tray onto the bedside table. He leaned toward her. "There's still work to be done, I'm afraid, if I'm going to accept all this. But, at least, I can pray that the murders will stop."

Whitney nodded. She tried to shake off the somber mood of their discussion. "I say we call in for Chinese."

"I think that's great," he said huskily.

"I'm going to phone Angela and let her know that I'll be late."

He reached out, stroking her cheek. "Call Angela, and tell her that I'll have you back in the morning," he suggested.

She smiled. "Okay."

It was an amazing night; the Chinese food was delicious. Whitney wasn't even sure what they ate. She teased him about being a cat person; he told her that cats were independent, and so, made very good pets. "Dogs are great animals, but they need a lot of attention," he said.

Whitney thought about her ghost dog. "They give a lot of love," she told him.

"That may be true," he said. "But cats rule. And," he said, pulling her close to him, "people can give devotion and love and all that, too," he said.

"Not to mention really great sex?" she whispered.

It hadn't actually been an invitation, but he took it as such. When they were exhausted and replete again, it was late, and they both drifted off to sleep, still entangled with one another, as if they needed to connect forever.

But that night, Whitney dreamed. She was back in her room at Blair House, and she woke because the dog was tugging at her nightgown. She didn't want to waken, but she did. She sat up. The dog wasn't alone. Her room was filled with women. Annie Doherty stood at the front of the group, her eyes sad and entreating. Behind her were other women; at first, she thought that they were all in period dress. But then she realized that there were four who were not. She recognized the face that Jake Mallory had created on the computer, the face of Sarah Larson. And there was Virginia Rockford, and behind her, Melody Tatum. And in the far corner, Jane Doe dry, the girl who still had no name.

One by one, they turned and started out of the room.

The dog remained, tugging at her nightgown, whining and thudding his tail. She was supposed to follow, she knew.

They led her down the stairs and out of the house, and the night was misty and dark. They walked down the block, and she could see faint lines, as if of a movie projection in the air, where the House of Spiritualism had once stood. And she could see the maw of the foundation.

Down to the depths, where the darkness writhed. It was the same shapeless…shape that they had seen on their screens.

Whitney didn't understand what she was supposed to see—the bodies of the women murdered at the House of Spiritualism had been discovered; the bodies of the current victims were at the morgue as well.

But there was something else there. And she was supposed to find it.

She felt as if the abyss were sucking her in, as if she were moving on some kind of astral plane in that direction.

She paused. The shadow rose from the ground and took form—the silhouette of a man in a cloak and a tall hat, and he held a long-bladed knife. She saw a woman walking near him, and saw the man reach out, and he jerked her against his form, his one hand choking her…

She began to slump against him.

He ripped the knife against her throat, and shadow blood began to spurt from the wound.

Suddenly, a loud screeching noise burst upon her. She awoke, startled, not sure where she was.

She felt warm arms around her; naked flesh, powerful arms.

"Just the phone," Jude said, rising by her side and fumbling on the nightstand for his phone.

He answered it. "Crosby."

His features went taut, his mouth pursed into a grim line.

"I'm on the way," he said.

Whitney stared at him.

"There's another victim—off Broadway. Her throat was slashed, probably half an hour ago now. She was discovered by one of the police officers patrolling the area. The blood was still oozing from her throat and her body was still warm."

14

Just like Elizabeth Stride, the fourth victim of Jack the Ripper. This woman's throat had been slit, but there was no sign of any mutilation on her body. The officer had come upon the killer, and interrupted him before he could carry out any further atrocity.

Hunched down by the body, Jude felt numb and dull as Dr. Fullbright performed his cursory inspection of the victim before the body was taken for autopsy.

Could he have stopped this anyway? Doubtful.

But he stood, searching the street. He looked over at Sayer, who was standing quietly about five feet away.

"Ellis—"

"Jude," Ellis said quietly, "I have our entire task force and half the beat police in the city walking the streets."

"There's going to be a second murder," Jude said. "There's going to be a second murder very soon, and when we find that body, it will be more horribly mutilated. This killer is definitely imitating the past closely, and the women in the Victorian East End were killed within the hour—the double event. Someone else is going to die soon—if he hasn't chosen his second victim already."

"I'd say she died just minutes before 1:00 a.m.," Fullbright announced. He looked up at Jude. "But you didn't really need me here to know that—Officer Grayson walked this street at a quarter to one and walked it again thirty minutes later and found Miss Laurie Thibault."

Jude felt as if he could barely stand still; he was powerless, and he loathed the killer with a frightening vengeance. They were being played, and in a city the size of New York, there was little that he could do about it. Hundreds of police officers were now searching the area.

They knew the victim's name because her handbag was still over her shoulder. She had performed in a burlesque show running in a tent near South Street Seaport, according to the flyers in her handbag. Since her cell phone was in her bag as well, they'd been able to call the director of the show, who had already told them that they'd been to a party at the Ritz downtown; she had left to get a cab home at eleven-thirty, and no one knew what had happened from there.

Jackson stood near him; he had already assessed the body. Whitney was at his side. The rest of the team was with the police, searching the area and desperately trying to stop the next murder.

"Oh, my God!" Whitney gasped suddenly.

Jackson looked at her, waiting. Jude walked to her, taking her by the shoulders.

"The construction site!" she said.

"We have cameras in there—we've observed from the beginning," Jackson said, frowning.

"The next victim won't be down in the deep section. We'll find her somewhere along the chain-link fence."

She turned, hurrying down Broadway. Jude, Ellis and Jackson followed her.

Jude damned the city for not having brighter lights in the area. Budget cuts, he thought resentfully. Running, he saw that there was some kind of dark blob on the sidewalk. A chill swept through him.

She had been right. Whitney had been right.

He got ahead of her, calling out for the others to stay back.

The woman lay on her back, her arms fallen to the side. Her palms were upward, and her fingers were slightly curled.

Jude hunched down. His hands were already gloved. He didn't touch her to see if she was alive—it was more than evident that she was not. Her one leg was crossed over her body; her abdomen was sliced open, and her organs had been ripped out and arranged around the body.

He steeled himself and took a deep breath.

How in the hell had the killer managed what he had at this time? The place was crawling with cops, and there were lights everywhere now...

He had functioned by sleight of hand, Jude thought. *While all the attention had been at the first murder scene, he had carried out his gruesome mutilations. He'd had to have known as well that he would be in extreme danger of being caught. Perhaps that had made it all a greater thrill for him.*

The double event. The killer had gone for the double event on the night that Angus Avery had been under house arrest. The body of this woman lay identical in pose and mutilation to that of Catherine Eddowes, fourth Ripper victim. When the autopsy was performed, he knew the findings would be nearly exact.

She was warm.

She hadn't been dead long.

He spoke into his radio mouthpiece. "Get Fullbright over here. Get him over here now. And get every man on the street moving. Subways, alleys—set up a road-block along Broadway. I don't care if we bring the entire city to a halt."

He stood, feeling as if his veins and muscles were made of ice, as if he had grown very old. Then he walked over to where the others were standing a distance from the body. "Ellis, stay with Fullbright, please. Keep every available person searching the streets. Somewhere nearby, we're going to find the words *The Juwes are not the men to be blamed for nothing* written over a doorway—and there will be a bloody piece of our victim's clothing beneath it."

He looked around the street. He stood and started walking. A bit in the distance, he could see the spire of Trinity church. He considered himself a decently spiritual man, if not a religious one. At that moment, he wished he could go into the church, fall on his knees and beg God to send them all a miracle.

He started for the church, but then he paused.

He knew where he would find the writing.

Whitney must have read his mind.

"Blair House," she said from behind him.

They were both right; the gate to the house was open. They didn't need to speak to one another to remember to touch nothing.

On the porch lay a bloody strip of fabric, ripped from the last victim's skirt.

And over the door of Blair House was written in chalk the words that Jude had just said.

The Juwes are not the men to be blamed for nothing.

"We'll get Forensics," he said wearily. "We're going to need several teams out here on the streets tonight. No one sleeps."

If the city had been in a panic before, it was afire now.

The papers and media carried nothing but information on the New York murders, and the hotels in Lower Manhattan were emptying.

Angus Avery screamed for his freedom, demanding that he be set free from his electronic monitor.

But because of the evidence against him, Deputy Chief Green could continue to hold him; it was more than possible that the murders had been committed by more than one person, and that Avery's accomplice had purposely timed the double event when he was under monitor and guard, therefore trying to prove his innocence.

Jude spent the day at the station reinterviewing every possible suspect and witness. He had in Captain Tyler and Major Radison, as well. He had in the best possible sketch artist, and he gave the sketch to both Hannah and Jake Mallory, and both returned the typical Victorian gaslight picture of the Ripper, excellent 3-D images.

He questioned both men further about the killer's face.

Captain Tyler proved to be no help. He hadn't seen the man's face; he had only seen the figure at a distance. Nor had his memory returned about anyone having been in his room. He'd had some water before he went to sleep...he often did when he could. But he hadn't seen anyone in his room.

Major Radison gave the question of the man's face deep thought. "It was very odd," he said.

"Odd how?" Jude asked him.

"Like—blank. As if he was wearing some kind of Venetian carnival mask," Major Radison said after a minute. "As if there was really nothing there, just a white face with no expression and nothing...live about it. Nothing real at all."

Jude sat back, drumming his fingers on the table. *A mask. That brought him back to costumes and make-believe—the movies.*

But it was true that Angus Avery had not left his apartment during the night. His ankle monitor had not gone off. Any device could be hacked, Jude knew, but several cops had been watching the director's place. It would have been damn hard for them all to be crooked.

He allowed the old soldiers who had tried valiantly to help to return to the veterans' home. They had become good friends, so it seemed, in the time they had been at the police station. Trying to help had seemed to strengthen them both, and Tyler was mortified that he couldn't help more. Jenna, at the station with Jackson, Whitney and Jake, assured the captain that he had done a great deal for them, and it was not his fault that he could remember nothing—it had been the drug.

He had Mrs. Allie Lipton, the wardrobe mistress from the movie set, brought in. At first, she stubbornly denied having made any mistake on her calculations; she knew that Angus Avery was strict. He had to stay on budget. He wouldn't stay on budget by having to replace costumes stolen by two-bit extras.

But then he asked her why one of the limo drivers had had to go to a fabric store.

She was an older woman, plump, somewhere over fifty. He saw her hesitate, though she quickly gathered her wits and said, "Costumes are always tearing, and I'm always mending something. He went for patches, thread, that kind of thing."

"And, of course, a receipt was turned in. I'll get a copy of that receipt," Jude told her. "Even if you don't have it, believe me, I'll track down your purchase."

She sat very still, and then her lower lip began to tremble. "One of the cloaks disappeared—they're actually caped coats, you know—regular coats with sleeves, and then a short cape over the shoulders. I didn't dare tell the director. He would have said it was my fault. And I could swear that every extra on the set returned his or her costume. I could swear it! Avery would have fired me for not having control. I can't get jobs as easily as I used to—you've got to believe me, Detective, the movies are run by the *young*."

Jude stared at her. He wanted to tell her that her lie might have cost lives, but it wouldn't have been true—

they had suspected that the killer's period costume had come from the movie set.

"When did the cloak disappear?" he asked her. "At the shoot at the construction site?"

"Oh, no—two weeks before that," she told him. "We'd been working on Staten Island. That's when the cloak disappeared. I didn't try to replace it until we had the same number of extras working again. That's why...that's why I didn't believe that its disappearance could be related to the killing that night. And the papers said that there were Jack the Ripper victims, but they didn't say that anyone had actually *seen* Jack the Ripper walking around. Please, please, you can't tell Mr. Avery. Of course, Mr. Avery has a court date now, but...oh, he couldn't have anything to do with this! Detective, I know that you have this information, but, please, please, please, don't report me to the powers that be at the movie company. I used my own money to buy the fabric to replace the cloak. Please."

He couldn't help but feel sorry for Allie Lipton. "I need the information for our investigation, Mrs. Lipton. I'm not the movie police."

He let her go; she could return to work. Apparently, the assistant director was filming action shots that day with the film's stunt performers.

Sherry Blanco came back in, her lawyer in tow this time. Jude was surprised, but he had nothing against the lawyer sitting in.

"Miss Blanco, we're not accusing you of anything, but I'm afraid that you were working with a murderer at some point during this film," he said.

She looked at her lawyer, and then at Jude. "I told

you, and I don't know why you don't understand this. I don't know the extras. Sometimes I don't even *see* the extras." She sat back, shaking her head, and then she leaned forward again. "Look, I'm not trying to pull any kind of…rank here, but I'm the *star*. Stars don't have to know the extras, or even the bit players. I don't eat with the others, I don't get warm and chummy with the others. And, hey, I'm not a nasty person. I do make friends, but you have to realize, people want to use me, too. I have to keep my distance."

He smiled. She wasn't going to give him anything. He was going to give her something to think about. "Well, I suppose that's good. Because the killer could still be working on your set."

"You've arrested Angus Avery, remember?"

"Two women were killed last night, remember?" Jude countered.

"Then maybe you should let Angus go," she said, smirking.

"Maybe. And maybe he has been working with someone. Killers who work together have certainly caused a great deal of death and agony over the years. But you are the star. I guess you don't have to worry, walking out of your trailer or getting into a limo."

She turned white.

"Detective!" her lawyer snapped.

"Yes? Can you point out what's untrue about my words?" he asked.

Her attorney wasn't a fool. He stood, drawing her up by the elbow. "My client isn't under arrest. She has answered all your questions, and we're leaving."

Jude stood and smiled. "Thank you so much. Enjoy your day, Miss Blanco."

When they left, he discovered that Deputy Chief Green wanted to see him in the lab. He knew that Whitney and Jake had been at the computers all day with Hannah, searching for any trigger in the background of any possible suspect or major player in the case. But he and Jackson weren't heading to the computers; they were off to see Judith Garner in the lab.

As they walked to the lab, Jude again felt a sinking feeling.

"A letter—we've received a letter," he said, seeing Green. In London, back in the day of Jack the Ripper, the police had received hundreds of letters from those wanting to solve the case, and those convinced they were, or knew, Jack the Ripper.

Green nodded grimly. "In the mail, postmarked Lower Manhattan," Green told him.

"And it's an exact copy of the letter sent to George Lusk, head of the Whitechapel Vigilante Committee— the 'From Hell' letter. It's one of the few letters they considered not to be fake, am I correct?"

"You are," the deputy chief told him. "It's not a photocopy, or out of a copier. The killer forged the handwriting. And," he added painfully, "it came from a tissue we believe to belong to the second victim last night."

In the lab, Judith Garner had the letter under glass as she prepared it for the many tests she would do. She greeted Jude with tight grim lips. "What do you make of it?" she asked.

He read the letter; he'd seen the copy at Scotland

Yard, but he hadn't memorized it. Odd to think that once, he'd thought of the Jack the Ripper case as little more than a social commentary, when he was learning about law enforcement, and a lesson in the improvement of law enforcement and new techniques in investigative tools over the years.

But he could remember the letter, and the words were the same, just as the stains on the paper seemed to be the same.

> From hell
> Mr. Lusk
> Sor
> I send you half the Kidne I took from one woman and prasarved it for you the tother piece I fried and at it was very nise. I may send you the bloody knif that took it out if you only wate a whil longer.
> Signed
> Catch me when you can Mishter Lusk

"He's dancing around us, Jude. He's making a mockery of one of the finest police departments in the county," Green said.

Jude opted not to remind him that he hadn't been entirely convinced that they had finished with the arrest of Angus Avery. They still had a killer out there.

He looked at Judith. "And the tissue that came with it?" he asked.

"Human kidney," she said. "I don't know yet if it will prove to have belonged to our second victim from last night."

"Do you have anything else?" he asked her hopefully.

"Hey," she protested, "I found the trace on the coat. My team found the blood in the limo. And I'm still working on that hundred-dollar-bill you gave me. So far, I've found a lot of cocaine, and fingerprints on top of fingerprints. We're still sorting them all out, but even then, we're going to have to go through hundreds and hundreds. We've worked around the clock in here, too, you know," she said.

"I know, Judith. Thank you." He looked at Deputy Chief Green. "I want to get Bobby Walden back in for questioning, too. I'm sure he'll come in with an attorney this time. And the team has been out at the garage where the limos are serviced and parked, but I want to see the place myself."

"That's all going to have to wait. Fullbright is expecting you in autopsy," Green told him.

"I've been through every extra hired by the movie company," Hannah said, leaning her head on the computer. "I studied the records of two hundred people. I found two medical students, but both were indisputably on duty at the hospital last night and the night that Virginia Rockford was killed. I searched out every record on Harold Patterson, the high-class pimp, and he's never even had surgery. I've gone through records and alibis until I can't see anymore," she moaned.

"Maybe we're actually looking in the wrong direction," Whitney said.

Both Hannah and Jake looked at her, frowning.

She grimaced. "The killer seems to know something about anatomy. He'd have to—right? Not like a doctor, but at least like a butcher. But we think he also knows something about law enforcement and crime scene investigation. All things easily obtainable online these days—but, as we all know, online information isn't always reliable, and crime shows and books are works of fiction. This guy has been really good. The first two murders—not the accepted five Ripper murders, but the ones we have in the files—might have been practice for him. Especially with Sarah Larson—Jane Doe wet. Maybe he messed up, and maybe he was afraid that he had left some kind of evidence on her, and that's why she went in the water. She was there at least a week, and her body was sorely compromised. With the woman who is still Jane Doe, he was careful and lucky—no one did miss her, but the way that she was stabbed, it was doubtful that, had she lived, she would have ever been able to speak. They weren't just victims he used to follow the Jack the Ripper path—they were experiments for him. And, I could be way off base, but who would understand forensic science and crime detection better than a cop or some kind of a crime scene official?"

Jake and Hannah stared at her. "Do you know how many people you're talking about?" Hannah asked woefully.

Jake shook his head. "No. She's on to something. He hesitated. "What about that detective—Ellis Sayer? He seems to follow a little too closely in Jude's wake. Perhaps he's someone who wants to be a bigger part of the case than he is."

"Ellis Sayer?" Hannah said incredulously.

"Just give a look," Jake said.

"It can't be Ellis!" Whitney said.

"That's exactly why we should investigate," Jake said.

They did. And they could find nothing on him other than the fact that he had been with the police force over twenty years, climbing the ranks through hard work and commendations.

"But we don't know where he was at the time of the murders," Jake pointed out.

"He was always available after," Whitney said. "Jake, look through all that and see if he ever did any work in film."

"Ellis?" Hannah asked. "You must be joking!"

They looked.

They found no film connection, and no medical training—and no work at a grocery store, butcher shop or any place that might have taught him a thing about anatomy.

"Hey, hey—go back a page!" Jake told Hannah.

She frowned and clicked a button. "We're on Face-book, Jake—what do you see?"

"On the side there—'friends' pictures."

"He was in a play!" Hannah said.

"It looks like a college production of *Hamlet,*" Whitney said.

"We can't hang him on a college theatrical," Jake said.

"No, but I guess he bears watching," Whitney murmured.

"Maybe," Jake agreed. "You know who else takes anatomy classes?" he asked.

"Who?" Whitney and Hannah said.

"Art students," Jake said.

Hannah groaned and threw herself at the computer.

"Hey, hey," Jake said, rubbing her back. "It's okay, kid."

"I think it's time to really look into the NYPD," Whitney said softly.

"You want me to sit here, on an NYPD computer, and keep looking up a bunch of detectives and officers who could get really pissed and get me fired?" Hannah demanded in a whisper.

"We'll do it from Blair House," Jake said.

"There are cops all around Blair House," Hannah said.

"Then we'll be safe," Jake said with a grin.

Whitney frowned. "Jude is attending at the morgue. Autopsy is scheduled for the double-event victims today," she reminded them.

They both looked at her.

"Excuse me just one moment," she said. She stepped aside and called Jude's cell.

"Hey," she said when he answered.

"Hey," he returned. He sounded weary and dejected.

"Are you going to autopsy?" she asked him.

"I'm on my way now," he said.

"I attended the others," she reminded him.

He was silent.

"There you go," she said lightly. "Sleep with a cop, and all of a sudden he doesn't want to call you for an autopsy."

She hoped that she had brought at least a flicker of a grin to his lips. "Whitney, I don't think that I even need to be there—I know what Fullbright will find. No trace, no evidence. The first victim will have strangulation marks, and her throat will have been slashed nearly ear to ear—like Elizabeth Stride. The second victim is going to have the same mutilations as Ripper victim Catherine Eddowes. I'm going to go and spend several hours and watch the horrible cruelty that an intelligent, narcissistic psychopath can inflict on another human being. I'm not sure I should be wasting my time. We're missing something. We're missing something that we should see clearly, and I just need to go over and over all the records and notes that we have." He was silent a moment. "Do me a favor, huh?"

"Sure," she said.

"I'm afraid that this killer sees us. He knows all of us who are cops, and he sure as hell knew that an FBI team was staying at Blair House. Be careful. Be really careful."

"Patrol cars are prowling all around Blair House, Jude. It's probably the safest place in the world right now. And you do know that I carry a gun, right? But, actually, you just gave me an idea."

"What's that?"

She lowered her voice. "We were going to head to Blair House to check out the NYPD, but I think I've just had a better idea."

"The NYPD," he said thoughtfully once she'd explained. "Someone on the inside. That's a terrifying thought."

"We're grasping at straws, maybe. But we knew from the beginning that it was a mammoth haystack."

"What's the idea I gave you?"

"We're going to stop in on your father."

Dr. Fullbright wasn't horrified; he was fascinated. "It's uncanny," he told Jude. "It's absolutely uncanny, the way this killer has replicated the past."

Jude stood silently. The body on the table was hardly recognizable as a woman. The killer had slashed her earlobes and her face. He had carried out the mutilations in very little time. He had planned it all carefully. He had staked out his victims, and he had somehow coerced them to meet him, or he had stumbled upon them.

No, he had selected his victims. He had gone to the strip club and selected Sarah Larson, a woman who had longed to be a Broadway dancer. He had selected Melody Tatum, paying cash to make sure that he'd have a woman where he wanted her.

He was attending burlesque shows, seeking those who might tend to be for sale.

He had money—he had paid cash for Melody.

"Is there anything you can tell me that can help me find the man killing these women? I don't need a lecture—I've seen the Ripper files," Jude said.

Fullbright looked at him, confused. "Jude, her clothing is over at the lab. I haven't anything on the body. We're in serious trouble when he decides to take his next victim. He'll emulate the murder of Mary Kelly, and you'll recall, he killed her at her apartment. He took his time, and he wallowed in a complete blood-bath."

Jude turned on his heel and left. He kept thinking about Whitney's suggestion that they might be dealing with someone in law enforcement. Someone who knew what the task force workers were doing—and how to avoid them.

It was a thought he didn't want to consider.

He looked at his watch; he wanted to get out to the garage, and he wanted an interview with Bobby Walden. He decided to deal with Bobby first, but when he checked with Ellis Sayer, Ellis told him that he'd been trying to pin down Bobby Walden all day.

"He was supposed to be filming some kind of a gang scene today, and he said that he wanted nothing more than to cooperate with the police, but he wouldn't be finished until five. Want me to get up to the set? I'm at the garage now. And you're going to want to see this. It's the most piss-poor security I've ever seen—there's a gate where the cars come in and out and register. And then there's a back fence with a gaping hole in it a mile wide. Anyone who knew where the keys were kept in the office could have walked through the fence and taken one of the cars out. Management has apparently planned on fixing it for months, but they just haven't gotten to it—never had any kind of trouble before, so they say."

"Make sure someone goes through all the cameras from the Brooklyn Bridge because I believe they might have caught something. The car had to have come back over."

"Yeah, we've done that," Ellis said. "I'm pretty sure

we found the car on the film, but we've enhanced and enhanced, and you can't see a face."

"The tags—"

"Muddied, front and back. We couldn't even go into court and verify it was the same car," Ellis said. "This is the most organized killer I've ever come across," he said. "I know my job, Jude."

"I'll go up to the set," Jude told Ellis. "I'm going to bring Jackson Crow with me. Maybe he can tell me if there's something strange I don't sense in any of the actors up there. Keep working the garage—look for anything that can help us."

He hung up, realizing that he didn't want Ellis questioning Bobby Walden. Ellis? He couldn't let himself become paranoid. *Logic, timing.*

Good old Ellis wasn't a killer. Unless he could teleport.

He still wished that Monty wasn't in the hospital.

And he realized that, since he'd spoken to Whitney, he suddenly mistrusted everyone. That was no way to run a task force, and yet, maybe it was the way that he had to be.

Andrew Crosby said it was fine for the little trio to come over when Whitney called him. He didn't question their motives.

But, first, they stopped by Blair House for Jake's laptop so that they could access his codes and programs. The street had reopened, but the police presence in front of the House of Spiritualism site and Blair House was still heavy. Will had remained at Blair House that day, following the police proceedings and studying the markings on the wall. Angela was with him, going through the film from the night before in hopes that one of the cameras might have caught something. They had both agreed that it would be good for the three of them to settle into Andrew's house for the afternoon, especially if they intended to look up records on New York's finest.

Whitney told Angela that as ridiculous as it might sound, she was wondering about Ellis Sayer.

"No, but it is curious, the way he was the one to *find* Captain Tyler. And it is curious that Captain Tyler was kidnapped from the veterans' hospital—and that *Ellis* found him wearing the coat," Whitney said.

"I think we'll get him over here later tonight," Angela said. "With just Jude, if we're growing suspicious of everyone else. I don't like to believe that the culprit could be a cop or an agent. But we can't eliminate any possibilities."

Angela watched her curiously as she spoke. "Hey, help me out in the kitchen for just a minute before you leave, will you?" she asked, "Hannah, you and Jake don't need Whitney if you're only going to grab a computer, do you?"

"Of course not!" Hannah said.

Angela drew Whitney into the kitchen and leaned against the counter. "I didn't get a chance to talk to you last night. You *knew* where the second victim in the double event was going to be found. How?"

"Oh, Angela, I was having the nicest evening of my life, and then I fell asleep. I dreamed I was here at Blair House, and the dog came to me—and all the victims. They led me back to the foundations of the old House of Spiritualism. And that thing—that seething black shadow we keep seeing on film—rose and became a silhouette of the movie image of the Ripper. I think… that the old ghosts were trying to warn me, except that others were with them—Sarah, Jane Doe—she didn't give me her real name—Melody and Virginia Rockford. Somehow, it goes back to the site. I wish I could figure out how!"

"We need to visit the site again," Angela said. "And you need to pay heed to that dog. He led you right to his mistress's grave site—and to the other skeletons."

"But last night was a dream, Angela. When we found the skeletons, I was awake when the dog came to me."

"We need to find out what that site has to tell us," Angela said.

Jake stuck his head into the kitchen. "I've got the laptop." He arched his brow. "You need more time?" he asked quietly.

"No, let's go on over to Andrew Crosby's apartment," Whitney said. "You never know what he may have to tell us."

The cast and crew of *O'Leary's* was valiantly struggling on, a man in a sweatshirt bearing the title of the movie informed Jude and Jackson. He was one of the film's executive producers, Griffin Byrd. They were having the assistant director work with crowd scenes that day, and they weren't avoiding Lower Manhattan, they were merely choosing sites to the north because there was obviously more space. Or so he put it.

"I can't believe that Angus Avery is guilty and, of

course, he has our support," Griffin told them. "This business is terrible—absolutely terrible. But you've had our cooperation all the way. We were out of the Broadway site before the investigation really began, and we've opened our props and costumes to the police, and the sets, of course. To our knowledge, everyone has cooperated fully. Sherry wasn't on the shooting schedule today, and I understand that she did come into the station. Bobby is just finishing a gang scene. I'll have him in here—" he paused to indicate the trailer where they sat, apparently Byrd's on-set office "—to speak with you as well."

"Mr. Byrd, if I were you, I'd shut down production until this situation is solved," Jackson said.

"But you're not me—shutting down would cost us millions," Byrd said.

"I thought this started out as a low-cost production," Jude said.

Byrd seemed to smirk at him. "Yes, that is *millions,*" Byrd said.

Jude forced himself to smile. "Mr. Byrd, the killer dressed up in a costume from this set."

"That's why you arrested Angus Avery, isn't it?" Byrd responded.

"Mind if we watch the filming?" Jude asked.

Byrd frowned, as if that was a confusing question.

"It's a closed set—there's been so much publicity," Byrd said.

"But I'm FBI," Jackson said politely. "And Detective Crosby is NYPD. We're hardly your customary gawkers."

Byrd apparently wasn't happy, but he couldn't think of a sound reason to refuse.

Jude was glad they had come out; the scene had just finished shooting, and Bobby Walden seemed to be hurrying away from the office.

"Mr. Walden!" Jude called.

Still in costume, breeches and a drab gray poet's shirt, Bobby paused. He turned back slowly, and then waved to them. "Hey, I was just going to change."

"We only need a few minutes," Jackson said.

A score of extras was walking behind the facade; flats that had nothing behind them except for the costume and prop tents that had been set up. The camera people were pulling equipment, and techs were running around as well, closing down for the day.

Bobby strode toward them. He smoothed back a handful of dark hair. "Bummer, huh? Who'd have figured old Angus, eh? And I guess he really was innocent—or had an accomplice."

"May we use your trailer?" Jackson inquired of Griffin Byrd, making certain that his tone implied that they wished to interview Bobby alone.

"Naturally. I'm just in from the West Coast, gentlemen, so you'll forgive me if I leave you for the day? I'm always available," Byrd assured them.

Jude glanced at Jackson, and he knew that they were thinking on similar lines.

Byrd didn't give a damn about any of the actors. He was a money man. He'd help the police; he'd hand over his own mother if that meant saving the movie.

Bobby came into the trailer and threw himself on the sofa, as if he were a nineteenth-century tough. He stared at them. "Guess you guys had something wrong, though, huh, what with what happened last night. There you go—another major bummer."

Jude realized he didn't like Bobby. He *really* didn't like Bobby Walden. But that didn't mean that he was guilty of anything other than being a self-serving prick.

"Bobby, we know that a cloak was stolen from wardrobe on this movie set, and worn by the killer who attacked Virginia Rockford," Jude said.

Bobby stared back at him, a flash of confusion in his eyes. "Yeah—it was worn by Angus Avery. I thought that was what you all figured." He sat up suddenly. "They don't include details on the news. Were the other women—the women killed last night—all chopped up?"

Jude didn't answer. "Bobby, do you realize that if you know anything at all, you could be charged as an accessory to murder? And if you can help us and you don't, other people can still die."

Bobby's eyes narrowed. "I don't know a damn thing. And if another woman is murdered, it's because you're inept." He stood. "*Catch me if you can*—isn't that what Jack the Ripper wrote when the London police couldn't find a bull's-eye ten feet in front of them? If a cloak was missing, and it was found with Angus's DNA or whatever, you've got your answer. Oh, but wait—Angus didn't kill anybody last night, did he?"

"Where were you last night, Bobby?" Jude asked him.

"On set until seven—and my limo driver took me home. My doorman saw me go in, and I promise you, he didn't see me go out," Bobby said.

"So, you were home alone?"

"What do you think? I was with a young lady. And if you want me to say more, you'll have to speak to my attorney. I don't kiss and tell. Why the hell would you suspect me? I'm a star!" he said, shaking his head. "May I change out of my costume now? It's been a long day!"

15

"Here's a reference to the Cult of Satan," Andrew said, bringing a book over to the desk where Whitney was sitting.

Jake and Hannah were busy at the computer. Since it was awkward for them all to stare at the screen—and Hannah and Jake were experts, and she was not—Whitney determined to let Andrew delve through his collection of books on New York history and tell her more about New York's past.

He produced a book. "I just read through this earlier. I'd heard rumor the Cult of Satan had a secret sign, see there—it was the emblem of Gilles de Rais."

"The serial killer who abused and murdered children—hundreds of them—in fifteenth-century France," Whitney said. "Yes, we've actually tossed his name around a few times since this all began."

Andrew nodded. "That's his coat of arms, with the blue edge and the fleur-de-lis. It was used as an emblem by the Cult of Satan. They would embroider it somewhere on their clothing, and show it to one another, because they didn't want their beliefs known. That book is on the cult. I guess it's not shocking. Life in Five Points must have been miserable, and poverty always breeds violence in one way or another. I suspect that the House of Spiritualism began as a place for tarot card readers and spiritualists, but Jonathan Black did move in and take over. Well, you've found the women he sacrificed. After I talked to you on the phone I looked up what I could find on the place, but there really wasn't much more. Except that I thought you might find this interesting. Satanists also valued reliquaries."

"Many religious tenets respect reliquaries," Whitney said. "I've thought about that as well—that a modern killer might be worshipping the body—or fragment— in a locket or a reliquary of some kind."

"Exactly. I think you were on the right track all along, and this may help you. In this book I discovered that Jonathan Black was rumored to have had an exceptionally 'holy' relic, if you will. He had a finger bone that had belonged to none other than Gilles de Rais."

Whitney stared at him. "And our killer *knew*, after more than three centuries, that he had the finger bone of Gilles de Rais?"

Andrew smiled. "Irish and Catholic here, Whitney. We believe in our relics, no matter how many years have passed. We cherish splinters of what we believe to be the true holy cross. It wouldn't be that different for a Satanist."

"I know, I know. We've talked about that, but I hadn't imagined anything so specific."

"We still don't know anything—it's a theory."

Whitney was thoughtful. She let out a sigh. "A good

one. Jonathan Black was supposedly killed and buried at the site when he scared even his own followers? I wonder if they saw all those women die—and began to wonder if they might be next."

Hannah came rushing into the office. "Guess what we found out?" she demanded.

"What?" Whitney asked.

"Dr. Wallace Fullbright has often been consulted for films and television. And, tada! He's worked as an extra in seven movies in the last ten years!" Hannah said.

"And," Jake said, coming in behind her, "we missed something in the records the other day. We didn't go back far enough. Ellis Sayer worked as a vet's assistant during his high school years. He could have assisted at many a surgery. Mammalian anatomy is pretty similar, when you're talking mainly cats and dogs. Not to mention the fact that the man has attended dozens of autopsy operations."

Jude and Jackson met up with the team and Hannah at the house at around seven; he was tired and hungry.

He listened to Jake and Hannah's new evidence. "No, we can let Ellis off the hook," Jude said, leaning back on the sofa, closing his eyes and gratefully taking a long swallow of his beer.

"Look, Jude, I know you work with the man—" Jake began.

Jude opened his eyes and looked at Jake, grimacing. "I don't deny that anyone can wear a mask, that we only *think* we really know people. But Ellis showed up too quickly on the scene to have carried out the last murders, at least, those which were carried out while Angus Avery was locked up. Ellis was with the first body last night when we found the second. The killer works with amazing speed, but Ellis couldn't have been where he was that fast. And I don't want to shoot down any theories, but Fullbright was at the morgue until he was called to the scene. I saw him arrive in the morgue vehicle. Hell, Fullbright is so excited about this rather than appalled, it has chilled my bones. But he's an M.E., and really good at what he does, and a body is a challenging puzzle to him."

"Jake, you've got to realize that what you're saying is true—and not true. Ellis Sayer had a right to be there with the body. Fullbright would have had the opportunity to destroy trace evidence on the body."

"I say it's one of the actors on the movie," Jude said.

"I don't think you're being fair!" Hannah said.

They all looked at her.

"My boyfriend has been an extra on movies. And he's the nicest guy in the world. You're being cruel to actors," Hannah said.

"Hannah, actors are fine people. Many are nice. Some may be crazy," Jude said patiently. He sighed deeply. "Okay, I don't believe the timing would have allowed Fullbright or Ellis Sayer to have been involved. But I'm close to the two of them, and I don't want it to be either one of them. I suspect an actor. Hannah is seeing an actor, so she doesn't want it to be an actor. We'll take the personal out of it. I've replayed the scenarios over and over in my head since I spoke with you, Whitney, and realized that yes, it could be someone really close," Jude said.

"I still say that Bobby Walden or Sherry Blanco are involved," Hannah insisted.

"Dr. Wallace Fullbright," Whitney said.

"One of the above. Or one of the other cops on the task force," Jude said wearily. "Or half the city of New York."

Will Chan was thoughtful. "Actors convince you that what isn't real is real. They have a talent to evoke emotion," he said.

"And magicians work off sleight of hand, convincing you that you're seeing what you're not," Whitney said. "A good magician can make you believe just about anything. Now you see it—now you don't."

"True. And it's a subtle talent. Bobby Walden might be a screen star, a personality," Jude said, "but a great actor he isn't. "

"Sherry Blanco won't be taking away any awards, either," Whitney agreed.

"We should have them all to dinner," Jackson suggested quietly.

Whitney grinned at him. "Jackson, neither Sherry Blanco nor Bobby Walden would accept an invitation to come to dinner here," Whitney said.

Jude looked at Jackson. "But, hey, we do take whatever we can get. The more people you eliminate, the better the focus on other suspects."

"The rest of the millions of people in Manhattan," Whitney said.

But Jude shook his head. "We know the killer. I honestly believe that—it's someone who is close to us, or someone we've had an interest in. And the killer—the second killer, because I don't believe that Angus Avery is innocent, just that we're supposed to think that—is high on his success regarding the last two kills. He feels that he is invincible. We've talked to and interviewed the killer, or he's someone we see every day. As far as wearing a costume and mask through his day-to-day life, he's doing that beautifully. But we know him, and he knows us, and that's how it's so easy for him to be a step ahead."

"And you really think we should ask Ellis Sayer and Fullbright to dinner?" Whitney asked.

"We are bound by the law. We've arrested Angus Avery because we had the evidence with which to arrest and charge the man. Our evidence trail is going nowhere. We have to trip this person up before they kill again."

"But what if we're wrong? What if it isn't Ellis or Fullbright?"

"And we may not learn the truth from a dinner. But at this point—what the hell? The two of them will accept an invitation. Let's go for it."

It was Whitney's turn to cook.

She'd decided on some down-home cooking and though she really should have had a lot more simmer time, she decided to throw together a jambalaya. Jude came into the kitchen while she was stirring her spicy mixture together. He slipped his arms around her waist and leaned low, inhaling the scent of her hair.

She was surprised at his action, but it didn't disturb her. The team knew about their relationship, and they all seemed to approve. She thought, too, that he needed a human touch that night.

"You all right?" she asked, turning into his arms.

"Hell, no, I'm scared to death. This guy is follow-ing in the Ripper's footsteps, but he isn't going by any timetable. More time passed between the second kill and the third and the fourth. Last night, he killed two. And if he manages to follow the Ripper's trail, the next event is someone indoors, and it will be the most gruesome murder yet. We have one man locked up who may or may not prove to be guilty, and it doesn't matter, because the murders are continuing."

"Stay here tonight?" she asked him.

He smiled. "Maybe. I know that I'm exhausted. This afternoon, I did mistrust everyone around us. But logi-cally, I realized I know who it *can't* be."

"You don't think it can be Ellis," she said gravely. "But you're still willing for us all to set him up."

"I don't believe you'll prove anything against him."

Whitney hesitated, looking at him. "I think it's someone who is a member of the current Cult of Satan."

Jude looked at her.

"The Cult of Satan was what Jonathan Black became high priest of—at least, I think," Whitney said. "I think that somehow, our guy was at the site next door—he may have even slipped in at night, like teenage kids are bound to do at dangerous but spooky places. He knew all about Jack the Ripper—and all the theories that the Ripper killed Carrie Brown, *and* he knew that Jonathan Black had been here, that he had a base of operations here. Whether any of these theories is true or not, it's as you once said—perception matters. I was with your dad today, and he showed me an emblem that all the members wore sewn secretly into their clothing somewhere. And he also told me that Jonathan Black was said to have had a cherished relic—something that contained a finger bone from the skeleton of Gilles de Rais—and he thought that his power came from the relic."

"Sounds reasonable," Jude said, and he smiled. "So, do I strip-search every suspect?" he asked dryly.

"No, but, if we do have a suspect..."

"Yeah," Jude said.

They heard the bell out at the gate ring. "One of our guests is here."

Whitney stayed with her jambalaya. Jude answered the door. It was Ellis Sayer who had arrived. She listened, as best she could as the others discussed the case with Ellis in the hallway. They seemed to be concentrating on the movie cast and crew, and Ellis was right there with them.

Angela came in to help her set the table. Whitney arched a brow to her.

"I'm feeling guilty. He seems like such a nice man. He has really humbly thanked us for having him over," she said.

"I know. I feel like we're beating a basset hound," Whitney said.

In a matter of minutes, the table was set. The doorbell rang again; Dr. Fullbright had arrived. He was loud and cheerful, thanking them all for having him for their get-together of the minds. The group moved in for the meal.

Will's place remained empty for the moment; he was still watching the screens.

The others began to sit, and Jude asked about drinks, offering Ellis a beer.

"Um, I don't know. Are we working tonight?" Ellis asked.

"I'll have a beer," Fullbright said. "I'm not working, and that's for certain. I don't care if more bodies come in. Tonight, I'm off!"

"Ellis, I'm having a beer, you can have a beer," Jude told him.

"All right. Thanks. I think this case is getting to all of us," Ellis said.

"In a way," Jude said, "it's still six separate murder cases, you know? So, tonight, we can throw out any speculation, any idea, because one thing is certain—this guy is damn good. Hey, Fullbright, what do you think about the killer's medical knowledge?"

Fullbright took a long swallow of his beer. Even in a knit polo shirt and jeans, he managed to look like a mad professor. "I don't know. I really don't know," he said, running his fingers through his unruly hair. "These days, you can learn just about anything on a computer. But there's a difference between seeing how something was done, and then actually managing to do it. Back in Victorian London, there were slaughter-houses and butchers everywhere, and people probably knew a lot more about mammalian anatomy than they do now, just in general. But did Jack—or our modern killer—have surgical skills? I don't think so. I think the old—and the new—have a basic understanding of anatomy. And that they're good with a knife."

"Actors?" Ellis said. He shook his head wearily. "Do you know how many we've interviewed? Some of them as nice as can be, and horrified, and helpful. Some of them scared of the cops—even when we try to tell them our investigation has nothing to do with a drug bust."

"Hey, any luck in the alley where Captain Tyler said he found the coat?" Jude asked Ellis.

"Nothing."

Jackson stood with his drink. "Cheers for this one evening, anyway, while we all seek the truth. To Whitney! Whitney is an amazing cook—she can whip up true Creole in a matter of minutes."

"Well, she is true Creole!" Jenna said.

"A total olio of humanity, actually," Whitney said, grinning at Ellis.

Whitney realized she felt horrible. She actually liked Ellis a lot. But then, Jude did, too. And he was willing to let them try to draw him out.

In fact, he was helping them get Ellis a little inebriated, or he was going to do his best to help.

"I think we have to look more and more closely at the actors in the movie, too," Jenna said. "After all, we're pretty damn sure that we have Angus Avery on Virginia Rockford's murder, but, obviously, he wasn't working alone. Or someone planted the evidence in his car. I still say it had to be the actors."

"I say that you need to look to the past," Fullbright said. He shook his head. "Jude, I don't want to depress you, but the original Ripper got away. Whoever is doing this is brilliant."

"Brilliant, but we all know that even the most brilliant criminal can get careless," Jude said.

"You haven't found anything, anything at all, on

the bodies?" Angela asked. "Dr. Fullbright, they really need you, you know."

"Look, what you all should do is force yourselves not to think about it for a night," Fullbright said. "Come back at it with fresh minds."

And then, when talk diverged into miscellany, Jude turned the conversation back to the case. "It was amazing how you found the captain—wearing that cloak," Jackson said.

"Yeah," Ellis said.

"Exactly where did you find him?" Whitney asked. "I know that when we were first looking for him, we searched all over."

"The City Hall subway station," Ellis said. "When you don't give us specifics, we keep watching the areas near where the victims were discovered."

He looked around the table at them all. "Someone knew that, right? Someone who has been watching us? I was supposed to find him, wasn't I? I was actually used, I think."

Ellis looked at Jude. "I—or another police officer— was supposed to find the captain. And he was supposed to have been arrested, and the public uproar would cause charges against Avery to be dropped."

Jude lifted his beer to Ellis. "If Angus Avery was being framed, then I'd say, yes, you were being used. You—or whatever cop stumbled across the captain. If Angus is one of the murderers, you might have been used, as well. He might have gone and kidnapped Captain Tyler, and planted the evidence, knowing that his partner was going to strike the next night and get him off the hook. Or, the killer is really relishing his accomplishments, and taking dangerous chances."

"Great. You think you're doing the right thing," Ellis said.

"You did the right thing. You did what you had to do," Jude assured him.

"Actors," Ellis said again, his basset head hanging.

"You were an actor," Whitney reminded him.

Ellis looked truly puzzled. He laughed. "I was in a play in school because I was madly in love with Briana Vanney. That's my theater experience!" He frowned and wagged a finger at her. "You investigated me!"

"I just happened to see a picture."

He shook his head. "You investigated *me,*" he repeated.

"We looked into everyone, Ellis. It was just curious. I thought I'd mention it."

"I had such a crush on Briana Vanney," he said.

"We all do strange things for love," Jude murmured.

Ellis stood. He wavered a little bit. "I have to go home. I have to go to sleep. Hell, Jude, I don't know how you do it."

"They've been long, hard days," Jude said.

"Hey, just go take a rest on the sofa," Angela suggested.

"Ellis, that's a great idea. Just go and lie down for a while. Trust me—I had to get through medical school," Fullbright told him. "You can't burn the candle at both ends forever."

"I should just go home," Ellis said. "Most of the guys—they're working in twelve-hour shifts, and somehow, they manage to go home and let it go for the hours they're off. Somehow, Jude, you can't do that with a case. Neither can I."

"Go lie down, Ellis," Jude said. "That's what I'm insisting you do right now—as head of the task force, I'm ordering you to get some rest."

Ellis looked at them all. Then he looked sadly at Whitney. "I'm not an actor. If I were, I wouldn't have been on the force. I'd be trying for fame and fortune, and I'd have appreciated it. And I'm a good cop. I sure as hell would never break the law on purpose, much less hurt anyone."

With that, he turned and walked into the living room.

"Cops," Fullbright said when he had left the room. "They can be just as aggravating as actors."

"Or M.E.s," Jude said.

"Hey, I'm not exactly Mr. Personality, and I know it," Fullbright said. "Why the hell do you think I work with the dead?"

By the time they finished the meal and cleaned up, Ellis was snoring softly on the sofa. Jude told Whitney that they should leave him there while he made some phone calls. She spelled Will, sitting before the bank of screens in the hallway, watching the strange rise and fall of the shadows in the foundations next door. While keeping one eye on the strange phenomenon that never changed, she fast-tracked the film from the night before. She realized that the killer had managed to dispatch his victim and eviscerate her just out of range of every camera that they'd set up.

At midnight, Jude and Jake came to find her; Jude

had been making phone calls, reverifying alibis, and Jake had been running more programs, delving deeper into the backgrounds on the actors, actresses and crew on the movie set. They'd gone back through the security tapes from the various ATMs on Broadway from the night Virginia Rockford had been murdered, but once again, the killer had eluded the film. Jackson had given Hannah a ride home around midnight.

"Back to me," Will told Whitney. "Go to bed."

She looked at the two of them. "Ellis is still on the sofa?"

"We're going to leave him there," Jude said.

She was surprised. "He's a cop. He has a gun. And we sleep in this house."

"Someone will be watching him through the night," Will assured her.

Jude offered her a hand.

She accepted it. Obviously, he was staying. It was probably far beyond the wrong side of protocol, but they seldom went by protocol. And every human being needed downtime; this was downtime.

The room was in shadow; she'd left the bathroom light on and it cast a gentle glow into the bedroom.

She'd barely closed her door before she turned into his arms. They wound up on the bed in a tangle of clothing, and as they clung to one another, desperate for the release in so many ways, they managed, bit by bit, to shed the annoying cloth that separated them. Guns wound up on either bedside table; shoes were kicked to the far corners of the room. Nothing felt so good, or so right. Immersed in his masculine scent and touched by the powerful heat of his body, Whitney felt the world disappear, and despite the urgent vigor of their love-making, she felt as if the world washed away. Energy and electricity seared through her, and she delighted in stroking the ribbed muscles of his shoulders, chest and abdomen. She found her own power in stroking his sex teasingly, and she forgot everything as their flesh rubbed erotically together, as he kissed and touched her intimately, and entered into her, filling her not just with delightful little orgasms, but with a sense that she was whole, and hungry for the ultimate climax. He moved slowly and almost teasingly, and she arched harder and harder against him until she felt the delicious, sweet burst of release, and in seconds, felt the shuddering impact of his body as he reached the same pinnacle. He fell down beside her, pulled her against him and whispered, "I think you've allowed me to survive this with a mind left."

They hadn't survived it yet, but she kept silent on that, brushing a kiss against the dampness of his chest.

They didn't speak again; they had been sleep deprived since she had come to Blair House. She wasn't aware then if he lay awake or if he had drifted; she only knew that sleep swept over her like a comforting blanket.

She didn't know if she was dreaming, or if she had wakened. She felt first the soft wet touch of the dog's nose on her hand, urging her to awake. She opened her eyes, and they were back.

Annie Doherty stood at the foot of the bed, and the other victims, past and present, were arrayed around her. She thought somewhat hysterically that it was getting crowded in her room; there were so many victims now. And they all stared at her beseechingly.

The dog whined. He barked, wagging his tail. He headed for the door; she didn't. He came back.

She rose, and started to follow the dog; the victims were disappearing through the walls that led to the upstairs landing and the stairs.

"Whitney!"

She heard her name, but it was as if she was being called from somewhere far away. She knew that whatever it was that she needed to know, the dog was trying to tell her.

She opened the door to the hallway.

But she didn't manage to open it. She felt arms on her shoulders and she turned to see Jude's concerned face. "Whitney, you're sleepwalking. And you're naked."

So she was. And now she was awake. But she still felt the urgency because of her dream. "Jude, we have to go next door."

"It's the middle of the night, Whitney. We'll go in the morning."

She shook her head vehemently. "Now, Jude. Now. I'll get dressed. We have to get the others, and we have to go next door."

She shook free from his touch and hurriedly gathered her clothing from wherever it had fallen on the floor. He did the same, and collected their guns and holsters from the bedside tables. Whitney raced ahead of him, banging on Jackson and Angela's door, and running along the hallway doing the same to the others.

Will, alarmed by the noise, came running to the bottom of the stairs.

Whitney heard Jude run down the steps to try to explain while she woke the others.

Jackson wasn't with Angela. He'd been downstairs with Will; they had meant to keep an eye on Ellis through the night.

Looking disheveled but quickly alert, the Krewe of Hunters assembled in the downstairs hallway. Whitney glanced at Jude. He wasn't protesting, but she thought that he was surprised that none of the others seemed to think that Whitney was crazy.

Ellis woke up, dazed, and then became alert. "What's happening? Oh, God, not another murder— not the Mary Kelly repeat!"

"Bring him with us," Jude muttered low against Whitney's ear.

"Intuition! It's our specialty," Angela said.

"Will, stay on-screen. Jenna, you're with Will. Come on."

Two patrol cars were on the street, watching the site. An officer emerged from one of the cars, flashing his beam at them. "Stop. NYPD."

Jude walked forward, showing his badge. "Detective Jude Crosby. We're going into the site."

"Uh, of course," the officer said. "Now?" he added.

"Yes, keep an eye out, please."

"Yes, sir!"

Whitney was beginning to feel like a fool. The dog and the women had disappeared when Jude had stopped her. A good thing, of course. If she'd made it past Will and Jackson in the hallway, she'd have been arrested by the officer for indecent exposure.

She bit her lower lip, waiting for Jackson to open the gate.

And then she saw the dog. He was halfway between the gate and the foundations, barking, wagging his tail, urging her forward.

"I see him," Jake whispered softly at her side.

"Yes," Angela said.

They followed the dog to the site, and down the stairs.

They had all been right. This special unit was special, all right.

The group of them started walking toward the hole, and they moved with purpose, or awareness of something he hadn't caught.

He felt as if cold fingers crept along his spine, but Jude kept his face as expressionless as he could, and followed. They were crazy, but...

They'd found the skeletons of the 1890s murder victims, and that had brought in an excavation, and the historians and anthropologists were still set up, painstakingly digging bit by bit. What was Whitney going to find that the experts hadn't?

He thought he heard a dog barking from somewhere, and then it seemed that an entire neighborhood of canines woke up.

He looked to the sky. It was a full moon as well.

Maybe the dogs were reverting to wolflike behavior, and baying at the moon.

Whitney stopped in the middle of the pentagram.

So far, the dig into the foundations had been kept to the other side of the structural wall.

"Here," Whitney said.

"Here, what?" Jude demanded, not able to keep quiet anymore.

Whitney looked at him. He'd come to know her very well. He couldn't exactly put a name to the way he felt about her, but he felt his body tense and his heart seem to tear apart. Shimmering and bright, she was someone in his life who was suddenly able to understand him. She was sensual, she was ecstasy and she was a sweet, cooling shower of light that eased him when he needed it most.

And she had to be…*special.*

She was going to lie to him; he could see it in her eyes.

"Something I read…or something your father told me. Here. We have to dig here."

"This is a historical site," he reminded her. "And we've already been digging here. We may disrupt something the historians or the crime scene techs have going."

He could just imagine the red tape. He could imagine what Deputy Chief Green would have to say to him. *"You were there? You allowed this, after teams of scientists had been called in?"*

He'd be back on patrol, or worse. His ass would be fired. Generations of New York City cops in his family, and he was the first who would be fired.

Jackson said quietly, "If Whitney is convinced, we need to dig. Now." He looked at Jude. Jude was the final barrier. "I swear to God, it's important if she says so."

Jude threw up his hands.

Oh, yeah. He'd be branded as *special,* too.

He thought about the corpse of the woman on the gurney at autopsy that day, and he lifted his hands in a shrug. "At this point, what the hell."

Once again, they headed to dig out the shovels and picks and spades. He, Jackson and Jake took up the picks. "I should help," Ellis said.

Whitney told him, "Look for an area that might have been dug in the last six months or so. You'll know because you'll hear something hollow, or you'll hit soft dirt."

The sound of the pickaxes striking hard brick seemed loud in the night. Jude felt his shoulders bunch and his muscles burn as he heaved hard and hit brick, and then brick again.

And then, something soft. He paused; the others had paused as well, hearing a hollowlike sound of emptiness.

He fell to his knees, digging at the mortar and earth around the bricks. The others were down beside him; they looked like a group of pups themselves, searching for a bone.

Nothing, just dirt, and more dirt.

"Keep going, please!" Whitney urged.

"Get the whisks from the other side," Angela suggested.

The others stepped back while Jude and Whitney carefully dusted away at the dirt. They came to the remnants of a large pine box and pulled it away.

Jude sat back on his haunches, stunned.

They hadn't found another victim.

"It's Jonathan Black," Whitney said. "The man who probably killed Carrie Brown, and made the world wonder if the Ripper had come to New York."

There, in a little cache that had been protected by the pine, lay another skeleton. A crushed stovepipe hat lay halfway over the disarticulated skull. Remnants of a cloak, vest and shirt seemed glued to bone by dark matter.

Whitney reached for a chain that lay around the neck.

"What are you doing?" Jude asked her, grabbing her arm.

"It's gone," she said.

"What's gone?" he asked her.

She looked at him. "Our killer was obsessed with Jonathan Black. He discovered where the cultists buried him when he went so berserk they were terrified of him themselves. The killer found the grave site, and he took the relic—the supposed finger bone of Gilles de Rais—for his own. He thinks it gives him power. The power of evil—or of Satan."

Jude was still puzzled. "Don't touch anything," Jude said. "Maybe…maybe here he left a trace."

16

It seemed that their nights were destined to be long.

Once again, scores of people were quickly called out.

The crime scene unit, let by Judith Garner, arrived, along with the anthropologists and the historians; evidence was sought while the historical scientists tried to preserve the integrity of the find. Jude had to control his impatience—he understood the importance of discovery for the sake of history, society and life to come.

He stepped in when Judith argued with one of the historians.

"Crime scene unit *first,*" insisted Jude.

Turning, he realized that Deputy Chief Green was on-site himself. He nodded, agreeing with Jude's action.

"I don't think there's anything more *you* can do here, Jude," Green told him. "And you look like hell—you should get some sleep. We've got more units from the FBI following up on the massive number of people to be interviewed, regarding all the victims. We have people on this, Jude. You're still lead, but you have to let others do more of the legwork. Right now, I want you at the station. I want a thorough report regarding this situation tonight. Then, I'm ordering you to go home. Don't show your face again for at least ten hours, do you understand?"

He opened his mouth to protest, and then he realized that Green was right; he would be worthless if he didn't get some sleep.

He walked over to where Whitney stood with her team, watching the proceedings. "I've been ordered to headquarters, and then to bed," he said dryly.

"Jude," Jackson asked him, "you keep files and notes at home as well, don't you?"

"Of course. My files can be accessed from the station or my apartment," he said.

"The one thing we're not up to speed on is the state of your investigation when you had your first two victims—Sarah Larson and Jane Doe dry," Jackson said. "I thought I'd have you bring Whitney with you. When you're finished at the station, you two can sift through those notes and see if there's something that might be pertinent now that we're sure the murders are connected."

"We really weren't certain that they were connected—until the third murder," Jude said.

"I'm too restless to sleep right now," Whitney said. "It's still the middle of the night. Jackson needs to get some sleep because he'll have to coordinate with the other FBI units tomorrow, Will and Jake are going to stay on the screens and research and Angela will watch over the dig here. Maybe I can be of use going through your old notes."

"I'll drop you off on the way to the station," Jude told Whitney.

Before he left, he walked back to speak with Judith Garner. "Judith—"

"Jude," she said patiently, "I know. Call you if I get anything at all. Well, we'll have all kinds of trace from the hole, I believe, but it will take time." She set a hand on his shoulder. "For a hot young man, you look like a dead rat the cat dragged in. You have to accept it—you cannot work this alone. And none of us can stop crime from happening."

"Judith, we *have* to stop the next murder," he said.

"We," she told him. "Don't take this all on yourself. I have a night team working away on fingerprints on that hundred, so just maybe—it's a long shot—but maybe we'll get a hit on someone, a print that matches up to a suspect, new or old."

"Thanks, Judith."

He left her, and Whitney joined him as they moved off from the site and headed down the walkway to the other side of the block, where he'd left his car.

"You can find your way around the computer room, right? I'll make sure you have all my access codes, and you can also go through the folders. I have tapes from interviews and hand-written notes in there."

"I'll manage fine," Whitney assured him.

He was still uneasy, though Whitney did carry a gun. Besides, no matter how *special* their team might be, she wouldn't officially be FBI if she hadn't passed strict standards on the target range.

At his apartment, he left the car in the street and walked her up to his door. He made a thorough search of the place.

Allison purred, standing by Whitney's ankles as she watched him. "What are you doing?" Whitney asked.

"Being paranoid."

He walked back to her, taking her shoulders and keeping his distance. "Whitney, what the hell happened tonight?"

He saw something pass through her eyes. "I guess I figured out something that I'd read somewhere," she said.

"You're lying."

Her head fell back, and she offered him a rueful smile. "You won't believe the truth," she told him. "And then again, maybe it is the truth—I read something, and it registered in my subconscious mind."

"What is the truth—as you see it?" he demanded. "Whitney, please, don't lie to me."

She looked at his face for a long moment. She was almost sad when she spoke at last, as if there was no choice but to say goodbye to a loved one. "There's a ghost dog that seems to like me. He belonged to Annie Doherty, one of Jonathan Black's victims. He apparently loved his mistress—he's trying to help us. Actually, I see the ghosts of the victims, too, but they're silent."

He stepped away, chills racing along his spine again. Was it true? Was it possible? He couldn't accept it.

And yet, he'd heard the barking of the dog that night at the site, and then all the local dogs had set up howling, as if in kindred spirit.

"I'm going to get through the report as quickly as I can," he said. His voice sounded hollow.

"You don't believe me," she said simply.

"I—I don't know what I believe. It doesn't matter what I believe. It matters that we find the killer. I'll be back as soon as I can."

"Jude, you're blaming yourself for all this," she said. "You can't do that."

He headed for the door, and then turned back. "Lock yourself in."

"You *are* paranoid."

"Yes. There are three bolts on the front door. Lock them all. There's only one bolt on each of the windows, but I've checked them all. And, of course, my father is right next door."

"Right," she said, staring at him.

He looked at her for one more minute, and then he turned and headed out the door.

Whitney felt as if she had been deflated. She had never felt about anyone the way she felt about Jude. Never. It had happened so quickly, and yet, it even seemed as if she knew him as she had never known anyone before. He was so intense. Honorable, reasonable… She loved the way his mind worked, she loved watching him when he was trying to be patient, and she even loved it when he felt he knew what was right or wrong, and bullied on in with his thoughts, opinions or actions.

And now he thought that she was a crazy woman, haunted by a dog.

He probably thought now too that every horrible

twist the movies had accredited to voodoo was true. Maybe he was beginning to wonder if she kept a dozen constricting snakes somewhere to dance with in rituals, too, and enjoyed sticking pins in dolls as a pastime.

She gave herself a stern mental shake. What anyone believed right now was of no importance, unless it pertained to the case.

She sat down at Jude's computer desk and keyed in his file code, bringing up the notes on Sarah Larson. She found herself smiling sadly as she read them. He had interviewed everyone on the waterfront, he'd gone through the Port Authority. There had been no way to trace the woman's movements because no one had known who she was.

She closed the file and opened the one on Jane Doe dry—the girl who was still unidentified, despite the fact that her picture had run in the newspapers and on television screens. How had she come to the city without anyone knowing or caring?

The world could be horrible, sad and cruel!

She'd arrived at the hospital, dripping and bleeding, from massive wounds. Unlike the other victims, she had been sexually assaulted. She had never spoken; she'd died en route.

Jude had taken her picture to every bar in Lower Manhattan. One bartender, an improbably mustachioed sort, had *thought* that he'd seen her in his bar, giggling with a man in one of the back booths.

Whitney jumped at the sound of a hard tapping. She instinctively drew her gun. She heard the sound of a door clicking and spun around, remembering at the last minute that it must be Andrew.

"Jude...you there?" Andrew called. He stuck his head around the door. "I don't mean to interrupt! Sorry about popping in when I shouldn't have. Jude—oh!"

He had the door open; he saw Whitney standing by the desk, her gun aimed at his head.

"Oh, whoa, sorry!" he said, stepping back.

Whitney let out a soft sigh and holstered her gun. "Andrew!"

"Where's Jude?"

"He'll be back any minute," Whitney said. "What are you doing up? It's still the middle of the night, or maybe close to the crack of dawn."

He grinned. "I'm a night owl." He beckoned to her. "Come to the doorway for just a minute and then I won't bug you. I wasn't sure what Jude would want, so I brewed coffee and poured him a good stiff bourbon."

She laughed. "I'll take the coffee, thanks," she told him. She stood and walked to the dividing door and looked inside. Her eyes widened. She hadn't seen this part of Andrew's place. It was Jude's old room, she thought. And he—or his father—was an eclectic collector of toys—and things. He had Indian totems, African masks, animal skulls and spaceships on the mantel, along with his books on the shelves, and even stacked on the coffee table.

"Cool place," she said. She narrowed her eyes looking at the skull of a steer; it was feathered, and rawhide ties held skins and bones in a ritualistic manner.

He eased her coffee cup into one hand. *They had begun to suspect someone close. Someone smart, someone who knew who was going to be where when.*

Her gun hand was free. "What's that?" she asked him, pointing to the skull.

But Andrew Crosby was Jude's father. A former cop. Impossible.

"What? Oh, that?" he asked, his eyes lighting up. "It belonged to a Shoshone medicine man. It was a gift to me from his tribe. Right before my senior year of high school, I spent a summer working on the reservation, and we became very close friends. The feathers help the soul fly, so he said, when a person dies, or, they help the sick person fly back to health. The bones give the person strength. That sac is filled with small otter bones, which help a warrior learn to swim. That big bone is from a horse—the prayers said that they help a person learn to be as swift as a horse. I think that one is a dog bone—it's for faith and loyalty. I gave it to Jude when he was a kid—he wanted to be an Indian. He believed that the Shoshone relic taught a man all that he should be. Can I show you anything else?"

Careful that she kept him in her line of sight, Whitney went over to study the skull. *Did anything appear to be a human bone? She didn't think so; she didn't know.*

She turned around to look at other relics and collectibles in the room.

"Great spaceship," she told him.

"Oh, I bought that at the first Star Wars convention Jude and I went to," he said, grinning. "It's just great, isn't it? They made toys so much better before. Oh, well, everything is becoming some kind of video game these days, and graphics are amazing on them, but as for real toys…"

She laughed. "Andrew, thanks. I have to get back to work," she said.

"Well, when you have time, come on over. I can show you Jude's childhood."

"I'd like that!" She kept him in her sight as she made her way back to the door. "Thank you for the coffee. I'll make sure you get the cup back."

Andrew waved a hand in the air. "Oh, I pick up all my stuff from Jude's once a week."

Whitney stepped back into Jude's apartment. She smiled at Andrew and then closed the door and bolted the lock on her side between the two apartments.

Back at the desk, she sat for a moment, stunned with her suspicion.

They'd thought it would be someone who was close. Someone who knew police procedure. Someone who knew them, and all about them.

Who better than Jude's father, a man who had access to his computer, his desk, to every bit of information regarding the crimes?

She called Jake Mallory; she didn't want to suggest to Jude just yet that his father might have a Satanist's finger bone in with the relics or hidden in a shaman's magic skull—a gift he had given to his son. She stumbled through her explanation of why she was suddenly suspicious of Jude Crosby's father.

It couldn't be Andrew's Crosby; it couldn't be.

And the relic had been, he had said, something he had gotten back when he'd been in high school. He had given it to Jude....

But at this point, it seemed that nothing was impossible.

"Get back to me quickly, Jake, please," she told him.

"You should get out of there, Whitney. I'll come and get you."

"How? You don't have a car," she reminded him.

"I'll get one of the police officers—there are still people prowling around next door, tons of cops."

"No, no, check out everything you can on Andrew Crosby for me first, please. And don't call a police officer—I don't want any of this on record. You have all the information, right?"

"I have it," Jake said. He hesitated. "Whitney, I know how you feel about Jude, and I'll—I'll be as discreet as humanly possible, but I'm glad you're calling me. About his dad, I mean. I'll call you right back, and then, I'm coming for you. I mean, coming for you. I'll get a cab, and we'll be together, at least. Hey, gotta go—Angela's on the radio. There's something wrong over at the site. Sit tight—no matter what, I'm coming for you."

"All right, thanks, Jake."

Whitney hung up. She tried to focus on the screen; she was armed. She could wait for Jake to call her back. She was in a locked room—far safer than heading out to the street.

She nearly jumped a mile when she heard something hit the glass at the back of the apartment; she rose quickly, and strode into the back. Nothing had hit the parlor windows.

She walked into the side room, Jude's den. The fire escape led from the window in this room. She walked over to it; the glass was cracked, as if it had been hit by a rock. Or something heavier.

Maybe a brick from an old building?

She jumped again; there was a thud that came from somewhere in the building. She was tempted to dash to the front door and run out, but she wondered if that wasn't what someone hoped she would do.

But the house was clear. She walked back to the desk, looked around and picked up the cup of coffee and took a long swallow. She should just call Jude; she was paranoid, but that was the way it was.

She heard another noise—a growl.

She frowned. The ghost dog was standing in the hallway, growling. There was something there that he didn't like.

She was startled; she'd never seen the dog anywhere else before, just around the construction site or Blair House.

"There's nothing there!" she said softly, and took another sip of the coffee.

There was something wrong with it now, she thought. She stared at the cup. Had it tasted this way, or had it changed in the last few minutes?

The dog barked at her, and then ran through the door to the hallway.

She dropped the cup and looked toward the door that separated the two apartments.

The thud!

The door was still closed, but the bolt had been jimmied open.

And she could feel whatever drug was now in the coffee beginning to take hold. Despite all the bright lights, the room was dimming, and her limbs were be-ginning to feel like water.

She could hear her cell phone ringing; she just couldn't answer it.

Jude glumly thought that at best he'd soon be pulled off the case. He started to fill out his report for the night, but paused. What did he say? *I was sleeping with an FBI task force member when she suddenly bolted up naked and started for the door; her ghost dog wanted her to get over to what is now an excavation site, and I'll be damned if he didn't show her where an old Satan-loving murderer was buried.*

The facts; just the facts. The FBI team had become convinced—through archives—that they now knew where the body of the historical killer lay; it was impor-tant that they unearth it, because the theories regarding the current killings were all pointed in the direction of the killer believing he was following in the route of the man.

Backtrack a bit.

We were trying to draw out a cop—and a medical examiner. And both appear to be exactly what they are—Fullbright almost flippant but honest and ear-nest; Ellis Sayer as hardworking and hangdog as ever.

That wouldn't look good on paper. But it felt good to think.

The offices were quiet. In the next room, he could see that a police officer had brought in two drunks who had apparently gone at one another in a bar.

He gave his attention back to the report swimming before him.

Expediency being the greatest necessity at the time, I deemed it best to dig, he wrote.

A creeping chill started up and down his spine. He felt something nudge his thigh.

Startled, Jude sat back. He didn't see anything. He felt the nudge again.

"What the hell?" He leaped to his feet.

He blinked. *He had been too intensely involved with the case.* His mind was playing tricks on him. He blinked again, but it didn't go away.

It was the outline of a dog. A big dog. Some kind of shepherd mix. Oh, God, he'd been playing with the crazies too long. His mind...

The dog looked at him and barked and kept barking. It padded away from him, and then ran back to him. The dog wanted him to follow.

He hesitated, looking around. The drunks were still there; the officer was still there, the desk sergeant was still there. None of them seemed to be hearing a dog.

He took a deep breath. And then he followed the dog, mumbling something to the desk sergeant on the way out.

Each step of the way, the dog waited for him. He knew where Jude's car was. He jumped through the door and waited for Jude to get into the driver's seat.

"Well, which way, boy?" Jude asked. "Or is this as far as the craziness takes us?"

The dog barked. Jude eased the car out. Traffic was minimal, but he didn't know where he was going. But each time he neared a turn, the dog went crazy until he veered his car into the right lane.

He had just realized that the animal seemed to be leading him home, when his cell phone began to ring.

He glanced at the caller ID. It was Judith Garner.

"Jude, I got a hit off the hundred-dollar bill. You're not going to believe it. I mean, I still can't believe that, good as we are, I got a known fingerprint off that bill!"

"Judith, you're amazing," he said. He'd just taken the turn down his street; the dog's tail thumped happily but silently on the seat next to him. "I'm going to kiss your feet later. Who?"

He didn't say goodbye; after she answered, he hung up and called Jackson Crow as he stepped down full throttle on the gas pedal.

The dog wanted him, and that meant...

Oh, God.

She saw him standing at the doorway to Jude's office, and she wondered if she was imagining a man again, because he was wearing black, with a dark brocade vest and a shoulder-caped cloak. His hat was a stovepipe.

But he had no face.

No. She wasn't imagining him, and he wasn't a ghost. If only he were. He had no face because he was wearing a white theatrical mask; it was the sad face of the duo that signified comedy and drama.

"I'd never thought that anything could be so good!" he said, staring at her. She was aware, although she couldn't see his lips, he was smiling. Gloating. "The others were really random. Well, I can tell you now, I guess—Angus picked the others. He said it was easy. People will do just about anything for a few minutes of fame. All he had to do was tell them that he could get them into the movies. And, of course, he didn't run around finding brain surgeons! They fell for his lines so easily. They went where he wanted them to go. They did what he wanted them to do. Anything—just for a chance to be in the movies. But, you know, the last girl he killed in London—before coming to the States—was Mary Kelly. Prostitutes then, prostitutes now. All they want is fame and fortune, and they want to use you to get it. Jonathan picked up a little cutie, even if she was a prostitute. But, you see, you're really no better. Young and gorgeous, and you're really kind of a whore, too, huh, sleeping with the cop when you haven't really known him long at all. You fit the bill nicely. And, imagine! You'll be found in the lead investigator's own apartment! Is that rich, or what?"

Whitney told herself that she hadn't had that much of the coffee; she could move. She had to move. She had to draw her gun from her holster, and shoot the bastard.

But she couldn't make her limbs work. He dropped his medical bag in the hallway, walked to her and stooped down and drew out her gun, studying it. "Yep, FBI issue. Not that it's going to do you any good now." He reached out and touched her cheek with his gloved hands. "Pretty, pretty, pretty thing! But you're really just a weirdo, you know."

He tossed her gun under the desk, still hunched down at her side.

Whitney was amazed when she was able to almost form a word. "Why?"

He grinned. "Angus Avery is going to make my

career skyrocket. And all the Sherry Blancos of the world will be nothing but dirt beneath my feet!" he said. "And, of course, he taught me all about Jonathan Black—and the power of Satan." He gave a little shudder. "Can't believe you figured out where Jonathan was buried. But Angus got it all right a long time ago. He is a New Yorker, and you're not, but…"

He stood again. "Time's a-wasting, girl! Your lover-boy cop won't take forever writing up that report." He looked at his watch and shrugged. "I should have had hours, but…well, I'll make do with the time I have."

"But…how?" Whitney managed to say.

"Ah, how, you ask? You never figured that out? You just don't understand the power of fame, and you should. Of all people, you should have understood. It was easy. I worked downtown on that movie. I knew the police station. I hung around as near to it as I could, and I watched who came and went, and I listened to everything said by everyone who came from the building and passed me by. All I had to do was a little flirting with a pathetic computer nerd."

"Computer nerd?"

"Hannah. She was the easiest. I met her at a coffee shop. I flirted with her. I told her I was going to make movies. She was so easy…I never let on who I was. I always pretended to be so flattered that she thought I looked like *the* Bobby Walden. I said I knew directors—I said I could get her extras work, that I'd done extras work…she was so gullible. She never knew how much she gave away!"

He couldn't resist bending down by her again. "She never will know. And if she begins to suspect that I'm not the man she thought I was...well, I've gotten really good at this. Angus taught me well. I know how to find little Miss Hannah, and make sure she disappears. If fact, when I finish with you, I think I'll pay a call on her."

He walked back to the hallway and picked up his medical bag. He opened it, and then held up a long, sharp knife. He glanced back over at her. "It's a Japanese carving blade, if you're interested. Light steel, and one of the finest."

He studied it with appreciation for a moment.

Whitney felt the seconds of her life dwindling away. Mind over matter wasn't working; the world was out of focus and she couldn't will her limbs to work.

But as he stood there, still admiring the glint of the steel, the door that separated the apartments suddenly flew open. Andrew Crosby—blood dripping from his head—reached for her, dragging her through the open doorway and into his apartment.

He slammed the door. Whitney felt pain in her hand as he stepped on her fingers. "Sorry, sorry, oh, God, he got your gun! I can't call for help, he smashed my cell. And yours...where the hell is your cell phone?" He patted her body. "Shit! It's on the floor in there somewhere. Whitney, do you hear me?"

She struggled to sit up and was intensely gratified to see that she could move again; the more she tried to move, the more she could.

"Help me up!" she told him.

He struggled and did so. As she gained her feet, they heard the force of Bobby Walden's body slam against the dividing door. It shuddered, and held, but he slammed against it again.

A second later, the door splintered and broke. Whitney struggled for the buffalo skull hanging on the wall. Andrew didn't protest as she dragged it down. As Bobby crashed like a bull into the room, she cracked it with all her strength on his head.

He fell between her and Andrew, and he quickly staggered up, the knife still in his hands. He let out a bellow and turned on Andrew.

"Here, you bastard! I'm the one you want!" Whitney screamed.

He turned, the white theatrical mask he wore seemingly cast in a puzzled expression.

"Andrew!" Whitney cried. He understood her. Bobby Walden did not. Nor did he seem to realize that now, even if he killed them both, he was caught. He was never going to move on to superstardom—his skin and blood were in the horns of the buffalo skull and Forensics would discover his identity for certain.

Andrew bolted for the door. Whitney tore back into Jude's apartment and dived beneath the desk. She couldn't reach her gun. It had skittered too far back.

And Bobby was coming.

For a moment, stars burst before her eyes, followed by blackness. She blinked. She came out from beneath the desk.

She was dimly aware that she heard a dog barking again, but she didn't know from where.

And a ghost dog couldn't help her now!

As Bobby Walden came in, pausing for balance against the door frame, Whitney stumbled into the living room, desperately seeking a weapon. She stood for a moment, swaying herself, darkness before her eyes. She blinked furiously. He was now stumbling his way after her.

She hurried for the rear den, falling against the door and then righting herself. There was only one bolt on the fire escape window.

It was like moving a thousand-pound steel object, but desperation, the fight for her life, sent adrenaline into her system, giving her strength. She got the window opened just as Bobby fell into the room.

She almost made it out the window; he caught her arm.

The barking was louder now.

He ripped her back into the room. He showed her his hands. "Was Mary Kelly strangled first—or did he just slice her throat? Your choice, Agent Tremont!"

She saw stars beginning to pop out in front of her eyes again, but when she blinked, they were gone.

And something was different.

The room was filled with women. Ghostly shades and figures, in contemporary and period dress. Bobby must have felt them somehow, because he hesitated.

"They're all here, Bobby," she told him. "They're all here, all the women you and Angus Avery killed. They're here to see that you're dragged to hell."

He let out a roar of anger, looking around.

He could see them, she thought.

"Bitches, whores!" he railed. "You got what you deserved! And she's going to join you, and we're all going to hell!"

He fell down on top of Whitney and his fingers wound around her throat.

Andrew, his face and scalp bloodied, was just running out the front door when Jude arrived, screaming for help at the top of his lungs.

Jude caught him. "Dad!"

"I'm all right, I'm all right. You've got to get in there—"

"Whitney?" he said desperately.

"Your place."

"Alive?"

"When I left. Hurry!"

The dog was ahead of him, barking insanely, as he raced up the stairs. Jude followed two steps at a time and tried to burst into his apartment. The bolts were solid; he'd seen to it.

Swearing, he rushed to his father's door, burst in and dashed through the splintered door to his own apartment.

The dog was ahead. He followed the dog.

Bobby Walden pressed his full weight into Whitney; she was tearing and ripping at his fingers, struggling desperately against him.

He would happily have shot the man, but the way that they were struggling… Whitney suddenly twisted and blocked his shot. He sheathed the gun and tackled the man who was on top of her, bringing them both off Whitney and rolling across his den floor.

Bobby Walden knew how to fight, but he didn't have Jude's size or strength, nor did he spend his free hours with a punching bag, learning how to burn off frustration.

Bobby only got in one good jab; Jude was furious, seeing red, and he pummeled the man. Until he felt Whitney's fingers, weak, but tugging at his shirt.

"Jude...no. He's got to stand trial. He's got to help us sort through it all."

He eased back; his hands were bloody. For a moment, Bobby Walden, wound in the cloak, the mask ripped away, lay on the floor. His face was swollen, his eyes were nearly closed. He was alive—Jude could see him breathing.

He stood up, reaching to drag the man to his feet.

"Bobby Walden, you're under arrest for the murder—"

To his amazement, the man suddenly screamed—a piercing, bone-chilling scream that sounded louder than anything Jude had ever heard.

The ghost dog started barking insanely again.

Jude twisted around, wondering what could cause such a shriek of pure terror.

He thought that he heard the swish of fabric. It seemed that there were shadows and strange forms in the air; he thought he caught a whiff of perfume.

"No! No! No!" Bobby suddenly screamed. He broke loose from Jude and ripped his clothing and his flesh, bolting through the window to the fire escape. "Ah, hell!" Jude raged, trying to fling himself after the man.

But it seemed that he couldn't get through the figures, as if the air had become water or rich honey, impossible to penetrate. But it wasn't the air; it was the women moving after Bobby Walden.

He made his way to the window, but Bobby's back arched against the metal rungs of the fire escape.

Before Jude could reach him, he fell…

He didn't hit the ground.

He was caught on the metal rungs of the fire escape, and there were sickening moments in which the man sputtered and choked…until he strangled to death on the heavy rawhide loop he had around his neck. A talisman was attached to the rope.

The relic that held the finger bone of Gilles de Rais.

The barking stopped.

The room seemed to be freshened by a sudden rush of clean air.

Jackson Crow and Jake Mallory burst into the room, guns in position, followed by members of the NYPD.

Jude came to where Whitney was slumped on the floor and fell down at her side. He took her into his arms.

There was a great deal more to be done by law enforcement at that moment.

But…

No man was an island. Law enforcement wasn't one man. There was a task force working this case.

They could deal with the situation now.…

No way he was writing another report tonight.

Epilogue

Whitney had been dosed with a powerful combination of drugs, all available to any good-looking marquee name. Jude was horrified to realize that the man had been using Hannah for information on what was going on with the case. Jude knew he'd have to talk to her, and he sat for long periods of time wondering about people in general. Some of the victims Angus Avery and Bobby Walden had chosen had been hungry for fame and a better life.

But Hannah had just been hungry for attention from a man who had really seemed to care about her.

Whitney was kept in the hospital overnight.

Jude stayed by her side.

He had a feeling they would one day discover that Bobby Walden had employed knowledge he'd learned about date-rape drugs earlier. He'd been an up-and-coming star, and those women he had accosted before he had fallen in with Angus Avery—and his particular form of the devil—had probably never reported that he'd raped them, if they'd realized it. Who would have believed them?

It was good that Ellis was just what he seemed. A good cop.

And it was good that Wally Fullbright was what he seemed, too. An eccentric little man with a keen interest in mysteries and a talent at autopsy.

He left Ellis to deal with Angus Avery as they used what they had learned from Bobby Walden to try to piece together exactly what had happened.

Avery's house arrest was revoked. He answered a few questions, and they learned that he was proud of all that he had accomplished. He'd known about Jonathan Black and been fascinated with theories about Jack the Ripper and Black since he'd been a child growing up by the seaport. He'd written the movie years before, and he'd known that he *had* to re-create the fear of the late 1890s.

Jonathan Black had told him so.

They didn't learn much more about the details of who had done what because Angus Avery strangled himself to death in his cell at Rikers Island with the sheet from his bed. His death surprised everyone; he hadn't been on suicide watch.

Whitney and Jude knew, of course, that he'd been prompted to his action by a different power.

Cops were supposed to believe in justice, not vengeance, Jude knew.

But he'd seen the bodies of their victims on the autopsy tables.

He couldn't feel any sorrow.

He was due to receive a commendation that he didn't feel he deserved. What he did deserve, and what he was taking, was a long vacation.

Ellis Sayer was one damn good detective, and the world of New York would be just as well served with Ellis holding down the high-profile realm.

He didn't know when Whitney's team would be called to another investigation; he just wanted every day with her that he could have. The team wasn't in a hurry to leave—they still felt there was unfinished business at Blair House.

One night, when he'd spent the afternoon next to Monty at the hospital, he headed over to Blair House in the early evening. Angela was preparing a roast. Jake's fiancée was joining them at the house while they finished up in New York, and the two were musicians. He'd been invited for a Krewe of Hunters evening, and he was grateful that they considered him part of their in-crowd.

When he arrived, he could see through the open gate that Whitney was standing in the front, looking perplexed.

"What's going on?" he asked her.

She looked at him and smiled sheepishly.

"One more time," she told him.

His heart thudded. "One more time?" he demanded.

She smiled and moved against him, lifting her head and coming on her toes to give him a kiss. "One more time with picks and shovels!" she told him.

He arched a brow.

"The dog, Jude. I have to find the dog. The excavation team dug up an old metal tag. A dog tag. It had the name Rufus on it. I think—I know you saw Rufus, Jude. I know that you did. I have to find him. We've decided that, between us, and with a fund from city donations, we can actually bury the victims from the past—and Jane Doe dry, until we find out who she is."

"*If* we find out who she is."

"We may never," Whitney agreed. "When we bury Annie Doherty, I want to bury Rufus with her."

"But you said they found his tag next door, at the excavation site."

"Right. I think Rufus tried to protect his mistress. I believe someone got a hold of him, but he escaped. He came back, and the owners cared for him, never understanding why he sat in the yard, staring at the House of Spiritualism, barking now and then, and trying to get someone to understand. Please, Jude, I know this is hard, but…"

"Let's dig," he said.

One by one, the others came out. Jude was silently glad to see that Jake Mallory's fiancée was a sweet and beautiful young woman. He couldn't help but see that Ashley and Jake were so close, and he had to admit that he had felt a twinge of jealousy now and then.

But Ashley dug in with the rest of them, not at all surprised that they were going to search for the remains of a ghost dog.

As Whitney had thought—though they did tear up the yard and make a mess of it—they found the remains of a dog. They were tenderly gathered, and wrapped, and set in a show box to await burial.

It was a beautiful night; it was the first night he had really relaxed, it seemed, since he'd been called in when the body of Sarah Larson had been pulled from the river.

He didn't leave until morning. Whitney, groggy,

golden and beautiful, reached out her arms to him when he was ready to go. He paused, returned to her side and kissed her. But she couldn't coax him back into bed.

"I'll be back," he promised her.

At the animal shelter, the attendant told him that they didn't have any full-blooded German shepherds at the moment.

Jude smiled. "I don't want a full-blooded shepherd. I want a mix. Something big and furry and lovable that enjoys people and needs a good home."

"Well, there's Ruff," the attendant told him.

"Who?" Jude asked.

"Ruff—that's what they called him when he was found on the street, I guess. Anyway, it's what we've been calling him here," the attendant told him.

"I'll take Ruff," Jude said.

"You haven't even seen him yet!"

"I know I'm going to like him."

And he did. Ruff was a mixture of shepherd and something big—maybe a wolfhound, or deerhound. He wagged his tail wildly when he met Jude, whined softly and slipped his wet nose against Jude's hand.

He filled out all the paperwork, paid the fee and left a donation, and left the shelter with Ruff, a shiny new collar and tags, and a long leash.

Whitney hadn't understood why Jude had been so eager to leave. When he called her to say that he was on his way back, she went out into the yard to wait.

They had the gate open, and she saw him drive up. He got out of the car and opened the passenger side.

The dog bounded to her as if he'd known her all her life.

Jude came behind, impossibly tall and sexy, his hair falling lightly over his forehead and a grin on his face.

"I thought you were a cat person?" she said.

"Yes, but…I'm in love with a dog person," he told her. "And, somehow, canines have really grown on me."

She laughed, threw her arms around him and kissed him. Then she drew back. "Jude, how are we going to work this out?"

"I don't know," he told her. "I only know that we will." He looked down at her for a long moment. "I know that I met you, and my world changed. I changed. I love you. Too soon to say that? I hope not. It's true."

She smiled. "What's too soon?" she asked him. "I love you," she added softly.

He pulled her close and kissed her. Ruff barked.

And Whitney knew that time and distance would mean nothing. Sometimes, that would be annoying.

But annoying could never interfere with anything this powerful and sure.

They would work it out.

* * * * *

MANHATTAN

The drink that typifies the five-o'clock cocktail hour in the city that rushes around with the speed of light? It could be named only for the borough itself.

But was it named for the borough? There are a number of stories that go with the creation of the Manhattan. Some say it was named after a bar called Manhattan. Some say it goes farther back, that a bartender in the 1860s created the drink for the first time.

Some even say the sewage system was so bad back then that the water ran brown with the color, and thus the drink was named Manhattan for the brownish flow of the rivers.

However it came about, it remains a classic cocktail with many variations.

Ingredients

2 oz rye whiskey
½ oz sweet vermouth
2–3 dashes Angostura bitters
Maraschino cherry for garnish

Preparation

Pour the ingredients into a mixing glass with ice cubes.

Stir well or shake.

Strain into a chilled cocktail glass (or serve on the rocks in an old-fashioned glass).

Garnish with the cherry.

Variations on the Manhattan

Dry Manhattan—Use a dash of dry vermouth and garnish with a lemon twist.

Perfect Manhattan—Equal parts of sweet and dry vermouth. Garnish with a lemon twist.

Brandy Manhattan—Replace whiskey with brandy.

Scotch Manhattan—Replace whiskey with Scotch.

Southern Comfort Manhattan—Replace whiskey with Southern Comfort.

THE PERFECT NEW YORK STRIP STEAK

While many around the world are turning to low-fat, heart-healthy diets and choosing fish and chicken over red meat, the classic steak house remains a New York staple. In the city, you'll find that there is an abundance of such establishments, and most New Yorkers with a taste for steak have their favorite. But even opinionated NYC chefs tend to agree on a few important steps for grilling the perfect New York Strip at home.

Shopping: Do spend the extra money on USDA PRIME cuts. Look for well-marbled meat—not too much fat, not big chucks.

Preparation: The New York Strip needs to sit out for approximately an hour, to achieve the correct temperature for the grill. Steaks right from the refrigerator will not cook correctly.

Coating: Never coat the grill. The coating goes on the steak. NYC chefs from different restaurants prefer different coatings. Some believe that *rubbing,* not spraying or soaking, a cut of meat in olive oil before adding seasonings is the key. Others prefer a butter reduction with the milk solids removed. Butter solids appear when you zap the butter in the microwave for a few seconds. They can be strained out through a coffee filter, or with a spoon. Some chefs prefer marinades, but those really do not constitute the flavor of the basic prime strip steak.

Seasonings: Some chefs believe there can't be too much salt, as the salt will form a crust. Most will suggest kosher salt, and many are turning to sea salt. And crack your pepper—none of that powdered stuff! Rub both into each steak after it's coated, and place the steak on the grill.

Perfect temperature is considered medium rare, not raw, but red in the middle extending to the perfectly charred outer rim.

Many steak houses sell custom sauces to complement your grill-at-home steaks!

And, of course, one of the best side dishes for the perfect steak has always been the baked potato. Russet potatoes are recommended, as they have a great texture for baking. The skin should be brown—no green patches. Potatoes should be scrubbed, and dried by towel or air-drying. Wrapping a potato in tinfoil will actually steam it, and leave a soft skin. For a crispy skin, do not wrap. Prepare the potato by rubbing it with olive oil or canola oil, and then rolling it lightly in kosher salt or sea salt. Optimum baking temperature is considered to be 350°F, and the oven should be preheated. Time is approximately an hour. A potato is done when the skin is crispy and its "meat" is soft.

A fresh salad always complements this meal. Iceberg wedges, dusted with bacon bits and blue cheese, a mixed salad or a Caesar serves as a nice final touch. So...sip your Manhattan and grill your steaks!

It's a meal that provides a pleasant evening in New York City. When the winter weather gives way to spring, Manhattanites head on home after work and like stepping out at night to enjoy the great weather! (Wait, many live in apartments without balconies. Okay, so...buy a little indoor grill!)

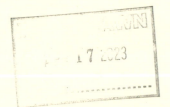